SAGE

•••••• IN THE RUGGED HILLS SERIES BOOK 1 ••••••

SAGE

DEBORA CLARK

TATE PUBLISHING & *Enterprises*

Published by Tate Publishing & Enterprises, LLC
127 E. Trade Center Terrace | Mustang, Oklahoma 73064 USA
1.888.361.9473 | www.tatepublishing.com

Tate Publishing is committed to excellence in the publishing industry. The company reflects the philosophy established by the founders, based on Psalm 68:11,
"The Lord gave the word and great was the company of those who published it."

Published in the United States of America
ISBN: 978-1-61663-656-2
1. Fiction / Christian / Historical   2. Fiction / Historical
10.07.06

*Sage: a venerable wise man, judicious;
an aromatic plant with grayish-green leaves used as
seasoning; the healing plant; the herb of happiness.*

ACKNOWLEDGMENTS

To God be the glory!

And to all of you who invested your time and hearts in this project (and you all know who you are), please watch for blessings to fall your way. I could never thank you enough nor list my gratitude in this short space; therefore, I have petitioned the good Lord to reward you as only he can. He knows.

CHAPTER ONE

"Somebody's coming, Pa," I yelled as I watched the approaching horse and rider with much anticipation. We hadn't had a visitor for over two months, and I was a bit lonely for news from beyond. I suspected the rider was the deputy from Crawford County, Johnny Simmons. He was real sweet on me, and no words had ever actually been spoken, but I knew he would ask me to marry him in the fall, and of course, I would say yes. Johnny was my only hope to ever move from this desolate, dried-up farm. The thought of leaving Pa and Lenny made me very sad.

Luvina, or Lenny, as we called her, was my older sister by six years. Ma died a decade ago, and Lenny had to step into her huge shoes of responsibility at the tender age of fourteen. Her only solace was the herb garden. Ma established it, and I suppose tending it was Lenny's way of keeping her alive. I understood none of it.

The rider was getting closer. I could hear the hoof beats now.

I hadn't heard Pa laugh much since Ma died. He was real good to us though. We never had a need unmet, and he taught us how to survive by example.

No! The rider wasn't Johnny. For a fleeting instant, my heart drowned in disappointment. He was much too tall to be the deputy. I watched intently as he approached. The closer he came, the slower my breathing became, as I was overcome with some unfamiliar force. The horse stopped at the gate, and the man, although well over six feet tall, dismounted with the grace of an eagle in flight. He tilted his head slightly, reached up, and brushed his hat while saying, "Howdy, ma'am. Would you have a cool drink of water for a tired horse and a mighty thirsty man?"

I could not speak; I had no heartbeat or breath. His countenance completely overwhelmed me. Never had my eyes beheld such a specimen of human beauty. Sensing my dilemma, he spoke again.

"Josiah Bozeman, ma'am. Just passing through on my way to homestead in Missouri." His deep, dark eyes smiled at me with a mystery, and yet they were so transparent that I could see all the way through him. I noticed his muscular shoulders that were as broad as Pa's ax handle, and his waist was so slim. I never heard the footsteps behind me, but I was jolted back into reality at the sound of Pa's voice. "Well, child, go get the man some water!"

"Paul Johnson here. So you're just passing through? You're welcome to stay for supper." They shook hands and led the sweaty horse to the trough.

I ran quickly to the house, dipped a long, cool drink and served him like royalty. His smile lit up the whole cabin. I looked at the dusty hat on the peg and then to his coal-black hair that hung loosely about his shoulders, clean, shiny, and miffed by the wind. His complexion was tanned, yet soft and innocent, and a dark evening shadow covered his jaw and chin. Underneath the long, black drover, he wore buckskin. His voice was deep, smooth, and soft and flowed out like fresh, thick cream. If I could touch that voice, it would feel like Ma's silk scarf.

I tried desperately to stay close to him and Pa, but there were chores. I did not want the magic to end. My precious, all-knowing Lenny understood and let me take care of the jobs inside. Lenny was always like that. She considered everyone else first, so unselfish, so giving, exhibiting these virtues by her love and devotion. She was quiet, very wise, and seldom displayed her dry sense of humor. I really didn't think of her as a mother, although she assumed that role and was my strength and inspiration. She knew how to do everything and taught me too, yet she never pushed me.

We busied ourselves with supper. Pa trimmed the lamps, and it thrilled my heart to see Josiah bow his head and close his eyes as Pa asked grace over our meal. The conversation with this stranger was mostly about the harsh winter of '58 and of the destruction of our barn by a fearless, eight-inch ice storm. The tone soon became more optimistic as Pa described his plans to rebuild now that spring had come. After Mr. Bozeman shared news from the far hills and gave us a glimpse of himself, Pa asked him to stay on a spell and help build the barn.

Oh, how my heart rejoiced! I could not take my eyes off him, and I only hoped he didn't notice. His eyes met mine for a brief second, and then after a pause he spoke to Pa. "Yes, Mr. Johnson, I'd be pleased to stay on and help you with the barn."

I didn't sleep a wink that night. Lenny and I shared the cabin loft, and we whispered until the wee hours. She dozed off somewhere between my deep sighs and dreamy imaginations.

With the first light, I was up and in front of Ma's looking glass. It was blackened around the edges and there were little black dots scattered across the middle, but my image was visible enough. Pa said that I was as pretty as a picture, and Lenny always encouraged me to take special care of myself. She helped me brush and curl my gift of golden, soft, waist-length hair. With fine attention to detail, she sewed simple fabrics into beautiful dresses for me. I wanted so much for her to share the glamour, but she insisted that she was plain and didn't have much time for imitation beauty. The blue gingham dresses were very fitting on her, and she nearly always wore Ma's white apron with the one lace pocket.

I heard the hammers, took one last look in the mirror, and hurried outside to begin my chores and to look at Josiah again.

Time seemed to stand still, so the day went on forever. I relished every moment I was near the man, and I felt the palpitations of my heart when our eyes met.

After supper Pa read his Bible while the three of us talked. And talk we did, as Josiah was full of amazing stories. Occasionally Pa would look up from his reading, smile, and even chuckle quietly at the tall tales. All the while Josiah's deep voice relaxed my every tension. Too soon night fell each evening and again we parted.

Two weeks went on like that and the barn was nearly completed. My light duty chores were as easy as sunlight during those days. I was basking in that magic and so caught up in my own dreams, I failed to be as good to help as I should. Lenny worked like a man carrying nails and heavy lumber to the men and jumping at their every request. She was indeed an asset to the barn building, and she did all her usual chores too. I never anticipated an end to my joy, but something Josiah said at supper reminded me that he only promised to stay on until the barn was up, so the possibility of his departure was near.

Rain woke me before dawn, and I thought I heard Lenny sniffling. I asked softly, "Lenny, are you awake?" No answer. She was asleep. Sometimes when Pa was hard on her or if she had had an especially bad day, she would cry very quietly when she thought we were asleep and wouldn't hear. I never had the heart to ask her about it because I was ashamed that I had so little courage and she had so much. I guess she really did miss Ma. Soon I too was off to sleep.

This time it wasn't rain that woke me but the banging of hammers. I was afraid Pa would be mad at me for sleeping late, so I hurried to the barn and noticed that the wagon was gone. Josiah said that he had gone for supplies. Oh my! I thought. An entire day alone with my Josey. But he worked harder that day than ever before and seldom took time to speak. At dinner he found an opportunity when Lenny was out of the room to tell me that he really needed to talk to me and asked me to meet him in the barn after dark. I could not eat another bite. I could barely breathe; even my vision was foggy. The afternoon dragged on and on and on. I thought it would never end and was highly disappointed when Pa came back so early.

I could not eat supper either, especially when Josiah told Pa how he had finished the barn except the doors and that he needed to head on to Missouri to build his own home. He thanked Pa for the hospitality and bragged about what good cooks and workers his lovely daughters were. The subject ended when Pa explained that he understood and was very appreciative of Bozeman's help and fine craftsmanship, and he presented the contractual payment.

As soon as the lamps were trimmed, we heard a wagon coming. It was a traveling preacher, so of course Pa took him in and they sat up until after midnight, visiting and discussing great Bible truths. He made me and Lenny go on to bed, and there was no way I could slip out of that dried-up old log cabin to the barn. I could not even cry for fear they might hear me and make a scene. So I lay there, afraid to speak to Lenny, just knowing that I would die before daybreak of a broken heart. Somehow enduring the pain, I did go to sleep, only to wake after the sun was up. I dressed without even a glance at Ma's mirror and literally ran to the barn. I found Pa sitting on a bale of straw, staring blindly into space.

"Where is he?" I asked desperately. "Where is Josiah?"

"He's gone," Pa answered slowly. "The preacher too."

I ran back into the cabin blinded by the tears. I searched for Lenny, but she wasn't anywhere in sight. I threw myself down across the feather-filled bed and sobbed and sobbed. I do not know how long I was there before my eyes spied the piece of paper on Ma's looking glass. It appeared as if it were once crumbled and wet and then dried and smoothed out. As I approached, I recognized Lenny's neat handwriting. It read, "Josiah and I shall always love you."

CHAPTER TWO

THIRTY-THREE YEARS LATER

Somebody's coming, I thought as I heard bare feet running on the boardwalk. I looked up from my needlework to the opened front door and waited to see who it was. The footsteps grew louder and stopped the instant he stood in my view.

"You have a package." He turned and began running back the way he had come. His footsteps faded with distance.

A package? I've never received a package, I pondered.

The postmaster's young son had delivered the message, and for no apparent reason, an uneasy feeling engulfed me. A difficult past had heightened my senses to impending pain. "What now?"

The baby began crying from the next room. My grandson, my joy, Bryson. He was sixteen months old. And it was sixteen months ago that I stood at my daughter's graveside; the warm bundle in my arms was of little comfort that day. My mind began to roam with my heart on times past.

It was autumn when Johnny married me, not long after a tornado destroyed the barn that Pa, Lenny, and Josiah built. Pa was so devastated that he piled up the remains and had a huge bonfire. He threw all of Lenny's things in too. He would be completely rid of her! She was the final blow of pain that killed him. He died before Thanksgiving.

"His heart," Doc Keith said, "just plain ticked out, too many disappointments for one man to digest, too many hurts." I was angry too, especially when I found out thirty years after the fact that Pa had arranged my nuptials by promising Johnny all of his worldly possessions. There was no real love; it was a bartered marriage. Although he was very kind to me, he never took my breath away or caused my heart to pound. I did miss Lenny and Pa. Pa was dead. Lenny was just gone, but as far as I was concerned, just as dead! Anger had been the emotion sparked each time I thought of her, followed by bitterness, and then sadness, for over thirty years. She abandoned me. Yet I still missed her desperately.

My three children were a great source of comfort and reciprocal love. The first, Leah, was born in our second year together. Little John came the next. It would be a great surprise seven years later when our precious Rachael came. She was beautiful, inside and out. I could relate to her more because she was like me. She had fallen under the spell of a dashing young entrepreneur. I understood the magic and encouraged the union, perhaps hoping somehow that I could recoup my losses through her victory. I never expected she would die, and I would take it all back just to hug her again. But I have the baby, and he is beautiful.

Leah and Little John moved their spouses to the city to chase their dreams. Between them there were nine other grandchildren for me to spoil terribly at Christmas. It was lonely with them so far away.

The proceeds from the sale of Pa's farm bought this comfortable home on Main Street, where from the front porch we have watched the world change drastically. The war and its colors came and went. Johnny went to war and came back, only to become sheriff. The community has deep respect for Johnny, and honestly, he has been a wonderful father, a good provider, and an adequate husband. Still I feel something has been missing.

Tiny hands tugged my dress, and me—back to the reality at hand. I looked down into that precious face that warmed me as only it could. "Let's get you cleaned up and go for a walk," I told him. With the baby satisfied and hugged, I took one last glance into Ma's blackened looking glass, straightened my hat, and we ambled toward the post office.

With kid gloves, the postmaster passed the brown-papered package into my hands, "It's from Missouri," he said.

I had never received any mail from Missouri. Oddly enough, my heart was unmoved. Even I was surprised at absolutely no surge of emotion. "Thank you."

Bryson and I strolled back up the boardwalk, sharing short greetings with others in passing. I carried the package like the mystery that it was.

I wasn't anxious to look inside or curious. Perhaps fear of some sort kept me at arm's length from the unknown. At home, I put the baby down for his nap, picked up the needlework, and sat to sew. But I couldn't take my eyes off that package, powerfully capturing my wonder. Johnny was gone on one of his political trips with the senator. *Should I wait until he comes home to look inside?* A clap of thunder startled me and I jumped. Clouds hid the sun, and the darkness suited my mood. "No, I'll open it now."

The box felt weightless and strange, neither hot nor cool, not good or bad. I did not recognize the handwriting. Ever so slowly I untied the string and pulled the paper away. The velveteen hatbox was rich, dark green in color. With hesitation I lifted the lid, almost afraid. Lightning flashed brilliantly and thunder roared across the sky. I jumped again and dropped the lid. A familiar fragrance drifted from the box. My hands trembled as I reached for the crumpled paper inside. It was a note from the same unfamiliar hand. It read:

> *Lenny's desire would be that you have this package. She tried but never totally forgave herself for leaving you. I buried her regret in the same pine box.*
>
> *—Josiah*

Now my heart *was* pounding. All those mixed and unbridled emotions flooded my soul. Tears filled my eyes and weeping would not wait. Lamentations, the unknown, and uncertainty filled the room and replaced the air in my lungs; it was most difficult to breathe. An unknown period of time elapsed and eventually dissipated some of that, so I focused once more on the green box. Peeking inside, I recognized the lace pocket of Ma's apron. The feel of the fabric on my hands was instant recall of a million memories even though the apron itself was tattered and discolored. It was as if Ma and Lenny both were with me. It was comfort and longing at the same time. I held the garment next to my face and felt the kiss of Mother. I breathed deep its fragrance and felt Lenny's shoulder. For a brief instant I was as happy as I had been in forty years. It was like going home. While still holding the antique material, I glanced back into the box. A small earthen jar was topped with a plug. It fit easily into my hand. Daringly, I pulled the top, only to again relive memories of the aroma. The matter was of faded grayish color, a dried, leafy substance, with a small piece of brown paper coiled in the midst. I unrolled the paper and acknowledged Lenny's neat handwriting.

Sage—the herb of happiness. The presence of Ma and Lenny again overcame me. Happiness indeed! There was one more item inside the hatbox. This one would require both hands, so I gently laid the jar and apron aside. The book was of old parchment paper neatly tied, as only Lenny could do, with gray twine. There was only one word on the cover. *Journal.* And I knew that it contained all those missing years. And I knew that she was no more gone this day than she was that sad, sad day thirty-three years ago, but this day I would patch the huge hole in my heart because this book would be the bandage. I pushed the needlework aside and snuggled down deep in Johnny's overstuffed chair. The rain pattered softly on the tin roof as the dark sky sifted in like a fog. I trimmed the lamp up and twisted the wheel for brightness. The apron was laid across my lap, the earthen jar by my side. I pulled the knot from the gray twine and opened Lenny's life to the first page.

APRIL 5, 1860

It has been almost one year, a year too full of newness and adventure to lend time for anything other than living directly in the moment.

Vividly I recall the emotions on that day. It was either the horses' hooves or my own heart pounding through my ears; I could not determine which. We rode away full of excitement, which only coated the remorse. I should have told Pa and my sister good-bye. But how overwhelmed I was at the opportunity to have a life outside that desolate, dried-up, old farm! My own life. The thrill exceeded the respectable and proper way to handle my departure. It was me, completely me, not Josiah, who chose to slip off in the night. He wanted to prepare them. I just couldn't say good-bye. I didn't have the guts! Totally uncourageous, a coward to the heart! Now I know that I shall regret that decision to my grave. I will press on with my eyes and mind open for the way to right my wrong. Pressing on, yes, but in the back of my mind and the pit of my stomach is that constant annoying tinge of guilt. I can't sleep it off or vomit it out. My prayer is that somehow they will forgive me. Not that I deserve it; I don't. But they do!

Josiah Bozeman was too big a prize to pass up. I was completely shocked when he asked me to be his wife and help build a homestead in Missouri. I never dreamed that he would look twice at me, especially since my sister was so beautiful. She was mesmerized with Josiah, but had committed her heart to Johnny. I never thought Pa would let her marry at sixteen, and considered she and Pa would have many more years together on that farm. They would be fine without me, and I would never again have such an opportunity. My mood of exhilaration blinded all common sense! Divine intervention! I believed. And in such, I justified my rash decision to accept Josiah's proposal. It seems selfish now.

Two weeks we rode. I was in great awe of the landscape, its majesty, its beauty, and I felt so ignorant of the mighty power of the Creator's work.

I watched Josiah carefully unfold the document of homestead. Nightly he read its contents. A dreamy look would cloud his eyes as he spoke of his plans and dreams. Those powerful hopes transferred into me as he held me close, and we indeed became one with a mission and each other. A justice of the peace heard our vows, and I became Mrs. Luvina Bozeman on April 27, 1859. However, in my heart I had been Lenny Bozeman since the first day I laid eyes on Josiah. And still today he remains every hope, dream, and wish a girl could possibly imagine.

The last day of our journey was perhaps the most exciting. We camped for the final night along an incredibly beautiful river called

Eleven Point. Josiah is quite a storyteller, and no matter how outlandish, I always believe him. His lips take on that warm grin, and he cocks his head a little to the right, and his eyes narrow a bit when he tells really tall tales. I humor him with wide-eyed surprise and drenching gullibility. We shared wonderful hours along this clear, musically rolling river. I thought of how our life mirrored the stream, beautifully flowing into unknown territory, carrying every dream like a fallen leaf.

The sycamore trees stood mightily along the banks, occasionally bowing to the river, as peasants would a parading king, their white and gray bark flaking off like peeling paint. It was too early for the leaves on the hardwoods to be anything more than a faint color of green, but the pines towered on the hillsides and their dark evergreen needles were quite the contrast to a brilliant blue sky.

We watched rabbits hopping through the underbrush while cat squirrels scampered across trees limbs. An occasional deer would sneak up to the water's edge for a cool drink. We saw raccoons washing their catch, and a polecat ran away quickly at the sight of us. There were an amazing number of birds that I had never seen before. Josiah is an expert, I suppose, as he schooled me on their names and habits. I was so taken by the mighty bald eagle as it soared great heights and nested in the tallest trees. The cardinal and robin's colors seemed brighter here. There were also some small, iridescent, blue birds that Josiah called buntings and he added that they were his favorite. I could have watched them all day.

Above the north side of the river, the Dresden sky began to darken into midnight blue outlined by silver. The sky to the west was dazzling! A huge sphere of orange melted into the tree line and clouds of purples, golds, and russets poured around it like an artist's spilled paints.

My hair was damp from the falling dew, and I shivered at the light chill. The blankets were wet too, and I drew them nearer the fire and crawled in. Josiah was studying his document. I could tell by his eyes that he was building. The man had the most practical and well-laid plans. This attribute earned him additional admiration from me. In fact, whether he is walking toward me or away from me, he seems eight feet tall. He is my Atlas. I believe that he shared all his mental designs with me, and although I could not see the plans as clearly as he could, I completely trusted his resolute confidence.

Upon waking that morning, I was startled by a loud, deep, rough-rolling sound that I had never heard. I learned quickly that it was a gobbler, and that springtime in these woods has its own agenda and takes on a special life. I was thinking how this must truly be heaven on earth as we packed up for our last day of travel. Before nightfall, we would be at the homestead. The spring mood affected me too, and I was giddy! I didn't know whether to pounce on Josiah and kiss him about the head or just let out a big squeal. I opted for neither and held it all in. Every time I remember that morning, I can actually smell that day, feel the sun, hear those sounds, and taste the salty breeze. My mind's eye can see those radiant colors twice, once on the hillsides and again mirrored in the water.

The horses nervously stepped and weaved from side to side as we packed them. They too sensed the excitement. The cool breeze easily moved through the leafless trees, along the banks, and the woods woke up and teamed with moving creatures. I breathed in deeply the cool morning air, heavy with dampness from the river. A foggy mist rose from the gentle flow. I stopped at its edge and grabbed a handful of watercress. I noticed the little black dots on the water's bottom that I recognized as freshwater snails. Pa always said that if they were present the water was safe to drink, as they only thrive in fresh, good water. This good water was so cold! My hands instantly turned red, then blue. I thought how fabulous it would feel on a really hot summer day.

Josiah doused the fire with water from yesterday's canteen and refilled it from the river. He looked around the campsite to make sure we had left nothing of our own, nor anything of nature's disturbed; then he turned and faced me.

"Lenny, my love, the next time we dismount, it will be at home." He gave me that Bozeman bear hug, lifted me clean off my feet and then sat me gently on the horse. He kissed my hands and mounted his steed. His eyes gazed into mine briefly before he nodded and jerked the reins. The horses moved in unison toward the winding waters. We followed the stream a mile or two before he was satisfied with a crossing. Here the shoal was of tiny, smooth, round stones, and the water was only ankle deep. It was so very clear that the bottom was magnified and the tiny stones looked like giant glass rocks. The whole river adventure amazed me to the point of unbelief. It was just too beautiful for words. It was spectacular!

Josiah prodded his horse to cross and I followed. I cannot express my excitement, but it soon turned to fright as I observed the looming hill above us. It looked straight up, and even I knew that it would be a challenge for the best of horses. He turned back east and once again we followed the river's course. He acted as if he knew what he was looking for, and sure enough, I saw him smile at the sight. It was a narrow path swallowed up in virgin pine. We took the path north and crisscrossed toward the hill's crest. I was tense, and it took all my concentration to stay mounted. My knuckles whitened. My back ached. I have no idea how long the climb really lasted, but the smell of sweating horses was very strong when at last he halted the ride. Only then did I take my eyes off the ground. The sight was incredible! My head was a tad light from the altitude, but I could see forever. I thought , *So this is the eagle's view.* Josiah did not speak, but looked at me with those I-told-you-so eyes, and we mentally agreed that this was indeed a most beautiful and almost sacred sight. The moment did seem deeply spiritual.

When the sun was directly overhead, we were deep in the thicket, and I could not see the forest, only the trees. It was quiet and so still, as if all the creatures were napping. We were the only beings moving. Up and down the hollers, over one hill, and then another, we pressed on. At the bottom of one of these, he pointed and spoke, "See this white oak?"

"Yes." I nodded.

"This tree is the southeast marker tree of our place." It was easy to see the pride beaming and sense his satisfaction. "We're home."

I really haven't the vocabulary to express my emotions at that moment. I couldn't speak, but I soaked in every visual image possible. We rode on for sometime northwest and then entered a clearing. I was quite shocked to see a small cabin in its midst. I did not know about that. As we rode closer, I saw movement from the corner of my eye. It was a boy. He looked about eight years old, and I wondered, *What in the world?*

The boy ran toward the horses, arms outstretched, and he began to yell, "Pa, Pa! You did come back!"

A boy? What in the world? After reading this I realized she did not know! She really did not know! Lenny did not know how I felt about Josiah. All these years I believed she stole him from me. What he wanted to tell me that night in the barn was that he and Lenny were leaving. He was never interested in me. How could I have been so foolish? I never dreamed that she longed to leave that old farm as much as I did. I am ashamed for how little I knew about her heart. Perhaps I was the one who needed forgiveness. But why did she never come back? Why did she just forget all about me?

APRIL 20, 1860

It never occurred to me that Josiah had ever loved anyone else, much less that he had a child! I sat speechless on that sweaty horse. I was dumbfounded! I was devastated. Instantly I realized that this young boy had a mother somewhere. Shortly I learned that she was in a shallow grave behind the cabin marked with a neat pile of rough limestone, like an Old Testament altar. Judith died during childbirth—the boy was raised by Josiah, and in his absence, Uncle Frank on the next holler north. Yet another surprise: these hills were full of Bozemans, all moved from Tennessee during the past decades. Funny he never mentioned it. Caution rose and my heart sank. *What in the world have I done?*

The boy ran up to Josiah, who had already dismounted. They hugged forever; then he politely introduced us. "Benjamin Wesley Bozeman, this is your ma. I expect you to treat her as such." Those dark brown eyes looked up at me sheepishly. He tipped his hat and said, "Howdy, ma'am." This child did not seem to notice that he was not nearly tall enough, as he reached up to help me off the horse. I obliged, and once my feet were firmly planted on the ground, he gave me a firm hug. It was a hug that longed for affection and acceptance. When he smiled at me, I was hooked, just like with his pa.

We were fast becoming friends. Other than to recite the story, Josiah has never mentioned Judith again. I suppose it either hurts too much, or else he just simply leaves the past there.

I spend my days cleaning, cooking, and building our nest. At night I sew and teach Benjamin to read. He is a very bright boy with an appetite to learn, which makes teaching him a great pleasure. He is such a hungry boy—hungry to know, hungry to please, hungry to love and be loved, and sadly, hungry to grow up. He is also a wonderful, hard worker. Together we have accomplished a great deal, and all three of us have really made a showing on this place. The barn is framed in, the garden spot cleared, and the perimeter framed with split rails. I have caught Josiah watching us work at times, and I do believe that I see pride in his eyes. His affection for Benjamin is apparent, and he spends plenty of time on me too.

The distress that I felt that first day here has gone with the wind.

APRIL 28, 1860

Today Benjamin and I took a stroll through the forest. We quietly walked beside a game trail, careful not to disturb this natural balance. Several times I thought I could hear footsteps behind us. When I would stop, so would that sound. I gathered up my skirt tail and tucked the hems in my belt, so they would not drag in case that was what I was hearing. It wasn't. Often I would turn and look behind, only to see the forest just as we had walked through it. But I continued to have the sensation of being watched. Very odd. I silently hoped that it was not a rabid wolf or panther hungry for fresh, warm flesh.

Benjamin took my attention off those thoughts when he pointed to a pile of deer scat and an area of leaves and peat moss scratched away by turkeys. He is sure that given the opportunity with a gun, he can keep food on our table all winter. We heard the scream of a pileated woodpecker and were scolded by annoyed squirrels. These hours I cherish and look forward to the next day we can share an adventure. I gathered old butternuts and looked for grapevines that will provide us with fruit in the fall. Benjamin is an explorer and doesn't miss a thing. His ample knowledge of the wild is obvious. I am not his first teacher.

MAY 1, 1860

Josiah took the mule to the river today. I'm not sure of the mission. But it ended up being a very special day for Benjamin and me. That child seldom misses taking the same steps his pa does, so it surprised me that he would choose to stay home. He works so hard at pleasing Josiah in every way. I would say that he most always succeeds.

Ben and I fed the hogs, cattle, sheep, and chickens, and then we started chopping brush. We soon tired of that and took a seat under the tall pines for a rest. A nice breeze blew the heat away, and Benjamin laid his little head down in the pine straw. "Look at the clouds, Ma."

The straw tickled my back as I lay on it too. Through the pine boughs, the fluffy clouds floated along like a sky river. He pointed out turtles and angels.

"How do you know what an angel looks like?" I asked.

"I've seen pictures in Aunt Anna's big Holy Book." Never had he spoken of his life at Uncle Frank's before I came, so I was taken aback. I had always wondered if he felt like he might betray someone if he talked about them, and I never asked for that reason. My hope was that someday he would trust me enough to share his heart. "What did it look like, the angel?"

"She had golden hair, and there was a yellow light over her head, bright eyes, a big smile, and wings that looked like goose down. Her robe was whiter than snow; she was beautiful! I love to look at that picture. I always imagined that she was my real ma. It helps me to think that. You understand?"

"Of course," I said. I knew not what else to say. This small boy was so thoughtful!

"Ma, can you tell me about heaven?"

I shared with him every scripture that I could recall, about the gates of pearl, streets of gold, walls of jasper, the river of life, and even about Paul's writing of the third heaven, and how we will be known as we are known.

"Tell me more."

"That's all I can tell you just now, Ben, but I'll be happy to read it to you straight from the Bible tonight when we settle in."

"Oh, please? Would you? I've just got to know if my ma is there."

I had no response to that. I knew too little about her, but I was sure that she was a good and decent woman, or Josiah would have no part of her. We lay on that pine straw in silence a while, and I mustered up the boldness to tell him, "She's there. I don't know if she can see us, but if she can, she is *so* proud of you! She loves you very much and is happy that you are doing so well. I suppose the most important thing is to make sure that you get there too when it is your time to leave this ole world."

He agreed, but I sensed that his mind had moved on to something else.

"Ma," he started, "I am so glad you came. I missed Pa terribly! He told me that he would come back in the spring; that's why I left Uncle Frank's and stayed here by myself. Aunt Anna sent lots of food, and I would go back for more when I ran out. They wanted me to stay with them, but they couldn't make me. Oh, Uncle Frank was good to me, Aunt Anna too, but I wasn't their child, and they really didn't have the room or time for me. But that isn't the bad part. Ma, if I tell you something, will you promise not to tell Pa?"

Reluctantly, I nodded.

"Uncle Dick is a bad, bad man. He beats on everybody. He only took one lick at me; I dodged him and ran away. Uncle Frank seems to be afraid of him. Rufus is just as bad and says that they all obey Uncle Dick because he keeps the money. I think it's because they are *all* afraid of him. He has killed several men already; well, nobody told me that exactly, but I could hear them talking. Ma, why would anybody want to be so mean?"

"I'm sure I do not know. I cannot answer your question, Ben. I have never met any of them." Then Ben gave a rather lengthy description of each family member.

A long silent spell followed, and I broke it by asking, "Have you lived with your uncles since you were born?"

"I can't remember. I know that when Pa was home, I stayed with him. When he had to be gone, I stayed with Uncle Frank. Pa knows better than to leave me with Uncle Dick. Their houses are not too far from each other, or either Uncle Dick can yell really loud, because sometimes we can hear him at Uncle Frank's farm."

Benjamin and I walked in silence back to the cabin. I was not ignoring him but attempting to sift this new information and comprehend the family hierarchy.

MAY 5, 1860

Not too long after I had scrubbed the biscuit pan, a lone rider came up the lane. Hidden from sight, I watched and wondered who he was. Josiah and Benjamin left right after breakfast to cut more logs for the new barn. Their lunch had been packed, and I had conceded to a day of chores alone. The gentleman on horseback wore the face of a man on a mission. Very coolly I greeted him. He obviously sensed my nerves and immediately identified himself as Reverend Tim Reeves, a Baptist preacher from the fifth ridge east. Knowing he was a man of the cloth eased me a bit, but I stayed on guard. He was looking for Josiah, and needed to converse with him on the local action of the war. I offered him a cool drink, of which he readily accepted, and made himself at home in my favorite front porch rocker. Reverend Reeves did not fill me in on the war rumors but did tell me of an Irish Catholic priest who somehow purchased a large tract of land near his settlement. It was quite clear to me that Reverend Reeves did not think very much of Father Hogan, nor his followers. It seems that some of his congregation had betrayed him and turned Catholic. I wondered to myself, *Well, how many gods are there?*

During one of his drawn-out stories about those miserable newcomers, a squeal came from his horse. "Gracious me!" he exclaimed. "I almost forgot what I came for." He jumped up and trotted out to the steed, unbuckled the saddlebag carefully, stuck in his hand, and pulled out a furry creature. "This is for Josiah's boy. Last year when they came visiting, the boy admired my stock dog and her puppies so much that I promised him the pick of the next litter. Here she is." I quickly hugged her tight. She was shivering. For some unknown reason, I shivered too. Reverend Reeves thanked me for the cool water, left Josiah a message of regret, and bade farewell. He spurred that poor horse so hard that it bolted like a bullet down the lane. Reverend Reeves never waved or looked back. Puzzled, I rethought the entire encounter several times. It made little sense to me, and I thought it curious that Reverend Reeves was the only preacher that I had ever been around that did not offer grace, even once. Just before dusk, my men drove the mules in pulling a small load of barn logs. They looked very tired and hungry, so I hid the puppy and busied myself getting supper. Ben was extraordinarily quiet, exhausted perhaps, while Josiah gave an account of the days events. Suddenly a high-pitched wail startled Ben out of his sluggishness, and he fell out of his chair. Josiah's eyes and mouth flew open, my own heart raced; then I remembered what I had forgotten—that poor little puppy. Once she was safely in Benjamin's arms, his meal was over and Josiah began to chuckle at the entire scene. Our laughter turned to smiles when we heard Benjamin name her Patches.

MAY 12, 1860

The mantle clock has just tolled two long rings. The men have long been asleep. I could not doze off, so I got up and lit the lamp to read. The words did not hold my attention, and I have been sitting and thinking about life as I know it, and I have decided to document a few things. I question myself constantly. I suspect that I inherited Mother's blood to a degree, although I dare not compare myself to her. She was a very intelligent, creative lady, and I do mean lady in every sense of the word.

Mother grew up in Philadelphia and was the daughter of a high-ranking public official. Her mother was a great pianist who traveled the world capitals, performing for important audiences. My grandparents insisted that Mother attain a first-class education and become as well traveled. She was sent to Europe by boat on her nineteenth birthday to experience the world. This was not a common practice. They had secretly set up meetings with the world's elite in hopes of a possible union. Mother had a mind of her own and strongly resisted. She had no intentions of marrying for any reason other than true love. She was quite the romantic and severely angered her parents when she left the city and rode west in that dingy, dirty, old wagon with Pa.

Pa was also raised on the East Coast by immigrant parents from the moors of England. They were staunch Christians and came to America to worship freely and live out their dreams. Those dreams failed to become reality, as debilitating illness struck, and their meager living was made on the dirty, rugged, and often dangerous docks. My father was their last great hope, and when they both died, he left that ruthless place to pursue all of those dreams.

The entire story was never disclosed, but Pa must have been quite dashing, as he made an undeniable impression on my mother. She only packed a few precious belongings before she stole away in the night to meet Pa at the park in front of Congress Hall. She never had to face the turmoil and proclaimed degradation of her choice. Mother truly loved her family and desired a relationship with them until she died. They were the kind of people who would rather ignore their own child than to face social embarrassment. She was never allowed to return, and they made no efforts to see her, or us for that matter. I know absolutely nothing about them other than the stories Mother shared. And furthermore, I do not care to. As far as I am concerned, she was the best of them!

None of that ever seemed to bother Mother. She had followed her heart and was always thankful for that choice. She told us so often. She loved Pa with every ounce of her being and all but worshiped me and my sister. Her most prized possession was her education, and she made absolutely certain that we girls learned everything she knew. That is possibly the reason that, after his stunning appearance, the most attractive thing to me about Josiah was his intellect. It was such a pleasure to meet a man who could not only carry on a clever conversation on most any subject, but he did not object to doing so with females. He seemed charmed by our articulateness.

The world as I knew it ceased to exist when Mother died. No one could ever tell me exactly why she died either. Doc Keith said she had digestive ails, and in fact, it was most probably the pain that killed her. In a short period of time she had become extremely lethargic, could not eat, and her skin and eyes took on a yellow tint. Within a few months, she had lost half of her body weight. She could not complete any task. She continued to pray and encourage us, and she never, ever complained. We did not even know that she was hurting. One cool morning I took her broth in and found her asleep in Jesus. That was the saddest day of my life. Pa had to forcefully make me let go of her hands and leave the room. All I can recall of the rest of the day was how fuzzy everything appeared through the water that never left my eyes.

I am including on this date my favorite poem that Mother wrote. She penned these words from experience, for her herb garden was only less important to her than God, Pa, and us girls. I cherished the garden to keep her close and alive to me. I have continued the herb garden here in Missouri, and it is doing quite nicely, I might add. I shall keep it always, as I find great solace and remembrance there.

Sage would be my favorite, and I share it with all that I deem friends. The mere fragrance brings back precious memories of Mother. Its flavor fills my heart and mind with a calm that only a mother can bring—peaceful. And that solace has once again calmed me.

Growing Grace

God gave us every herb that is upon the earth's face.
His reason and purpose surely wrapped in His Grace.
Below you'll find some rhyming words to practice if you will;
The art of living, the art of loving, the art to climb life's hill.
Sage is the herb of *happiness,* a most important thing.
A glad heart it takes to bear the load that life for sure will bring.
Thyme is the herb of *wisdom;* ingest all you can
To learn, to grow, and to keep His Word is the entire duty of man.
Mustard is the seed of *faith;* keep it growing all your life.
It can be the guide that helps you cross the mounds of pain and strife.
Basil represents *honesty,* a trait to humbly wear.
If trust is lost, your word's not good, and there's no way to repair.
Mints are the herbs for *healing* when your body is tossed and torn.
A cup of tea will lift you up if you are sick or tired or mourn.
Parsley is the herb of *friendship;* there's no greater bond of men,
And far more precious than what's at the rainbow's end.
Catnip is a natural *lullaby,* for all of baby's needs.
It soothes the tummy and calms the cry, a mother's help indeed.
Lavender is a form of *peace,* and peace a must to have.
Its aroma alone relaxes like a miracle-working salve.
Rosemary is the herb of *beauty;* look closely if you're smart.
For beauty is only beauty if it is found within the heart.
Ginger reflects *compassion,* so when you get the news,
Don't hastily judge others till you've walked within their shoes.
Dill is the herb of *pleasure;* one needs fun and rest and joy.
Because all work and no play makes a very boring boy.
My garden blooms of integrity, fed from comfort rain above.

Here I find solutions in my precious herbs of love.
So do not use them sparingly; share and spread them all around.
Be the best that you can be, and satisfaction will be your crown.

I had heard that poem before but could not remember where or when. Reading her words made me very lonesome. For a fleeting moment, I could see Mother very vividly, I could hear her sweet voice singing, and I remembered what she smelled like. How odd that I did not know the story of my parent's elopement, I suppose I never asked. The emptiness Mother's death left in my soul has always been present, but Lenny felt it so much stronger than me. I never considered that.

MAY 15, 1860

I went to the forest again today while Josiah and Benjamin were gone over the north holler to help Uncle Dick with some secret chore. Since the vegetable garden hasn't been too fruitful, I constantly search the meadows and woods for additional foods. Josiah kills plenty of game for the meat table, but I enjoy baking a sweet bread or two. I carried a cloth bag that was half full of nuts and felt a strange sensation. I had that sense of being watched again. Every time I've wandered there I've felt it. I stopped and listened and then slowly turned and looked behind me. Of course there was nothing there. But when I was walking, I swear I could hear footsteps. When I stopped, the sound stopped. I have decided that the whole thing is my guilty conscience.

The men came home long after dark. They told tales of the country splitting up and war getting closer to our hills. All the talk of war scared me so much. I recalled Mother's history lessons and even those bloody battles from the Old Book. I could not even imagine our quiet existence disturbed by war or for what reason anyone would have a need to fight in this desolate region. I silently prayed that it was just talk and that we will never see any danger. Uncle Dick was notorious for troublemaking, and that is what I accounted all this nonsense to. It is obvious that he uses fear to control those around him. Uncle Dick will not control me!

Benjamin has just awoken from a frightful nightmare. Just wait until I see that devil Dick Bozeman! It is easy to understand why he has earned that nickname. I fully intend to give him a piece of my mind. After an hour of comforting, the boy returned to sleep. He is precious to watch, so innocent, so at peace. His little heart is so sensitive and pure. He is kidnapping my heart, like a hero bandit.

Although I spend the biggest part of my days alone now, I am so busy with chores that I seldom just sit and ponder. Josiah does things a little different than we did on the farm. I have had to learn and adapt some new ways of getting things accomplished. And I might add, I love it! It is a sincere joy to please him, and this place is becoming my home. I do find myself talking with God, scrutinizing the present and reflecting on the past. At times I long for a quiet place to just visit with my Maker. I should determine to do just that and discover the way to change my poor attitude toward Josiah's kin.

JUNE 1, 1860

Today, I officially met the family. Uncle Dick; his wife, Katherine; Uncle Frank and wife, Anna; and a wagonload of children that I have yet to get straight in my mind who belongs to whom. The wagon pulled up totally unexpected with its load of kinfolks and food—thank goodness!

There was no question as to the leadership of that bunch, not a body moved or so much as an eye blinked until Uncle Dick climbed down, and then only when he cocked his head sideways and jerked it did the others offer to unload. He may be the head honcho, but

I noticed that he did not bother to help any of them, and that instantly hardened my opinion of him. Uncle Frank climbed out next, and as soon as both of his feet were firmly planted, he turned and helped each woman and the smallest children out of the wagon. One tiny towheaded girl did not want to take her arms from around his neck. She appeared to be about two years old, beautiful, and quite shy. The bigger children bailed over the back of the wagon and ran straight around the cabin to the rope swing. I could not count them, but it was obvious that they had been here before. Benjamin was excited! He works so hard all the time, but he is still a little boy who needs to play. I am glad for him that his cousins came.

Katherine and Anna, both much older than me, went right to work gathering food and corralling the little ones. Uncle Dick never spoke, just gave me a long, once-over glare, and then headed for the barn in search of Josiah. Uncle Frank came right up without hesitation and gave me a great big welcome hug. He was a sweetheart to let me know how happy he was that I had come, as Josiah wanted and needed a good wife so bad, and Benjamin desired a Ma. Of the two, Anna seemed happy and outgoing. Katherine was very quiet, looked downward most of the time, and carried herself in a most insecure manner. When Uncle Dick was near, she curled up inside herself like a beaten dog and appeared to be a bundle of nerves. She never spoke first and at all times walked about five steps directly behind him. Her body language alone proved to me that Uncle Dick was less than charming. It is quite difficult for me to mask the dislike that I harbor toward him. He did not speak directly to me the entire day, but he did cast a few commanding looks. It is certain that I shall never bow to that evil man, and it will be a cold day down below before he tells me what to do! I haven't shared this with Josiah yet, but I shall!

I learned that the two couples, with seven children between them, had moved to the adjoining sections several years prior and were instrumental in coaxing Josiah to these hills. (I learned a lot today!) Josiah's own father had been killed by a cyclone. His mother married again, a man that the Bozemans never approved of, and made her life unbearable.

Anna also told me that Dick was beastly to Katherine and their boy, Edward, who is not mentally right, and her opinion was because Katherine took a beating before he was born. Edward does look a sight! His face is very round, and his eyes are like slits that disappear into two lines when he smiles. His mouth is big and his lips very full. He cannot speak plainly, even though he is sixteen years old. He moves slowly, and he's sluggish. It broke my heart to see the other children push him around, and even his mother tried her best to ignore him. Anna said that his brain did not work right and that Dick never wasted time, food, or clothes on him. The poor boy had to take whatever might be left over from all the others. That gave me better understanding why Katherine was unkind to her strange son, although I could never accept that, and I was shocked that this behavior was occurring right before my eyes. She probably took more abuse if she gave anything at all to that boy, including attention and especially affection. Like the weakest of my little chickens, Edward was definitely at the end of the Bozeman pecking order—injustice at its highest form. What can I do? I'll think of something!

I had never seen anyone like Edward, and I found myself watching him closely all day. I wanted to protect this strange boy and hug him. I wasn't sure if that would be acceptable, but I decided that it did not really matter, and as soon as I could tell Josiah and make sure that it would cause him no grief, I would do exactly what I wanted. I was proud of Benjamin when he asked one of the bigger boys to stop hitting Edward and insisted that they give him a turn on the swing. Since the swing belonged to Benjamin, he was the boss (that is just how it is in these hills), and although physically Edward is nearly grown, he still behaves like a six year old. He grinned real big and laughed so hard as he went back and forth and round and round on that swing. It was clear that Edward understood and could motivate in little more than the basic human instincts. My heart bonded with that unloved boy.

Tara, Frank and Anna's oldest daughter, was incredibly beautiful! Her eyes were very kind, and our spirits were kindred. She hung near me, and though she seldom spoke, I sensed that she liked me and felt comfortable here. My hope is that we can become good friends. Her baby sister, Tressie, was the sunshine of the day and eventually overcame her shyness and climbed into my lap. I rocked her to sleep. The feeling of a small person at rest in my arms was wonderfully new and strange. I did not want to lay her down; I wanted to hold her, touch her soft curls, and smell her baby breath until she woke up. But there were plenty of other mouths to feed, so I laid her on my best quilt, kissed her sleeping face, and went to the big room to help the other women prepare the meal.

A feast it was! Katherine baked a huge dish of apples, and there must have been a hundred soft, flaky biscuits. Her new potatoes were boiled to perfection. Anna proudly produced her infamous hickory nut cake and old pan dowdy. A wooden crate contained pork hams and chops, venison, and chicken that had cooked all night in a covered pit. It all smelled so wonderful! Fortunately, I had a huge pot of beans cooking, which went well with the fresh vegetables gathered and prepared from their gardens. We laid old sawn oak planks across the fence rails in the shade that served as a long table and spread the dinner. Of course the men ate first, and then we made sure that all the children had plenty. I took it upon myself to fix Edward's plate and did not flinch one bit when Uncle Dick gave me the evil eye. When everyone sat to eat, I thought we needed a topic of conversation, and I mentioned the impending rumors of war. Bad idea! Uncle Dick shot me a killer keep-your-mouth-shut look, and Anna's eyes got so big I thought they would pop right out of her head. Katherine immediately hung her head and stopped eating. Frank could not say a word as his mouth was full of ham, which seemed to get bigger with every chew. It was Josiah who saved me when he broke the silence by sharing his plans of the afternoon's barn building. Anna told me later that the war was, in no uncertain terms, absolutely *not* discussed by women. *Well!* I thought, *Maybe at your house.* I had to silently count to one hundred as a method of holding my tongue and slowing my anger. I did not know that I could get so angry!

Rufus, Uncle Dick and Aunt Katherine's oldest son, is a skinny young man with dark, hateful eyes, and I do not believe that I heard him utter one word all day. He was a hard worker though and did the labor of two grown men. Toby is fourteen and the loner of the bunch. He stayed off to himself and seemed angry, or maybe unhappy would be a better description. He never smiled or talked. I noticed that his hands were so rough, and instantly harsh thoughts toward his pa filled my head. Temperance did not only look hateful, she exercised that personality to the hilt! In fact, she refused to join us women and stayed in the barn with the men. I thought of how Katherine was so brow beaten herself that she had little goodness left to share with her children. What a sad lot! I attempted to get Toby's attention, to acknowledge him, share a smile, or approval of sorts, but he purposely avoided my eyes. Toby would be a hard one to reach, and I have vowed to pay attention and not let him slip through this wicked web that will forever scar his inner man's heart. Here I go again, trying to take on the whole world when my own closet is stained. Forgive me. I watched Josiah sitting with his kin. Oh, how he did shine! He is much taller, much more tanned, and a million times more handsome! Most importantly, he has heart, and without a doubt, a deeper intelligence. He was kind to each and every one of them. He made a point to rub every boy's messy hair and gave each of the girls a big hug. They liked it too! He asked each of them about their pets and their lessons. The children reacted to this attention in such a grateful manner that my heart burst with pride. They adored him. Josiah is possibly the most thoughtful human on earth.

Earlier I watched the three men and four sons working like well-paid hired hands on that barn. It was hot, and most of them were shirt-less. Josiah's biceps puffed out like melons. His abdominal muscles looked like the rippled sand beneath the river's water. His tanned skin glistened with perspiration as he singlehandedly lifted heavy beams high above his head. Josiah Bozeman is physically the strongest man that I have ever known, yet it is his gentle demeanor that actually gives his silent strength credence. Watching him is as stunning as watching great acrobats performing death-defying feats in a traveling circus. I do believe that his kinfolks admire him greatly, even Uncle Dick.

Suddenly I heard a loud thud and an excruciating moan. We jumped and ran, only to find Toby lying prostrate in the dirt below the unfinished loft. His face was powder white, and his eyes were wild with pain. All the while Uncle Dick was yelling obscenities from above, ordering him to get off his sissy behind and back to work. We dared not intrude but helplessly watched him struggle to get up. The boy's arm was dangling uselessly from his shoulder. I could not help it when I cried, "My Lord, Josiah, the boy's arm is broken. Help him!" Uncle Dick stopped his hollering, and Josiah steadied Toby's walk until we got him to the cabin's porch. A splint was quickly fashioned from slab ends and cotton cloth strips. I made some willow bark tea for his pain and rubbed the swollen skin with chamomile. Toby accidently let his guard down when he thought no one was paying attention and seemed grateful for Josiah's gentleness. He did finally look me in the eyes; I saw a sad, sad young man full of gratitude but helpless to express it. He never spoke. He did not have to; his eyes said it all. Toby became rather fidgety and would have no part of sitting still. He said his legs and one arm worked just fine and shortly was back at the barn. Anna was nervous about the whole episode. Katherine showed no emotion at all. Uncle Frank was sympathetic. I was exhausted from the entire ordeal.

Work at the barn resumed, and we women cleaned and packed up and then took up our needlework. Tressie took a nap. Edward got very quiet as he watched me run that tatting shuttle back and forth through the thread. His eyes never missed a knot, but his face took on a puzzled expression. I made a feeble attempt to explain and show him the fine art of creating lace. He never understood yet never tired of watching. Tara lounged in the shaded grass and became absorbed in a book. Anna worked on the most beautiful piece of petit point. Katherine just sat on the edge of her chair, staring at the barn, sitting at attention, waiting for orders until she could move. I directed several questions and made pleasant comments to her, but it was very obvious that she was not interested in small talk or conversing of any kind. I respected that and left her to her misery. Anna and I had quite a chat. Well, actually, she did the chatting. I had to hurry up just to listen. She is the self-appointed family historian and needed little encouragement to tell it all. Honestly, it was way more than I wanted to hear and was thankful when Tressie woke up. I focused all my attention on that beautiful baby girl. Edward seemed almost jealous when we giggled. I enjoyed the day to a point, but I must confess when the sun began to sink, so did my energy level. After the late evening meal, where nearly every morsel of food was consumed, the Bozeman clan loaded up and headed out. I was glad to see them go, all that is except Tressie, Edward, and Tara. Benjamin was asleep before the wagon rolled to the next hill. He had piled up in the finished barn with Patches for the night. Josiah has gone to the porch, and I can see his eyes are closed and his breathing slow and deep. He has had a long, hard but fruitful day. Just a few moments ago he thanked me for my hospitality to his kin with a sweet good night kiss and a tender pat on the head. Now that the day is done, I am not sure how I feel: angry at Uncle Dick, sad for Toby, worried about Edward, exhausted from Anna, indifferent toward Katherine, happy with Tara, amazed at Tressie, and very, very thankful for Benjamin and Josiah.

JULY 4, 1860

Today I strolled through the forest on a blackberry hunt. Again I had that sensation of being watched. I had great liberty today to take my time, so I decided to settle this once and for all. I carefully chose my steps and turned my body just enough so that while looking down I could also see behind me. For several hours I walked and gathered the juicy berries. Several times I practiced the method that I had just formulated in my mind. I never saw anything odd except my purple fingers, but I never lost that sensation either.

I fancy myself having keen ears because I can hear birds call and insects humming a great distance off. I can hear hoof beats and wagon wheels long before they reach the cabin. I swear I can hear footsteps behind me in the forest. I never have a fearful feeling, just one of not being totally alone.

The brush moved ahead, and I jumped almost out of my skin! I saw the white flag and recognized a doe as she made quick graceful leaps, leaving my view within seconds. "So she's the one that's been watching me." After my heart stopped pounding, I continued my adventure and gave it no more thought. I did stumble upon a beautiful spotted fawn lying in the underbrush not far from where its mother bolted. The little creature stayed perfectly still, and I know it thought it was invisible. I am again awed at nature's way.

A few moments later I stooped over for berries on a low stem, and my head began to swim. I could feel the blood draining from my brain like a curtain falling at the end of a European play. I dropped to my knees, buried my head on them until the sick feeling passed. This was the second time this had happened in as many weeks. I need more rest, I think, and maybe more greens instead of so much meat. When I raised my head, I saw it. I would have never seen it had I not been sitting on the forest floor. The pine needles were pricking my legs, and my head throbbed as the blood returned. So I wasn't for sure that I saw what I thought I saw. Slowly, I stood and walked in its direction. "Perfect! This is it!" I said out loud. "I have been searching for this very spot since I unpacked at the cabin my first day here."

The clearing was shaped like a crooked heart. The ground was covered with a deep blanket of peat moss and pine needles. It was soft to walk on. Huge pine trees and a few tall white oaks flanked every side except the south toward the river. One patch of white flowers blossomed alone. These roselike flowers were white with golden centers, just daintily gracing the clearing like a queenly centerpiece. In the middle was a very large boulder. This huge rock was a mixture of earthy colors, white and blackish specks, and tiny flowing veins of browns and grays. I guessed it to be about five feet in diameter, with an awkward heart shape to it, much like the clearing itself. The top of the rock was only two feet from the forest carpets and at first appeared flat. I climbed up and noticed a slight contour in the center, a perfect seat, of which I took. In a cross-legged position, the view to the south caught my attention. It was much like the one that Josiah and I had gazed upon at the top of the river the last day of our journey here. I could see again forever! The distant hills seemed to roll into each other. One folded in from the right into one on the left and then another and another. I knew the elegant Eleven Point River was at the bottom of one of those folds because I could see a mist rising. The greens blended together like a patchwork quilt and the sky was bunting blue. A few cottony clouds drifted along, which made me aware of the wind. Its musical whistle stirred the boughs above me, and as I looked up I saw them dancing a waltz. The forest smelled like clean dirt under fresh-cut, damp straw. No, maybe it smelled a little like sage. Yes, that is what it was—happiness! This place held so much peace that I thought I had accidently stumbled through one of heaven's gates. I have no idea how long I sat there soaking it all in. My thoughts began to wander, and as they did, my eyes filled with tears as I envisioned Pa and my sister, and the pain of missing them grew as I faced my love for them. The guilt began to grow again, and I told myself that this would be the place, if there ever was a place, to meet and make it right with God. I told him of my agony. I asked forgiveness, for the selfish way that I had left them. I asked for guidance and protection for my family. I spilled the beans, you might say, and began to feel much lighter. I spent plenty of time in thanksgiving too. But it was only when I asked how to fix life for Edward and Toby that thoughts other than my own entered the space. *It is not your job to fix anything, Lenny. That's my job. Your job is to love me and keep my commandments.*

It was during this deep meditation that a strange experience occurred. Scenes and words rolled through my mind like a vision. This is what I only know to call a revelation. I saw a scene of God calling to Adam and Eve after they had partaken of the fruit and had hidden from him. He issued curses on them and on the generations to follow because of their disobedience, but he also forgave them and they got to start all over, yet on different grounds and with different circumstances, ones much less than perfect. Just like that, I understood that he had forgiven me, and even though I was forgiven, I would never forget, because I realized that as a result of my foolishness, my curse was to spend a lifetime without Pa and my sister. I then felt great obligation to attempt restitution since he also gave me an opportunity to begin again. This is the first time in a year and a half that I have had any relief at all from that awful load. By direction and help from above, I made up my mind right then and there that I would ask their forgiveness and make right the horrible wrong that I had done my family.

Only when my eyes strained to see clearly did I realize that it was getting late, and I had to hurry to reach the cabin before dark. I took one long, last look around and began walking in the direction I thought was home. So that I could find my way back, I broke small limbs along the way. The next time I go, I will tie scrap fabric markers so as not to lose the way.

So thankful was I to have found that special haven. I will call it my Prayer Rock. And I will go there as often as I can afford the time. I will grow there and get nourishment and rest for my spirit. My heart was happy and at peace as I reached the cabin clearing and noticed that either Josiah or Benjamin had trimmed the lamps. I jumped like that doe when I heard the scream.

It was Benjamin. "Ma! Ma!"

I quickly answered, and we ran toward each other. He almost knocked me down when he grabbed me. As he hugged my guts out he cried, "I thought you were lost and dead! Oh, please don't ever leave me again!"

I had no idea that he cared so much and felt awful for causing him agony. It was definitely unintentional, and I told him so. As I hugged him back, he eased his squeeze and said for the first time, "I love you."

It was a very good day!

JULY 7, 1860

Today is Saturday. Although there are still daily chores, this day of the week has become a free day of sorts, and we all three afford one another the brief liberty for self-indulgence. That liberty for me today will be seeking forgiveness from my pa and sister by way of letter. I slept on it all night. I wrote that letter over and over again in my mind, and now as I sit to write, massive fear grips my soul! I am so afraid! I do not even know where to begin or what for sure to say. I cannot find the first word. I was so absolutely certain that the Spirit was guiding me this direction. Was it only wishful thinking? Why must I second-guess everything?

After a few moments of deep thought just now, I can almost hear my mama's sweet voice reading. The words roll off her lips that we should not have a spirit of fear but of love and power and a sound mind; we should resist the devil, and he will flee from us. So I have laid down the quill and wrapped Ma's apron around me. Somehow it makes her feel close to me. How I desperately need her guidance and genuine love at this moment. She would understand. She walked in these same shoes. Oh my, I have only just now realized that I have committed the same felony of slipping away from my family in the middle of the night just as my mother did so many years ago. But realizing that doesn't lessen the pain or the responsibility.

There was a great struggle and wrestling with the inner and outer powers. I did finally write the letter. I was startled by a deep growl, and then barks from Patches. I recognized the cracking sound of rocks underneath wagon wheels. Someone was coming, and I was ashamed to admit that in pure dread, I thought, *Oh, please don't let that be Uncle Dick.* Josiah and Ben were off to the river to exercise their liberty in a fishing contest. I seriously did not want to confront that evil man alone! My second emotion was apprehension, as I thought of the war rumors and secret discussions. I mustered up the courage to wait on the porch and quiet the dog. From under the hill, the carriage top glistened. It was new, modern, expensive. I could make out two figures: one dark, one light. One in front, one in back. My curiosity grew with each increased heartbeat. The two heads nodded hello in unison as the horses were jerked to a commanding halt. Then the blackest man I had ever seen jumped out of the driver's seat and all but ran to the back and helped down a beautiful, elegant lady. Her parasol popped open and her many petticoats puffed out the huge silk skirt that flowed like a river spring from the bustle. I saw the pearl buttons on her lacy blouse reflect the bright sunlight, and the feathers on her bonnet moved like the breeze that seemed to gently blow her toward me. Within touching distance, her eyes smiled larger than her lips, and her right gloved hand reached out to take mine. Her voice was pleasant, kind, yet with authority, as she proudly introduced herself as Beth Mae Conner from St. Louis. I offered them both a cool drink and a chair, of which they accepted with much grace. At first the black man backed away, his white eyes wide and questioning toward Miss Conner, but when she smiled and nodded approval, he seemed to relax and be overjoyed.

These two were on their way to a place called Rich Woods to conduct business. They had stayed the previous evening with a group of Irish settlers who directed them down Panther Springs Road, north to Simpson's Mill, then westward to their destination. They had obviously taken a wrong turn or had been given erroneous directions. It was getting late, and I offered them a haven for the evening. Old Zeke, the driver, was instructed to stay in the barn by Miss Beth. She and I talked as the sun disappeared and then rose again. What a wealth of information! She was fluent in current world events and history, and knowledgeable about people and places that I had only read about. For the first time since Ma had died, that empty feeling left, and I was comforted by this sagacious woman's presence. I knew that we had established a relationship, a strong and well-bonded one. I am positive that just as Ma taught, what we have bound on earth will be bound in heaven. I listened more than I spoke, although Miss Beth did hear a brief rendition of my own history. She gladly offered to take the all-important letter to the postal service. She assured me that she understood the gravity of its importance and would make its safe delivery her utmost mission. I trusted her, and I loved her immediately.

Josiah and Benjamin returned with a basketful of trout early in the fortnight, and although very surprised to see such dignified visitors, enjoyed preparing a mountain feast for them. Josiah knew of this place called Rich Woods and explained how it was referred to now as Thomasville. He gave directions for safe passage the next day. Miss Beth was ever attentive as Josiah talked of money matters and business. She took on a serious countenance, and I watched them lost in conversation, oblivious to the world, and wheels turning in their heads. I was impressed with Benjamin's perfect manners; for sure we have made genuine friends.

JULY 28, 1860

It's Saturday again, our free day. Although hot and muggy, we finished chores early. Josiah wanted to spend the day fishing on the river again. I shared my experience of finding the rock, and Ben opted to go with me to see it. I feel so blessed that he gives my inklings attention. He acts like most everything I do, say, or think is of great interest to him. I hated to see Josiah go fishing alone, but I was grateful for the company. This day I packed us each a picnic. Josiah expressed an interest in our plans, but I think he liked the idea of me and Ben spending some special time together. We hugged at the yard gate, gathered our flour sacks of lunch, and went off our separate ways, Josiah on horseback, Ben, Patches, and me on foot.

The summer brought out its own critters, and we hadn't walked very far through the tall grass when Ben stopped to pick off a deer tick. "They sure are pesky little insects. "Ma, what purpose do they serve?" he asked.

Well, that was something that I had never considered. "Maybe they are the leeches of the wildlife world. Perhaps they suck out tainted blood." Actually, I hadn't a clue. "Let's ask your Pa tonight." We both let out a belly roll laugh. It had become an inside joke between us, the fact that Josiah has such a head full of knowledge. Of course, we had no way of knowing if all his facts were truth or if he just always had an answer.

We chatted all along the way until we came to the first broken branch. The fabric strips that I carried in my pockets were brightly colored and would be easy to see, so I tied one there. Then we searched for the next broken branch.

"Over here, Ma."

"Okay, you found it, you tie it on. Really tight please." And so on the journey went until at last we entered the heart-shaped clearing.

"Wow, it is so peaceful." Ben was amazed. We had lunch on the rock, careful not to make a mess, as it is a tabernacle in the wilderness of sorts. "This view is beautiful, Ma," he said. "You should paint this scene on canvas."

I explained how costly paints and canvas are, and he promised that when he grew up, he would earn enough money to purchase a huge supply. All I could ever want or use. "Ma, what are those white wildflowers?"

I had wondered that myself, as I hadn't see them growing anywhere else.

"Let's pick some," he shouted as he jumped off the rock.

I followed. Suddenly I had that sensation again, even though I had not heard any footsteps this day. It was unnerving! Standing near that small patch of roselike flowers made them look larger. Their fragrance was enchanting and they seemed sacred, like the rock. So I asked Ben if we could leave them growing there, as they would wilt before we could get them in water. He agreed. Almost before we settled that issue, he spotted another.

"Look, Ma." Just beyond the flowers was a trail. "Do you suppose it is a bear's road?" he asked.

I told him that I did not think so, but it most certainly was a game trail. I told him of the day I jumped the doe and watched the spotted fawn nearby.

"Let's follow it," he begged.

"Oh no; we should never walk in a game trail."

"Okay then. Let's walk beside it."

Nothing would do but that we walk down into the holler beside that faint path. I reminded Ben that we would have to walk back up the hill and that it was getting hot. A small stream trickled in the creek bed. The water was very cold, so for sure it was a spring branch. I scooped up a drink with both hands. Oh, it tasted good! Ben lapped the water like one of Gideon's army, which yielded a chuckle from me. He looked upward for the sun, pointed, and told me that it was two o'clock. He also told me that the holler would lead us right back to the farm. "Are you sure?" I asked. He explained to me how and why it would indeed. Very reluctantly I agreed to his plan of following this holler home rather than climbing the hill to the rock. After all, this was our free day!

The thick forest canopy provided wonderful shade, and the cold water cooled the air; the walk was most pleasant. Around the first bend was the water's source. Here the earth let forth its bowels and a crystal-clear water gushed forth. Clearly this had happened for hundreds of years, maybe thousands, perhaps the nearly entire six thousand years since creation itself, as the deep gray limestone walls showed signs of liquid wear. Ben was delighted at our discovery! He mentioned the glory of being the first humans to have ever seen this majestic burst of nature. I too wondered and knew that I would indeed return to this spot with the box of chalks. The local culture and wives' tale is that if a person drinks the water, he will always return, so just in case that is true, we both drank long and hard from that beautiful spring. Ben pushed the leafy ferns back and climbed toward the top of the rock wall to take a seat on the smooth, flat ledge. As he climbed up, I was helpless when his hand jerked back quickly and he winced. "Ouch!" he exclaimed, as I saw the blood trickling from his fingertip. I knew immediately that a timber rattler had bitten him because their natural habitat is cool, shady, deep forest rocks. "It was just a sharp rock, Ma," Ben spoke quickly when he saw my face. By the time his sentence was completed, he had reached the top, sat down, and was looking for whatever had pricked him so that he would not sit on it too.

"Ma, get up here! You have got to see this!"

And so I did manage to climb that ledge, and he was right. I couldn't believe it!

Neatly rowed in layers at the back of the ledge were fifty or sixty ancient Stone Age tools.

"Arrowheads," he said. "Knives."

"How do you know that?" I asked.

"Pa told me."

"Figures." I laughed to myself.

"We found one in the field while plowing last year. Pa says that the Osage Indians lived here before we did. I guess we are not the first people to drink these waters." He seemed so disappointed.

We scratched through several layers of peat and dusty matter, only to uncover more tools. There were many! All sizes and colors. Obviously they had been purposefully and meaningfully placed there: a secret stash, a dowry, or a war or hunting campsite; one could only imagine. As I slowly dug with my fingers, I spotted something of a different color, smooth rather than cut, so I found a small stick and carefully dug it from the earth. When the soil was loosened and gave way, it rolled out: a small clay jar. It was beautiful! I climbed back down and washed it off in the swift water. The fingerprint dried on the bottom's baked clay intrigued me to the point of wondering who it might belong to and what the world around him or her was like at that time long ago. Benjamin was more interested in the pink-colored points and the long, slim, matte-black knife blade that looked like pine bark.

"Can we keep them?" he asked.

"Well, they clearly have been here for a very long time. I doubt anyone alive will be returning for them. It seems that they have become a part of the forest. Sure, let's show your Pa."

With that decision, we loaded our empty flour sacks and pockets. "We'll call this place Osage Springs," Ben declared.

"And so we will," I concurred. Secretly, I felt like Cortez discovering a lost city of gold!

Ben glanced at the sun, pointed a direction, and we walked a ways up an incline to the holler's edge when his feet slipped and he fell to his knees with a thud and a groan. I rushed to catch up and help him. His pants were torn and both knees bleeding. There was nothing to do but spit wash them and continue on our journey. I prayed that Benjamin was right about this holler's end! How horrible would it be to get lost in these woods! The bleeding stopped. He was bruised but fine, just a few scratches. Then we noticed the source of the injuries. The forest floor at that very spot was a solid mass of tiny, flat, very thin rocks, all different shapes and beautiful colors. It was like gravel in the river, only not round, smooth stones. I dug my heel in and drug my foot backward. They were deep, maybe two inches.

"Chips and flakes," he spouted.

"What?" I asked.

"Chips and flakes," he repeated as he pulled out a newfound knife. He pointed out the work on this piece and explained how the ancient people used antlers and other stones to chip off the flakes to shape the points. "Knapping," he called it.

I looked at him with great wonder while shaking my head and smiling. What I have here is a miniature Josiah. What could be better than having two of them? We marveled at the heap of colorful pieces and verbalized our imaginations that maybe when an Indian would get injured or too old to hunt, he, or maybe she, would sit on a hillside like this and knap tools all day. Or maybe certain members of the tribe were natural-born artisans and their station in the clan was this, their craft. But we will never really know for sure. So we tied another marker and continued up the holler.

I walked in absolute fascination! I laughed at myself as I thought, *Sister, you will never step on a snake or spot a rare bird, as from now on your eyes will be peeled to the ground.*

Thank goodness for suspenders, as Ben's pockets were so full of the heavy stone work that his britches were trying to slide off. My sack became heavy too before we reached the cabin. But the clay jar was carefully wrapped in a hanky and stuffed in my shirtwaist. I would save it for something very special. And doggone and a thousand wonders! That holler *did* lead back to the farm; it came out just below the barn. We even beat Josiah home and couldn't wait to show him our cache!

When he did survey our find, his eyes widened in glee!

"Paleo," he spoke.

I did not even ask.

AUGUST 18, 1860

Saturday. The garden has burnt up in this extreme heat. Chores were minimal this day, and Josiah wanted to go with Benjamin and me to Osage Spring. He was seriously interested in witnessing our discovery with his own eyes. This was a first! It was the first time that Benjamin and I knew something that Josiah did not. Perhaps we may have been a little too puffy chested, but we were thrilled to lead the way.

The markers were no longer needed to show the way, as the path was well worn. Josiah stood in the heart-shaped clearing for quite some time in silence. When our eyes met, he smiled and nodded his head in great approval.

He said, "Come with me." We followed him back to the path, but rather than go the way we walked in, he continued on the ridge. We had not traveled fifty feet when he stopped. "Just as I thought!" he exclaimed.

Benjamin and I had not ventured this far in the forest, so we had never seen it. The tree was bent ninety degrees, the bend being about waist high. The trunk was a good thirty inches in diameter, and the treetop grew just off the ground and pointed to the holler's bottom. Two knots stood out on either side right at the bend and looked like eyes. From this angle the tree looked like drawings of pachyderms that I had seen from the other side of the world. The three of us discussed this for a moment when Benjamin said, "We'll call it the Elephant Tree."

Josiah called it a thong tree. He told us how the Indians would bend a young sapling so that it pointed to something of importance, such as a water source. They would secure the sapling's position with a leather strap or thong. The tree would continue to grow into that permanent shape, long after the thong disintegrated. Even though he had never been there, Josiah said that if we walked down the hill to the holler's bottom in exactly the direction that the tree-top pointed, we would come out at Osage Spring. We did.

"How old do you think the Elephant Tree is?" I asked.

"Couldn't say exactly," Josiah answered. "I would guess about sixty or seventy-five years old. We would have to cut it and count the rings to be sure."

We explored the spring for hours. Like the tree's age, one would have to count how many more artifacts we found. Hundreds. Josiah thought we should leave them be. He said we would not use them, and there may have been some sacred reason that they were left there in that manner. The spring and its surroundings did have a mystical beauty and deep peace. He wanted to respect that. We did.

On our way home, Josiah too was amazed at the knapping hill, and I could sense his mind working, imagining days of old, or maybe how to make good use of these colorful, manmade flat gravel. We traveled home without much talk, as we were each absorbed in our own musings. I do believe that we brought the peace of the springs home with us. I feel very blessed tonight.

SEPTEMBER 3, 1860

Last Friday morning over biscuits and ham, Benjamin informed us that he had been thinking; in fact, he hadn't slept a wink. I tried not to let him see my smile because, in fact, his snoring woke me more than once. His dilemma: he needed to earn some money, and he had devised a plan. He figured that everybody would always have to eat, and so his vision started with food.

"Ma, we only have two hens and a rooster. Sometimes they lay and sometimes they don't, so this plan will help us too. I have designed in my head a poultry house. There will be nesting boxes and a separate room for chicks. I will build feed dispensers so that their scratch will be delivered automatically and stay clean. That way it will not be wasted like it is now. I'll save feed costs." He paused briefly and surveyed our faces for approval thus far. Josiah nor I spoke, only nodded, so he continued. "This is how it works. I'll construct flat baskets with handles on each end from wire, deep enough to hold large eggs and line the bottom with straw. Each day I'll gather the eggs at the same hour; that way the hens will learn a routine and know when to expect me. The baskets will stack neatly on top of each other so the eggs do not break on shelves that I build in the springhouse, where they will stay cool in the summer and warm in the winter." He paused again, searching our faces.

The corners of Josiah's mouth were turned downward, and his furrowed brow formed the number eleven. Benjamin had his absolute attention. "And your customer base will be?" Josiah asked.

"That's the good part." Benjamin had only begun his delivery. "Pa, if I could use Old Buck, and by the way, I'll pay for his upkeep and even buy him from you if you want, for my transportation. Out of leather, I'll sew huge egg basket holding saddlebags, and we'll take it real easy when we stop by every farm within a day's ride, the same day of the week, of course, that way my customers will learn the routine and know when to expect me. I'll be the egg supplier of the county! People won't even have to keep chickens anymore, and that will be one less thing to worry about. Soon the word will get around, and I'll have to establish routes, so I might not be able to help you around here, Pa, but say maybe two or three days a week. Sorry. I know, I know, you are wondering about the money. It is true; very few people in these parts have a great deal of money, but

I've thought that out too. You see, if they cannot pay me in coins or paper, I'll barter with them for something else. Then I'll sell or trade it at the next stop, and on and on it goes. If I should end up the month with more goods than money, then I'll take them to Thomasville and sell them to Mr. Woodside at the general store. That will become a routine, and they'll know to expect me. Heck, even the people in the village will know to come and see what I've got. Why, they may want me to deliver their goods on our trip back, and I can make money both ways." By now the boy's voice had grown louder and louder along with his excitement. His plan just kept enlarging itself. He was out of breath by the time he finished his presentation and sat back in his chair, waiting for our verdict.

Josiah ate another whole biscuit with honey and drank a long cup of coffee while he digested the morning so far. This was torture to poor Ben. I dared not speak a word.

Josiah set down his tin, cleared his throat and spoke. "Son, that is quite an idea. It provides a service, a product not particularly in demand, but maybe your marketing could create the demand. It's wholesome. It's honest, and it will be a hard day's work for a good day's pay; that is, if you can make it all come together. I am rather impressed by your ambition, your consideration of the family, your attention to detail, and your long-range vision."

Benjamin never took his eyes off his pa as he rendered that opinion and was stone faced.

Josiah rested his elbow on the table and then rubbed his chin with that strong, tanned hand. His eyes turned upward some, as if in deep consideration. I became totally lost in this father-son exchange; it was almost a sacred passage of manhood moment.

"I'll tell you what. After chores, let's build a rope net, take those old sawmill slabs that we have no need of, and build that main room of your hen house. Then tomorrow when we go for supplies, we'll pick up your first brood. You'll have time to build your nesting boxes and wire baskets on the porch at night, and by the time your chickens are laying, you'll be ready for business. And I'll loan you Old Buck, no charge, the first month."

That young boy beamed like a lighthouse! He seemed to suddenly grow another foot tall! He leaped from that chair, hugged his pa, and ran outside to get his chores finished. I barely caught him say, "Thanks for breakfast, Ma. I love you, Pa."

Sure enough, yesterday evening at dusk, they rolled in with twenty or more new hens and two roosters, all squirming in that rope netting. By dark, they had been lovingly introduced to their new home by a creative boy with a heart full of dreamy hope. He beamed with pride as he poured scratch in the feed boxes, and it flowed just as designed. Never had I witnessed Benjamin so enterprising, nor had I seen such strategy from Josiah. He is an incredible pa, giving his son the liberty to learn, grow, maybe fail, and rise again, all while standing far off with support, encouragement, and a shovel to pick up any pieces that might fall.

It was as if Benjamin suddenly realized that I had never commented about his Bozeman's Fresh Eggs and Oddities business, and he asked what I thought. He was still on cloud nine.

"I am very, very proud of your effort and especially your integrity, Benjamin. You are a very bright young man! The only thing that I might add is advice from my pa, who always said that any new venture should be dedicated to the Lord and conducted for his glory. You might consider that. I offer you my deepest support and great encouragement." His smile was ear-to-ear wide.

Earlier while I sewed by the fire, Benjamin gave me a big hug and climbed that loft to sleep and dream. I could hear his mumbled prayers. Josiah was already fast asleep.

Just now Benjamin came down from the loft. His countenance had fallen and so did my heart when I saw his face. "What is it, honey?" I asked.

"Ma, I've been thinking about your advice, and well, how in the world am I going to baptize all those chickens?"

OCTOBER 2, 1860

This has been the weirdest day! It is Tuesday. Josiah and Ben were not back from the journey to Thomasville. Tara left right after breakfast. I love that girl! She has been with me since the ten minutes after the men rode off Sunday morning. I never cease to be amazed at how things just fall into place like that. I did not look forward to spending these days alone, and just like that, she shows up. I think she longs to get away from her big sister duties occasionally, and she is after all, a young woman, old enough to start her own family. She must be thinking of that herself because she quizzed me at length with a thousand questions about how Josiah and I met and what I felt and thought, and what it was like to be married to him. Of course I became all tongue-tied when I attempted the answers. She even blushed at my blushings. I believe that Tara adores me as much as I do her, and I am eternally grateful for our friendship. With Frank and the other children to care for, I imagine her mother is just too encumbered to build a close and special bond. I don't want to be her mother; it seems much more valuable to have a friend relationship. She asked me to teach her to tat, so I dug through the old tin box of threads and found the bone shuttle that belonged to my own mother. Gently she held that lace-making tool as if it were a great treasure. It is to me! She was a natural, swiftly caught on, and was soon tatting long rows of very pretty, dainty, and nearly perfect lace.

She had not been gone ten minutes and probably not even out of earshot when I became terribly lonely. Without the men at home, my chores were few, so I decided that a walk through the forest would be the cure. The leaves had begun to turn, so I grabbed my wooden box of chalks, donned my bonnet, swept up the nut basket in my other hand, and set off. Maybe I would gather the first fallen nuts (maybe that was just to cover up my guilty feelings of wanting to entertain and medicate myself by drawing, rather than working). I trudged onward, straight down the well-worn path to the rock. Not far into the woods, the footsteps behind me were obvious. I could sense panic rising into my heart. In my mind I could hear Josiah's voice. "No matter what comes, remember, don't panic." *Too late.* I stopped. More than once. Maybe as many as eight times. So did the footsteps, every single time. And each time I turned around, I very slowly and earnestly searched the landscape. Nothing. I scolded my silly self, and by only absolute stubbornness went on to the heart-shaped clearing. The sketchbook and chalks were scattered near my feet on the rock when that acorn hit me on the head and scared the ever-lovin' daylights out of me. I didn't scream, but I did nearly wet my pantaloons. I swear that squirrel was laughing at me. Well, this day's drawing left a lot to be desired, so I wrapped it all up and headed home. In another two weeks the color in these hills should be brilliant; maybe then I'll have a drawing worth its salt.

I must have stayed focused too long, as it was way beyond dusk by the time I made it back to the cabin clearing. I will confess the trip home frightened me more than ever. I let my imagination get the best of me, and besides hearing the footsteps behind me, I am sure I also heard huffed breathing. A light in the window of that cabin was one of the most welcomed sights that I have ever seen. My men were home! I was safe! Thank you, Lord! They had already eaten and were getting ready for bed. I was greeted with two generous hugs, one from each, and an extra kiss from Josiah, along with a sweet scolding for staying in the woods so late. My nerves were still a bit raw, and I wasn't at all sleepy, so I thought I would start my next morning's chores. I gathered the soiled clothing from the saddlebags and heard paper crinkle. The paper I pulled from Josiah's pocket was a newspaper article, torn neatly on every edge from its page. The headline instantly confused me. I did not understand it, nor why Josiah would have it. And so it went:

Friday, May 09, 1851 *The Memphis Enquirer*
"Unknown Creature Sighted in Arkansas"
"Wild Man of the Woods"

During March last, Mr. Hamilton of Green County, Arkansas, while out hunting with an acquaintance, observed a drove of cattle in a state of apparent alarm, evidently pursued by some dreaded enemy. Halting for the purpose, they soon discovered as the animals fled by them that they were followed by an animal bearing the unmistakable likeness of humanity. He was of gigantic stature, the body being covered with hair and the head with long locks that fairly enveloped his neck and shoulders. The wild man, for we must so call him, after looking at them deliberately for a short time, turned, and ran away with great speed, leaping twelve to fourteen feet at a time. His footprints measured thirteen inches each. This singular creature has long been known traditionally in St. Francis, Green and Poinsett counties. Arkansas sportsmen and hunters having described him so long as seventeen years since. A planter indeed saw him very recently but withheld his information, lest he should not be credited until the account of Mr. Hamilton and his friend placed the existence of the animal beyond cavil.

I'll not sleep a wink all night, nor will I *ever* complete the drawing from the rock.

OCTOBER 3, 1860

I really did not sleep well! While Ben was drawing the morning's water, I asked Josiah about the article. He looked puzzled and took it from its place. He read the story as if he had never seen it. He looked up at me in silence for a moment, then the number eleven between his eyes disappeared and he began to laugh. "My dear Lenny, did you not see the other side?"

Well, no I did not. I was so mortified by the wild man story, I could scarcely think of anything other than my own spooky adventure of the day. It seems that on the backside of that newspaper story was an article commemorating the official opening of the University of Missouri ten years prior. Josiah said he tore the paper from a wall at the general store (there were many layers of glued newspaper there for insulation) to give to Miss Beth on her next visit, as she was an alumna, and he was sure that she would appreciate the clipping. He never even read about the wild man … so I never shared my feelings about it, as he found it so amusing—and I did not.

OCTOBER 20, 1860

Tara came calling again, but today she brought her cousin, Edward. It seems that Uncle Dick is on a tangent, and Tara offered her Aunt Katherine a brief reprieve. She would take care of Edward for a few days. How sweet! That girl is very special! She fills some of the emptiness I harbor from my sister's absence. As always, their hugs and smile were like good medicine. Tara told her story of how Edward completely attached himself to her when he saw her tatting. He was fascinated at that shuttle moving back and forth so swiftly, the same way he did me that first day we met. Odd thing was, he never offered to touch the threads, shuttle, or finished product; the movement alone seemed to mesmerize him. His delight was so obvious, I had to wonder why his mother did not notice and tat herself, for no other reason than to entertain him. Then I remembered Uncle Dick's rage and disdain toward the innocent boy. My hackles begin to rise, even as I write. I have to talk myself off that high horse every single time that man crosses my mind. He is nothing more than plain and simple evil, at least in my opinion! I don't dare even think, *Yes, but how does God look at him?* because I would rather just not like him!

The day was perfect! Four or five indigo buntings fluttered before us on the trail. That autumn nip was in the air, a tiny hint of chill, and the sky was brilliant blue, not a cloud in sight. A picnic at the rock would be the order of the day. I had wanted to share the sight with Tara anyway, and Edward would have a great adventure too. He skipped ahead of us along the trail until it ended. Once inside the clearing, his mouth made a pie shape, and he jumped up and down. Tara asked him to speak softly, as this was a quiet place. She sensed it too, I saw, and Edward totally understood. We enjoyed our lunch on the rock. There were only a few of the little white flowers still blooming, but their stocks were lush and green. Tara walked closer to get a better look. "Oh my, they smell so delightful!" she exclaimed. I agreed, and she asked if I thought it would be okay if she spread her blanket nearby.

Edward went right to work clearing the rock of fallen cones and tiny twigs.

Now this is true peace, I thought as I climbed off the rock to investigate an unfamiliar bird call. As I scanned the branches for the singer, I noticed the huge, fluffy, white clouds lazily drifting across the sky. I glanced at Tara, who had by now fallen into a nap. Edward's noise-making had stopped, so I turned back toward the rock to see what he was doing. He was just sitting there. Just sitting there like stone with a slight smile on his lips. His eyes were turned upward, as was his chin, staring into space, perfectly still and silent. I have no idea how long I stood there watching him, like time itself had stood still, but suddenly those white fluffy clouds broke open, and a lone, brilliant ray of sunshine fell on the touched boy. Just him. He looked as though a box of candles had been lit behind his head as a thin beam of light seemed to encircle him. Then just as suddenly, the light disappeared. I looked up the moment the clouds closed and then looked back to Edward. His eyes were shut now, but his mouth formed an upward crescent moon shape, ear to ear. His hands were clasped together as if in prayer. It was one of the most beautiful few seconds in time that I have ever witnessed. "No," I whispered to myself, "*this* is real peace."

The spell of the moment was broken by the repeated balk of a pesky old jaybird. Tara awoke, and Edward climbed from the rock, took her hand, and pulled her toward home.

"Looks like it's time to go." She smiled.

We chatted merrily all the way back while Edward picked every wild aster in his path. I never told anyone about what I witnessed. The words of mortal man are simply not enough. It is a treasure that I cannot share by speaking out loud, lest I dare lose it.

The two headed for their own homes long before nightfall. Their tummies were full, and they left well hugged. Edward's treasure for the day was the ball of tatting thread ends that had been growing for years, and Tara tucked away a small, tied, cloth bag of happiness. Sage, that is.

JANUARY 1, 1861

The year turned over today, a place to start again. It is understood that history started one second ago, and a person can decide to begin again at any given moment or place, but the first day of a new year has always presented itself to me as the perfect occasion to reflect and refresh. Especially this year! I need to be sure about everything! My belly is very swollen, and Josiah says the baby should come before the geese begin to fly north. I have no idea when that is, but it shan't be long now. It has been over six months since Miss Beth took the repentance letter to my family. Although we haven't heard from her, I trust that it has been delivered. Delivered! What a word—and exactly what I am waiting for, and wanting to be— delivered—from the guilt, and of this new person growing inside of me. Now more than ever I miss my pa and my sister! I have to wonder if a person ever pays in full for a bad decision. I am positive that my sister would greatly rejoice at becoming an aunt. And Pa, oh, my dear, precious pa, how often he spoke of grandchildren. He never said it out loud, but I could tell that it was very important that he honor his own parents' dreams by continuing the family. I am sorry for him and Ma that they had no sons. At this moment, I am determining to raise this child in a manner that will fulfill his dreams and hopes with great honor. Writing has become difficult just now, as tears have blurred my vision. Had I known the power of this pain, I would have never left them the way I did!

Benjamin has taken over all my outside chores. Josiah demanded it since the baby is so near. Thank goodness the winter has been mild so far and unseasonably warm. He hasn't allowed me in the forest for weeks now, so I make laps around the barn to keep my muscles firm, with Patches right on my heels. We have decided on the baby's name. If it's a boy, we will call him Daniel Seth Bozeman, after Josiah's pa. And if a girl, we will call her, Lucy Leah after my sister. The old middle-wife (as Benjamin called her) who helped deliver Anna's children died of exposure a few winters back. Josiah has laid the plans. When the time comes, Benjamin will take the fastest horse straight through the woods and bring Tara to help. She is well aware of these arrangements and has her bag packed and ready. This will be the first baby that she has actually delivered on her own, but she has assured me that she knows just what to do, as she watched the granny woman bring in the last of her four siblings. She says the old granny woman rubbed her head three times to pass on the enchanted skills because she had the true calling. But Tara also told me that she is quite nervous about the whole thing. So as to not forget, she laid out Josiah's sharpest knife on the bedstead. That frightened me so! I asked what she intended to cut, and she said, "Just the pain. I'll toss it under the bed as soon as I get here."

"What?" Well, she should know; she's the one the old granny woman anointed and passed the mantle of middle wife to. I chuckle as I write this, but truly, I am apprehensive too. I do believe that every person born is a precious soul sent from God. So I take great comfort in that.

Patches is barking. It's Miss Beth. I must be clairvoyant!

You truly did love me, didn't you, Lenny? You planned to name your baby after me. I love the way you treated Tara.

It's the same way you always treated me. I cannot help but harbor a bit of jealousy toward her, but am so grateful that she was there with you.

And now a baby! Lenny, why? Why didn't you find me? I missed so much! And you missed me too! I can tell you did.

JANUARY 4, 1861

I cannot believe the beautiful layette that Miss Beth and Old Zeke brought. There are the softest blankets, gowns, caps, and even store-bought cotton diapers with fasteners! I was so shocked! The beautiful lace and delicate fabric was more elaborate than any I had ever felt. "Straight from Paris," she said. Old Zeke's eyes misted up as he witnessed my joy and great delight. He obviously adored, admired, and respected Miss Beth a great deal. I think that is a two-way street. More amazing than the French delicates was how she knew about the baby. She confessed that she saw it in my eyes that first moment we met, and she knew that I did not even know it yet. "That surprise discovery is far too special the first time." She did not want to spoil it for me, so she never said a word.

They spent three days and two nights with us. I cannot describe the visit; it was like Christmas morning, like finding that Stone Age cache, like the first time I heard Josiah say I love you. It was so wonderful! We shared and laughed, and our bond strengthened. During the day, Old Zeke worked with Josiah and Ben, Miss Beth helped me with my chores while talking of their ventures, and as we drank the afternoon tea from England, she schooled me on what to expect at the birth and motherhood, and she taught me how to take care of a baby. How could I ever show my gratitude? But I think she knows.

As always, there were small tokens and gifts. She had for Benjamin a book titled *Moby Dick* and thought it was a good primer of sorts. She said that if his reading was not up to the level, I might read it aloud to him, "Good idea," I agreed. There were newspapers for Josiah, so that he might keep abreast of the world's current events and money matters. Old Zeke proudly handed the exotic box of teas to me. "This'll halp ya feel a mite better, Miz Lenny." We did not require gifts; their presence was more than a present itself, but Miss Beth was all about manners and the bread and butter gifts.

The most important part of the visit was about the letter. Over tea the first afternoon, her face took on a solemn twist. She reached into her leather bag and produced an envelope. From across the table, it certainly looked well traveled. She never spoke as she slid it across the table toward me. I took my eyes off it only briefly to look into her hers. What I saw was great pain, and my heart sank. The envelope was the same one that I had sent, with someone else's handwriting all across it. Miss Beth took my hand before it touched the envelope. "Child, I am so sorry. After we left you last summer, I had Ole Zeke take me straight to the mail hack in Thomasville. I spoke directly to the postmaster and gained the assurance that your letter would be delivered. On the way here, we stopped at both Thomasville and Alton to check for anything that might be coming back to you. This was the single item." She stopped talking, squeezed my hand, and then gently lifted hers away, leaving me liberty to move forward as my courage would allow. With great anxiousness I picked up the dirty envelope. It read:

Return to Sender:
Ms. Lenny
Oregon County, Missouri

As new postmaster in Crawford County, I regretfully inform you that this mail could not be delivered to the addressees. Neighbors near this locale have reported that a tornado ripped apart the farmhouse, barn, and outbuildings at this farm on October 31, 1859, and the whereabouts, nor well-being of the owners can be determined.

I remain,
Postmaster Samuel Stevens

JANUARY 5, 1861

I have stewed all day, and here is the final gist of it;

I believe that God is just and faithful to forgive, as he promised. I will accept that. But since my letter could not be delivered, and my Pa and sister are obviously dead themselves—they can never accept my apology, nor offer or decline forgiveness.

So I take back everything I said on the rock last July.

How can I possibly forgive myself?

I cannot!

Oh my goodness! You thought we died in that tornado! Lenny, your heart must have been breaking to think of us dead. How horrible of that postmaster to send such untruths! Lies! Even if he did not realize he had errone-ous information, those falsehoods changed a lot of lives! Forever! Oh how desperately I wish you had known that I was still alive!

FEBRUARY 16, 1861

Two days ago, Josiah woke me, "Look at the sky, Lenny."

It was incredibly beautiful! All shades of lavender and coral.

"It's too warm. Way too warm for February," he said.

In a jesting manner I replied, "Should we take warning, Captain?"

His stern look made it clear that he was very serious.

"I've seen this before," he said rather gruffly, then busied him-self, which finalized the conversation.

I was a bit taken back by his actions and attitude, as this behav-ior was completely out of character. So I arose and got busy myself. Before long Ben ambled from the loft, his tousled hair a sight. Normally I would have giggled, but that wasn't the mood in our cabin that fine morning. "What shall I do?" I asked Josiah.

"Prepare."

I wondered for what, but for the first time ever was afraid to ask, afraid to engage in any conversation with him. I had never witnessed an unkind streak in Josiah. Perhaps it wasn't unkindness at all, maybe it was genuine worry or concern, although I had never witnessed this either. Maybe my emotions were getting the best of me, as I realized that I was *so* tired. Tired? Good grief, I only just got out of bed. But I am always tired these days, as it is very difficult to wag this huge belly around, especially since the baby in there must be a prizefighter! This child is constantly jabbing and poking my ribs, as well as all my other innards.

We let the cook fire go out, as the cabin became sultry, even in the early morning. I could feel stickiness seeping all over my body; even my hair felt extra heavy. I soon adopted Josiah's mood and became sullen myself. Benjamin was unusually quiet, and so we carried on our daily duties without speaking. After washing up from breakfast, I just had to lie down. I didn't think I could take another step, and I wanted to scream to that baby, "Can't you just be still?" When I awoke, it was already midday. Thankfully Josiah showed no signs of disgust or aggravation, as I had prepared no meal. He and Benjamin had cut leftover biscuits and covered them with ham from the smokehouse. I thought Ben overdosed his with the wild honey, but before I could comment, my own thoughts overpowered me, "What in the world is wrong with you, sister? You are being a horrible woman!" Of course I didn't, and wouldn't, offer an answer to my own question. Fortunately, I just kept my mouth shut. Josiah was in a better humor and back to doting on me. He even brought me a bite to eat in bed and then wanted to know if there was anything more he could do to help me be more comfortable. What a prince!

As soon as they went back to work, it occurred to me his issue. He was fearful! Yes, that huge, strapping, wonderful man was afraid! I hadn't thought of it before, but when Benjamin came into this world, his mother left it. Poor Josiah, he must be reliving those painful days, and I was not helping by being a selfish, spoiled, rotten crybaby! In its own way, his bad mood was simply a product of fear, which only made me understand how important I really am to him. Well, that revelation uplifted my spirits, and before I could smile inside, I was back asleep.

The heavy rumbling woke me in the middle of the afternoon. I can't say I actually jumped out of bed—my mind did, but my body lagged a bit behind. From the front room window, I gazed toward the barn; nothing was moving. The stillness was eerie, and the sky took on a greenish tint. The northwestern direction caught my eye. I do not know a name for it, but the cloud was unlike any I had ever seen. It looked like a tilted granite wall sitting on the horizon and angling halfway up the sky. A solid mass of black. Coal black. The top edge was perfectly straight, and it was moving ever so slowly in my direction. The stillness gripped me again, and I became aware that no birds were singing, and no creatures wild or otherwise were stirring. I could not see any cattle, sheep, horse, or even chickens. I walked out on the porch and called for the men. No answer. My back began to really ache, so I went inside and got off my feet. The pain eased a little when I propped them up. I noticed the perspiration across my nose top. The sensation in my stomach wasn't pain or nausea, and that's when I realized that the baby was calm and motionless. I could only wonder what that meant, and suddenly I felt desperately lonely and longed for a familiar sound outside. I did not know what to do other than be still. So I did, but I also began reciting the Lord's Prayer over and over in my head. When I was certain that he had heard that quite long enough, I switched to the Twenty-third Psalm. The fourth time I got to the line about still waters, it hit! With such force that it felt as if the air had been sucked right out of my lungs. Darkness had moved in with that wall cloud and rain was pounding the cabin so hard that it was actually shaking. I looked at the mantle clock—five forty. At that moment a severe pain shot from the center of my back waistline in a circle to my belly. I knew I should not have sat in that position so long, so I got up and went back to the window. The air whistling through the cracks now was bitter cold. Before the brilliant flash of light faded, the ear-shattering blast erupted. As I jumped away from the window, I heard Josiah's muffled yell and caught a glimpse of two bodies running toward the barn. I could see the silhouette of horses bolting from their stalls and hear frantic bawling of cows. I could not see clearly through the deluge, and my heart raced hysterically. That sharp pain wrapped itself again around my waist from back to front, both sides. While moving toward the fireplace, I noticed the clock—five forty-five. It was then that I remembered Miss Beth's lectures and decided that maybe I should pay more attention to the pains and to the clock. Surely to goodness this would not be the time for a baby! From across the room I stared at the window; I couldn't see much. The storm was delivering hailstones now, and I was attempting to rebuild the fire; it was getting so cold. Then the window shattered and the storm came inside. I heard my own scream, then I saw it—the flames, licking out of the barn like evil tongues straight from hell. Oh my Lord! Everything near and dear to me was fighting that fire-breathing dragon in the barn! The flames had to be from hell, as no fire could sustain itself through that much rain and hail.

Oh! The pain again. I could see the flames reflecting in the clock's face as I read—five fifty. "No, no, no, not now." I knew I had to get to the bed. The stabbing pain paralyzed me just at the bed's edge. I grabbed the knife that Tara had placed there and flung it under the bed. The pain was *not* cut, but when it did subside, I crawled in and everything simply disappeared: the cold, the noise, the flames. The next thing I remember was feeling the dampness and the pain around my middle. The storm was even louder than before, but the darkness was dissolved by the light of the flames. *Is the house burning too?* I remember thinking. My eyes scanned the room, empty, not another living soul, and I wondered if my passing would make it unanimous. The glass on the only bedroom window was still intact, and I glanced its way. I screamed again, even louder. The figure that I saw quickly vanished. It was the most hideous, grotesque face, if indeed it was a face at all! "*I must be delirious,* I thought… then I heard soft footsteps. The paralyzing pain took over the fear… and lasted so, so long. When it eased, I felt a rough hand brush my cheek and a warm, damp cloth was placed across my face. I could hear a low-pitched voice making a *shhhhhh* sound. I could smell a musty old, leather odor. "Thank you, Lord, Josiah is here," was the last thought before I blacked out again.

I was semi-conscious and felt a strong pressure on my waist, like hands pushing down. I heard that deep, soft voice; it was very calming. Now I could smell smoke, the hail had stopped pounding, and there was only a gentle rain hitting the rooftop. I saw no flames, only a lamp above my head, and I could barely make out the shape of a person bent over my feet, much too small to be Josiah or Benjamin. "Thank you, Lord, Tara has come." I was out again, with absolutely no sense of time.

Relief. Relief was the next feeling I remember. Relief from the pressure. Relief from the pain, but that gasp and shrill cry from the bottom of my bed woke me completely. A small warm bundle was laid on my chest. Long locks of thick, dark, wet hair were showing from the bunting. I could not see a little face, but the skin that showed was glowing in the lantern's light, a rich, tannish shine. This entire episode was surreal. I could not mentally put it all together, and exhaustion consumed all emotion. I pulled the bundle to my face, felt its warmth, and breathed in that baby breath fragrance. I thought of Tressie.

Josiah's voice brought me back. "Lenny, Lenny, my precious Lenny! Please, God, please don't take her!"

Before my eyes popped open, the smell of smoke and burning flesh nearly choked me. I could see his blackened face in the pale light. Sobbing came from across the bed. Benjamin was crying his little boy heart out. *What has happened?* I thought. Then I remembered the storm and that very strange dream.

"Lenny, Lenny! You're back! Oh, thank God above! Speak to me, please!"

I reached up and touched my husband's soot-covered face. He too began to weep.

When Benjamin leaped onto the bed and grabbed my other hand to his face, tears busted forth from my eyes as well. Not one of us three could speak, only sob.

And then, a fourth cry broke out from the end of the bed, but this one came from a newborn baby girl. Josiah kissed my face before he cuddled her, and made no attempt to stifle the tears. Dazed and confused, I was!

Benjamin whimpered in short sentences. "Ma, Ma, I thought you were dead, Ma! We didn't know! We didn't know the baby was coming! The storm blew in. Lightning struck the barn! We were trying to save the cows, Ma. I'm sorry! I'm sorry, Ma."

With the little strength that remained, I wrapped him in my arms and kissed his smoky, dirty head. "Shhhhhh," I whispered as comfort. "Oh my Lord!" I remembered.

Josiah's eyes lit up and a smile creased those tearstains down that black ash on his face. "Lenny, you did it! It wasn't the plan, but you did it! You delivered our beautiful baby daughter, and you are both fine." He immediately bowed his head and began to praise our Maker with genuine thanksgiving. I dared not interrupt his prayer, and yet heard not a word of it as I desperately grasped for remembrance and answers. I realized I was strongly tugging on his burned shirt. He winced, and I saw his own wounds. The burns were deep, but even that wasn't my greatest concern at the moment. "Where is she, Josiah? Tara brought the baby in!"

"Lenny, sweetheart, you are weary and delusional from this trauma. There isn't another soul within miles."

"You didn't send for Tara?"

Now Josiah's face took on that fretful look as he replied, "No, dear, we had no idea that the baby was coming."

"Josiah, somebody brought this baby in, and it sure wasn't me!" I spouted as my eyes scanned the room for the missing piece of confusion. Ben became gravely quiet; his face turned ghostly white as he stared at the only doorway into the room. I followed his gaze with my own eyes. "Oh my Lord! Josiah!"

He turned and saw it too. There was a moccasin-booted leg showing from behind the open door. The only sound was that of our breathing and the popping fire in the chimney. I took the baby, Benjamin covered his mouth with both hands, and Josiah slowly walked over and closed the door with his boot. I squealed! For it was the same face I had seen through the window.

The beady black eyes stared wildly under the layers of draped, bronzed wrinkles. Two tiny, brown hands with bulging veins lay crossed on the chest. The hair was thick, matted, and gray across the head until it separated into braids at the shoulders, where it turned as black as the eyes and was again as long as the buckskin's fringe. I smelled it again, a musty, old damp leather.

My pounding heart, Benjamin's shallow breathing, the baby's gentle smacking, Josiah's footsteps, and the popping fire was a horror symphony playing loudly in my ears. No one in the room blinked, not even the baby.

In the shadows the creature's face looked like a peeled apple that had been left in the entire summer's heat; it was dreadfully wrinkled, shriveled, and very tanned. As straight and still as a French statue it stood, supported by the doorpost, caught and cornered. Josiah stopped within arm's length.

"Weti! Weti!" The sound escaped the pruned lips. Its voice was deep and raspy. She tapped her fingers on her chest. "Weti!" The creature bowed into a motion that resembled a curtsy of sorts.

Josiah backed away, and as he did, the creature stepped into the light. We were spellbound but no longer alarmed. She looked like an ancient one. Her hands unfolded as they extended toward us. "Weti," she spoke again.

Benjamin was the first of us to speak and did so in an innocent, childlike manner, "Are you an Osage Indian?"

The old squaw shook her head slowly from side to side.

Josiah asked, "Do you understand our talk?"

This time the shaggy head nodded.

"Did you bring our baby?" he quizzed her kindly.

Again a nod. "Weti," she again tapped her chest.

"You are called Weti?" Josiah questioned.

A crooked smile moved the wrinkles on her face when she nodded.

Josiah moved forward, took hold of her hand, and gently kissed it. "I owe you my life, Weti." A million questions swarmed through my brain. The scene was dreamlike. Just as before, Lucy Leah broke the silence with her own announcement.

Weti moved like a feather toward the bed. I squeezed my hold on the baby, but without speaking she asked, "May I?"

As if under her spell, my eyes answered yes. She reswaddled the infant and snuggled her to my chest. Lucy hushed.

Weti then reached into the deerskin bag tied to her dress and pulled out a leafy substance and then motioned to Josiah. Her presence commanded the room, and he obeyed. His burns were severe, and he winched once she sprinkled her medicine on them.

"You are Cherokee," he spoke without waiting for confirmation. Weti nodded.

After the shock dissipated, fascination flooded in. Even though communication was limited, Weti insisted that I must have rest. I remember very little else of the evening except that Benjamin finally did climb to the loft, and Josiah pulled our best chair to my bedside after he washed the burnt barn away, determined not to leave me.

Weti came back in with a damp cloth smelling of strong mint and placed it on my forehead. When my eyes closed, my mind went back to the rock. My eyes popped back open. "Weti, are you the footsteps in the forest?"

Those black eyes disappeared below the wrinkled-gathered eyelids, and a toothless grin rippled the crevices of her cheeks. She nodded.

I turned to look at Josiah, and when I looked back toward her, Weti was gone.

FEBRUARY 28, 1861

Weti returned for the first time since Lucy came. She gave both the baby and me a good going-over. That wrinkle-moving grin expressed her pleasure with our progress. The deerskin bag now filled with new medicine; she insisted that I drink her tea.

I had no idea what she sprinkled on Josiah's arm that night, but the burns healed quickly—proof of her effectual herbal lore. He and Weti communicated remarkably. Somewhere along the way, he picked up some of her native tongue; couple that with gestures and they understood one another. Yes, he has become our resident interpreter. Why am I not surprised?

Benjamin has even decided that he wants to become an Indian and has vowed to learn the language.

I was not comfortable taking Weti's medicine. How could I not trust this old soul who saved both of us? Again a thousand questions rolled through my mind, and I desperately wanted to be able to talk to her. I have determined to pay closer attention! Why the big mystery of stalking me through the woods? Actually, I have pondered that since the moment of her confession. Maybe that is why I cannot fully trust her.

Weti brought Ben a bag of nuts, seasoned and roasted over an open fire. They were delicious! She brought Lucy Leah the most beautiful deerskin moccasins, although much too large just yet. The soft leather pouch she brought me was to carry the infant in, much like a papoose in front. She skillfully modeled how to wear it, and reached out both hands begging to hold the baby. Weti cuddled our daughter tightly to her chest, but rather than sit in the rocker, she went to the hard rock hearth. She sat there the longest time, rocking back and forth as that raspy voice hummed a tune and sounded much like a breeze blowing through the forest canopy. The totally contented baby went sound to sleep. Big tears filled the deep wrinkles on Weti's face. *Why*, I wondered, *would she cry?* We could not verbalize our thoughts to each other, but I could feel her heart, and I know now that she is a safe person; truth is, she first loved me.

Weti carefully placed the baby by my side and patted my head. "Shhhhh."

Watching a sleeping baby is like looking into heaven. I never tire of that, but when I looked back up, Weti was gone. How does she do that?

After supper tonight, Benjamin, Josiah, and I sat by the fire. Benjamin rocked his baby sister while Josiah told us what he had learned this day about Weti. Even her name had deep significance, as in her native language, Weti means *faith*. She was thirty-two winters old when the white men forced her from her home in a land they called Georgia, which they thought contained a great wealth of gold. Her home community was Red Bank, and her husband is buried there. Their little daughter was only five winters old, and it was very, very difficult for the little girl to keep up each day on the long journey. Many of Weti's friends and family died along the way.

"Where were they going?" Benjamin interrupted.

"To Oklahoma," Josiah answered. "Five different tribes were moved by the government from the southeastern region of America to a reservation; that is a place reserved especially for these people. But it was cruel and unkind, I have heard; in fact, that atrocity is being called the Trail of Tears. I counted up the moons Weti spoke of and figure it was the fall of '38 when she and her daughter, under the cover of darkness, slipped away from their captors, and by faith ran toward that North Star until they could run no longer. They traveled a few more nights and only stopped running when they found a cave to hide in. Until Weti heard the geese flying overhead, they never came out of the cave while the sun was directly overhead. That cave is somewhere nearby."

"Where is her little girl?" Benjamin asked.

"Well, if I understood correctly, she died three years after their escape," he answered.

"Do you mean to tell me that old woman has been living alone in these woods all these years?" Benjamin could not imagine that.

"That is what I understood," his pa replied. Then Josiah looked at me. "Lenny, she is sorry that she frightened you. She saw you the first time you ventured into the woods, although you could not see her, and you never will because she has only survived by learning how to become invisible. She knew you were inexperienced and knew a baby was coming, so she watched over you like an angel of God. How thankful I am for her! I *do* owe her my life for saving my family. I trust her, Lenny. We must respect her ways and not intrude, as this property has been her home long before it became ours. Son, she watched over you too all those times I had to be gone. Let us always remember to entertain strangers, as we may be engaging angels unaware."

A sweet, sweet spirit filled our home tonight. It was a spirit of thanksgiving, compassion, and charity. As I gaze on this precious, beautiful child, I cannot see how it would be possible to love her more. If God loves his own children more than I do this baby, well, I cannot even imagine how that could be possible, but I am beginning to understand the unconditionality of that agape love. Awed, I am!

MARCH 2, 1861

"The buzzards are back," Josiah announced. "Time to plow the rest of the garden."

We had already planted potatoes and sweet garden peas in the snow. I couldn't believe it! But Josiah assured me that it was timely. I could only help during Miss Lucy Leah's naps. She is such a little creature, yet she demands so much attention. Okay, I confess, the largest sum of my attention is voluntary. I can't help it. She's just too cute. And sweet!

We have not had any visitors all week. Over breakfast Benjamin mentioned how long the winter had seemed to him, and although he enjoyed his new sister, he sure would like to see his cousins. After agreeing that the baby and I were up for a trip, we planned the excursion. None of Josiah's family had met Lucy yet, and I could not wait to show her off and to have Tara hold her. It was settled. We would leave right after the plowing was finished. And that we did. The mood was festive, so much so that I did not even dread Uncle Dick. It has been almost two years since we married, and I have never been to their homesteads. Lucy was a great traveler; of course the steady gait and bounce of the wagon put her right back to sleep. The way was so much farther than I had imagined; it was early afternoon when we rode up to Uncle Frank's. The cabin was larger than ours, the clearing not as big. I did notice a rope swing in the backyard. I had expected children to be running everywhere, laughing and playing. Not so. I had expected Tara to run out, squealing, and greet us. Not so. I had imagined Anna standing on the porch, drying her hands in her apron. Not so either; in fact, the place seemed deserted. We stayed in the wagon while Josiah went to the cabin and knocked. Eventually, he went in and then shortly came out, shrugging his shoulders. The only sign of life was a single smoke curl floating from the flu. "No one home," he yelled. "They must be at Uncle Dick's."

Benjamin's smile turned to a frown. Nothing to do but travel on to the next farm. We were a bit more somber, but Josiah attempted to change all that by singing, "She'll be comin' round the mountain when she comes."

Benjamin and I busted out in laughter, and Lucy jerked. You see, as handsome, kind, and strong as Josiah is, he is that poor of a singer. He is completely tone deaf. Couldn't carry a tune in a bucket. Sure, he knows all the words, but he has never heard the melody, which makes me sad for him. Why, it's like not being able to see the colors of a sunrise to not hear a melody!

He stopped singing and his face took on a hurtful expression. When we finally quit laughing, we took up the song where he left off. He joined in too, and I don't know if Lucy liked it or not, as she never woke all the way up.

When we reached the split rail fence, Josiah turned the team through the opening and down the lane. There were fields on either side. The black cattle ignored us and kept grazing.

"The fish are biting," Benjamin said. I gave him that question mark look, so he continued, "Well, Ma, if the cattle are all standing up eating, then the fish are too."

The roofline and the chimney appeared from the back of the field. A huge pine thicket surrounded the cabin on three sides. I could see people moving about. Male figures were busy in a small clearing to the left of the yard. They had shovels. Girls' bonnets bounced sporadically through the meadow behind the cabin. They had baskets. So far, no one had acknowledged our presence. I saw a ball of curly blonde hair dancing across the porch toward us. It was Tressie. She was shouting, "No, no, go away!"

Josiah jumped out and got to her first. "What's the matter, Tressie?"

"You cannot take him!" she cried.

"Who, Tressie, who?"

"Edward! My friend Edward! He's hurt."

By now Tara had heard the commotion and run out. She looked horrible! Her eyes were red and swollen; she could barely speak. "How did you know?" she asked.

"Know what?" Josiah begged.

"Edward. He's d—d—d..." She could not speak the word *dead;* it just would not come from her lips, and she began sobbing uncontrollably.

"Oh, my Lord!" My own voice sounded foreign. Because my baby was so new, I had to ease out of the wagon. Benjamin was frozen in place. I covered Lucy real tight, squeezed Ben's hand and then went to Tara. Josiah had Tressie in his arms, her head buried beneath her golden curls in his chest. His face showed shock. I grabbed Tara and held her tight until she could get hold of herself. By this time Katherine and Anna were on the porch. Frank, Rufus, and Toby were digging the grave. Temperance came around the cabin, her basket filled with spring's first flowers.

Josiah quickly surveyed the situation, handed Tressie to Tara, and said, "Come on, Benjamin." They took off toward the working men.

None of the women spoke, only Anna, Tara, and Tressie showed signs of being emotional. "Could we go inside?" I asked. They turned and reentered the large open room. I went back to the wagon, swept up my sleeping bundle, and followed. Once inside, still no one spoke. I couldn't take it any longer. "Where is he?" I asked. They all looked at me as if I had spoken in an unknown tongue. So I asked again, "Where is Edward?" Only Tressie responded by pointing to the adjoining room. My heart broke in two when I saw him. Edward was so white and so still lying on that feather bed, his slits for eyes now closed forever. A huge knot had swelled from his left temple. His already large lips were twice again as big and black. There wasn't any blood, thank the Lord. Who knows how long I stood there staring at him in disbelief—long enough for a steady line of tears to run down my fingers and soak the French, laced blanket.

When Lucy let out her wake-up cry, I jumped out of my skin, and all the women in the other room began screaming at the top of their lungs. Overcome in their grief, not even one of them noticed that I had a baby. Given a different set of circumstances, this might have even been a bit humorous. They quieted down when I walked back in the room and uncovered our beautiful Lucy Leah. Tara started weeping again, Temperance stomped out of the room, and Tressie just wanted to touch her. The other mothers were not impressed, as a baby was old hat to them, although Anna did force a half smile and whispered, "Congratulations."

I had to get out of there before I lost my composure. I found a rocker on the porch. Tara joined me. "What happened?" I inquired.

Tara spoke in a muffled tone. "At the supper table last night, Edward reached for a second biscuit. This angered Uncle Dick, as it was the last one, and evidently he wanted it. He backhanded Edward across the mouth so hard that the whole chair went over backward. Edward yelled when the back of his head struck the hearth. Uncle Dick slung his own chair against the wall so hard that it smashed in a hundred pieces. He ran to Edward and began kicking him in the head while screaming, "Get up, you simpleton, worthless excuse of a human being!" She said that Edward became still and never moved again. The family remained silent at the table until Uncle Dick sat in Edward's chair and finished his supper. He only said, "Clean up this mess," as he went outside to enjoy his tobacco. Tara's rendition of these events were told me secondhand, as only a few hours before did she coax this truth from Katherine.

Out of that relentless fear did the family tell anything other than, "Edward's chair turned over backward, and he hit his head," which is a half truth. Or half lie.

By this time Lucy was fed and sleeping again, and the men came in from the makeshift cemetery. I found an opportunity to whisper the question to Josiah, "Where is your uncle Dick?"

His disgusted eyes only met mine briefly as it seemed he had asked Toby the same question. The emotionless answer was, "He rode away at sunrise."

Speaking of emotion, Katherine showed none. She could not be comforted; she was too far removed. Even Anna did not try. Outright fear emitted from all the others.

My energy was spent on Tressie, Tara, and especially Benjamin. He was distraught.

The men wrapped Edward's body in some old, tattered horse blankets and laid him in the back of the buckboard. Toby bravely guided the old mare to the fresh grave. The rest of the family walked in tearless silence behind the wagon. Josiah would not let me walk and carry the baby, so we followed in our own wagon. Not Benjamin, he was right there beside Edward's body. Tressie rode in Josiah's lap. Katherine looked sheepishly weak while Frank and Anna took on slightly regretful expressions. Tara was genuinely mournful. Heartbroken! Clearly in unspeakable pain. Even though the sky was bright and cheery, it was a dark, cold day at the Bozeman homestead.

Edward's body was laid face up in that hand-dug grave. Katherine covered him one last time in the quilt she made during the nine months that he rode inside her. I do not want to believe that it was relief I read in her face .

Josiah rendered an impromptu eulogy, and his prayer was holy spiritual.

Uncle Frank began to sing, "…tempted and tried, we're oft made to wonder…"

Half of us joined in as the last words were sung. "Farther along we'll know all about it. Farther along we'll understand why. Cheer up, my brother, live in the sunshine. We'll understand it all by and by."

Toby began covering the quilt with a layer of lime. Then he snatched up the shovel and began slinging rocky soil.

Josiah grabbed the arm of this angry young man. "Wait, son, let's get your mother and cousins back to the house." Toby turned into a statue.

The girls walked by the grave, one by one, and dropped their flowers in.

Josiah helped me in the wagon, but I asked him to give me a moment. He gently took the baby and nestled her close to him with overwhelming protection.

I made my way back to the grave, knelt over that lifeless body, and reached into my pocket. Tears fell with the tatting shuttle as they all landed silently on my precious friend. "I loved you, Edward. I really, really loved you!"

Our ride home was very quiet, except for my soft humming to the baby. I watched Benjamin closely. How I wish I could ease his pain, his confusion, and the anger that he had yet to feel. Josiah was running all of this through his head as well, I could tell.

"I loved Edward too, Ma." Ben broke the silence.

"He knew you did, son." I smiled at him; though he couldn't see it in the darkness, I pray he heard it in my voice.

"That's the first grave that I have ever dug," he humbly spoke.

The stars sparkled so brightly overhead, my thoughts lost among them. "If you love me, keep my commandments. If you love me, keep my commandments," kept running through my head. *How odd,* I thought. *All this pain and confusion and agony, and turmoil and misunderstanding. Why would this scripture capture my mind?*

"If you love me, keep my commandments."

Then I got it. But I had to ask, "Lord, oh, Lord, *why* did you tell us to love our enemies? I *know* I love you, Lord. But *how* can I love that man? How can I keep that commandment? How *dare* I?"

Now I understand completely why he is called Devil Dick Bozeman. He is indeed!

MARCH 5, 1861

I have struggled for these three days since Edward's passing. I cannot get a hold of the senseless act, the great waste, nor any peace. I cannot tell which rages greater inside me, the sadness or the anger. Josiah and I have spoken very little about the episode; what is there to say? Benjamin is so confounded that he is having great difficulty just getting back on our daily routine. We all are. A tragedy of this magnitude just does not roll off like water from a duck's back. I realize that the mundane tasks must continue, but I know myself well enough to know that I will not feel whole again until I settle this matter in my mind and in my spirit! That is why after the necessary duties were accomplished this morning, I bundled Lucy up and we journeyed to the rock.

On the way, I felt Weti watching and took great comfort in that! I climbed on to the rock and folded into the seat while gently rocking the baby. She soon drifted off into sweet slumber, and I felt the liberty to let the tears fall where they may. And fall they did! I knew better than to ask why, so I asked how. How do I get through this? How do I sit here in the exact same spot where I saw heaven actually shine down on that precious, curious soul? How? Then through my mind the words rolled: "Sorrow not, even as others which have no hope." I pondered these words for such a long time and then asked again, "Is Edward there in heaven?" I waited and waited, but I received no answer to this query, and just before my mind wondered on, the same words came again: "Sorrow not, as others which have no hope."

He is there, I decided. He must be. For no being in heaven would be cruel, unkind, or ignore him there.

I could feel peace flowing into my heart, and my spirit was strengthening. More tears fell; these were of thanksgiving. Truly this peace is not as the world knows it. Now rather than have a vision of Edward with that huge knot on his head and being mistreated, I can only imagine him in a heavenly realm—happy, whole, and wanting for nothing. I can do that.

Now for the other side of the unbalanced equation; I cannot find solace where Uncle Dick is concerned. I vividly remember the scene from this very spot that I experienced many months ago concerning forgiveness, and yet I am having immense difficulty applying that forgiveness for this horrid infraction against Edward. I did not even know what questions to ask. Evidently no questions were required, as my mind filled with stories of Job and how the evil one was allowed to wreak all manners of havoc upon Job and his family. The man's life was altered beyond comprehension, and yet he survived with blessings.

"The sun rises on the evil and the good, and the rain falls on the just and the unjust."

I understand that, but what relevance has it here?

"The righteous are spared from the wrath to come." I pondered that thought for some time. My understanding of it was that regardless of how he made an exit from this world, Edward's soul is far better off than it would have been at Uncle Dick's farm in the years to come, and even though the evil man sent him to eternity, he did the simple boy a great favor by helping him enter glory.

So am I supposed to be grateful that Uncle Dick killed that precious boy? I am supposed to be thankful to this evil man? No more words or thoughts came. Nothing. I watched my sleeping baby, and it finally dawned on me: Edward is safe. Edward is whole, thanks to Uncle Dick.

Lucy's eyes were wide on the way home.

This was almost too much to comprehend! I have never known a man to be so evil! So dastardly! Thank you, Lenny, for holding your own with Devil Dick! You were always the brave one. You made Edward's short life here better, Lenny. And Weti! Oh my, wasn't she a godsend? How wonderful life would be to have known a Weti! Lenny, your journal reads like a battle of good and evil. I was simply sick, to have missed it. I felt so helpless reading your words, so unworthy, almost like a bad sister.

MARCH 26, 1861

Even with those revelations at the rock, it has been most difficult to find great joy these last few weeks. Edward's death brought a very dark cloud of sadness over our life. The silver lining is this precious baby girl. I am fascinated at the way her tiny face changes every day. She is growing, and how marvelous it is to watch her discover the world. The day she found her hands was hilarious, and then when she realized that those feet were attached and she could touch them with her hands, it was a thrill. Those beautiful green eyes watch with great interest each movement and every different color. I do believe that she has my keen sense of hearing, as she leans toward her Pa's voice, and when she hears a bird call, those curious eyes flash to and fro. She is my heart outside my chest.

Benjamin's chickens are in a full laying frenzy. We have prepared eggs in every way imaginable! Josiah and I both agree that he has thus far been successful. His baskets are ready, Old Buck is groomed, his route mapped, and the Bozeman's Fresh Eggs and Oddities business is ready for the maiden voyage.

The apprehension that I have is because the trek will take two days, it means that he will have to stay overnight someplace. Not that I am concerned about any of our neighbors; it's just the war issue, the whispers about it, and tension in the air. . With immense thoughtfulness Ben has offered to prove his ability to survive the elements to comfort my uneasiness. He has planned an overnight campout on the forest's edge at our property boundary. We accepted his proposal and Old Buck has been loaded with everything that a person might possibly need and the egg business supplies, minus the eggs. The boy made camp, cooked his supper over an open fire, and bedded down for the night. The night air had a bitter chill, and I was worried about him getting cold. I could not sleep and spent most of the night on the front porch. Sometime in the wee hours, the coyotes began to howl, and howl they did! Loud and long. I sat there imagining that Benjamin was hearing them too and getting frightened and being afraid to ride back across the field to the cabin. I worried that he may have left some food out, and that would attract some hungry beast. I just knew that he was scared to death!

So before the sun was up, I put Lucy in the bed beside Josiah, prepared a warm drink, saddled the horse, and rode across the property to that scared little guy. When I rode up, I saw nothing moving. I became fearful and urgently called out, "Benjamin!" No answer. *Oh my gosh!* I thought, *Something has gotten him.* "Benjamin," I cried again. Still no answer or motion.

There was a heap of blankets and quilts that I approached and shook with my right arm. Suddenly a little head popped out. "What?" he said. "What is wrong?"

"Nothing is wrong," I replied. "I just came to check on you."

"Ma"—his disgust was evident—"why did you come over here? Now you cannot say that I stayed out all night by myself."

"Well, I thought those coyotes screaming would scare you and—"

"Ma, I never heard a thing all night. I was sleeping good until you woke me.

I feel terrible about ruining his adventure. I guess it is hard to accept that he really is an independent little man. I will have to back off and let him be.

The prelude camp out was two days ago, and as I write this, night has fallen and the stars are twinkling, but no sight of Benjamin. But I cannot help fretting. The boy has been gone for more than forty-eight hours. I swear that Lucy missed him because she has been fussy all day. She refused to go to sleep this evening, a behavior never exhibited before. Josiah may say not to worry, but that number eleven is deep between his eyes tonight. He warned me about making too big of an issue over this, as it might discourage Benjamin. I can see his reasoning and agree; however, that does not make me less concerned. Patches is on guard as well. It was quite difficult to hold her tight as Benjamin rode away. He has never before left without her, except for his camping adventure. No telling where that boy is, but I would guess that he is bunked up somewhere nice and snug. My prayer is that he is well fed, sleeping sound, and that his pockets are full of change and his egg baskets empty.

Well, I may have to concede to his independence, but I still find it difficult to sleep.

MARCH 28, 1861

Last night I was sitting in the large rocker on the front porch when I heard the horse's slight gallop. I quickly went inside. I took Josiah's advice. I did not want Benjamin to think that I had no confidence in him, but I was torn because I did not want him to think that I did not care either.

I could hear Benjamin ride on to the barn. It seemed like enough time to untack and groom Old Buck, but then I heard nothing for a great long while. Finally, Benjamin did come in and attempted to tiptoe toward the loft ladder.

"Is that you, Benjamin?" I called.

"Yes, ma'am."

"Are you okay?" I queried.

"Can I tell you in the morning?" he asked.

"Of course," I told him. "Good night."

Benjamin had a deep frown at breakfast. Josiah finally broke the silence. "So can you tell us about the first run of the Bozeman's Fresh Eggs and Oddities?"

Benjamin's head hung so low. "Pa, it was nothing like I planned or thought it would be. I first stopped at Uncle Frank's; he wasn't there, but Aunt Anna said that they did not need any eggs. They could not eat all they had, but she thanked me for coming by. The other boys laughed at me as I rode on. With that kind of reception, I had no desire to go to Uncle Dick's. So I rode off, and the more I thought about it, the more I was almost embarrassed and began to think my idea was stupid. After nearly two hours, I came to a fence and lane, so I spurred Old Buck up it. There was a nice cabin, and a young woman came out and said they had chickens too and needed no eggs. She told me that I had better ride on and be careful because she had heard that Union troops were in the area. She must have been afraid of me too because I could tell she did not trust me and would not offer her name even when I introduced myself. By this time I was really doubting. I only made one more stop that day and was greeted by a double-barrel shotgun. Pa, I tried to find my way to the Irish settlement, but I must have taken a wrong turn because I rode until the sun was almost at the treetops and never saw another home . I found a nice flat spot surrounded by tall pines and made camp. I could not get a fire started, so I ate my supper cold. Then it started sprinkling, and my bedding was soaked. I wasn't afraid, but it sure was miserable. Since I could not sleep, I lay there and thought about how I could improve my sales pitch. I had to convince myself that this was a good idea. I decided that I was not going to let a few bad calls determine my future business, so before the sun was up, I was packed and ready to ride. I did find the settlement at Eden, and I enjoyed visiting with those folks but they also had plenty of eggs. This old woman named Lessie tried to give me a penny for my trouble, but I would not take it. So she insisted that I take a gunnysack of down in exchange for two dozen eggs. I asked her why she wanted to do that since she had chickens, and she said that hard work should be rewarded, and she would send the eggs to a family who would be grateful to have them. I am not exactly sure what all that means, but I thanked her. Oh, yeah, she fed me a mighty fine meal too. She gave me directions to a few other homesteads and said I should start back. So I did, but I ran into the same situation as before: no one needed eggs. I put ten dozen eggs back in the springhouse last night, and left the bag of down on the porch."

By now his eyes were moist, and only his bravery kept tears from flowing freely. In silence we finished breakfast, and Josiah spoke, "Benjamin, you have made a valiant effort to realize a vision. There is no shame in your endeavor. Envy often provokes embarrassment when misinterpreted. Any shame should be on those unknowing boys who laughed; they did not know better, so please do not be unforgiving toward them. Let us be thankful for Miss Lessie. She is indeed a dear! We shall have to express our gratitude when we visit in the near future. Benjamin, I want you to rethink your business plan, understand any lesson you may have learned, and we will discuss this again next week. In the meantime, all is well, and your parents are extremely proud of you."

Lucy laughed. It was her first laugh! The smile lasted a long, long time.

I do believe that she was happy to have her brother home.

APRIL 3, 1861

Benjamin called a family meeting. He took his pa at his word and desired to give a full report of his first business venture. I think he really just needed to get it off his chest, so he could move on.

"Pa, I have been thinking about what you told me to do. I have really tried to think of what I learned last week. I was so sure that my idea was great and that I could make lots of extra money. Up until this morning, I have been feeling like a big, fat failure. So I slipped off to Ma's rock and had a good visit with the Maker. I was determined to stay there until I had something sensible to tell you."

It was obvious that this young boy had struggled to find the words that his pa would find acceptable. Earning Josiah's respect was so important to this little man. Ben's eyes are always wide when he speaks to Josiah, surveying his pa's face for any signs of assurance. That amazes me some, as I see Josiah as a kind, understanding, and gentle father. We had a discussion about this a short time ago, and Josiah explained that a boy desperately needs approval from his father. Approval from others, even his mother, is not the same. To become a real man, a boy must be validated by a man, and that man should be his own pa if possible. Josiah said that he well understood this and aimed to do his level best to make sure that Benjamin knows beyond a shadow of a doubt by the time he is grown that he has what it takes to be a genuine man with no reservations! *However did Josiah become so wise?* I wondered. I can see how Josiah's own father's absence made a huge difference, and it's almost like he has to make up for that loss with his own son. Whatever the reason, he is a magnificent father. Perhaps this sort of situation is why often we suffer: to better someone else's life.

Benjamin looked down for some time before he began his dissertation of the wisdom gained. It was clear that he was uncertain where to start. Josiah too noticed the boy's struggle, so he spoke first. "Son, I will tell you again, the business venture was a valiant effort, one of which I am extremely proud."

"Pa, I have many feelings. Like I already said, defeat came first, but I constantly resisted that one. Why, sometimes I just ignore it completely and try to think of something else, but it always came back. So I understand that I should replace that feeling with the facts, so here is how I see them." He cleared his throat, took a deep breath, and continued. "Pa, I worked as hard as I could. I kept everything clean, even the chickens. I babied the eggs and brushed Old Buck. I made sure that I took the very best care of all of them, so they would be the best they could be too. I do understand that they were the root of my business. So I do not feel bad about my work. If I made a mistake, it would have been in my selling methods. I was not pushy or demanding, and I think the fact that even though I believed in my product, I did not believe in myself, and that showed through to my customers. We did not lose any money in the venture, but we did not make any either. It cost me several days and many, many hours, and you pulled my weight on the farm while I was away. But it did not actually cost us any money. I have decided that unless I can turn a profit, anything I take on will just be a pastime. Pa, if I decide to take up a pastime, it will be something fun, like fishing! Another mistake was not researching the area. I should have made that ride through the country and asked if anybody needed eggs before I ever invested the money and time in all those chickens; then I would have known that eggs are not a big necessity. Also, I want to thank you and Ma for trusting me, believing in me, and giving me the chance to try out my idea. I did learn a lot about business, and someday I am going to try again, but before I invest, I am going to count the costs, all of them."

APRIL 5, 1861

I was up before the sun. Well, the truth is Lucy prompted my rising. As usual, she was wet and hungry, and my greatest delight is easing her discomforts. (I may hold her too much; I'll have to ask Miss Beth about that.) Honestly, I did not know what to expect from motherhood, but even in these short three months, I have come to a better understanding of my own mother. I knew she loved us, but I had no idea how deep that love was. I miss her now more than ever, and as soon as the dew dries this morning, Lucy Leah and I are going to the herb garden.

My well-laid plans for the daily chores changed when Weti appeared. She would not eat with us, and I wondered, *Why? What does she eat?* Her intentions were apparent, and as always, her wish was my command.

Weti commanded me to drape on the deerskin pouch. She gently snugged the baby in. It felt so natural, and Lucy was especially content. What a great way to travel. It was like holding the baby tight with no hands. Weti suggested that we pack some dried fruit and eats in a bag and then took my hand and led us out. There was longing in Ben's eyes to go too, but Josiah's firm hand on the boy's shoulder was a gentle, "Stay with me." I wondered what those two were up to because Josiah wore that all-knowing grin.

Much to my amazement, this time I followed Weti straight to my rock. Of course she would know the way; she trailed me there enough times. Once in the clearing she took my hand and led me past the tabernacle to the lovely patch of white flowers that were just coming up and starting to bloom. Their gorgeous fragrance filled the air. She lovingly touched the baby's face and then mine. That deep raspy voice began to roll, and I strained my ears to listen intently. The words she spoke deliberately and slowly were understandable.

The gestures of her entire body together with those crude words began to come to life, and by golly, I understood her story. It was as if I were interpreting an unknown tongue. A whole new world opened to me.

The long, long journey had been so cruel, and the Cherokee mothers had grieved so profoundly that their chiefs prayed for a sign to lift the mother's spirits and give them strength to care for their children. From that time on, every place that a mother's tear touched the ground, a beautiful white flower would grow. The flower's center was gold, representing the gold that was taken from them, and the seven leaves on each stem represented the seven clans that were forced on the journey.

I was so taken by the legend and her emotional rendition that it took several minutes for the significance of this spot to soak in. Weti's own little child was buried beneath this garden of Cherokee roses.

"Oh, Weti!" I cried. And I could not help myself; I forgot not to intrude. I wrapped her in a bear hug. She did not resist, but melted in my arms. "Dear God," I whispered, "we are all your daughters!" The moment was brief, but I sensed that it was the fulfillment of many years of longing for her. I dared not imagine the loneliness of her years, for my heart would surely stop with pain. My clutch on her softened, and she slipped from my hug. We moved to the rock and took a seat. I prayed silently and knew now that my prayers were not the first from the holy place.

Weti passed the fruit slices from the flour sack. We ate in silence while being serenaded by nature's music. Lucy Leah was asking for attention, so I obliged. Weti was gone when I glanced back her way.

The baby and I stayed another hour, during which time I observed a pair of buntings building their nest. I had never seen a bunting nest, as they are very illusive birds but so stunning!

I pondered our blessings, especially little Miss Lucy. She is barely even here and already exposed to a world of culture—laces from Paris and deerskin from an old Indian wise woman. She must be special, sent here for a great purpose. I asked God to guide my feet, which ultimately would guide hers.

When we did venture home, yes, I heard the footsteps, but this day I smiled at the sensation of being watched because today it felt like love.

APRIL 30, 1861

Tuesday. The garden is growing nicely. While hoeing today during Miss Lucy's nap, Patches announced the callers. Rocks were popping. *Wheels*, I thought, *oh, if it were only Miss Beth and Old Zeke*. The hoe was steadied, and the sun shielded by my right hand. I gazed down the lane. The first thing I saw was the fringe. "Thank you," I whispered. The second thing I noticed was Old Zeke's white teeth shining. What a heart that man has! I forgot that hoe faster than a bee's buzz and was soon hugging Miss Beth. She was just in time for afternoon tea. Old Zeke hunted the men up, and we girls enjoyed a catching-up chat session. My good friend was appalled at the story of Edward's death. She was both angry and sad and was extremely compassionate toward my own suffering. She called Uncle Dick "dastardly."

Naturally, she was more excited about Weti and wondered if she would ever meet the old Indian wise woman. I told her that I did not know, as Weti materialized at her will only, but she was well aware of all their comings and goings. Miss Beth believed that Weti was supernaturally posted here! All that I can be certain of is that she did save my precious baby, and me for that matter, and like Josiah, not only do I owe her my life, but my baby's also. Miss Beth left two silver dollars for Benjamin and his Bozeman's Eggs and Oddities business, as eggs were on her list to purchase for the next stop, and how fortunate for her that she had found them so handy. What a charming darling! Miss Beth could not wait for Lucy to awake from her nap. She had to lift her from the crib and rock her eyes open. The baby was content and comfortable in her arms, almost as if Miss Beth were her natural grandmother, and Miss Beth played that part like a master thespian.

After supper, we enjoyed twilight from the front porch. Our guests brought a stack of newspapers from across the country. Miss Beth asked if we knew that a new president had been seated in the nation's capital. I did not; Josiah did. Without an invitation, Old Zeke drove Miss Beth right up to the east portico of the unfinished capitol building and watched the entire inauguration of Abraham Lincoln. The revelry was beyond words and emotions mixed. I could not believe those two could be so brazen! But what an amazing story! The information that I most revered was a conversation that Miss Beth recounted where an individual asked Mr. Lincoln if the Lord was on the North side of the war. Mr. Lincoln's reply was,

"I am not concerned about that, but it is my constant anxiety and prayer that I and this nation be on the Lord's side."

Lucy had passed into deep slumber long before the night's conversation ended, and Benjamin was so enthralled that he was up past his normal bedtime. Josiah was energized by the dialogue. I too was captivated by their dissertations, but my heart was so happy just to have them with us again.

The mantle clock struck twelve, and we all agreed to sleep on this newfound climate of our country, however disconcerting.

AUGUST 12, 1861

Two weeks ago Josiah left for Queen City to gather more equipment and hardware to finish the barn. Uncle Dick and his hooligans went too. I suspected that bunch was up to something far different than fetching salt and sundries. These days the men talked in private and whispered their gossip. But I did know that the war was raging just beyond our ridge. Perhaps they were simply attempting to protect us. Josiah had made it very clear that he wanted no part of it, the war that is.

As darkness fell I watered the chickens and noticed a dead indigo bunting near the coop. It made me very sad, as these birds always remind me of Josiah and our last day of travel here. The little bird represents all good things to me, and I wondered how and why it died. I scooped out some soft earth and buried it. I heard a wagon slowly coming up the lane as I placed rocks on top the bunting's grave. The dog barked. I ran to the cabin, from where Benjamin and I watched eagerly, as we both missed Josiah and longed for his homecoming. We could finally make out the dark shape of the horse and buckboard against the silver horizon, but could see no driver. The horse halted in front of the cabin. Nothing else moved for a long time and the silence was menacing. Rumors of violent Union troops made us wary of running out, especially in the dark.

But after too many minutes, I could stand it no longer. Benjamin said, "Wait, Ma, listen."

I did, and we both heard a faint, steady drip. It was not raining. The sky was filled with stars. "What in the world?" I grabbed the lantern, lit it, and we crept near the wagon. The dripping sound grew louder as we approached. I could see a thick liquid running out the back of the wagon and splashing in the dirt. Little clouds of dust puffed up with each drop. "Oh my Lord!" It was blood! I gasped and pushed Benjamin behind me. Never had I been so afraid! I did not want to look in, but I knew I must. My worst fears were confirmed: Josiah was lying in a pool of blood. He was breathing. His eyes were closed. His right leg was gone.

It is nothing more than a miracle that Josiah was still alive. Benjamin went for help. He and Uncle Frank were sweating profusely and out of breath when they rode up from the neighboring ridge. Benjamin told me later that he prayed and cried at the top of his lungs all the way across that ridge as he rode for help. I never told him, but I was doing the same thing as I cradled Josiah's head from the first second he took off on Buck until they were back and dismounted.

Uncle Frank had me build a fire and burn off the end of a small fence post log. When the log had burned down to about twenty inches in length, he took the unburned end by both hands and pushed the glowing hot end into the stub that was once Josiah's leg. The smell was putrid. Josiah was still unconscious, but he flinched and jerked grotesquely. "Weti! Weti," my heart, in its deepest despair, silently called for her. "We desperately need you now! Please, Weti, where are you?" We mixed salt and lamp oil to pour over the wounds and burnt flesh. He had Benjamin gather up all the cobwebs he could find and stuck to the nasty mess for clotting. I put mint on to boil. It was time for healing.

Four days passed before Josiah responded at all. When he did become coherent, he was crushed beyond measure. He thanked us all for his care, but I wonder if he questioned the reason he remained alive. His actions reflected emotions of feeling less than the man he was before. He drank heavily the chicken soup but gained strength slowly. Weti came on the fifth day. She was recovering from snake fever and was saddened that she had not been there to help us. She did work her medicine, and Josiah was quickly much better. Only once did he talk about what happened, and he made us vow that we would never mention it again.

Josiah left ahead of Uncle Dick's bunch on purpose. Two days into the journey, he realized that the roads were teeming with union troops. To avoid confrontation with either side, he opted to ride slowly through uncharted lands. He stayed clear of all roads and footpaths. He claimed to be surprised at the rebel troops doing the same and wondered why the bluecoats had not figured this out. One night he camped with a group of men on their way toward Ozark. They had no fire, naturally, and spoke softly, sharing their tales. The captain appointed a scout to survey the situation at daybreak each morning. For three days they could not break camp and move because of the surrounding enemy. Josiah spent long hours with a soldier named Johnny Simmons. Johnny had been married a few years and bragged about getting a nice farm with his bride, which he sold for a hefty sum. (For a fleeting moment, I thought that Johnny Simmons might be the one I knew from Crawford County, but logistics would make that impossible.) They mostly talked about the war and their hope of the aftermath. This guy, Johnny, prayed that he could stay alive to see the child that his wife was carrying. He expressed his fears and the difficulty of understanding what the War of Rebellion was all about, but at the same time he spoke with great pride and undying loyalty to the Confederation. His confidence in Josiah created a bond of camaraderie.

Josiah voiced his own opinion that the only real attribute the South had to fight with was their pride, and how because of logistics they could not possibly win this conflict, but they would die with honor and what a waste and foolishness the entire ordeal appeared to him. Josiah hated the turmoil and was glad to be uninvolved by choice, at least so far. Finally one morning, the coast was clear. The camp broke and the rebels headed north while Josiah rode west. His keen ears had saved him more than once, and this day was no exception. He hurried into the brush just as a band of Union officers rode up and stopped right beside him. They never had a clue that he was there, but they were so close that he could hear every Yankee vowel they spoke. It seems that they knew all about the rebel camp, and the Union spies had reported the camps break and move. They were well aware of the Confederates' travel plans and had a troop lying in wait to massacre the boys in gray. Without any thought of himself, Josiah immediately determined to rush after the band of rebels and head off the impending doom. As soon as the officers were out of hearing range, he headed northeast at breakneck speed, all the while his eyes peeled for blues. He did catch up with Johnny and his men. But it was at the same instant that those Yankees fired the cannons. As Josiah sped between the fire and Johnny's horse, the ball meant for Johnny took off Josiah's leg and killed his horse.

The entire band retreated and let Josiah lay. He reported that his entire life moved slowly before his eyes; then he blacked out. When he came to, the smoke had cleared, and he was in a safe harbor. Little did either side know that Uncle Dick and his crew were firing on the Yanks from behind. The blues were totally unaware, and every one of them bit the dust. That's when Johnny pulled Josiah out of open sights. Josiah could remember little after that.

We now know that Uncle Dick is responsible for getting the wagon full of Josiah home, although he had bigger fish to fry and continued on his mission. That rebel band made its way to Wilson's Creek, where they sustained heavy casualties, but they did win that battle.

I shall always wonder if Johnny made it home alive. I privately thank him for pulling Josiah to safety, but I resent the great sacrifice. And somehow it just doesn't even out. I must get to the rock.

I cannot believe that happened! I am not surprised at all that a man like Josiah would risk his life for others, buy why? Why God, would you reward him this way? Especially since he was so adamantly opposed to the war. I remember how scary it was when my husband left for battle. But the war ended for us, he came back home whole, and our lives went back to normal. In fact, Johnny never spoke of it, and I never asked. Josiah, your life could never be the same. Lenny's either! How could I have felt so cheated all these years, when I never experienced any horrors of this magnitude?

SEPTEMBER 29, 1861

Saturday. We have not taken advantage of our free day since Josiah returned from Wilson's Creek. There is plenty to do, and this family is all about teamwork.

Last spring Josiah brought seeds from Thomasville for the garden and surprised us with popping corn and peanuts. I remember when we planted these the little rhyme mother always recited during planting. "Who plants a seed beneath the sod, then waits to see believes in God."

Today, Benjamin and I will harvest the popcorn.

Weti's deerskin pouch was fabulous! It allowed me to continue all my chores with Miss Lucy onboard. Little Lucy never complained about the free ride. Lucy would reach for the corn stalks, so I had to pick the corn a good arm's length away. I feared that the sharp edges of the slender, browning leaves would cut her tender arms. She was fearless and only giggled. I did make the mistake of giving her a shucked cob; of course it went straight to her mouth. She fretted only briefly when I took it back and dropped it into the basket with the others. This summer's extreme heat had dried the corn early, and by the time it was all picked, this day's sun was directly overhead. Time for the little one's nap. Benjamin hauled the baskets to the porch, where the three of us would clean it while the baby slept.

I had seen a cast iron sheller, but we only had six natural shellers—our hands. Let me tell you, my hands did not feel anything like cast iron when the day was done! We would hold the cob with both hands side by side and then twist in opposite directions. The kernels would easily pop out and fall into the pan below. It wasn't long before every cob was clean and the pans were full. I wondered how we would ever get the corn clean enough to eat. I should never wonder or worry; as usual, Josiah showed me. He had Benjamin lay out a clean bed linen on the ground just under the porch's edge. He rolled his chair there and lifted the pan of shelled corn high over his head and slowly poured the kernels to the linen below. The heavy kernels dropped straight down, but the chaff just blew away in the wind. Not a speck of it ended up with the corn. Mother's readings from the Book came alive right before my eyes! It was easy to see how the grain can be separated from the chaff.

We scooped up the clean corn and stored it in tightly closed crocks. When darkness came this evening, a chill did too, so we built a fire. Josiah sent Benjamin to the smokehouse, and he returned with a deep, tightly woven wire basket attached at the end of a long handle. I had seen it out there but did not know what it was. I thought it might be used to strain berries. Wrong! Josiah threw a handful of fresh corn in the basket, then holding the long handle, positioned the basket just over the flames. Before long, popping sounds and this wonderful aroma filled the cabin. Once off the fire, he threw in a pinch of salt and shook. That popped corn melted in my mouth like warm snow. It was too delicious because it disappeared faster than Weti.

OCTOBER 3, 1861

Our little Lucy is growing so fast! She is sitting up, crawling as fast as a blue racer, and cutting a mouth full of teeth. She loves her pa! That baby's hair is so curly and shiny, and those eyes are the deepest shade of green. They remind me of the river's water: tinted, yet clear enough to see through. I remember playing dolls as a little girl, and having a real baby is nothing like that at all! Life has been good, but some days it is hard to remember what it was like before she came, and she is only eight months old. I suppose every mother feels this way—blessed and wealthy! What amazes me is that I never tire of her nearness or demands.

Tara rode up this morning, to my pleasant surprise, with Tressie in tow. Lucy took right up with them and chose Tara over me most of the day. I do believe that is the way the good Lord intended because Tara was in dire need of an emotional uplifting. Bonding with the baby was just the ticket because when the sun set that evening that beautiful smile was back on her face. Tara is still devastated over Edward's demise *and* Josiah's missing leg. I am thankful that she feels comfortable coming here for her escape from the mundane routine of her life. The duo came prepared to stay a few days. Oh, how this place will liven up with those two beauties here!

Josiah was so kind to let Benjamin finish his chores early so that he could play with Tressie. He adores her. Those golden curls just bounce when she giggles, and he enjoys making her laugh, so they are a grand combination. Benjamin thinks that Tara is the most beautiful girl on earth, and his face turned twenty shades of red when she hugged him tight. Benjamin and Tressie walked hand in hand to the barnyard to see the new but unexpected baby pigs; Tara and I settled in for a good visit. Today she wanted to start a quilt. She also brought a basket full of tatting for my inspection. Her needlework was remarkable! This young woman has extraordinary talent! Her tatting was as precise, even, and delicate as any I have ever seen. She has definitely mastered that art; no wonder she wanted to move on to another one. I say she is talented because not only had she designed this quilt in her mind, but she also has dreams far beyond. Most pioneer women build quilts from standard patterns like the log cabin or star—not Tara; she is an artist. Her quilt is to have squares depicting specific events, a textile historical document, if you will. She produced a drawing, and I produced a crate of fabric scraps, scissors, and tapes. It occurs to me just now that our friendship is piecing together and growing just like the quilt! Tara and I had quite the conversations today. She asked if I believed in God and if I believed he really heard prayers. I told her that, yes, I did believe, and yes, I believe he hears and answers prayers. Although I did confess that I did not understand nearly enough about God or his ways, I would like to know and comprehend better. She confessed to me that she had been sincerely praying. I did not pry, and she did not reveal the subjects of her prayers. I think she wanted to tell me, but for some reason she did not confess any further than the prayer vigil. So tonight when I visit with the good Lord, I will ask him to have his will in her life and give her the desires of her heart; that is, of course, if they fall within his will. We also talked today about homemaking, children, and marriage, so I highly suspect that I have the right inkling about her desires. She is such a lovely person, and I do not know how I could possibly love her more. She is tender hearted and so kind. In the few years that I have lived in these hills, I have not met any young man that I would approve of, as if I had that right. For some reason I feel so protective of Tara, and my own desire is that she has all the fullness of life, a happy one. The man who wins her heart will be a very fortunate individual!

At the supper table, Josiah gave thanks for our company, along with our other many blessings. He loves these girls too, and we would keep them with us if they would stay. I think that Tressie wore Benjamin out, as he was yawning before the last bite even made it on his fork. Little Lucy went to sleep long before the rest of us even sat down, perhaps watching us scurry around all day wore her out too.

Tonight as I write this entry, everyone is fast asleep. Tara rolled out the feather mat just in front of the fireplace. The last time I looked, Tressie was curled up in a little ball so close to Tara that I am surprised either of them can breathe. For sure they will not get cold, as there is a definite nip in the air these October days. They looked like angels in slumber. I will close with heartfelt thanksgiving!

OCTOBER 5, 1861

Friday came and all of us loaded up and headed to Thomasville. Tara and Tressie had planned to leave this day anyway, and since it was closer for her to go home from Thomasville, she would take her wagon and go home from there. So Lucy and I rode with Tara, and Tressie rode with her buddy Ben, and Josiah. The men's wagon led the way, and Tara and I laughed our heads off as we could hear them attempting to sing. Josiah would belt out a hardy, "She'll be coming 'round the mountain," and Ben would mock him, singing in a monotone voice. Tressie would laugh and put her hand over his mouth. She was right; it wasn't a pretty noise.

Lucy soon fell fast asleep with the gentle sway of the wagon. We rode under the forest canopy for many miles, and then the road climbed roughly to the top of a ridge. Off to the left was a very deep holler, and the meandering stream at the bottom was easy to see between the giant pines. We were all startled by a loud yell, and then a shot rang out. Josiah and Tara pulled back on the reins immediately, and our horses halted with a strong jerk, waking the baby.

The band of horses and riders was moving toward us at breakneck speed. They pulled to a stop only when they had our wagons surrounded. "Who goes there?" a gray-suited man sitting very tall in the saddle commanded.

"Josiah Bozeman and family. Who's asking?" Josiah answered with authority.

"Not your business, man. What's in the wagon?"

"I have already told you: my family. Would you kindly move aside so that we may continue our journey to Thomasville?" Josiah spoke with the same authority.

"You related to Dick?" the smart-mouth man asked.

"My uncle," Josiah replied.

"You lose that leg at Wilson's creek?"

"Not really your business, man, but since I have nothing to hide, yes, my leg is somewhere in a hundred pieces near Wilson's Creek. Please move out of our way."

The tall man in gray jerked his head to the side, and the other riders moved to our rear, clearing the road for our passage.

"We have been notified that there are Yanks scouting the area. You might reconsider your journey just now," were the last words the man said as he spurred his horse and took off as quickly as he rode up. The others followed suit, leaving a dusty cloud blowing in our eyes.

Well that was rather unnerving, I thought but said not a word. My heart was beating a bit faster than normal, and Tara's face was as pale as butter. Tressie's giggle broke the silence when she laughed at their red legs, and Lucy's cry followed.

"Everybody all right back there?" Josiah turned in our direction.

"We're fine," I answered.

"Let's go," he shouted as he shook the reins and then started another verse of "Oh, My Darlin' Clementine," but nobody was laughing now. It was sometime before Tara spoke and then only in a hushed tone. The jolly mood of our outing had been shattered.

The rest of the trip was uneventful, other than the red fox family that ran under Josiah's wagon wheels. Unbelievably, not one of the five were injured, and they moved faster than lightning getting away from us, as if they were in a war of their own.

At Thomasville, our happy mood was somewhat restored, as the place was bustling with people and activity. Most of the folks knew Josiah and Benjamin, and they were kind to make my acquaintance. Tara shared a few hugs with old friends, and Tressie delighted the crowd with her golden locks and sweet smile. As usual, Lucy stole the show just by being the new baby. Tara and I selected the batting for the quilt and dreamed of more designs while admiring the colorful fabric and notions. I noticed a box of chalks, much like the one Josiah had brought to me some time back, and was shocked at the price. I could not believe that he might spend that much money on something as frivolous as drawing chalks. I told myself to find some special way to thank him later. Tara supposed that they shouldn't tarry long, as they needed to get home before dark, and she was fearful after that episode on the ridge. Josiah and Benjamin discussed the situation and agreed that the girls should definitely not travel home alone. Benjamin volunteered to ride with them and borrow Uncle Frank's horse to return to our home tomorrow. So that is what transpired. I was unhappy about the plans and would have rather us all gone back home together, but Uncle Frank and Anna were expecting their children tonight. My heart was so heavy when we parted ways, and I watched that wagon full of young people that I dearly loved roll out of sight. Josiah evidently shared my distress, as that number eleven between his eyes was deep, and he had even fewer words than usual.

Our wagon was laden with batting, sugar, meal, and a few other necessities before we rolled toward home too. There was little conversation, and my eyes seldom ventured off the road ahead or behind. I expected any moment to be rushed upon by the enemy, whoever that was. Josiah's shoulders were straight and his mission clear; he too was watching in earnest. We saw not one wild creature other than birds the entire trip. Lucy was a dear and slept. As the wagon bounced and bumped along, I pretended in my mind that we were on the rock, and I sought the good Lord's protection over that other wagonload of precious cargo headed north. Time seemed to drag on and on. I thought we would never get home, and several times I was tempted to ask Josiah, "How much farther?" but refrained. I realized what was going on inside my head, and I determined not to give in to the fear. I would be as brave as Josiah. I ran that whole episode over and over in my mind and grew even more proud and thankful for him. A hero, that's what he is! He is more of a man with one leg than any man that I have ever known with two, in fact, mightier!

Finally I recognized the forest trails near our home and relaxed some. That did not last long, as for the first time I saw movement from the corner of my eye. It was a brownish shadow moving at the same speed as the horse parallel to the wagon. Josiah saw it too. We jumped at the same time when Weti popped out into the road ahead of us. "Weti!" Josiah yelled. "What is it?"

Weti calmly explained with her own expressions that all was well at our place and that there was no need to worry because she knew that the other wagon had safely reached its destination and that Tara and the other children were also safe and fed.

When she finished speaking, she turned and disappeared into the pines, never waiting for our words of gratitude. I have learned to stop wondering how, what, where, and why she does what she does. I just try to be mindful and thankful for her. In fact, my sense of security, especially these days, is elevated just by the knowledge that she is always somewhere nearby.

I have just now been awakened by Patches's barks and a horse's hoof beats. The pulse pounding in my ears drowned out the barks and hoof beats. Josiah sat straight up too and without a word grabbed his gun and hobbled to the front room. I knew to stay put. Lucy was fast asleep and never moved nor uttered a sound one. The length of silence seemed forever, but it was broken by a familiar voice.

"Pa, it's just me." Benjamin was home. Said he needed to be here tonight and had to take care of us too. Yes, that boy is my hero number two.

OCTOBER 15, 1861

Rain had set in for the day, so after the necessary chores, Benjamin curled up near the small fire, reading.

The last thing we expected today was visitors. As usual, with great caution, Josiah approached the riders. The two men were well dressed and obviously lost. They were invited in for dinner and obliged. The tallest gentleman bowed low at the cabin's door, his wide-brimmed straw hat was removed and swept toward the floor as he said, "Good day, ma'am. Samuel Clemens at your service. And may I introduce my brother, Orion."

"Good day." I returned the courtesy and wondered if I too should bow but did not. "It is a pleasure to make your acquaintance. Please do join us." I gestured them toward the table, and the two gentlemen took a seat. Their appetites were as hearty as their fancy clothes. Ben was mesmerized by the storytelling of Mr. Clemens.

The brothers were raised in Hannibal, Missouri, and Benjamin was so fascinated with their life story that he asked a hundred questions. On the mighty Mississippi, Samuel became a cub pilot on a riverboat and learned to navigate that rushing river by night and day. He told a sad, sad story about their youngest brother, Henry, getting killed in a steamboat accident. I could see Ben's dreamy eyes wishing he could ride the river on those boats because Mr. Clemens made it all sound so real, alive, and adventurous. What young boy can resist an adventure? Two years ago, Mr. Clemens became a fully licensed riverboat pilot, but the war broke out and all travel on the river ended. So after a brief stint as a soldier, the two were headed to explore Nevada and California. How exciting!

They did not tarry as long as we would have liked for them to, but Samuel thanked me for the fine vittles and Josiah for the directions to get back on the right road to Queen City.

Mr. Clemens rubbed Benjamin's head, kissed Lucy on hers, and again bowed low before he and his brother mounted their steeds. Only when they were really out of sight, did we look at one another and realize that we had been exposed to something larger than our life.

As I cleared the table, I noticed a small folded paper. A note scrawled there:

Thank you, Mrs. Bozeman, for a very lovely afternoon. Your family is indeed a treasure among people. Please accept this small token of our appreciation. I shall be watching for an appropriate replacement for your husband's missing leg, as a fine man as he should enjoy all the

fruits of life. Your children are precious. I look forward to having my
own someday and hope that mine are as perfect.

Until we meet again,
Samuel Clemens

Four coins covered the small sketch of a riverboat and the words
For Benjamin.

We would have never accepted this token, and Mr. Clemens
probably knew that. They were too long gone to catch them now.
I do wish we had gotten more information, as these men are of the
integrity to be mighty fine lifelong friends.

I am never ceased to be amazed at the characters just passing
through this wilderness. One never knows what, or who, a new day
will bring. Evidently we are not as isolated as it sometimes seems.
Another good day!

NOVEMBER 23, 1861

The weather has been uncommonly warm for this time of year, and
today we had an unusual adventure! The decision was unanimous; it
was far time this family had a day of fun. Benjamin and I had been
taking care of most everything while Josiah's wounds healed, and
he thought that we deserved a much-needed break, so at his insis-
tence I took the reins, he took the front seat, and Benjamin helped
tie Lucy's traveling basket tight in the rear of the wagon. Ben was
happy to ride back there with the picnic basket too. Patches started
out running alongside. I watched for Weti, as I so longed for her to
be with us, but alas, she was invisible.

Off we headed east and south, to a beautiful place that Josiah
had often spoken of approximately eight miles away. We traveled
atop the same ridge for quite a while. The day was beautiful, as
were the woods and wildlife. Several spots along the way the timber
thinned enough to see just how high this ridge was. Magnificent!
Breathtaking! A lush green valley zigzagged at the bottom between

and through the smaller hills. "It looked like a meadow river," Benjamin said. After nearly two hours, we stopped in a shade to enjoy biscuits and cider. Josiah's spirits seemed to be soaring with the eagles we spotted. I had to wonder if these were the same birds that we had seen nesting along the river on that delightful journey to this new life two years ago. He told us how the river flanked us on the right, and even though we could not see it, we could smell it and occasionally hear ripples, or maybe we just imagined that part.

By now Patches was content to ride in the wagon with Ben and Lucy. The road was very rough, and even Josiah laughed out loud as he bounced around like a pumpkin. (His one leg wasn't strong enough to steady him yet.)

I hoped all this jarring would not cause him pain. Benjamin wrapped his arms tightly around his pa, but they both almost bounced right over the seat. We all got so tickled, the horses seemed confused. I suppose they had never heard such laughing. The day was perfect already. I could not remember a day when all of our spirits had been so light hearted and free. This was indeed medicine for our souls and our relationships.

This light-heartedness continued until we topped a high hill and the road was so steep that it actually disappeared from sight. "Slow," Josiah commanded. Not that he had to, as I had already pulled the horses to a complete stop. Now, I am not sure that I would have ever attempted this road on my own, but I had confidence that Josiah would never harm any of us, so I prompted the horse to move but held the reins tight with no slack. As if they had made the passage before, the horses stepped carefully and sure footed. At the bottom of the hill we could hear water rippling, and through the trees saw that beautiful Eleven Point River flowing lazily along, oblivious to the world around it. I gasped at its beauty, and the flood of memories rushed into my thoughts. No one spoke as we each admired the landscape, even Lucy. Glancing up I saw the pine lodge house ahead.

Several folks were standing on the porch to greet us, although the closer we got I noticed the shotgun pointed right at us. "Josiah

Bozeman and family here," Josiah shouted. The shotgun never moved. I could almost feel the crosshairs on my head and was near panic for my children's safety when I heard an old crotchety voice holler, "That really you, Josiah?"

"Yes, sir, Mr. Van Winkle. And my family too. Glad to see you are well."

"I'm not well, sonny, but I am alive, at least for today," he spouted back.

Josiah laughed at that, but I failed to see the humor. Benjamin was grinning. He had already met this crew on his egg-selling adventure.

"Hope you did not bring me anymore dang eggs," the old man belted.

"We did not, sir. Just us. Thought you might like to lay your eyes on my beautiful wife and our new baby girl."

"Well, shut my mouth!" the old codger crowed. "Josiah's done gone and got himself a woman and made another baby." And with that the shotgun was laid aside.

The old man grabbed Benjamin with one arm around the neck and with the other hand rubbed his knuckles into the mop top until Benjamin's hair was standing straight up. Benjamin cringed in pain but never made a sound, as if he showed respect by letting this old man abuse his head. Josiah laughed until Mr. Van Winkle said, "Good Lord, man! Where is your leg?"

"Left it at Wilson's Creek last August," Josiah answered.

"Don't dare tell me that you went and joined the wrong side, son!"

"Did not join any side, sir. Just got caught in the middle," Josiah explained.

"And that, man, is precisely why I sit here with the shotgun ready. We have already had some of those men in blue snooping around. So far, we have held them off. Tim Reeves has pretty much got this community organized, and we get each other's back.

"Father Hogan's bunch don't take too kindly to us, nor we to them. Shame it is; we all live here together. Too bad we can't get along. Got to watch them like a hawk."

In a most serious tone, the old man asked, "How are you moving with it? With one leg."

It was this comment that opened my eyes to the old man's real sincerity, and I was immediately glad that we had a friend like Mr. Van Winkle.

"Physically, I manage; mentally, I still have two legs. It is a struggle to accept reality, for sure. But it is what it is, and at least for today, I'm still alive." Josiah was laughing when he finished the sentence. They all laughed, but I heard something in that remark that I had never before. *A struggle,* I thought, that he had never allowed me to see.

The lanky, lean man holding up a lodge pole with his back laughed too. He bowed low to me and Lucy. I curtsied back to Mr. Van Winkle's handsome grandson, Jebediah Huddleston.

"Watch out, miss, ole Jeb here is a heartbreaker!" his grandpa warned. "The women in these hills chase him like a rabbit. Wish one of them would catch him; he's eating me out of house and home. Now give me that baby," the old man demanded.

Josiah took Lucy and sat her in the old man's lap. She gazed at him with big eyes, but she never fretted. Jeb and Ben struck up their own conversation and took it to the barn. Mr. Van Winkle and Josiah began to discuss nonstop the latest goings-on. The dialogue between the two old friends was entertaining, and Lucy and I were content to take it all in. In less than an hour, more visitors rode up, but this time the shotgun stayed put.

"Hoooowwwdeeeee," came rather shrill from the wagon still a ways off.

"Miss Lessie, good neighbor, she's got to know everything that is going on, but a fine woman," Grandpa said.

"Well, if it isn't the dashing Josiah Bozeman! Heard you had a new family, and that boy, my, my, he has grown, and into business ventures, is he? Josiah, you did a fine job with that child. Last

March when he came by selling eggs, I swore I had never met a more polite and respectful person. Eggs were good too. Did you bring more today? Oh, glory be, a baby! I have got to wrap my arms around that precious one; give her here." Miss Lessie never took a breath. She swept Lucy up and danced a jig across the porch. Lucy giggled, but I was looking for her lunch to spew forth at any twirl.

"I'm sorry, honey." Miss Lessie directed the statement toward me. "I didn't mean to ignore you. I am Lessie, Lessie Simpson. In case you didn't know, you have a most wonderful husband in this country, and this baby, oh, gracious me, is the most beautiful child I have ever laid eyes on. But then she belongs to Josiah, and you, of course. I would have known who her daddy was just by looking at her; why, she looks just like him. Welcome to the Hills. You won't have to wonder if I'm your friend, honey, I am. And if you ever need anything, you send for me."

"Thank you." I managed to get the words in edgewise. "It's a pleasure to make your acquaintance. Benjamin told us how kind you were to him. Thank you."

"The pleasure is all mine. Oh, and I see you staring at my hat. Don't mind that price tag jangling, I like people to think I just bought it." Lessie let out a huge guffaw and then turned toward the old man. "Old timer, where are those handsome grandchildren of yours? I need a hug from Jeb, and do you suppose Miss Caroline could make us up some of her famous tea?"

"You'll have to wait on your hug, Lessie girl!" he hollered real loud. "Put the tea on."

I could hear the sound of pots and pans banging inside the home. And looking up, I saw a pretty set of eyes looking through gingham curtains.

"Please forgive this one, Miss Lenny. She ain't exactly all there," the withered man explained.

"Oh, she's good as the rest of us, Harold. You just want to keep her to yourself," Lessie touted back. "Don't pay him any mind, Lenny. He's the one that ain't exactly right."

Before long, a very attractive girl came out carrying a large tray with cups, saucers, and a teapot. Caroline served the tea with grace and beauty. I was shocked at such a lavish treat so deep in the woods.

"Shocked, are you, Lenny?" Miss Lessie asked.

How I wish I was not so transparent. "Well, I am surprised at a tea party. What a delightful treat!" I responded.

Caroline smiled and curtsied when I thanked her for her kindness. She never spoke, and I was told that she never had. But it was clear that she could hear, see, and smell better than we. I sensed that she had a deeper understanding and knowledge beyond ours. Sweetness just oozed from her persona. I looked forward to getting to know this young lady.

The tea party had not ended when Tim Reeves rode up. He wore the same scowl that he had on the day he left Patches at our farm. Patches did not bark but ran up to him wagging her tail. She remembered him. That surprised me too. Maybe he wasn't such a bad guy after all.

Mr. Reeves talked the war, his church, and Father Hogan (although that is not what he called him), and wanted the details of Josiah's brush with death at Wilson's Creek.

Josiah gave him limited details and quickly changed the subject. He also let Mr. Reeves know that he had no interest at all in this war and kindly thanked him for keeping it as far from us as possible. I sensed that Mr. Reeves was a bit insulted, but he appeared to respect Josiah and his opinion. I particularly enjoyed his story about a church he had started years before in Arkansas. It seems that he had sent a letter, which included the date of the revival he intended to hold there. The church sent a note back explaining that they did not need to have a revival. On the date specified in the first letter, Mr. Reeves showed up at the church, walked to the front, pulled the revolvers from the holsters on his side, laid them on the pulpit, and then said to the congregation, "I understand that you do not believe that you need reviving, so if any of you would like to stand just now and tell me why, I would like to hear it." Of course no one stood or spoke, so he started preaching and carried on the revival meeting as planned. The opinion that I formed about Mr. Reeves upon our first meeting has not changed. After he left, Miss Lessie told me that he was a Baptist preacher and had a passion for starting churches all over the area. She then told us of an upcoming revival next spring, a brush arbor meeting. The speaker would be a traveling evangelist rather than Tim Reeves. I determined to write down the dates and plan to attend. I could use a good sermon. Miss Lessie offered to accommodate us in her home for the duration of the revival. How sweet! I thanked her again and told her I would like that very much.

Josiah decided we should head home, so there was a lot of hugging going on. He invited all of them to come to our place anytime and offered whatever help he might give for whatever circumstance. We said our good-byes and waved until my newfound friends were out of sight. The goodies that Miss Lessie packed up for our trip home were so good!

The children were fast asleep long before nightfall. I feel my life has enlarged itself because of the new friendships and the bonds strengthening my family. Other than some talk, we saw nothing of this war.

Thank you, good Lord, for all of it!

The air was dark and bitterly cold, we had all gone to bed. Patches started barking frantically.

"Help! Josiah! Ben! Please help!" we heard Toby yelling as he jumped off the running horse.

While Josiah and Benjamin dressed, Toby explained how Tressie had disappeared around noon. The entire family had been searching for her since, to no avail. Sleet was bouncing off the roof. The situation did not look good.

I could not leave my baby and assist in the search, but I could pray. And pray I did the rest of the night. To date, this may have been my greatest test of faith. Lucy woke up shortly after sun up and the sleet had pile an inch high. Only after the mantle clock struck eleven did the men ride in. Their faces were strained. Ben put the horses away and speechless Josiah could only hold Lucy and me. As hot coffee warmed them around the fireplace, Ben shared the details. Josiah organized the family to search in rows, which they did all night, shouting her name and shaking every bush. Just after dawn Toby spotted something black and still in an open ditch. It was Tressie, covered with sleet, one shoe missing. Since she did not respond to his call he thought her dead, but when he drew very near, those golden curls bounced and she lifted her face and reached out her hands to him. Of course the family was overjoyed and celebrated in a mighty way. Tressie told how she had followed a rabbit because she wanted to see where it lived, and then about the mysterious, dark man, taller than the barn who wrapped his cape-like arms around her while it was so dark and cold until Toby woke her up.

Josiah says there is no earthly way a child could have withstood those elements, and that a power far above our human understanding must be at work.

I could not sleep, I had to get up, light the lamp and look up the story in 2 Kings where old Elisha asked God to open his servant's eyes so he could witness the hills covered with chariots of fire. I did not read about those chariots being manned by dark men taller than the barn, but I bet they were. Tressie is alive. My faith is stronger and deeper. How can I ever doubt again?

JANUARY 7, 1862

Patches barked early, and the group on horseback came into view. It was the uncles and their sons, come for the slaughter. This was the annual kill and butcher day. At least I must admit that Josiah's family does right by him. As soon as I saw them, I knew that the next few days would be dark. Each time a task came along that Josiah could not manage alone, he became quiet, despondent, and depressed. No words were spoken, but the light inside him would just grow dimmer. I suppose any decent man would feel the same way, but I wish desperately that he could accept our unchanged admiration, respect, and unconditional love. He cannot; it isn't enough.

The fat hogs have been shrieking for several days, and it has not been because of the flies, as there are none this time of year. Maybe they could sense their time drawing near. There is a shallow snow on, so the meat will keep good.

The boys busied themselves building the fires. Benjamin seemed excited; he does like to have company. Josiah hobbled right out in the middle of this circus. His spirits seemed elevated too. Uncle Frank knocked the fatted calf right between the eyes with the blacksmith's hammer. Rufus helped him string it up to skin. Uncle Dick did not hesitate when he lifted the hog into the scalding box and then poured boiling water over it. While the meat cooled, little Miss Lucy helped me (well, she watched) mix up the pickling brine. She is almost one year old and walking like a Greek athlete. She is very beautiful too. And she is trying to speak. So far we can only understand Papa, Mama, and Bubba. The rest of her jargon is much less understandable than that of Weti, but, my, she does jabber!

The casks were full of the cut-up pork and ready for the brine. The meat floated until the large flat stones weighed them to the bottom of the barrel. Sometime in March we will remove the meat and hang it to smoke.

Toby was in charge of the sheep and put aside the tallow for candles and soap later. Benjamin kept the fire hot under the big cast iron kettle where we rendered the lard. When ready, Josiah would ladle the liquid into cooling pans. Later we will store it in tins and jars.

Little rivers of melted snow flowed away from the fires, and the stench was far less than pleasant, but our bellies will appreciate these efforts all year long. It was an exhausting day but a fruitful one! I am indebted to and thankful for Josiah's kin. We will not go hungry. God truly does supply our needs and uses whom he will.

FEBRUARY 12, 1862

Rufus, Uncle Dick's oldest, rode up this morning to say good-bye. He showed Josiah the orders. He was officially enlisted in Confederate Regiment Missouri Infantry and was headed for Alton to report for duty. I do not know why he came by, as he is such a bitter, mean person, just like his pa.

Benjamin and I excused ourselves to the barn so Rufus could have some privacy with his uncle Josiah. From the corner of my eye, I saw Josiah lay his hand on the young man's shoulder; Rufus hung his head and then took a seat. I had no intentions of eavesdropping, but as we walked back up from gathering the eggs, I overheard the conversation.

"Uncle Josiah, I *have* to go! I have no desire to live the rest of my life in Pa's shadow. I can do nothing right or good enough in his eyes, no matter how hard I try or what sacrifices I make. The more I act like him, the more trouble comes between us. This is my ticket out, don't you see? Besides, I am very angry about what those Yanks did to you, and I will avenge that!"

"Vengeance is not ours, Rufus."

"Oh yes it is!" he replied. "At least if we have the gumption to take it. And that is exactly what I intend to do. Uncle, you are my cause; in fact, you are the only positive influence in my life. I could never say these things to my Pa, and I would not be sharing them with you now except that I feel that I will never return, and being honest with you may be the only honorable thing that I ever do." Rufus took hold of Josiah's hand, shook it strong, mounted, and rode away without looking back.

I was wrong about Rufus. Shame on me. That young man has been jerked in so many directions that he has absolutely no identity, but he does have heart. How sad that he has never had the freedom to be true to it. Maybe now he can.

Josiah was quiet the rest of the day. Again, my heart swelled with pride at his respectful influence and genuine concern for others.

Benjamin adopted the silence, and he took Patches to wander into their own private world of imagination in the barn. He was sad too, without completely understanding why.

I *must* remember to pray for Rufus daily!

FEBRUARY 14, 1862

My goodness, it does not seem like a year has passed since Lucy was born. I try not to think about it too much because that was such an extremely emotional day in our history. It is impossible to relive without being overcome with serious dismay, that is, of course unless I only concentrate on the new baby part. Now that is not entirely true because Weti also came into our world that stormy night. Lucy is walking and laughing and basically brightening our days. Benjamin woke her this morning as he could not wait to give her a gift. He had taken old lumber scraps and built her a miniature barrow, one like his, only much, much smaller and lighter. She loves for him to push her around and around the garden and through the orchard in that contraption. Now he has built one just her size. I suppose he thought she could push her doll around in it or help him with the chores. Her little sleepyhead did not show the response that he was looking for, and I am afraid that he was a bit disappointed. When she realizes what he has done for her, I am sure that sheer delight will replace those drowsy eyes.

Josiah struggles without that leg. He does not talk as much, and that spark is missing from his personality. He is not unkind to any of us; quite the contrary, he cannot do enough for us. But since he made that comment at Eden last November, I have been paying much closer attention. I am completely uncertain of what to do about it. With Ben's help, he can do almost everything that he did before, yet it is almost like a part of his soul left with that leg.

The men went to chores and Lucy, and I walked to the rock, even though it was bitterly cold. The sun was bright and the sky cloudless. She crawled up on the huge quilt that I covered the rock with, and I climbed in beside her, and wrapped us up tight with the ends. Lucy has come to know this place as her naptime space, and immediately she went to sleep. Josiah was weighing heavy on my mind this day, so I began to visit with the good Lord about him. "And we know that all things work together for good to them that love God, to them who are the called according to his purpose," rolled through my brain. *How can that be?* I wondered. Nothing. Absolutely nothing else came.

I was so deep in thought that when Weti sat down beside me, I jumped and squealed.

Of course, this woke Lucy, and she puckered up to cry until she saw Weti, and the giggles started. She crawled in the wise woman's lap, and Weti gently stroked the toddler's dark hair. Was that a tear dripping from her eye? Weti dared not look at me just then, and I respected her privacy and pretended I was busy with the quilt. Weti pulled out a small pine needle basket, complete with lid, and handed it to Lucy. I wish Lucy had been more tender with Weti's handiwork, but after all she is only one year old. Weti did not mind, and somehow she must be a baby whisperer because Lucy seemed to understand Weti's grunts and utterings and opened the basket only to find a beautiful, beaded hair band. Evidently that was not enough, as she reached inside the buckskin dress and pulled out another pair of deerskin moccasins (somewhat larger than the first pair she gave us), with the beadwork matching the gorgeous head-band. Lucy knew exactly what to do with the footwear and immediately attempted to pull off her little boots and replace them with Weti's birthday gift. Weti's smile said more than any words could have. Weti then looked me square in the eyes, gently took hold of my arm and in her broken English said, "What a man does is very much louder than the words he speaks." Her rough hand squeezed my arm and then relinquished its hold, and she returned to stroking the baby's hair. With her words burning in my head, I began to fold the quilt for our trip home and heard Lucy say, "Bye-bye." When I turned around and moved the quilt from in front of my eyes, Weti was gone. Lucy was giggling. That little squirt understands Weti and her comings and goings. Wish I did! I picked her up and held her close for one last prayer on the rock. She was so quiet, and Josiah's face manifested in my mind's eye, along with Weti's words. Our trip home was cold, yet uneventful, other than the footsteps behind us of course, and I felt enlightened.

MARCH 14, 1862

"Ma?" Benjamin's voice startled me this morning. "Do you know what day it is?"

"Friday the thirteenth?" I answered.

"No, Ma, it is the fourteenth."

"Okay, what makes this day so special?" I quizzed him.

"Today is my birthday! I am eleven years old today."

It never occurred to me to ask about his birthday. Immediately I felt bad about that.

"Oh, I am sorry, Benjamin," I spoke as I wrapped him in a hug. "I should have known. Happy birthday, son." I kissed his forehead. "How can I make this day special for you? Anything you desire, in the realm of possibility, that is."

"Could you bake me an apple cake? And could you put that really sweet, gooey icing on it? And could you fry some chicken? And could we *not* have green beans today? Would you cream some corn? And tonight can we sit by the fire, eat some popping corn, and listen to you read?"

I processed the list of requests. "Of course! And let's just call it a birthday party."

"Pa! Pa!" he yelled while running through the cabin to find Josiah. "Ma is going to have a birthday party for me!"

I declare, I do not believe that I have ever seen that boy so excited. I asked if he had ever had a party, to which he replied, "Never." Then he proceeded to tell me that no one had ever acknowledged his birthday, and that the only reason he even knew when it was is because of that the date is written on the flat stone atop Judith's grave, and he knew that she died the day he was born. He said that knowing this would be important to me. It is. Oh my, what a load for a little guy to carry. I have never noticed this stone he spoke of. Next time I go near, I shall have to take a look.

We barely finished the conversation when I heard the baby laugh, and Josiah say, "Well, hello there." Weti was here. Weti's mission this day included Benjamin only.

"How did she know?"

She asked if she could borrow him until the sun was there, and her withered, crooked finger pointed to the three o'clock sky. Josiah and I looked at each other with the question and both shrugged our shoulders. "Sure," we told her, "if that is agreeable with him."

All eyes were on Benjamin. "Are you going to teach me to speak Indian?" he asked.

Weti did not utter a reply but only smiled that toothless grin and held out her hand toward him. They disappeared together in the brushy holler that lead to Osage Spring.

I spent the day preparing Ben's order and getting ready for the party, yet I kept my eyes on the sky.

When that boy returned alone at exactly three o'clock, he was on cloud nine, and the day's adventure had to be shared right then. Benjamin had us gather on the porch, Josiah and I in our favorite chairs, while he attempted to corral his little sister on his lap. That did not last long, but his story went like this:

Benjamin and Weti did go to Osage Spring. They sat on the ledge above the spring, and she taught him to weave a miniature basket of pine straw. He proudly produced the basket she made from his bib pocket. I cannot believe how intricate and delicate it was! The second basket that he pulled from the other pocket was not quite as proportional. We bragged on it, and he assured us that with practice, he could make one equally as lovely as Weti's. We agreed. But that was far from the most exciting event of the day. After the basket-weaving lesson, Weti served him dinner.

Benjamin was not sure what he ate, something like jerky, but the flavor was wonderful. She then led him back up the hill toward the elephant tree. Halfway up the hill, she stopped and just stood there. Ben thought she had seen a bear or something worse. Eventually, he tugged on her sleeve, so she pointed straight ahead.

Frightened a little, Ben scanned the jutting boulders and was quite surprised when he clearly saw it. A small white oak grew directly beside this three-foot opening on this side of the hill, and a grapevine was tied around the tree's trunk and vanished into the hole. "Is that where you live?"

Weti nodded and then motioned for him to draw nearer. He wanted to go in so bad, but was somewhat fearful and did not want to be intrusive. At her urging, he mirrored her movements and slithered down the vine. It was not all that dark inside, as the opening was a natural angled window, so he figured that not much weather came inside, but the perfect amount of light did. The floor was damp, and a small stream lined the cave's wall eventually disappearing into another dark opening. There were rock ledges on two sides that served as her pantry, as there were tools, food, and many, many small clay vessels much like the one I found at Osage Spring. Weti explained as best she could that these clay jars contained her medicine. A high side of the cave was dry, and there was a pile of goose feathers covered with tanned hides, which Ben thought was her bed. There were drawings on a flat wall that appeared as little circles and straight marks. (Josiah thought this was her calendar.)

Not more than three minutes were they in the cave when Weti motioned for him to climb back up the vine. He did, and she followed. They walked in silence back to the spring. He asked her if all those arrowheads and knives were hers, to which she responded no by shaking her head from side to side. She pointed to the sun and then pointed to our home and then held her hand up as to say,

"Bye." Benjamin headed back down the holler, and of course when he turned to wave, she was gone.

We were puzzled as to why Weti chose to disclose her home to Benjamin. Josiah decided that she knows that she is aging and wanted a trustworthy person to know where she stayed. I suppose she will tell us why in her own time.

The birthday feast was laid out, and Benjamin's expressions were those of a king. We had so much fun putting this all together. It would be our first real party together. We were only halfway through supper when Patches began to bark. Gravel was popping, so I knew that wheels brought our company. Darkness was just beyond the trees, so we could see that our visitors were Miss Beth and Old Zeke. Benjamin yelped with glee, and Lucy's eyes lit up at his excitement. My heart leaped with gladness too, but Josiah frowned. These friends had not visited since Josiah was cheated out of his leg. He did not appreciate the attention that his mishap conjured. I jumped up and gave him an assuring pat. "It will be fine." I picked up the little girl and met our guests on the front porch. I have not near enough room to write everything, so here are the highlights:

It had almost been a year since their last visit. Old Zeke was grayer, Miss Beth more gracious. We invited them to join our party, and party we did! As usual, Miss Beth had gifts for each of us. They were very impressed at how much Lucy had grown and how beautiful she is. Old Zeke watched her like an adoring grandfather, and she was intrigued with his dark skin. She could not help herself, but she had to touch him and run. "Hurt?" she would say. We got tickled about it, and Old Zeke was a dear, as he did not mind at all.

Benjamin was delighted to have birthday guests. The visit could not have been more timely.

When Josiah came out of the shadows, his new appearance caught them off guard, but no big scene was made. They never asked what happened, and they did not treat him any different than before. Miss Beth pulled a chair close beside him and shared the latest news from across the country. This really brightened his day. I was thankful that war talk was minimal. Lucy clapped after we sang "Happy Birthday," and Benjamin's apple cake was the hit of the evening. Except to Lucy that is, who was totally fascinated with Miss Beth's hat. The pink ostrich plume floated back and forth with every gesture of her head, and the toile that wrapped around the rickrack base was like a pink cloud drifting on her head. And, yes, before the night was over, Lucy Leah was sporting that fine millinery. It was very difficult to get her away from the mirror. Tonight was the first time that I had noticed how very much she looked like my sister. Other than the dark hair, she was the same beauty!

We opened the last crock of popping corn, and it tasted even better tonight than that first night right out of the garden. Was it the occasion, or that Josiah had mastered the art of corn popping? Old Zeke called it manna.

Bedtime came too soon, but our young son had a wonderful birthday, and when I kissed his head good night, he was still beaming. He thanked me with a tight hug while he whispered, "I love you, Ma."

Perhaps the best word to describe the mood in our home is contentment. A perfect day! Happy children, godly husband, true friends, full stomach, warm home—what else could any person on earth yearn for? This state is most easy to be content in!

Happy birthday, Benjamin!

MARCH 15, 1862

At Miss Beth's orders, Old Zeke stacked a good number of hatboxes in the bedroom, and when Lucy had eaten breakfast, she put on quite a fashion show. Miss Beth would situate each hat, Lucy would gaze at length in the mirror, and then stumble and crawl around the room, pausing before each of us. What fun! I can see right now that plain gingham dresses will not satisfy my little prissy daughter. Where did she get that?

A healthy pile of newspapers was left for our reading pleasure and information. Miss Beth and Old Zeke were headed for Queen City. I asked if traveling in this climate of conflict was safe. Miss Beth said that she was not sympathetic to either color, and depending on who asked, she had a set of pat answers when they were stopped and questioned. Old Zeke played mute and deaf. So far it had worked beautifully. These two should be in the theater! She assured me that they would stay put this time until the confrontation was won. "How much longer can it possibly last?" she asked jeeringly. "We'll be fine."

Patches danced merrily beside the carriage, and whether a rock or stumble I could not tell, she slid underneath those huge spinning wheels. Of course the surrey bounced, and Old Zeke reined the horses to a stop. He jumped out and began to cry, "Oh, Misser Benjerman, I done gone an kilt yur dawg! Laud halp me! Laud o' mercy! I'm a sorry, I'm a sorry!"

Fortunately, Benjamin was at the spring house restacking the eggs. He did not witness the mishap. I laid Lucy in the rocker and ran to the accident. Patches was not dead, but she was not moving either. There was no blood, and her whining was soft. Old Zeke rolled the carriage forward, and we inspected the injuries closer. I assured him that he had nothing at all to do with this tragedy, but he would not stop crying. He lifted that speckled dog and carried her to the barn and built a bed from old blankets, all the while crying a mournful song. Benjamin hugged him and told him that Patches would be okay. Of course he too was heartbroken, but he did not want Old Zeke to feel bad about what could not be helped. Miss Beth became an instant babysitter while all this hullabaloo was taking place, and Lucy was screaming her head off from the front porch. One can imagine the sight that greeted Josiah as he rode back up the lane from his morning livestock check—a screaming baby, a crying black man, and a whining dog amidst a flurry of activity. I do believe Ben's hug worked magic, as that is the only thing that hushed Old Zeke's tears, and my cuddling Lucy the only thing that quieted hers. Josiah got everybody back on track, assured the visitors that Patches would be fine, and helped them back on their journey. Benjamin began his long vigil by Patches's side. Is there no way to protect a young boy's heart from pain? I could not bear to see him hurting! "Oh, Lord, please let me hurt instead of him!" I whispered the impossible prayer.

But, my dear, he has to experience pain. The choice is not yours. The words passed through my head.

"Auuuuuuggghhhh!" my heart cried inside itself.

And, my eyes teared up as that surrey rolled out of sight.

This was not a good ending to a time of celebration.

MARCH 22, 1862

It has been a week since Patches was injured under Miss Beth's carriage. It appears that her tail or backbone is either broken or badly injured, as she cannot stand up on her back legs. She has not eaten or drank anything for six days.

Poor Benjamin. He has offered her fresh milk, water, squirrel, even chicken and broth, all to which she only turned her head. He is devastated.

The only thing we know to do is keep her comfortable. Unfortunately the air temperature has not been very warm, and yet that boy has slept by her side every night. He made a bed in the barn and has refused to leave her alone at night, proving that a boy and his dog are a most important element of boyhood!

Lucy does not understand that Patches is impaired and still wants to pat the black spot on the dog's hip. "'Atches, 'Atches," she cries. Benjamin has tried to be patient with his sister, but he asked me to keep her out of the barn until his beloved dog gets well. This may be the first sibling rivalry issue, and if so, it isn't too severe. I think we can handle this one.

Only today did I scramble four eggs in butter on a whim and take to the makeshift infirmary, and much to our amazement, Patches lapped them up. We now have hope that she will make it. And we could not believe it, but while eating supper we saw that dog walk out of the barn! She was ambling toward the cabin on her two front feet. Her back legs were lifted up over her head and just dangled as she hobbled along. She looked like something from a traveling circus. "What resolve!" I exclaimed.

"No," Benjamin countered. "That is God answering my prayer!"

I looked at him in great admiration. If only I had his wealth of faith!

APRIL 5, 1862

Josiah and Benjamin have gone to run their traps for the last time this year. They should be back in two days, as it just takes so much longer with three legs rather than four. Josiah still amazes me with his determination and inventions. I suppose that is why I was so surprised when he told Mr. Van Winkle about his struggles. I have no doubt that those two will return with the wagon overflowing with pelts.

Tara and Tressie showed up just after Lucy and I had biscuits and gravy. We had plenty left over for them. Tara had made pretty little twin rag dolls for Lucy and Tressie, and they entertained themselves the rest of the morning. Tara caught me up on the well-being of the family. They were all fine except Temperance, who had slapped her mother and caused Katherine's eye to blacken and swell. "What is ailing that girl?" I asked. Tara assured me that she had no idea, but that no matter how hard she had tried, all of their lives, Temperance just would not have anything to do with her. "She acts like she despises the very air that I breathe," Tara expressed.

We decided that our conversation about Temperance was bordering on gossip, so we changed the subject. Against my better judgment, I asked about Benjamin's mother, Judith. Tara told me that she was a lovely lady, kind, and hard working. Judith was not beautiful on the outside, but as sweet as anyone she had ever known. She had traveled here from Tennessee with Josiah while expecting Benjamin and the trip was more than her body bargained for. Josiah had blamed himself deeply for her passing, and the family thought he would mourn to death for her. Then Tara apologized for telling me all of that and that she loved me far more than anyone and would not hurt my feelings for anything in the world.

I assured her that I was not bothered by her revelations. The truth is that I feel almost guilty for asking, as if I have betrayed Josiah somehow by talking about his past behind his back. That was never my intention, of course. I am, in fact, very secure in our relationship, and I only want to be the very best wife that I am capable of.

Tara went on to say that the entire family, except Uncle Dick, was ecstatic when Josiah brought me home, and the general consensus is that I was good medicine for Josiah. Tara said that she probably should not tell me this, but that Josiah was the most sought-after bachelor in Missouri until he showed up with me, and there were a great number of women who cried in bewilderment and disappointment. Well, that shocked me and actually made me feel a little special, until I remembered that I dare not exalt myself.

The little girls disrupted our deep discussion with needs of their own, and the balance of the day was filled with their wishes and chores.

Before Tressie drifted off to sleep, she told me again about the dark man as tall as the barn and made of glass that wrapped himself around her in the woods that icy night. I was fascinated by her story, and Tara said that no matter how many times she tells about the episode, she always tells it exactly the same, and her little eyes get big and bright as she tells of how warm his wing arms were. It was a great blessing to kiss both of these little heads good night. They looked like precious angels sleeping on clouds of feather pillows.

After they were fast asleep, I unpacked the special quilt that we had started last fall. Tara was delighted at the finished product. She wrapped up in it, and her faraway look made it obvious that she was dreaming of her future.

As we admired our handiwork, Patches began to bark. "Someone is coming," I told her. That fear and dread rose up immediately. Josiah had warned me about strangers and soldiers milling about. He told me to keep the guns close and loaded.

"What shall we do?" Tara gasped.

"Just be quiet and still. I'll get the guns," I answered as I handed her the pistol.

"Oh, I hope I do not have to use this," she declared. I sat down and never released my clutch on the shotgun.

Footsteps came across the porch, and there was a knock on the cabin's door. "Mr. Bozeman?" a man asked.

"Who goes there?" I asked.

"Mrs. Bozeman, it is Jeb Huddleston. I am alone, unarmed, and looking for Josiah."

I relaxed, breathed a sigh, released my clutch, and opened the door for him. It was indeed the handsome grandson of Mr. Van Winkle. As he walked through the door, I happened to see Tara's face. Her pretty dark eyes widened with surprise. A blush quickly covered her cheeks, and she stopped breathing.

When I looked at Jeb, his eyes were locked on Tara, and time had evidently stopped for them both. "Jeb, this is Josiah's niece, Tara Bozeman." I broke the spell.

"It is indeed a great pleasure to make your acquaintance, Mrs. Bozeman," he bowed low.

"That's Miss Bozeman," Tara replied as quickly as I have ever heard her speak.

With that his eyes too lit up, and he bowed again.

More than a few seconds of silence passed, and it was clear that he had completely forgotten his mission. "Jeb, Benjamin and Josiah are running their traps and will not be home until the day after tomorrow."

"Oh."

"Is there something we can help you with?" I asked.

"Actually I am on a mission of sorts." He remembered his reason for being here.

"Grandfather is ill, not near death or anything, but he sent me to inquire of Josiah about the old Indian woman's medicine."

"What is wrong with Mr. Van Winkle?" I queried.

"He hasn't any get-up-and-go; he tells us that his get-up-and-go has got up and went. He is sleepy all day long, yet he sleeps all the night through too. He has lost his appetite for Caroline's cooking. That is how I know that he is seriously sick! Nobody can pass up her cooking!"

I wondered how they knew about Weti. It seems that these woods are full of ears, and I wonder how everyone else seems to know and I do not.

"Well, Jeb, if you know of Weti, you also know that we cannot call on her, as she comes and goes at will, even though she does always seem to know when she is needed. It is late and dark. We obviously can do nothing this night. You are welcome to stay, and we will work on the problem in the morning." It was all I knew to tell him.

"Thank you, Mrs. Bozeman. I will be happy to sleep in the barn or on the front porch." He sounded grateful enough.

"Please call me Lenny," I told him. "I'll get you some bedding."

"Thank you, Lenny, but I have provisions. I will leave you ladies and get some sleep. It was nice to meet you, Miss Bozeman." He bowed again toward Tara.

She had not spoken a word up until that moment, but she said, "Please call me Tara."

"And so I shall. Good night, Tara. I look forward to seeing you both in the morn." And with that he turned and exited the room, gently shutting the door behind him.

We spoke not as we listened to his footsteps fade in the distance and his horse snort when the saddle came off. Patches was not barking, but I could imagine her tail wagging as she followed him to the barn and would be glad to have company herself.

It was all I could do to keep a big smile from spreading across my face when I looked at Tara. She had this shocked look on her face, and I knew exactly how she felt. I experienced the very same reaction the first time I laid eyes on Josiah. Tara was speechless, so I had to help her out. " You never met Jeb before?"

"Never," she said and sighed.

"He is a looker, isn't he?" I teased her. Shame on me.

Tara did not answer, only nodded her head up and down .

"Do you think we had better turn in too?" I asked.

"I suppose so," she answered, "but I don't think I can sleep now."

I should not have, but a huge laugh burst out before I could muffle it. I apologized as I prepared for bed, but she did not even hear me. Oh my, that girl has been smitten. I would not swear to it, but it appeared that Jeb was bitten by the same bug. I have no idea what kind of person he is, but if his heart is as wholesome as he is handsome, then they are a perfect match. The morrow should prove to be extremely interesting. With Tara's pallet made near the girls, I said good night and climbed into my own bed, mentally reliving the day, and just now as I pen these last words, a movement in the window caught my eye, and a familiar, wrinkled face smiled at me. Weti let me know that she is on guard. I will sleep sound, Tara will only catnap, and I suspect that she will be up before the sun, brushing her hair and pinching her cheeks, and I would guess that she will wear a fresh dress and fuss because she did not bring her prettiest one.

Time to talk to the Maker. I shall ask for direction, and for the safe passage of my men, and give many thanks.

APRIL 6, 1862

Sunday morning, and the sunrise was incredible. It was as if mighty lights were shining right down on this farm, a magnificent stage, and a production was opening with great fanfare. Tara was up, primped and primed way before I or the little girls even woke up. She asked if we could prepare a special breakfast. Of course I went right along with her plans. I had never seen Tara nervous or antsy, but she sure was edgy this morning! She was so disappointed when we heard voices on the front porch, far too long before a knock came. When we answered the door, there stood Jeb *and* Weti. Tara was startled, as she too had only just heard of this old wise woman and had never seen her in person. They both came in, and we enjoyed the meal together. Tressie was afraid of Weti, but Lucy demanded that she have her breakfast right from Weti's lap. This pleased Weti, but made Tressie a bit jealous.

Before the morning was over, Tressie too was climbing on the old woman. Jeb was given a deerskin pouch of powder for his grandfather, and I sent a small muslin bag of my favorite healing substance, the aromatic sage. However did Tara and Jeb manage to elude the rest of us and take a very long stroll down the drive? As they neared the cabin's clearing, I overheard him ask her if he could call on her, to which she replied that she would be honored. The air just had a special feel today. I watched them from the corner of my eye as they stood beneath that towering cedar and noticed a pair of buntings chasing one another around those fragrant branches. Ah, spring fever! Well, it certainly has arrived in these hills.

Weti disappeared shortly before the girls' naptime, and Jeb rode off just after dinner with his bags of healing and perhaps much more than he came searching for. He promised to send word one way or another about Mr. Van Winkle's recovery. I thought Tara never would stop waving, and she wasn't worth a flip the rest of the day.

We did very little other than the necessary tasks. As I survey the day's events, I am not at all surprised at the budding relationship of Tara and Jeb, but I am stunned and puzzled by Weti's behavior. She has avoided any other white people, and she suddenly shows herself to not only Tara and Tressie, but Jeb too? I absolutely do not understand. One thing I can be sure of is that she deems all of them safe, or she would have never appeared. Also, if her stamp of approval is on anything, I trust it, so she must have been letting me know that Jeb is of good character and harmless.

I am looking forward to sharing this entire episode with Josiah and getting his take. Tonight's sunset was as incredible as the day's beginning, and the curtain did indeed close on a wonderful production of a beautiful Ozark spring day. I am drifting off to slumber, knowing that a new chapter in Tara's life is opening, my men are headed home, and Weti is out there somewhere, happy to have the blessing of little ones loving on her today, watching out for us, but especially knowing that my Redeemer liveth! As soon as the visitors leave tomorrow, Lucy and I shall venture to the rock.

I could see myself in Tara, the way she was so mesmerized by Jeb. Looking back, I saw how selfish I was to not notice Lenny's attraction to Josiah. It was difficult to accept the fact that I am responsible for a portion of the relentless pain in my being all these many years. More than ever I understood now how massive waste consumes our lives, a product of foolish pride. I'll never have my sister back! She was precious!

MAY 11, 1862

We are in hiding this night. I have to write quickly and extinguish the lamp.

Two Union soldiers casually rode up our lane today. I hid the baby under our bed and begged her to keep quiet. Poor little thing must have sensed my horror, as her eyes were as round as a hedge apple; the same angels that shut the lions' mouths for Daniel came and closed hers, as she never made a peep.

The crash of Josiah's chair and loud voices attracted my attention, and from the window I saw the men in blue backhand him and call him a cripple traitor. Josiah lay prostrate and was out cold. They laughed and went toward the barn. *Oh my Lord, where is Benjamin?* I thought as the noise in the back of the cabin startled me. My heart was pounding in my ears louder than that noise. Thank you, Lord! It was Benjamin. He crawled through the window in full panic.

"Ma, you and Lucy have got to hide!" he cried in a whisper.

"No," I said. "Stay here." Yet he heard not a word, and when those men disappeared into the barn, he crept to the porch and pulled his pa's colt revolver from the secret shelf under his chair, tossed a rifle to me as he ran through the cabin, and then crawled back out the window and crept to the chicken house.

I loaded the gun and waited.

One of the men came out of the barn with our milk cow tied to his horse. The other followed with Old Buck tied to his. The smaller man came back to the cabin, walked up on the porch, and kicked Josiah again. I guess he was quite satisfied that he had killed my husband and just walked right into our home. He looked all around and touched everything on the mantle. I had slipped under the bed with Lucy and the rifle. Those black, dirty boots walked into our bedroom, and he began emptying drawers and boxes. He was ransacking our home! Suddenly he stopped, slowly turned, and walked toward the bed. He patted the bed with his gun. His knees came into my view, and then that nasty face and filthy eyes glared at me. "Well, what have we here? My, you are a pretty thing, and this little one even prettier. Looks like I will not have a bad day after all." He reached for my baby, and without thought or hesitation, I pulled the trigger.

The smoke was still burning in my eyes when I heard another gunshot. This one came from outside, in the direction of the smoke-house. Fear was out of the question; I was way past that! I dared not move, but that also meant that I could not reload. The decision to do so or not was made for me by the footsteps near the front door. Ever so slowly, they crept through the cabin, slower and slower; then they reached the bedroom door. By now this blue's blood was pooling across the floor and dripping through the cracks. Dripping blood, a familiar sound and pure horror! Before I saw the boots, I heard a familiar voice, "Ma! Ma!"

"Thank you, dear God!" It was Benjamin. Without releasing my grip on the toddler, we were both out from under the bed in one quick motion, and the three of us embraced. Benjamin could only speak when his breath returned. He figured these men would attempt to steal our food, and the huge, burly, hairy, smelly man did go into the smoke house and was pulling down the hanging hams when he spotted Benjamin in the rafters. He tried to grab the boy and got angry when this swift kid eluded his grasp, so he said, "I'll just kill you, boy," and went for his gun. Benjamin already had the man's dirty hair in the sights and pulled the trigger before the man's pistol had cleared the scabbard.

Josiah began to moan from the porch. "Lenny, Benjamin." We ran to him. His lips were bleeding, and two huge goose eggs had popped out on his forehead. Quickly, we gave him the details of what had just transpired. "We've got to bury those bodies," he said. "Quickly!" He held tight the crying baby.

I wrapped the mangled heads in flour sacks, and we drug them to the lane, loaded them in the buckboard, and hauled them far from the clearing into a dried-up pond bed. This land is far too rocky to dig, and we were too short of time to use a pick, so we covered the bodies with brush and fallen limbs. We determined to burn them later. Benjamin emptied their pockets. "Son!" I exclaimed.

"Ma, I'd hate to burn money," he reasoned.

With the day's wash water, I cleaned the bedroom floor, and Benjamin sprinkled lime through the cracks, and then he raked sawdust into the dirt floor of the smokehouse. It wasn't until we went out for more water did we see the smoke curl coming from the barn. "Oh my Lord, Josiah, they have set the barn on fire!"

I heard him curse for the first time.

Benjamin and I ran with all our might, careful not to lose the water in our buckets. Fate was with us this hour, as only a small stack of straw was smoldering, and the water we had was sufficient to snuff it out.

"Ma, what are we going to do with their horses?" Ben asked.

"Let's put the tack under the brush pile. We'll burn it too."

Under the cover of darkness, Benjamin led the horses to Uncle Dick. I am sure these acquisitions will not be old hat to him, as the words *horse thief* are commonly associated with his name.

Josiah believes that the men we killed were deserters.

Weti showed up just at dusk, medicine bag in hand. She doctored Josiah.

Lucy would not release her hold on me. How in the world will she cope with this day's experience? I asked Weti. She was of no opinion. The old woman looked especially weary. Satisfied with her work, she took a seat on the hard hearth and did not disappear until Benjamin returned safely.

He was wide eyed, and I knew not how to comfort him. We all knew that sleep would not visit this night. Ben emptied his pockets and sifted through the blood-speckled belongings of those evil men. There was nothing of value, only a note to family graphically degrading our way of life, to which Benjamin spouted, "I am glad we killed them!" as he tossed the paper into the fire. Our unspoken pact: this day will remain an untold story.

Josiah's demeanor was one of utter failure. Well, he can just move over with all of that and give me a seat because today I became a murderer. I am no different than Uncle Dick.

Oh, Lenny! I could not even imagine having to endure this tragedy! Lenny you could never be a murderer. You were a hero. You saved your child and your home. I heard so many horror stories during the war, but they were only stories. I forgot them and moved right on. The world as you knew it changed that very moment. My world never changed.

MAY 12, 1862

It is true that a leopard cannot change its spots, nor can a man change the color of his skin, but war, yes war, changes everything in its path. Determined to finish our business himself, Josiah insisted on going with us to light the fire. We soaked fabric strips in oil and stuffed them deep into the brush pile and poured a bucket of red-hot coals on top. The red chips sifted down through the pile, and there was just enough breeze to catch it all up. We continued to stack more dried brush to the flames. The smoke blew away from us and was an odd blue color. Ironic, isn't it? The smell was putrid. I ran behind the pines and threw up. I did not want Lucy to see me . Good grief, Lenny! As if she did not see enough yesterday to mark her for life!

Yes indeed, war changes life, all four of us now harbor battle scars. I have no idea what will come, but be assured it will be greeted with different perspectives. My son is changed. One click of a colt's hammer sent him directly from childhood to manhood.

MAY 13, 1862

Josiah's banging on the loft ladder woke up the whole house this morning. That may not be the correct verbiage, as none of we four have really slept since Sunday.

The events of the past two days have us on an emotional ocean. Our senses have sharpened, we see every movement, and we are alert at any sound. We are fearful and semi-guilt-ridden, afraid that more Union troops will come and discover what we have done. The source of the guilt cannot be identified because, given the identical circumstances, we would have behaved precisely the same.

Benjamin bailed from the loft on the verge of hysteria. "What is wrong, Pa?"

"I need your help; let's go," Josiah ordered.

"Don't you want breakfast?" I asked.

"We will eat when we return."

When they returned, long after noon, Josiah would not say a word, but Benjamin reported.

Josiah told Benjamin that he had had it! He was sick and tired! Sick and tired of being an invalid, and he would have no more of it!

He would never again be in a situation where he could not protect his family. "I must walk again!" he explained. "And you are going to help me." He had the boy get my ball of twine, which they used to measure the length of his arms and legs. Benjamin cut forked hickory limbs to length, padded the forks with my quilt batting, and sewed a cover. "There," he said, satisfied with his invention. Josiah scooted to the edge of the porch and dangled his leg. He had Benjamin stand up the hand-fashioned crutches on either side of him, positioned the pillow-top ends under his arms, and finally put all of his weight on the leg as he stood. "Get behind me, son. If I stagger, you steady me. I have a notion that the muscles in my leg and arms are pathetically weak." Benjamin hopped to his post and Josiah set the crutch ends a foot in front of him. He took his first step in seven months. It was a great accomplishment!

I did not know how to react to this new development. Josiah must have sensed my dilemma because he said, "I am sorry, Lenny. Giving in or giving up just isn't in me. As often as I have heard that old adversary whisper in my ear, 'Just give up; quit,' I considered that. But the voice in my other ear repeats, 'I never promised that the cross would not be heavy and the hill would not be hard to climb. I promised to show up and take you through the fire.' This day I have chosen which voice I shall hold fast to."

JUNE 10, 1862

Old Miss Lessie at Eden was right about the upcoming revival. This morning a slow horse sluggishly sauntered up the lane, and the rider looked as haggard as his charge. Reverend Evan Penn is a circuit rider and visiting all area homesteads, inviting the families to the evangelical camp meeting near Mr. Van Winkle's farm in Eden. Looks can be deceiving because he was a delight to visit with and seemed eternally grateful for the drink and rest stop on our front porch. After last month's episode, I was extremely cautious as to every move and remark that I made, as well as Reverend Penn's. There was a marked and definite change in Miss Lucy. Obviously our skirmish with the deserters has planted a seed of insecurity in this baby girl, as she never let go of my skirt tail and was very anti-social. This business about not trusting anyone is so foreign to me, and I do not like it! Such is life in the midst of war.

The reverend seemed completely harmless, and after the first hour we both relaxed a bit. I was glad when Josiah and Benjamin came in for dinner after the morning chores. I watched Josiah's inter-action with this gentleman, and I am satisfied that Reverend Penn is indeed who he claims to be. The reverend invited us to the camp meeting and gave brief details. Without being pushing or demand-ing, he made it sound like our life and future depended on our atten-dance. He assured us that we would be revived, inspired, and filled with hope and peace. He asked us to bring any instruments and join in the music worship and told us that in years past, the food was so good that it would make you want to slap your pappy.

After all the meeting information had been presented, we spoke of our mutual acquaintances living on the river and other neighbors. He became gravely quiet when Uncle Dick's name came up. All he would say was "Christ died for all." We had a nice meal together, and the men sat in the shade of that huge cedar another hour or two. Josiah invited the reverend to stay the night, but he declined and said that he must be about his Father's business. That tired old horse never lifted his head as he carried the reverend back down the lane and out of sight. And so a new and hopefully, long-lasting friendship has been fashioned.

The camp meeting starts August first and will last as long as the Spirit leads, a minimum of a week. I have never been to a brush arbor camp meeting and have no idea what to expect, but from the account of Miss Lessie, it will be quite a time, and I am excited about going. Josiah said unless there was more trouble, we would make every effort to attend. I asked if we could invite Tara to accompany us, and he agreed. The only problem is going to be the daily chores because Ben-jamin is looking forward to the adventure too. Josiah said that if Toby wasn't going to the meetings, he would offer him that job. So it is set! We will pack up and go back to Eden in August.

It is amazing how having something to look forward to changes an attitude. And we surely need a diversion from this gloom of impending doom and destruction from the threats and dangers of a two-colored war clashing all around us. Josiah did voice his concerns about our safety but reminded himself of the stronger one inside us.

JULY 5, 1862

Today's visitor was James Hanger from Virginia. Like so many passersby, he was not lost but on a specific mission. An old acquaintance had called back a favor and requested Mr. Hanger specifically to our homestead. His boxed in wagon was laden with numerous strange contraptions, and our curiosity got the best of us as Mr. Hanger, an ex-soldier himself, limped slightly when he walked. First, he told us that his old friend, Samuel Clemens, had sent him our way, and he was not only under obligation to Samuel but also had a strong, sincere desire to help wounded soldiers.

Then he told of his invention, the Hanger Leg, that is a device under patent. Josiah was very apprehensive until Mr. Hanger lifted his pant leg and showed us a wooden leg made from barrel staves that hinged at the knee. He told of how he had lost his leg during a skirmish and was considered the first amputee of this national conflict. He was determined to walk again and felt that the good Lord had given him the wisdom to design this contraption, replacing catgut in earlier models with rubber bumpers to control the arches and the ankle's flex by using a plug fit wooden socket. Mr. Hanger could sense the apprehension and continued his story of how there were tens of thousands of wounded soldiers with amputations and that the U.S. government guaranteed artificial limbs for all veterans who had lost limbs during the war. His invention had become so well known that his own state legislature had commissioned him to manufacture this Hanger limb for all limbless veterans. Josiah immediately explained to Mr. Hanger that he had never been, nor would ever be a soldier for either side.

The fact that Josiah was not a soldier was of little relevance to Mr. Hanger, and he retrieved his measuring devices and proceeded to map Josiah's body for an appropriate fit. Benjamin watched all this with wide-eyed amazement, and I do believe that we were all quite shocked and taken by this turn of events. Josiah interrupted the man's work only once more when he attempted to explain that we had no monetary compensation for this great service. Mr. Hanger assured Josiah that all expenses had been paid in advance and to not let that be of any concern. All I knew to do was prepare the greatest feast within my ability for this incredible man working wonders right before our eyes. Benjamin became Mr. Hanger's gopher and ran back and forth from the wagon to the porch with staves and tools and other strange gadgets. Benjamin's excitement grew as this Hanger Leg evolved from parts and pieces into a new life for Josiah, and the rest of us. Not an hour after dinner, Mr. Hanger announced that the leg was completed except for adjustments and insisted that Josiah sit for the fitting. The contraption was fastened on with leather belts, and Mr. Hanger ordered Josiah to stand. Reluctantly Josiah stood with ease. "Walk," insisted the leg's maker, "toss those crutches aside!"

Benjamin and I held our breaths. The smile on Josiah's face was the first indication of success; that smile was contagious and soon spread to all of us, especially Mr. Hanger, who was overjoyed to see a lame man walk. His just reward was witnessing the recipient's joy and astonishment. "It will be sometime before you master the new leg completely, but you shall," he said with calm assurance. Before the accomplishment totally sunk into us, Mr. Hanger had all his gadgets loaded and was uttering his good-byes.

No matter how hard we begged, he would not consider staying with us, determined to make it to Thomasville before nightfall. There is no way in this world that we could show our gratitude to

Mr. Hanger. He had obviously been in this situation before and assured us that he had by far reaped the greater benefit of this endeavor. And so he rode away the exact same way that he had arrived, unannounced and unexpected.

Josiah never sat down the rest of the day and half of the night. I helped him unstrap the wooden leg before he got into bed. He has already learned to maneuver himself around the house without the crutches. Benjamin thought we should have a celebration and burn the crutches, like a sacrifice in the wilderness, but Josiah said that maybe he should keep them for a backup, and so he hung them high in the barn loft. We ended our extraordinary day wishing we knew how to contact our friend Samuel Clemens. We exercised God's promise, and the three of us gathered and asked the good Lord to bless and prosper Mr. Clemens, wherever in this large world that he might be.

AUGUST 11, 1862

Finally! My family is down for the evening, exhausted, yet full, full of groceries and spirit. We only this day arrived back home from the revival at Eden. It has been an indescribable week! Since I am having difficulty finding sleep, I must at least attempt to pen the experience.

For nearly a week before departing, the entire family joined in preparations for an undetermined hiatus from this homestead. I do believe that we were all looking forward to what we thought would be a mysterious adventure. Toby had no desire to spend his week at a camp meeting and agreed to reside here and tend to the place. He assured us that he would be fine. Josiah had faith in this young man, and ever since that day in the barn when Toby's arm was broken, the young man has had a mighty respect for his Uncle Josiah. I do believe that he would live with us without much encouragement.

Tara did accompany Josiah, Benjamin, Lucy, and me to Eden. We were all disappointed that Uncle Frank and Anna would not allow Tressie to go too. But since they nearly lost her this year, I guess I can understand. And of course the threat of the war still swarms the hills. Our wagon was so loaded that there was scarcely room for us riders. We sang and chatted all along the way. Tara's excitement level grew the nearer we got to Eden. She had never been there, but the three of us had told her so much about the beautiful place that she felt she knew it well. What she really knew was that Jeb Huddleston would be waiting for her, and she longed to see him and experience that feeling again. As far as I know, they had only written a time or two since they met at our home last April.

We had gotten word that Mr. Van Winkle had indeed recovered from whatever ailed him, and he gave Weti all the credit. Since none of us had ever attended a camp meeting, we had no idea what to expect. The ride there was uneventful, other than Lucy having a very dirty diaper quite a distance from any water source. She was a stinking little girl until Josiah found a path to the river.

Benjamin picked out the perfect spot to set up our temporary home under the shade of a huge white oak. It looked like we were some of the first to congregate. The men took care of the horses, set up the campfire, and set up the poles for our makeshift tent. Tara and I unloaded the wagon, and prepared the bed rolls and food. Miss Lessie drove up soon after we had unloaded and was wound up tighter than a tick! She seemed a bit disappointed that we were not going to stay at her house, but she was so excited about the upcoming revival that her excitement rubbed off on us, and we hugged as she left some delicious baked goods. She also offered to be of any assistance that we might need and headed to the next campsite to welcome the other visitors.

Reverend Penn had taken up residence for the week at Mr. Van Winkle's. (I think he knew about Caroline's cooking.) Mr. Van Winkle was as full of it as ever, and when he saw Josiah walking around the campsite, he slapped him on the back and wanted to know if the old Indian woman had special magic that made his leg grow back. Josiah found no humor in that question and did not qualify it with an answer, but he explained the Hanger Leg and his gratefulness for it. So few people had seen Josiah without a leg; no one else commented except Reverend Reeves, who was rather nosey about the costs, Dr. Hanger, and any other details that Josiah was willing to share. Miss Lessie never even mentioned the new leg, just as she had never acknowledged the missing one. She may be old fashioned, but she does employ proper manners.

There is no way that I can write about all the people we met, as there were hundreds! The road into Eden was itself a river of wagons, horses, and folks on foot all that day and far into the night. In fact, the entire week it was a one-way road in, as many came but no one left until the camp meeting officially closed. It was exciting! The days were filled with cooking, storytelling, children playing, fishing, exploring the banks, flat cone-shaped papers on sticks fanning the elderly women, and friendships forming.

The atmosphere was one of cheerful, spiritual relief. It was the first time in several years that the threat of impending doom from the war did not seem to loom over our heads; it were as if that heavy, unspoken darkness was not anywhere near this beautiful, peaceful place along the slow rolling, crystal-clear river. Or so it seemed.

Tara was handy when there was work to do, but she was nowhere to be found the rest of the day. On the third day, Benjamin came in to watch Lucy while I went to the river to wash her diapers and whispered that he had seen Tara and Jeb holding hands. He did not know what to think about that and was absolutely beside himself. I assured him that it would be okay, but I am not so sure that he was satisfied. Jeb did spend a lot of time at our site, and we got to know the man that he is, and I must say that I have come to like him a great deal. That might be an understatement for Tara. I do hope that she took the sermons to heart, but I cannot be sure that she even heard them. I have so enjoyed witnessing this budding romance! Josiah is reserved as always, and I do not expect an opinion from him unless I ask, which I will not.

On the first day, several men fell trees, some built rough benches while others dug holes for the felled trees that became the bearing beams for the side rails, and the chopped brush that topped the primitive structure. Underneath this arbor a platform was built that served as the preacher's roost, complete with a rough pulpit, and perhaps the most important of all—the mourners' benches. Straw was strewn all underneath to keep down the dust, and a corner was set aside for any musicians who wanted to play or sing.

At dusk that first day, a loud trumpet sound rang out, and word was passed from camp to camp that a meeting had been called. We all dropped what we were doing. I picked up Lucy, and I followed Josiah to the brush arbor. Reverend Penn was on the platform in front of the pulpit, and with his arms raised up, palms outstretched toward the crowd, silence overtook the throng, and the rippling of the river's water was the only audible sound. Reverend Penn waited a few moments before speaking and then informed this multitude of the schedule of events, and what would signal each. He offered up a very lengthy prayer, asking for God's visitation among this crowd, his healing power to flow down, and his will be done to its fullest. Lucy's squirms were the only movement that I was aware of, and I was impressed by the reverence displayed by all the attendees. We were dismissed and made our way back to the campsite and bedded down. It was very difficult for me to find sleep in this air of excitement, and I was not the only one because I could hear soft muttering all through the camp.

With dawn came the sounding of the trumpet, which signaled formally the beginning of the camp meeting. We had time only to dress and freshen up before the second blast sounded, which meant that prayers were to start in each camp. We were still in silent prayer when the third trumpet blast came, a call for all to gather for public prayer in the arbor. After this a community breakfast was served, and we were free until the afternoon prayer meeting. It took a few days for us to get the routine down, but oddly enough, the excitement was never reined.

I had no idea that so many people were blessed with such great musical talents! Why, the music alone touched hearts, and each night I saw tears falling, arms raised toward heaven, eyes closed, and shouts of glory rang throughout the congregation during the music service. Some folks swayed with the music, some danced, others hummed, and those who knew the words sang along. Poor Josiah, he joined in, but although his voice is deep and rich and as smooth as butter cream, he cannot carry a tune. He had been reluctant to sing, but when Reverend Penn shouted, "Make a joyful noise unto the Lord!" Josiah took him at his words and belted out the songs; it was indeed a joyful noise to me, so I am positive that the good Lord enjoyed him too. Jeb surprised us when he picked up a fiddle and lit up the night with his composition. This inspired many others, as soon that corner was full of men, women, and little children playing in great harmony instruments, of many which I had never heard. The energy created by the powerful music was enormous, and I noticed twigs and leaves falling from the arbor, as it seemed to sway with the melodies. Occasionally a star could be seen through those branches, and they too had an appearance of dancing.

When Reverend Penn knew that his congregation was stirred up enough, he called the music to a halt and took off preaching with a lengthy exhortation of how truly brief life is and then went into the dangers of unprepared and sudden death, especially in this climate of war. Using Scripture seldom heard, he explained in great detail the horrors of hell. His sermon ended with a deep, soulful pleading to all sinners present to come to repentance. He appeared totally spent when he fell to his knees and began to plead with God to enable hearts to accept the Holy Spirit's call. The hanging oil lamps spilled out an eerie light as someone in that corner began to softly play a stringed instrument and we all stood up, and I noticed several people making their way down those makeshift aisles and falling at the mourner's benches. Before long those altars were crowded and the music got louder and louder. I jumped out of my skin when a scream sounded, and Benjamin wrapped his arms around my waist and shouted too. His cry was of fear; the other scream was somebody slain in the Spirit, I learned later. Mighty zeal overflowed this crowd, and the singing and shouting continued on far into the night. There may have been as many as a hundred converts that evening.

The second day and night were much the same, except that this night we witnessed the jerking. People were even more touched by the power that fell. One large lady got happy and started jumping benches, then fell down in some sort of trance, and Miss Lessie turned a flip. After the second night's meeting, Benjamin queried Josiah and me back at camp. The boy was completely confused. Josiah talked with him over an hour, explaining that many people's actions reflect their emotions, and that the Word of God is so very powerful that it overwhelms folks, and most do not know how to channel that power. He told his son that we were not to quench the Spirit, but that all things should be decent and in order. He put in plain words how we must live by those words, and not our emotions because we cannot be happy and excited every hour of the day, and as we well knew, circumstances can change our lives in an instant, and all of life is not necessarily pleasant. Therefore, we must keep, believe in, and behave according to those words, regardless of the world that rages around us. Benjamin seemed to understand that part, but he was mortified of hell and asked a hundred questions. Josiah upheld all that Reverend Penn had preached about hell and shared that hell is mentioned in the Holy Book many more times than heaven is.

In spite of this parental guidance, the young boy had nightmares the first three nights. He finally confided in me that he was afraid that those men we killed were in hell and that we put them there. What a huge burden for a little guy! I must confess that the same thoughts had crossed my mind, so the next morning at our camp prayer, we agreed to seek God's wisdom concerning this secret matter. That night's atmosphere was more powerful than any before. I wondered where all these people came from, as every night the crowd grew, and each night the mourners' benches were covered with tears and fists. Much to my astonishment, Benjamin was among them, and I watched closely as he kneeled, laid his crossed arms on the bench, and rested his head there. The boy never went into a trance, jerked, nor exhibited any other manifestation, but eventually stood, walked straight to Reverend Penn, reached out his hand, and shook the preacher's hand in gratitude. He quietly returned to his place beside me.

The boy was a foot taller and free from fear. I never asked him about his experience, but he shared with us during the ride home. He told us that each night during the preaching that he relived that day in the rafters of the smokehouse when he was staring into the black eyes of that deserter, and glimpses of his short life rolled before his eyes, and he knew that he was going to die. He said that he never considered pointing the gun at that man and pulling the trigger; it just happened before he realized it. He said that he knew he had unconfessed sin and that no matter what else the Book had to say, hell was a place that he did not want to live forevermore, nor did he wish any of those he loved to live there. Josiah, Tara, and I assured him that hell was not our destination, and that eased his deep concern.

I shared with him the reassurance that I had received about that horrible day in March. Each of us eventually chooses where we will spend eternity, and as stated in the Holy Book, there is a time to be born and a time to die, and that day last March was the day those ex-soldiers were to die, and it was *not* our day to leave this world, as our purpose has yet to be fulfilled. Not only all that, but those men are in the eternal destination of their choice, and we had nothing at all to do with that. Benjamin concurred with me and added his similar revelations. He also vowed to live his life as close to the Book as he possibly could, and he would appreciate our patience with him. I thought to myself, *Oh, if he only knew how I personally struggle in my walk with the good Lord, he would not have confidence to ask for my patience but would have to exercise his own endurance with me.* Nonetheless, Josiah and I are elated that our boy has chosen this path for his life when there are so many that he could have chosen in this day and time. We expressed our pride and encouraged him to stay on the straight road. Josiah cautioned him that his life would not be easy or smooth but a massive challenge. It would require constant communication with his Maker and faith that one who knows is always in charge would be the catalyst for success in that challenge.

There may have been as many as thirty other preachers at this camp meeting, and when Reverend Penn was exhausted, one of them would jump up onto the platform and take up where he left off. This was especially helpful the last day because beginning that morning, the baptismal service began. The summer had been especially hot, and the sumac and walnut trees had already begun to turn red and yellow. The sky was its bluest blue and the river's water cold, clear, and swift. The congregation gathered near the shore, forming a huge semicircle around the preachers and the converts, each waiting his or her turn to make public his or her profession of faith. Reverend Penn walked out to the middle of the flow and raised his hands toward heaven. The crowd quieted, and then his prayer began and ended as he reached his hands toward the converts. He invited the preachers to line up beside him in the cool river. They did so, leaving about three feet between one another. Then one by one, the converts entered the water, one flesh-covered soul to each reverend. Each preacher's right hand was placed under the person's chin, the other behind their head, and after Reverend Penn raised his right hand to the skies and asked blessings on each new child of the King and deemed that he baptized them in the name of the Father, the Son, and the Holy Ghost. Each preacher would dunk the new saint under the water and hold him or her just long enough for the water to wash his or her sins away. The converts would pop up from that cold water with gasps, squeals, shouts of hallelujah, or tears flowing . They would wade to the river's edge, meeting the next in line somewhere near the middle. The wet converts were greeted by relatives and friends with hugs and more tears and shouts of joy. From the back of the crowd a beautiful, single voice was heard, "Shall we gather at the river, where bright angel's feet have trod? Gather with the saints at the river that flows by the throne of God. Yes, we'll gather at the river, the beautiful, the beautiful river. Gather with the saints at the river that flows by the throne of God." Soon those who knew the words joined in, and the harmony drifted up toward those billowing, white, fluffy clouds and out through the thick forest and just above the river's flow in perfect harmony. It was incredibly spiritual! My own tears fell like rain, and Lucy stayed perfectly still and attentive to this spectacular display of holy presence. The singing continued, "Soon we'll reach the shining the river, soon our pilgrimage will cease. Soon our happy hearts will quiver with the melody of peace. Yes, we'll gather at the river. The beautiful, the beautiful river, gather with the saints at the river, that flows by the throne of God."

The song was sung over and over, and by the time someone changed hymns, we all knew the words to every verse. We sang "Onward Christian Soldiers," "We're marching to Zion," and many others that I did not know until the tree's shadow grew very long. After the last candidate for baptism was dunked, Reverend Penn dismissed the other preachers from the water. It was only then that I realized that Reverend Reeves was not among them. Reverend Penn ended the camp meeting from his stand in the middle of the Eleven Point River by requesting God's blessings and safekeeping on all his children and that he constantly remind the others of the torments of hell at their end of life so that they would turn from their wicked ways and follow Christ.

My mind was in a fog as we packed the wagon for our journey home. Our new friends promised to visit and invited us to their humble abode in the Irish wilderness. Miss Lessie hugged and hugged, and all the Van Winkles showered us with salutations and invitations to return. Jeb had not left Tara's side for three days, except while she slept, and the two of them were finding it difficult to say good-bye in the midst of the crowd. I could almost feel their hearts breaking. Half of the attendees had ventured up the long hill from Eden before we ever had completely broken camp. I do not suppose there was a big rush to leave, but we really did need to get back home and relieve Toby. Josiah agreed and thought that with all the traffic, we would be safe enough traveling beneath the stars, and so we did.

We were an hour away from the river at Eden when we heard gunshots in the far distance to the east. We were still so full of the Spirit that fear did not immediately overtake us. Fifteen minutes after the first shots, Josiah pointed to the eastern sky, from which came a bright glow. The night sky had turned to orange, and yellow sparks were spewing upward. A roar filled the air so loud that the sound of gunshots faded, and a burning stench had already wafted within the air we were breathing. "Is the Lord coming back?" Benjamin shouted.

"I do not believe so, son," Josiah answered abruptly. "It appears to be an extremely large fire."

"Where do you think it is, Josiah?" I asked.

"I could not swear to it, but I believe it is at or near the Irish settlement."

Immediately I thought of our new friends and prayed that what Josiah thought was not true. "Should we go?"

"I cannot risk the life of my family," was Josiah's reply. "I must get all of you home safely. By the look of that glow, there would be little that we could do at this point. Let's be very quiet until we reach our property."

"Pa, is that what hell looks like?" the boy asked.

"I am sure that I do not know for certain, son, but from the Word's description, I would think possibly so."

And so it was, the balance of our journey home, was made in silence, save only the cracking of gravel under the wagon's wheels. Once we arrived at our home place, Benjamin found Toby sleeping in the barn, and all looked fine. Tara opted to stay another day with us and helped me gather Lucy and only what we needed until the morning from the wagon. The men unhitched the team and got into bed about an hour ago. Well, exactly what Reverend Penn said would happen has—the fiery darts of the evil one are flying. He does not like to see victory on the Lord's side, and I must say that there was indeed great victory in Jesus this week.

OCTOBER 25, 1862

Uncle Frank stopped by two days ago with very disturbing news; at least it was to me!

He was on his way to Thomasville in preparation for Tara's move there. His wagon was loaded with her belongings and furnishings for her new residence, and he planned to have everything set up when she arrived.

Evidently Jeb has decided to sign up with the Confederation, and since Tara cannot become a soldier, she has volunteered to take a station at the hospital. It must have been a rash decision because she never mentioned this notion.

Yes, I realize that is an extremely noble cause, but I do not want to lose my friend! Tara will be a wonderful nurse; she just has that natural talent. But I am going to miss her with all my heart, and I will worry my head off about her living in that rough place.

Tara arrived yesterday morning, and we shared an understanding hug before sitting down with a pot of tea and muffins. Lucy sensed something out of the norm and stayed especially close; in fact, the only time she got out of Tara's lap was when Weti showed up, and they took turns cuddling her.

Tara revealed the events that had transpired since our camp meeting at Eden. Besides the many letters sent back and forth, Jeb had visited twice, and during the last visit he explained his burning desire to serve the cause, and so he was enlisting. He clarified that his greatest desire was to spend his life with her and asked for her hand in marriage. In fact, the trip itself was actually to make this request by asking her pa. Uncle Frank gave his permission and his blessings long before Jeb bent his knee, gently kissed her soft hands, and then asked if she would be his wife and the mother of his children. Tara told this story with dreamy eyes and immense gush. He told her that if her answer was yes, he could go to war now with a great reason to stay alive and a future to look forward to, one that dwelling on would help him endure the miserable existence on the battlefield. She readily accepted his proposal and decided to join her fiancé by contributing to the cause, helping care for other fallen warriors. Jeb was not 100 percent for this, but he could not condemn her decision since it was because of his that she made it.

So the plans were well laid. Tara promised to keep in touch and call on us if she needed anything at all. Tara brought Lucy another beautiful rag doll, a new quilt pattern she had designed for me to work on, and a tin of beautiful beads for Weti, who thanked Tara with moist eyes, as a hug was not in her makeup. Weti was gone the first time we turned around. We had a pleasant supper, and Josiah asked in a special prayer that Tara be watched over and all her needs supplied. And for the first time, I heard him ask for safety of those fighting this irrational war.

Tara and I stayed up long after the others went to sleep and talked about our dreams, hopes, fears, and talked of the fun times we have had and those we plan to have. Tara asked my advice on planning a wedding, something I have no experience in, but I assured her that I would help her and her mother any way that I could. She said that Jeb wanted a big, bona fide celebration with all the trimmings. They had discussed getting married at Eden, just above the river at the cave opening, and would attempt to have Reverend Penn come back and perform the ceremony. She asked if I would make her dress, and she sketched the most beautiful gown that I have ever seen. Perhaps together we can stitch it as beautiful. They have yet to set the date, but given any unseen circumstances, probably next fall.

Weti was on the porch at sunrise with a pine straw basket filled with trinkets and medicinal powders for Tara. She did not linger long and only left after touching Tara's shiny hair briefly. This was the first time that I ever saw Weti physically leave.

Toby rode up early this morning to escort Tara to her temporary new home in Thomasville. He had breakfast with us and was very graphic in his description of the war hospital there. He told us that the enlistment center was getting larger every week, as well as the cemetery.

Toby has a way of taking all the sugar coating off life and getting down to the raw and realness of it. Today was the first time that he carried on an authentic conversation with me, and either he is growing up, or he is becoming a total Rebel. He promised me that he would look out for Tara as if she were his own sister. He assured me that people in Thomasville knew who she belonged to and would not bother her because of that. I am not certain exactly what that means, but I assume that it is something to be thankful for. They rode away, and for some reason I felt like my life had changed somehow.

Josiah knew of my concerns and sadness and babied me this evening. He is so precious. Benjamin told me in his man voice, "Not to worry, Ma."

OCTOBER 30, 1862

Another weird day! I woke before the sun and wondered why our fire had gone out during the night, as it was downright freezing in the cabin. I placed an extra quilt on the little one as I passed her crib. By the time Josiah buckled his leg on, I had gone out to gather firewood and saw the crystal world. The precipitation that fell as we slept had turned to ice. No wonder it was so cold! I asked Josiah if the winters came so early in this part of the country, and he told me that he had never witnessed this phenomenon. Benjamin was fascinated by the ice covering, and when the sun had been up about an hour, it reflected off and through the frozen crust and was incredibly beautiful. Josiah would not let him attempt chores until it melted some. He took my salt crock and sprinkled it on the porch steps. Breakfast was especially tasty as we sat in front of that roaring fire, but I thought of Weti and prayed that she was okay.

Benjamin mentioned Jeb, who had stopped in for a few minutes yesterday on his way to Thomasville by way of Uncle Frank's to visit and pick up a few more of Tara's things. Benjamin had admired his extra tall, blond horse, and Jeb offered to trade him for Old Buck. "No way!" Benjamin told him. "You have a mighty fine-looking horse there, Jeb, but I could never part with Old Buck."

Jeb intended to enlist at Thomasville and said that he just could not come so near without stopping in for a visit. He assured us that his grandpa and his sisters were fine, as well as the other neighbors near Eden. It sure was good to hear about old friends. The sad news he shared was that many of the homes and barns in the Irish Wilderness area had indeed been torched by invading troops. Our worst fears were confirmed; that glow in the night's sky we witnessed on our way from the camp meeting *was* a mighty fire destroying the entire community. Jeb reported that most of the farms had been pilfered and ninety percent of the inhabitants left starving, with only the clothes on their backs. He seemed to be in a rush, and I suspect that he was in a hurry to see Tara. He was kind enough to take her a few more little items that I had put together, and he assured me that he would give her a big hug from me. I thought, *I'll bet you will.*

He had nothing new to share about the upcoming nuptials, except that he hoped his two years of enlistment would pass quickly so that he could start building the home he had designed for Tara. I like him more every time he comes around. It is almost like I have adopted Tara as my little sister, and I am constantly thinking of her as if she were my sibling. Maybe I do that to appease my guilt, or maybe it is longing for the relationship that I injured and the tornado finished off. Since I will never see my own sister this side of glory, Tara has sort of filled that empty, lonely place in my heart, and I would protect her with my life.

By noon the sun had come out bright and the temperature climbed so fast that all the ice had melted away, leaving the ground wet and even muddy in places.

We got all the outside chores done and took a wagon ride across the fields, looking for possum grapes to make this winter's jelly.

If I could not be there, I am thankful that Tara was! I have to remind myself that you thought me dead; otherwise, I would be hurt all the more. Reading of the bonds Lenny and Tara shared, made me want to meet her someday.

NOVEMBER 7, 1862

Josiah and Benjamin had been fishing at the river, and a floater docked near the deep, blue hole. It was an old friend, and my men shared their lunch and campfire. The brown bass bite good these cold days in that swift water below the big spring, and today was just the ticket to catch a mess. Josiah allowed Benjamin to tell the story tonight, and after the boy went to bed, confirmed the accuracy of the account. I asked Josiah how much confidence he had in this friend, and he was certain that if this man told anything, it was valid, and he added that the story was only revealed when he had inquired of this gentleman about the well-being of his niece and her fiancé.

I never thought to ask the man's name; I suppose it matters not, but his report was that Tara had settled in her new home, and the sheriff was personally looking after her, as her beauty had stirred up the young gents, and remarks rendered did not set well with him. The hospital was filling up fast, yet most of the casualties were not soldiers. Nonetheless, Tara had more work than she could say grace over. His sense was that she was a natural at nursing, the setting fit her well, and the doctors were mighty proud to have her.

Jeb, on the other hand, was not faring as well. It seems that he was riding alone up that steep ridge just east of Thomasville that morning last month when the unexpected ice fell and his horse slipped. He and the horse rolled down the wooded side of the ridge and spent the night at the bottom of the holler. The horse's leg was broken, and Jeb's collarbone was cracked. His right arm suffered a compound fracture, and his knee smooth out of joint, not to mention all the scrapes and bruises and the frostbite. Only when riders atop the ridge the next afternoon heard Jeb hollering at the top of his lungs was he discovered and carted to safety. His horse had to be shot and was left in the holler as fodder for the coyotes and other carnivores.

The townspeople thought it odd that one of Tara's first patients was her own betrothed. Jeb would heal, but he was not allowed to enlist and was not promised much hope of ever enlisting, even if he healed completely. It was reported that his dreams of fighting for the cause were dashed, and he was saddened about that but ecstatic to be near his dear heart. This storyteller had no notions about what would become of Jeb when he was released from the hospital or when that might occur.

Well, that just proves that plans do not necessarily always come to fruition. I have always heard that if you want to make God laugh, just tell him about *your* plans. I do wish I could talk to Tara tonight!

The floater also told Josiah that his other niece, Temperance, had ridden into town with her pa and stirred up a heap of trouble. When she found out from the town gossip that Tara and Jeb were engaged, she had a nine-yard fit, went to the hospital, and threatened to whip Tara like a dog for stealing her beau. The doctors had to call the sheriff, and he escorted her straight from the premises to her pa, who whipped her in front of everybody in the saloon. She spent the rest of her stay pouting in the back of their wagon, shouting profanities at anyone who walked by. Jeb confessed that he had no idea what Temperance was talking about, as he had only seen her once in his life, and that was when she and Toby made a mysterious visit to Reverend Reeves and got caught trespassing on Mr. Van Winkle's property. The meeting was brief and very unpleasant. Tara was mystified but not surprised by her cousin's behavior and was completely satisfied with Jeb's knowledge of poor, crazy Temperance.

The man also told Josiah the sheriff was between a rock and a hard place because he, like most folks, was mighty scared of Devil Dick Bozeman, and he simply ignored that girl's unlawful behavior; yet he knew that he was not upholding his oath to keep the taxpayers safe from such vulgarity. This sort of episode was becoming commonplace in Thomasville, and most folks did not depend on the law anymore to keep order; in fact, no one really knew who the law was or who was really in charge.

Now that comment causes me great concern and brings great uncertainty of our future. Josiah did not voice an opinion, but his concern was evident as those dark bushy, brows of his furrowed into one.

DECEMBER 25, 1862

This Christmas Day should have been a joyous celebration. The entire membership of this household is still shaken! We spent most of yesterday preparing for this special day. A big snow was on, and after the necessary chores were accomplished and the animals cared for, Josiah popped a basket of his famous corn. Benjamin fetched the sewing tin, and the three of us strung popcorn as a garland for the tree. Benjamin had gathered pinecones and holly berries to embellish the small cedar propped in the corner. Well, I say propped; actually it was tied to the wall. Benjamin accidently knocked it over twice, so he had the joy of decorating again, and we all shared a good laugh, but, oh, how that fragrance filled the cabin, along with the genuine Christmas spirit! Four socks gently hung from the mantle and candles were glowing brighter than ever as we sang every Christmas song we knew more than once. The hot cider tasted so delicious! And the cookies that Miss Lucy helped bake the week before made our mouths happy. With fresh cream, sugar, and new fallen snow, Josiah mixed up heavenly ice cream. I thought Benjamin would be as sick as a dog because he ate so much. Yet no tummy ache could dampen our spirits. Josiah has become so proficient with the Hanger leg that he can almost outwalk me, and this special holiday is even more precious this year because our lives are somewhat back to normal. His determination to overcome the handicap is phenomenal. That man is the most inspirational person that I have ever known. I find no reason to complain or even acknowledge any aches or pains. Benjamin has adapted the same attitude, simply because of Josiah's example! For some reason this season just seemed more significant.

So, Josiah had laid out the Holy Book for his traditional reading of the Christmas story, and we gathered around the fire while he went for wood. Not Benjamin, Lucy, nor I noticed the shadow sneak into our merrymaking. In the middle of our song, we were hushed instantly by a loud and angry, "Shut up!" We were so startled that before I could reach the baby, this menace already had her snatched up and bound tightly.

"Temperance!" I yelled. "What are you doing?"

"Put her down!" Benjamin ordered.

"Not on your life," Temperance hollered.

That is when I saw it, the same knife that I had thrown under the bed the night the baby came was now held beneath Lucy's tender little throat.

"Do not move, or I will slice her in two!" Temperance ordered.

"Oh my Lord!" I cried.

"No need to call on a myth," she shouted. "No one can save her."

Josiah's voice was most welcomed. "Temperance, what do you want?"

"I want you, Josiah. I want you! I hate your wife and your children. You belong to me!" Temperance screeched like a wild woman.

"Temperance, whatever are you thinking? You are as my sister. I know, in fact you are my cousin, but I admire you as a little sister. Please release my daughter," his voice resounded with authority.

"No, Josiah, no! I will have you; I have always loved you! You belong to me. You do not know, Josiah! You have never understood! I am *not* your cousin! I am *not* your sister! I am no relation to you at all! I aim to get rid of these children and your stupid wife! I have a colt in my coat pocket, and I intend to use it! I *will* have you at last!"

"Temperance, I have no idea what you are talking about. I ask you once more to put down that knife and give me that child!" Josiah spoke with a calm but commanding tone.

"No! Josiah, I will not give you this screaming kid; you must know!"

She had to yell at the top of her lungs to be heard over Lucy's screams. Josiah walked toward the two, and she shrieked, "Do not take another step, Josiah, or I swear I'll cut her head smooth off!" Josiah stopped instantly.

"I am not your cousin; I am not your sister! Your stepfather had his way with my mother, Josiah, and I am the product! You see, we are no blood relation, and your Uncle Dick hates my guts! He has tried to kill me just as he did that stupid boy, Edward. My mother hates me; I am an outcast. You, Josiah, you are the only human being that has ever given me the time of day, and I know you are in love with me too. I can see it in your eyes; I can hear it in your voice. Oh, why, oh, why, did you bring this woman here? You and I would have been so happy. I cannot tell you that I killed Judith, but I wished her dead too. I was so happy when she died. I hated her too! You did not come to me then, but I knew you would. I hate Benjamin because you give him love that was meant for me! I could not harm him before, but now I see that is the only way that we can be together. He has to die too. Josiah, you are not brave enough to do it, but I can. I can do this, for us. Say good-bye to this girl. She has to die now."

At that moment, a mighty yell burst forth as Benjamin jumped on her back at the same time he snatched the hand that held the knife and snapped her wrist. In her fit of rage to Josiah, she never saw him slip into the shadows and creep up behind her. Lucy hit the floor hard, and her yelping stopped. That same instant, Josiah leaped forward to help Benjamin subdue Temperance, and I grabbed the baby and held her close to my heart. She was severely frightened but unharmed.

Quickly I removed her from that scene, shut the bedroom door, and gently rocked her on the bed's edge. She eventually quit shivering, but her sniffling continued into the wee hours.

Back in the front room, Josiah had to manhandle Benjamin too in order to keep him from strangling Temperance. They managed to tie her with leather straps, as she would not settle down. She would not stop screaming either, so he had no choice but to tie a rag across her mouth. Josiah did find the loaded gun in her pocket. The young woman's wrist was obviously broken; Josiah attempted to set it with small stove wood and cloth strips. Benjamin was livid!

Perhaps shock best described our emotion. The snow was deep, dark, and had well enveloped our world, and we had no idea what to do with this clearly insane woman. Her energy spent, she finally went completely limp. Josiah offered her drink. She refused or else had not enough strength to open her lips. She flopped over like a bag of potatoes. We did not know if she was comatose or asleep, but whichever, her bellowing had ended. Of course, Lucy was the only one of us that could find sleep, and I could find no tears for Temperance, only fear. An hour or two passed; no words were spoken, and shortly after the mantle clock struck ten tolls, Josiah stoked the fire, picked up the Holy Book, and read the story of Christmas from Luke. I wondered if the fear those shepherds experienced at the sight of angels was as strong as what we were feeling. Peace on Earth. Peace on Earth. Those words kept ringing in my ears, circling through my mind.

I excused myself and trouped through the snow to the outhouse. Although the chamber pot was handy, I had to get out of there. As I shivered on that cold, hard, wooden hole, I visualized the rock and mentally escaped there. I thanked the good Lord for the safety of the children and life in general but asked for understanding and wisdom in and of this current situation. I sat there until the cold overtook the feeling in my fingers and toes, never receiving an answer.

Josiah's relieved look greeted me at the cabin's door. Benjamin's wide eyes were locked on the crazy, unconscious woman. Josiah shrugged his shoulders but spoke not. We sat in silence until the sun came back and glistened across the snow. Lucy woke up crying. I did not want her to see Temperance, so I fed her in the bedroom. Still the big question mark loomed. What to do with this person, this possessed stranger. That answer came in the form of barks from Patches. It was the first time ever that I was truly glad to see Uncle Dick. He and Uncle Frank rode up fast and all but knocked the door down getting in. "We followed her tracks in the snow. She confided her plans to Toby, who came clean before sunup. He did not believe that she was serious, but when she never returned, he decided that he should tell somebody," Uncle Dick spouted.

"Is everybody all right?" Uncle Frank asked.

"Her wrist is broken," Josiah replied. "The rest of us are only stunned."

"That stupid girl! I'll kill her myself!" Uncle Dick went into a rage.

Josiah grabbed him and spoke in a calm, yet dominating manner, "You'll do nothing of the sort."

"Let him kill her, Pa," Benjamin chimed in.

Josiah cut his eyes toward his son with a scolding stare.

"There will be no more killing or talk of killing in this house," Josiah announced.

"Come on, Frank, let's get her out of here," Dick shouted as he jerked Temperance to her feet. The gag was now gone from her mouth, but the leather ties were still in place. She obviously had no fight left in her, and as the two men manhandled her out the door, her feet left two solid trails in the snow. They flung her over the back of the horse and then mounted the other horses.

"I cannot allow her back on this property, uncles," Josiah said.

"Don't worry." Uncle Dick snorted. "She'll not be a bother to you ever again."

There was nothing to be said as we three watched them disappear into the whitened forest. The silence was spooky. And the hoof prints from our porch to the woods edge were eerie, especially about halfway, where drops of red became a solid scarlet line. Josiah outfitted up for the morning chores and Benjamin followed suit. I began to prepare breakfast and thought, *Are we supposed to simply carry on, as though nothing at all has happened?* Well, what else could we do? Sit down and cry? I thought of Temperance and really did not care what became of her. Something is terribly wrong with me to feel this way; I know it.

I suppose Josiah thought it time to clear the air, as he sat Benjamin and I down after Lucy was fast asleep. He expressed his sadness and disappointment at the unbelievable turn of events. He also commended Benjamin on his bravery. Just as in the case of the Union deserters, he asked that we get this all talked out and then bury it.

He did not know how to fix what was broken here, but he trusted the good Lord to take care of the healing. He hoped desperately that we would not live in a mode of fear. He explained that he believed a calm voice could turn wrath, to which Benjamin interrupted and expressed his own opinion that the crazy woman intended to kill his little sister, and his instincts took control and they did not include calm talk. His anger was evident. Josiah had to agree with the instinct issue and again hailed his brave son. He assured us that life would go on, and as in all tragedies past, we would survive.

I had to wonder how deep loyalty should be considered when killing is the topic. Would Josiah have been so merciful had the intruder been someone other than family?

As this Christmas comes to an end, I can write that it is not at all a silent night or a holy night; our spirits are definitely not calm, and nothing seems very bright.

MARCH 2, 1863

The war is raging. To hear it told, these hills are crawling with blue and gray uniforms, tattered and torn maybe, but moving. There is no point for our men to attempt keeping the big secret; even if they never spoke a word, it is written all over their faces. The difficulty is not only being fearful of the unknown but the uncertainty of who the enemy even is. After the Christmas Day ordeal, how can any of us be sure that our own family is real, and even if we know for sure, whose to say that even *they* are not the enemy? Too often now we hear of brothers taking different sides, wearing different colors, and fighting each other in the name of what? I do wish someone could explain all this war to me! I just do not get it! The fear is taking its toll on our sanity, and our nerves are raw. Why do we just continue our daily chores and pleasantries as if nothing is amiss, pretending that all is well? I am so weary of the threat of death looming over my children and husband. I suppose we have no choice other than to continue on. We could curl up and die, lie around and cry, or just go crazy and shoot the world up. After scribbling these words, it is clear to me that we are simply doing the very best we can. Surviving.

Today I woke up wishing that I could recall the feelings of that sweet peace and glory that washed over me at the camp meeting last August. As hard as I try, I cannot get a hold of that power. A big blessing today was when Weti showed up and parked on the porch. Little Lucy was in an especially reserved mood this morning. Even Weti's visit did not appear to excite her, although she did crawl up into that well-worn lap and play peek-a-boo. Weti has got to be the most observant human being on this earth. She always has exactly what we need in her smelly, leather pouch. She is an artist with her hands and never ceases to amaze me at the trinkets and useful tools that she makes for us. Lucy soon tired of us grown-ups and jumped off the porch to search for the first flowers of spring. I just felt so bad today, and Weti noticed. She asked if I wanted to share.

Honestly, I did not know what was bothering me or what to share. I expressed this to her. She was quiet for a long while, and when I looked at her, she was staring at me, those beady black eyes never moving and never blinking. *What?* I thought. *What is she doing? What is she staring at? What does she want me to say?* No sooner had those thoughts left my mind and she spoke. "You afraid?" she asked. You know I am, but when she made me say it out loud, it felt different. "You sad?" she asked. I did not realize that I was sad, but I was—sad because of the war, sad because of Josiah's loss, sad for losing Edward, sad for killing those men even though they would have killed us, sad for missing my own sister and Pa, and I was just down right angry at Temperance! All of that spewed out before I could even think about stopping it, and as the sound of the last words left my lips, tears just started pouring from my eyes and my heart.

Weti just sat patiently until my little fit had passed. "Oh, Weti!" I cried. "Do you have any medicine in your bag for me?" All those pent-up emotions flowed like the river from my soul.

The old Indian woman nodded her head. She reached into that pouch and pulled out a white powdery substance and offered her hand toward me. "Do you know this?" she asked.

I shook my head, as I had not a clue.

"Your people call it hemlock. It is great poison. It can kill very quickly."

The shock of her statement dried up all the tears, and although I had never been afraid of Weti, I felt like backing away from her, especially since I had never heard her use such vocabulary. Another mystery. Weti is full of surprises!

"Your eyes show surprise," she spoke gently.

"Well, I am, Weti. I do not understand why you would offer me something like that," I told her.

"I no offer this to you," she explained. "This you have drink for many moons."

The fear left, but the puzzlement overwhelmed me. Weti was silent for maybe three minutes and then spoke again. "Did you hear the big man on the wall wailing out to forgive others?"

For a minute I thought Weti had lost her mind and gone crazy on me. I struggled to understand her, and then it dawned on me. "Are you talking about Reverend Penn at the camp meeting?"

Weti nodded her head.

"Were you there, Weti?" I squealed with delight. "You were there!"

Still nodding, she spoke, "Yes, I listened with big ears, and I believe. The Great Spirit has led me always, and I shall follow his footprints wherever they guide. He has my papoose, and he is waiting for me. Did you not listen with big ears?"

I was stunned. First of all, I could not believe that she followed us all that way. Why am I so surprised? Weti's observation and comprehension skills are as sharp as her creative talents. And of course she can remain invisible. I answered her question. "Yes, Weti. I believe that I listened with big ears. Weti have you always been able to speak so clearly?"

"Your Benjamin teach me. We barter. He teach me to speak, I teach him good medicine. Now, you understand about the poison?" she asked.

"No."

She patted her chest. "In here. You are full of it."

"Full of what, Weti?" I quizzed her.

Her hand opened toward me, again revealing the hemlock. "Poison."

"When have I taken the poison?" I asked .

"Temperance. You have bad heart for her. It is like you take poison and want *her* to die," Weti explained. And with that she walked to the edge of the porch, slung her arm toward the sky, and the poison blew across the yard with the wind and disappeared.

"Throw it to him," were Weti's last words as those deer skin-covered feet carried her toward the forest and out of sight.

APRIL 17, 1863

Toby brought mail today, a letter from Tara. His attitude and mannerisms mirrored his pa, much to my disappointment, but I cannot help but believe that there is a goodness inside him Tara's letter was a breath of fresh air with happy, happy news. She and Jeb have set their wedding date. They will tie the knot on June 5 at Eden. Reverend Penn has agreed to return and perform the ceremony, and Miss Lessie and Caroline are preparing a feast. Mr. Van Winkle has deeded property for their home place, and even Tim Reeves is cutting logs to cure for their home. Tara wants me to come to Thomasville the next trip and pick up the fabrics for her dress and take her measurements for a perfect fit. She had a list of thirty-three questions about wedding details and asked me to have the answers when we come. Her letter was full of excitement and gush, and I could not help getting caught up in it too.

She wants me to be her matron of honor, Lucy to share the flower girl duties with Tressie, and Benjamin to be the ring bearer. And she asked that Josiah bless the union with an opening and closing prayer. What a great occasion to look forward to! Other than the camp meeting, there has not been an event to eagerly anticipate since the rumors of this ugly war commenced. I am going to put my whole heart into helping make this special day one that Tara and Jeb will cherish forever!

Tara's letter contained a post script that Jeb had taken a job as a clerk at the enlistment office and that the wounds from his mishap on the ridge were healing nicely, and other than scars and a minor limp, they were not obvious at all. He did not like his job but planned to save his wages entirely for the expenses of their new home.

This news shifted the mood of my entire family to one of hope.

MAY 14, 1863

Tara's wedding dress was the most beautiful I had ever seen. *Had,* being the key word! I have only just now put the garment out of site, as it has become a source of great pain. Yesterday afternoon Frank and Anna came for a visit. Frank was friendly as always, but when he was out of earshot, Anna let me have it! She made it very clear how angry and displeased she was with me. For fifteen minutes she ranted, and would not allow me to speak nor defend myself. She went on and on about how horrible I am, and how the family does not care for me. Anna literally murdered me with her tongue. I could feel my heart bleeding! She is angry with me because Tara asked me to sew her dress, and to assist with the wedding details. I was so completely surprised that I just stood there speechless. Anna stomped back to the wagon while spouting her final say, "I will never forgive you!"

MAY 29, 1863

The big wedding is only a week away, all preparations in place, just waiting on the bride and groom to arrive.

Josiah, Uncle Frank and the rest of the family finally got Anna to settle down after her outburst. The truth did come out, and it seems that she had ingested a large quantity of poisonous mushrooms. Only Weti's powerful medicines brought Anna out of the comatose condition, but the old Cherokee woman's prognosis was that serious damage had occurred and Anna would never be the same. Even though there was mutual consent that the mushrooms were the culprits of her delusion, Uncle Frank was over apologetic, and so remorseful. The fact is, Anna's feelings had indeed been hurt, and for *that* I am regretful. I should have been more considerate, and wise in the matter. Nonetheless, the wedding will proceed.

JUNE 5, 1863

The big day has come and gone. Although they went to bed hungry, Josiah and all the children are fast asleep in a well-deserved slumber. Benjamin is watching out the window. And I am writing by the soft glow of Miss Lessie's oil lamp; she has so graciously made her home ours.

Jeb and Tara rode off in Mr. Van Winkle's best wagon, which was completely covered with wild roses, asters, and foxglove, and where Miss Lessie found all that satin ribbon is beyond me! The two newlyweds were sitting so close together, Mr. Van Winkle said, "It must take both of them to drive."

The chuckles were kept to a soft roar, and I could only smile as they disappeared into a sunset as magnificent as I have ever witnessed in these hills. We are rejoicing more than most, I suppose, as it is no less than another miracle that any of us are alive this evening.

Josiah looked so very handsome in that dark drover coat and hat. I was transported back to the time and place when I first saw him, and I swear, my heart skipped a beat right there. From that moment on, the ceremony took on a different color, and it felt like Josiah and I were the bride and groom. Josiah asked the guests to join us in prayer, and every head was bowed. He asked the good Lord to bless this union and open their hearts to receive the words that Reverend Penn would speak. Then he walked to the wedding wagon and took out an odd-shaped instrument.

It was triangular with strings much like a fiddle, and as he pulled the bow across those strings, the sweetest music drifted down like the water flowing on the rocks high above us from the cave. The music was soft but right on pitch and soothed the soul. The water's rhythm and Josiah's melody melded into splendor. I stood there with my mouth gaping open and only realized it when I glanced at Miss Lessie, and her smile was wide and knowing. But that was only near the end of the rendition—no telling how many flies went in and out before I pressed my lips back together. I was shocked that Josiah could play music, and was that instrument the psaltery? (I found out after the service that the psaltery is the very type of instrument that David of the Old Book played to soothe King Saul.)

As soon as the music began, Tressie and Lucy floated down the aisle of that old camp meeting setting, dropping primrose petals from Weti's delicate pine straw baskets. Those little girls looked like angels straight from the streets of glory, and my heart filled with both happiness and pride. Benjamin followed with the rings on a pink pillow covered with Tara's tatted lace. He did not resemble an angel quite like the girls but more like a fish out of water. In those fancy clothes, he looked like a miniature Josiah. I had never really noticed before how much he resembled his pa, and this seems more so the older he grows.

The music stopped, Reverend Penn asked all to rise, Josiah began to play again, and I was watching Jeb's eyes, which widened and gleamed as Tara stepped into the aisle. Her beauty was unmatched, and a sweet, sweet spirit filled the place, much like it did during the camp meeting. She stopped far short of the front where Jeb was anxiously waiting. Reverend Penn read the scripture explaining how Jesus would someday come for his bride, and he asked Jeb to go and get Tara, which he symbolically did. There was not a dry eye in the place!

Reverend Penn delivered a most precious ceremony. He read more scriptures, and before he had them say all the I dos and I wills, he explained that they were marrying each other for all the things that they liked about each other, but many mornings would come when bad breath and bad moods would attempt to overshadow the bliss they were feeling today. He told them that when those days came to remember *this* day and especially to remember those things that they so loved about each other, the very reasons that they got married. I thought it was an odd deliverance, yet so very true. Josiah confessed before he went to sleep this evening that he felt like Reverend Penn's words were being spoken directly to me and him, and it was so spiritual that he felt like we were the ones getting married today.

Jeb's face turned bright red when Reverend Penn told him that he could kiss his bride. He just stood there dumbfounded, so Tara reached out, took him by the shoulders, pulled him to her, and gave him a big smack right on the cheek. The crowd went crazy with laughter, and Jeb's face became even redder. The preacher introduced them as Mr. and Mrs. Jebediah Huddleston, and they marched back down the aisle hand in hand. The wedding party followed, and we all gathered in the mess hall for a feast. And feast it was! Caroline and Miss Lessie had outdone themselves, and we were all stuffed when the shots rang out.

The company of men in blue disrespectfully rode those horses right into the building. They even fired a shot into the wedding cake, and the leader pointed his revolver right at Reverend Penn's head. It was Josiah that stood and confronted these intruders. "Sirs, as you can clearly see, we are having a wedding. There is no war in this place. Would you kindly take yours elsewhere?"

"Do you honestly think that we will just heed your orders and turn and leave?" a crusty, dirty one said. "Are all you hillbillies that ignorant?"

"Ignorance has nothing to do with this situation, sir. This is an ordained ceremony before the eyes of the almighty Creator, and you would be far better served to address him than ransack this couple's most important day."

"Well. Since you have enlightened us, it would be sacrilege to bring bloodshed, so we will join the celebration." He dismounted and began to stuff his pockets with the uneaten food. The other soldiers followed suit, and soon there was not a morsel remaining, not even the cake. I was shielding Lucy and Tressie, who were still, quiet, and scared to death. Benjamin stood on guard behind us, and the other men positioned themselves as best to protect their own. Josiah never backed down from his stance, and I feared that they would slay him right before our eyes.

It was late afternoon, and there was hardly a breath being taken when a running horse stopped at the front door. "Captain Wilson! Colonel Reeves is not here, but we have just received a report that he has been spotted at Warm Fork," the rider shouted with a tone of urgency. With that news, the men were ordered to mount up, which they did, and just rode away, but not before that crusty old one fired two shots through the roof and stared us down with an evil eye, but no one was physically harmed.

When the smoke from that episode settled, Jeb insisted that we finish our revelry, but honestly, that celebratory mood had been destroyed. We did watch the couple open a few gifts, after which they loaded up to drive off into happily ever after.

I pray they had safe passage to their new home across the creek. The home was only finished a week ago by the entire community, an extreme effort made by all as a gift for the young couple.

I quizzed Josiah about the psaltery, and he said that he did not see his talent to play as a big deal. He just always could play instruments and that it was singing that he had trouble with. That psaltery belonged to Mr. Van Winkle's wife, and no one else could play it, but Jeb had requested it be played in honor of his grandmother so that her presence would be felt by those who loved and missed her so. Benjamin will not relinquish his watch, so I think I will turn in now and at least attempt to sleep. This has been a much-anticipated day; the anticipated portion could not have been better, the unexpected could have been far worse, and it angers me that the evils of this war of rebellion must intrude uninvited into our lives and wreak such havoc!

OCTOBER 25, 1863

Saturday. Little Lucy was already asleep late this evening when Josiah and Benjamin drove in from their monthly trip to Thomasville. The air had that sweet, autumn nip, and the foliage was very bright. My offering up thanks when the men return from anywhere these days is becoming commonplace. Of course, I was anxious to hear the news they had to share from this latest excursion. Also, I was excited about getting the fabric scraps ordered so that Tara and I could begin our special baby quilt project.

Benjamin was unusually hyper and hurried to unhitch the wagon and groom the horses. Hugs were in order too, especially after a night apart. The fabric was beautiful, and the treats they picked up delightful. We had a small pile of posted mail, but nothing earth shattering or even interesting. I secretly hoped for a note from Rufus. No one has heard from him since last February when he stopped to tell Josiah good-bye. I suppose shame controls my feelings concerning him, as I wrongly judged him and had not the opportunity to make it right. I just want to know that he is okay. This whole war issue just baffled me. I cannot wrap my mind around it or understand its reason. I just know that tensions are great, loss is huge, and fear runs rampant. Any news received these days is consumed by it.

"Will this ever end, Josiah?" I asked. "Since March I am so fearful of those men in blue!"

"Yes, my dear. One way or the other, it will end. We can only pay attention, be as prepared as possible, and trust in the good Lord above to watch over and help us. This is not our war, but the rain falls on the just and the unjust. We will survive!

"Lenny, I notice you fretting at times, and I would like to tell you something my mother always said," Josiah added.

I was quite shocked, as I had never heard Josiah reference his mother, so I listened with ears wide open. "Today is the tomorrow you worried about yesterday," he proudly quoted, "evidenced by the miraculous well-being of our precious Tressie, after she survived that night in lethal weather."

OCTOBER 27, 1863

Toby stopped by today on his way home from some secret mission to Yellow Bluff for his pa. That Uncle Dick has no concern for the well-being of his children; what a selfish individual! Here I go again, being his judge, shame, shame. I must learn to trust the Lord for his vengeance and leave the judgment to him. I did think it odd that Toby would go home from Thomasville by way of our farm, but whatever reason, he ate with us and felt free to share some interesting information, although it may have been more than we needed to know. Toby's countenance has changed lately, and I cannot decide if he is leaning more toward the civil side or to the outlaw. Josiah thinks that he just needs a firm foundation and is being swayed in too many different directions. He says that Toby is at the crossroads of his life and is trying to make sense of it all in order to choose a direction. We all hope that he does not follow in his father's footsteps, and I have to wonder if Josiah is the only trustworthy person he knows.

Toby described the activities near Thomasville that shocked me a little. He said that he had watched several horse races and was amazed at the wagers being placed by men he had never seen and many that he knew well. He told of the many times that he had watched fast horses being traded and sold and that Thomasville had become the South's center for that sort of horse business. He also told that the same place was a depot for a national horse-smuggling business and that certain people, whom he would rather not name, are getting filthy rich. Toby had even made one such delivery for a nominal fee to a dealer in Ironton, Missouri, and was asked to take his lot on to St. Louis but flat refused out of sheer fear. I do not know who Toby is hanging out with or around, but he is obviously involved in situations that are less than lawful and dangerous.

Oh my, this young man was further gone than I thought. I asked Josiah what we could do to help him, and he said that we had better mind our own business but let Toby know that we love him, care about him, and will always be here for him. Josiah says that when people stray, they always come back to the love. He also said that it is imperative that we exalt that charity toward Toby and others because the world at this juncture in history is demonstrating very little. Certainly I agree, and this could be why some of those doomsday preachers are calling these the last days and telling folks to prepare for the world's end.

DECEMBER 24, 1863

Christmas Eve again, and as every year, the cabin smells of the fresh cedar tree (that has been toppled over twice and is now tied to the permanent nail hammered into the log well above eye level, specifically for Benjamin's tree). Josiah, myself, and the children loaded up the wagon a few days ago and rode through the forest in search of the perfect tree. We let Benjamin decide and only rejected the ones that were taller than our cabin walls. Isn't it funny how trees always look smaller in the woods? Benjamin had to saw the trunk off twice before the star did not scrape the ceiling. Popcorn is strung between year's last possum grapes, and chalk-colored paper shapes adorn the branches. Lucy drifted off to sleep on the third verse of "Silent Night," and the men followed shortly. Even though our taxes have been paid, the trapping year was less than profitable, and there are not any extra cents for store-bought gifts. I have sewn the children some new clothes and written Josiah a poem. After learning a new and very pretty lace pattern, I tatted the edge of a pillowcase set for Tara and Jeb, but there will be no fruits and candies this year.

Last night Josiah lectured that we need not get so caught up in gifts because that is not the reason for the season, and we must remember why the holiday is special. That is why this morning was so remarkable and, as usual, proves him right. I was admiring the beautiful sunrise from the kitchen window while washing the breakfast dishes. At first light, I could see something moving way out across the field, and I knew that it was a creature of some sort. The brightening sun revealed that there were several critters; I counted as many as twenty-three. They were moving slowly, inspecting the grasses with their beaks. These birds were huge! The solid white feathers were quite a contrast against the winter woodland color. The entire family rushed to look, and it was then that Josiah confirmed their species as snow geese. Benjamin nor I had ever seen a snow goose and were amazed.

We must have watched the graceful birds for an hour and discussed why they had chosen our field to stop in and why in the world they never flew off, as when the sun disappeared tonight they were still there. Josiah guessed that they were in the migratory pattern but were deterred by a weather matter. Honestly, I do not know what he was talking about, but he said that perhaps there was an ice storm in their route, and they were waiting for the front to pass. Benjamin said that he thought the birds' visit was a Christmas gift from God, and we all agreed that he was correct, and nothing purchased could near compare. Before I turn in, I will put out some token gifts in the socks hanging from the mantle and thank the good Lord for the snow-white birds that visited this day that taught us a powerful lesson.

JANUARY 4, 1864

I am sick! Sick in my soul! And I am angry!

Through the foot of snow and ice, Jeb brought Tara this afternoon. They have gone to bed in the loft now, and I can hear her crying as I write this.

Last month as we watched the snow geese and were in such peaceful bliss, a great atrocity was happening across the county. Miss Lessie had taken Mr. Van Winkle and Caroline to her brother-in-law Pulliam's farm for a Christmas banquet. Many family and friends had gathered at this annual tradition, and a hungry, cold, group of Southern sympathizers that had camped nearby were invited too. Although unrelated, Tim Reeves was there and had asked the blessing on the special meal. As the unarmed men and family were eating and making merry, a troop in blue raided and massacred the lot. Rumor has it that up to sixty people were killed.

Jeb said that he really did not know exactly what had happened; he just knew that the dead were buried in many different places and that he buried his grandfather, sister, and dear friend in the family plot at Eden next to his grandmother. Jeb is consumed with hate over this, to the point that I am frightened at what he might do. Tara is devastated, and Jeb has threatened to join Reeves. Tara and Jeb did not attend because they are expecting a baby, and rather than share this wonderful news with gladness and joy, she had to tell me between the sobs. My plan is to find Weti in the morning and ask for aid because although I am no doctor, something is very wrong with Tara's description of her expectancy.

Lucy has no idea what is going on, but she can detect the agony and was fretful this evening. Benjamin, on the other hand, totally understands, and I saw that defiant, rebel attitude rising up in him, which makes me more fearful! Josiah was crushed to learn of his dear friend's demise, and although he showed no extreme emotion, he was deeply compassionate toward Jeb and Tara, but this night had no answers, no fixes, and no words of wisdom. When they all settled in for the night, I sat for another hour holding Miss Lessie's wide hat with the hanging tag that Jeb gave me and quietly wept until no more tears would come.

How can hell be any worse than war? When I compare our Christmas Day to the Pulliams, I almost vomit. How could two extremes of good and evil exist in such close proximity? I am too heartbroken to even approach the throne tonight. I tried to sleep, but it would not visit, so got up, lit the lamp, and picked up Josiah's Holy Book. It fell open to Deuteronomy 29:29.

JANUARY 5, 1864

Weti was on the front porch at daybreak. She would not eat breakfast with us. She was solemn, and her weathered skin sagged. I inquired if she was ill, to which she shook her head slowly. She sat patiently until everybody was out of the house other than Tara and me. Benjamin asked to take Lucy with him to the chicken house and did.

Weti took Tara to the bedroom and had her lay across the bed on her abdomen. The old, wise woman rubbed her hands along Tara's spine and then around her waist. Tara was not crying this morning and lay as still as a stone. Weti had her roll over and laid her old wrinkled ear to Tara's belly. We held our breath and watched in wonder as this old soul worked. Weti's expression was grave, and after she straightened Tara's underskirt, she motioned for me to sit down. Weti's prognosis was not favorable; she said that there is a good chance that Tara's baby will not live, and she instructed Tara to drink a glass of spring water each morning and night with a pinch of the pinkish powder tied up in the tanned bag that she gently placed in the mournful girl's hand. This new information further overwhelmed Tara, and Weti explained that a struggling soul would decrease the chances of the baby's survival and that Tara must somehow channel the agony away from her belly. The big question: how? Weti quietly slipped from sight when I was helping Tara dress.

Jeb and Josiah were very troubled at Weti's diagnosis, and Benjamin asked, "What about Tara?" Josiah assured him that either way where the baby was concerned, Tara would endure, but the losses of late would take time to heal and that we must be mindful of both she and Jeb.

Tara and Jeb left this afternoon, as she was homesick for her mother and needed to check on her family. Our afternoon was spent in grief, and before dark Weti appeared and just sat in silence, as if she knew that her mere presence brought us comfort.

FEBRUARY 19, 1864

This was the first day that the temperature has been over freezing in three weeks or more. We did not expect visitors, but Uncle Frank and Anna's wagon rolled up the lane just after dinner. I had already put away the food but asked if they would eat. Dinner was declined, but they would appreciate a warm drink, which I promptly prepared. I did not ask any questions and was fairly apprehensive as to the purpose of this visit. Josiah was close at hand this day and did most of the talking. It was very obvious that there was a purpose, but Uncle Frank took his sweet time about getting to it.

The two men engaged in small talk, and Anna never said more than hello and only nodded when spoken to. The subject of Uncle Dick came up, and the men spoke in hushed tones so that I missed that discussion. Oh, that Devil Dick! A bad cloud just follows him around. We were told that Temperance had beat Katherine again and that Toby had taken a hickory to her. She then pulled one of her pa's guns on Toby. Thankfully it was unloaded, and he took it from her. Uncle Dick locked her in the smokehouse, and they shoved food under the door to her. That is all too bizarre for me to comprehend! My emotions concerning Temperance are so mixed. She is not poison to me any longer, but I would just as soon never have to have any dealings with or about her.

I asked Uncle Frank about Tara, and his eyes became very sad. They had received a letter from Tara last week confirming that she had for sure lost the baby. Tears popped out of my eyes before I could stop them.

Anna stared at me so mean and said, "It's all your fault." She then looked away and spoke no more. The men did not hear her remark, and I did not qualify her statement with a reply. Anna is still angry with me because I, rather than she, sewed Tara's wedding dress, and those poisonous mushrooms she ingested last year has affected her memory and mental state. I do not know how to make that right.

Truly, after I heard Tara's disturbing news, the rest of the day was a blur for me. Our company left in time to get home by dark, and I was thankful for their departure. I asked Josiah if we could go to Tara, and he said that he would check the safety of travel and then consider the trip. He was very gloomy about the baby and told me that Benjamin was worried that Tara would die too; at least that is how Benjamin explained the holes knocked in the barn walls.

It is nights such as this that I have difficulty sleeping and long for the comfort of my mother. She would know about this lost baby; she might help me understand the why of it. Tomorrow I shall look for Weti.

JUNE 13, 1864

A band of bloody killers rode through several weeks ago. Bush-wackers. This war has created monsters. Fear has taken hostage the country's emotion. No wonder the men wish their women not to speak of war; perhaps this is their feeble attempt at protection. Josiah has only just now returned from Uncle Frank's. The whole family is again in upheaval. Uncle Dick called the outlaw band PawPaws, as they live along the bottoms of the state's border with Kansas. Josiah said that he was not convinced that is who these people were, as the name Cantrell came up too many times. None-theless, this bunch boasted of murderous raids on families loyal to the Union north of us. Horrible tales they told and only laughed about them. Maybe they really *were* headed to Texas, for who could believe such a ruthless band? Uncle Dick fed and boarded them; well, Katherine did at his command. I would never let those people near my children! I truly wish that I could write that I cried at the rest of this story, but I cannot even will any tears.

This band of killers included the brothers Frank (who befriended Uncle Dick at Wilsons Creek in '62) and Jessie. After hearing the horrid tale of their experiences with deranged soldiers,

I can understand how violence inflicted at an early age would drive a person to rebellion, but these men are nothing less than brutal killers. Ugly Temperance was so enthralled by these outlaws that she donned her brother Rufus's clothes and rode off with them on a stolen horse. Toby found her naked, beaten body two hollers west. They buried her next to Edward.

I have to be very careful not to let pure fear seep into the deepest marrow of my bones. I must keep those words in red, constantly in the forefront of my mind: "Do not be afraid. Fear not. Let not your heart be troubled. Be not overcome with...the cares of the world." What a tall order! Is it even possible? It must be, or else he would not have spoken this. I will try!

OCTOBER 21, 1864

Lucy Leah is such a source of amusement! This afternoon we were sitting on the front porch rocker. She was gazing across the yard and pointed past the fields and wood line. The bright blue sky only magnified the leaves that have once again turned into the brilliant colors of autumn. She looked up at me with those beautiful large eyes and said, "Ma, did you know that God made the trees?"

"Yes, he did," I answered.

"Did you know that God made the birds? And the grass and all the critters?"

"Yes, I did know that."

"Ma, he even made me!" she was so matter-of-fact that I had to smile at her confidence. I wondered how she became so sure about it. And the words about how we must come as a little child to God ran through my mind, so I decided to quiz her further and get inside that pretty little head of hers.

"So, how do you suppose God made you?" I asked of her.

That little girl jumped out of that rocker, threw those hands on her hips, and gave me that I-can't-believe-you-don't-know look and replied cockily, "He had a patter-in!"

It was very difficult to keep a laugh from bursting forth. "And where in the world do you suppose he got the patter-in?"

Now she was really beside herself (I had a glimpse of what my future may hold), as she again was incensed; because not only were those hands planted more firmly on her hips, but her head was lunging forward, and without she hesitation raised her voice in response, "At the Thomasville general store!" Like where *else* would one get a pattern?

Thankfully, Lucy's attention span is rather short, and she moved on to other topics of discussion. But Josiah and Benjamin both enjoyed the story as I recanted it after she was fast asleep.

FEBRUARY 14, 1865

Our precious little Lucy Leah is four years old today, and just like the day she was born, dark luminous clouds blew in from the north.

At daybreak, I went to the porch for a dipper of water, and there sat Weti. She was poised like a statue, just patiently waiting for the rest of the world to wake up and join her. She smiled at me, and I saw something in her neatly folded hands. Today was an important anniversary for her too, as she is single handedly responsible for bringing this baby into this world. I have to wonder if she doesn't always think of her own little daughter where Lucy is concerned. Regardless, I am ever thankful for this ancient one who so lovingly and graciously adores us and, like a guardian angel, is timely for every disaster or celebration. She will not allow us to do one thing for her. It is as if her reward alone comes from doing for us. Only my mother has taught me more about life and living than this treasured Indian woman who has adopted my family. I really love her. I only hope she knows and understands this.

Tiny footsteps turned our heads toward the cabin door and out ran the birthday girl. Before I could hug her, she was seated in Weti's perfect lap.

Weti was smiling as Lucy dug into those folded hands and pulled out a soft leather doll. This baby doll had long, black hair, a fringed dress, and tiny, little, soft leather shoes similar to those that Weti brought to Lucy on her second visit, only much smaller.

Lucy squealed with delight and hugged the old woman so hard that I thought Weti was hurt, but the toothless smile that followed that bear hug proved me wrong. This was the first time that I have ever actually heard Weti laugh out loud. The whole scene thrilled my heart, and I wished that Josiah and Benjamin could have witnessed it too. When I heard them laugh from the window, I realized that they had indeed shared the moment. They burst out the door, and Josiah swept up that little darling and kissed her all about the head. Lucy laughed and laughed, and Benjamin made it worse by tickling her tummy. After a huge celebration breakfast, the men left to start chores, and we girls cleaned up a bit and then played with the new doll. Lucy named her Carla.

The balance of the day seemed somewhat uneventful. Weti was so attentive and adoring; she seemed to enjoy herself more than any of us. When Lucy laid down for her nap, Weti patted her head softly and whispered in her ear. I left the room to give them private time, and when I walked back by the door, Lucy was fast asleep, and Weti was gone.

Patches's barking lured me to the porch, and I gazed down the lane. I too heard the gravel popping under turning wheels. When in sight, I did not recognize the wagon. The canvas cover was painted with bright colors and looked much like a magazine advertisement. The jolly driver was loudly singing a peppy yet unrecognizable ditty. His eyes met mine, and the mouth music stopped as he tipped the wide brim straw hat in my direction. "Good day, ma'am."

I nodded back with great curiosity.

"You would be the lovely Mrs. Lenny Bozeman? Or would that be the lovely Miss Lucy Bozeman?" he queried.

I thought this stranger knew a bit too much about our business, and before I could answer, I heard Josiah's voice. "That would be Mrs. Lenny Bozeman to you, sir, and you are?"

"Dr. Holcum, sir. It's a pleasure to make your acquaintance, Mr. Bozeman, and you, Mrs.," nodding his head toward me. "Dr. Holcum at your service. Fixin' what ails you, supplying your basic homestead needs, and full of bull, which happens to be included in the price of any of my goods and services."

Wow! That was a mouthful, and I wondered how many times he had made that speech. But it did tickle me, and I was humored by his delightful manner.

Josiah was not. He was remembering the war and its strangers.

"Your neighbors insisted that I stop by and offer my goods. Not that they think you have a problem or anything; well, truthfully, that is just the line I use to get my foot in the door. What I really aim to do is prove to you that your blood can be cleansed with my own remedy snake oil. Triple H, it's called. Holcum's Humble Healing Sauce. Surefire way to cure what ails you. Do you ever feel tired and droopy? Lose your appetite or cannot get enough food to satisfy your tummy? Or maybe you can't sleep? Or even if you sleep too much; hey, could be that you have a little one that needs weaning? Or do you bleed too free? Do you have a deficiency of any kind? Or are you losing your hair? Do you have worms or parasites? If you experience an abundance of gas or bloating, and if the ole ticker just ain't ticking timely, my HHH will solve all your issues. Warranted! Guaranteed! Yes, indeed! Buy a bottle for ten cents, and I'll throw another in free, but wait, if you will purchase right now, I'll throw in this iron skillet and fancy kettle tool. How many can you use?" Dr. Holcum finally took a breath. Why, I was thinking of pouring a bottle down his throat to help him.

"Not interested," Josiah said without amusement.

I, however, wanted to laugh and hear more of this fancy man's rambling. He was so comical. At the risk of aggravating Josiah, I prompted the man for more. "Dr. Holcum, what have you in that lively wagon?"

"Glad you asked," he replied. "Do come take a look."

Josiah grabbed my arm. "I'll look," he barked. I too remembered the deserters and was thankful that he went first.

"Mama, Mama," was the cry from the porch. Our little angel had awakened. "It's my birfday!" she reminded us all.

I ran and hugged her up. Her bright eyes were surveying Dr. Holcum's colorful wagon with great question when we heard him exclaim, "Why, this must be the infamous Miss Lucy Leah."

"I left Thomasville yesterday, and Mr. Woodside at the general store asked if I was traveling this way. I told him that I follow my nose and go where the wind blows. He told me about a package that had arrived for a Miss Lucy Leah Bozeman that needed delivering. I figured it was a great opportunity to meet you folks, add you to my route, and attempt to sell my goods, so I volunteered to deliver this special box." And with that he disappeared inside the wagon, only to return promptly with a huge, brown paper wrapped box.

By now we had settled on the porch, and Dr. Holcum sat the box before Lucy. She squealed and then looked at me for approval. Before I gave that to her, I searched the package for markings or clues to its origin. It had been posted at New Orleans. That could only mean one thing. "Okay, birthday girl, you may open your gift."

We watched intently as she peeled away the craft paper only to reveal a multicolored wrapping, complete with a wide, pink ribbon. I thought how pretty that would look tied in her dark hair. Josiah had to help with his knife, and it was all Benjamin could do to keep from jumping in and ripping the paper for her. We were all so curious that patience became longsuffering. That little girl made a long, drawn-out ordeal with this surprise package, which was exactly what the sender had hoped for, and I could not wait to report it. Josiah helped her remove the lid and pulled out a very large, beautiful, dark green, velveteen covered box, complete with fringe and a braided handle.

Lucy opened the round box and pulled out the cutest hat I have ever seen. It was shaped much like a bonnet, made of the same green cloth as the hatbox, with a wide brogan ribbon across the top that tied lusciously under her shapely, tiny neck. Unlike Miss Beth's hats, this one was designed especially for a little girl's head, our little Lucy. She bounced around that tree, and the green ostrich plume sticking out from the hat's back mimicked her every motion. The fabric was well chosen to match her beautiful, sparkling eyes, and I knew at once that I must make the next trip to Thomasville and select a lovely material for a fancy dress to match.

That Miss Beth, she is a sweetheart! Ever thoughtful and always right on time. Why she does it, remains a mystery. I looked in the green box, and it wasn't empty. There was a card, inside it read:

Happy fourth birthday, you beautiful child! Wish we could be there to celebrate with you. Please enjoy your very own hat, and we look forward to your style show the next time we visit. We love you.

Old Zeke and Miss Beth

The mood was broken by the snake oil man. "Now that is a rather expensive hat! Looks like you folks know people in high places; I'm for sure adding you to my stops. Now, might you oblige me and take a look at my wares?"

Josiah's heart had softened toward the pushy man, and I did feel obligated at this point to at least look at his goods. He did, after all, deliver a great deal of joy to our baby girl and us. Benjamin entertained Lucy, or maybe it was the other way around, while Josiah and I toured the loud wagon. Dr. Holcum was indeed a traveling salesman and assured us that if he did not have something we desired, he would make every effort to have it the next go round. Josiah dismissed the Triple H, but he did purchase a leather tool. I found a stack of cotton goods that would be perfect for the new quilt Tara and I planned, and by golly, the price was right. I noticed that Benjamin had watched this event with wide eyes and digested Dr. Holcum's every move and word. It was easy to spot this young boy's passion; he was a businessman at heart. We watched Dr. Holcum drive out of sight while listening to his joyful, loud ditty disappear with that bright wagon into the tree line. We agreed that his horses even appeared to be dancing to the tune. What a day it had been thus far! A loud clap of thunder startled us back into the cabin, and the lightning flashed and the rain pounded while I prepared supper. Josiah lit the lanterns, but the candles on Lucy's cake really made the room brilliant. We sang the birthday song, and then at Lucy's request sang it again to her new baby doll.

I checked on her shortly after Josiah put her to bed. Evidently she had gotten back up, as her green bonnet was hanging on her bedpost and Carla was wrapped tightly in her arms, but she was fast asleep. And as I watched her in beautiful slumber, I got a whiff of that baby breath and the smoke that had filled my nostrils on this same night four years earlier. I glanced at the dark shadows behind the door and halfway expected to see that moccasin foot, but there were only shadows, bittersweet, like the memories. I shook off that gloomy mood even though the storm raged outside, and I looked back at this precious child that the good Lord blessed us with, and my heart filled with gratitude and thanksgiving.

Happy birthday, Lucy Leah!

My only regret is that your grandpa and Aunt Lucy did not get to love you too today.

Good night, beautiful!

It just did not seem fair that I missed my beautiful little niece's birthdays, not to mention all the other special occasions of her life. I was saddened that she did not grow up with my own children. After reading this journal entry, I vowed to find Josiah and never miss another important day with Little Lucy. I had to wonder if Lenny ever told her about me, and that we shared a name.

MARCH 27, 1865

Our little Lucy is fascinated with birds. I watched her from the window this morning as she played in the yard. Patches's head would cock from one side to the other in quizzical wonder, and I had to laugh out loud. It took a while for me to figure out what this child was doing. She would hold her arms out straight to her sides and then run straight and fast. She would lift her feet off the ground and, of course, crash and roll. That poor baby's legs and arms were scratched, bruised, and bleeding, but she continued to try to fly.

This child keeps us in stitches! Yesterday she asked why I always made her pa the cakes and cookies, to which I replied that he had a sweet tooth. After her fingers rolled around her mouth, she proudly announced that she had six sweet tooths.

Last week I watched her sit cross-legged for an hour. When I could no longer stand the suspense, I went out and inquired to her antic, and noticed an egg in the middle of those precious little legs. Before I could ask she exclaimed, "I'm trying to hatch an egg, Mama."

APRIL 12, 1865

Hallelujah!

Toby's horse was soaking wet with sweat when it stopped running, and its rider likewise out of breath. One of Toby's arms was in the sky waving wildly and his shouts could be heard all the way to the river.

"It's over! It's over! The war is over! General Lee has surrendered in Virginia!"

Could it be true? I thought. Is this horror really over?'

Josiah quickly came from the barn, Benjamin right on his heels, and Patches yelping as loudly as Toby. Toby just kept repeating his announcement, which frightened Lucy because this was not the reserved, mild-mannered Toby that she knew and loved.

We all joined him in the yard, and he gave us details between his gasps for air.

"Does your pa know?" Josiah asked.

"I do not know where he is," Toby replied. "Uncle Frank was there when the news came. A postal rider's horse fell dead as soon as he halted right in front of the Thomasville general store. The guy jumped off screaming at the top of his lungs, and Uncle Frank had to douse him with water to shut him up."

"Well, has anybody notified the troops roaming throughout these woods?" Josiah asked.

"I could not tell you," Toby replied. "All I know is that it is over! Many of us that heard jumped on our horses straightaway and took off to inform our families."

Benjamin was silent, but I could see the wheels turning in his mind, trying to grasp the magnitude of this turn of events. Josiah asked Toby to stay and join us for supper, but the young man said that he must get to Eden and share the news with Jeb and Tara, and he rode off the same way he rode in, full steam ahead.

We stood there dumbfounded, with hopeful hearts, hopeful that this news was accurate, and somehow, someway, we could get back to a normal life, free of fear and destruction. I am surprised at how shocked we are. Had this fearful way of life become the norm? I cannot remember what normal is.

MAY 20, 1865

As soon as I squealed at the sound of their wagon, Lucy ran and put her green dress on, as she was already wearing that green bonnet. That girl was prancing across the porch before Old Zeke could halt the horses, and their laughter roared. Miss Beth was clapping and laughing the whole time Old Zeke helped her down.

"Why, who is this gorgeous lady?" she inquired.

Lucy performed a long and low curtsy, to which Old Zeke mimicked and returned.

"Lucy Leah Bozeman at your service," my little girl spouted as she rose slowly from her presentation.

"My, you are a picture of pure loveliness," Miss Beth returned. "May we join you?"

"But of course," Lucy responded. I suppose all our days of playing theater had paid off, and I never thought she was paying all that much attention.

Hugs were lavished on one another, and a tall cool glass of water served before we got comfortable for a long catch-up session.

Old Zeke went to find the men, and we girls set up the tea party. Miss Beth's yellow-trimmed hat was wide, and the big orange flower had Lucy's complete attention. But before we could start our party, Miss Lucy insisted that I too have a hat, or else I dare not attend the party. Miss Beth thought this was hilarious, and nothing would do, but she dragged out a shiny brown, net-covered, sprawling straw head topper that nearly covered my eyes.

"That's better," Lucy chirped, and the party was on. I must admit it was fun, but I felt like Benjamin at Tara's wedding—totally out of my element.

We thanked Miss Beth for Lucy's custom-made green bonnet, and I gave full details of its perfectly timed arrival on Lucy's birthday. Miss Beth seemed very pleased, and when I questioned her about its shipment from New Orleans, she explained that she and Old Zeke had somehow managed to elude either army and made their way to New Orleans from Queen City under the cover of darkness. I wanted to ask why, but I thought that if I needed to know, she would tell me. It really did not matter because their being here was a thrill! Her spirit was lighter, and the subject of the war and its results were dismissed at the onset, and our talk was of pleasantries. Before the tea party ended, Lucy was wearing the large yellow hat, and Miss Beth had on the green bonnet.

With supper done and the children tucked in, we four enjoyed the late spring summer night on the front porch swing and visited until the wee hours. We had lots of catching up to do. Miss Beth had never received my letters (and I wondered who had), so there were many stories to share. Tears were shed over our friends' deaths at Eden, and gasps of unbelief at the intrusion of the army during Tara's wedding. It almost seemed that Josiah and I were doing all the talking, so after two hours he changed the tune of the conversation, "So what adventures have you two had?"

They shared the horror story of President Lincoln's assassination. I was stunned Josiah knew of the demise. I have to wonder what the complexion of the country will take on now. Lucy went to sleep with her bonnet on. She isn't worried.

JUNE 19, 1865

Reverend Penn was with us this Sunday morning, and he led us in a small service of worship. We sat on the porch as the breeze made its way through those cedar branches and then swept across our faces. The birds were singing loudly, as if to join our hymns. I noticed the indigo buntings bouncing from limb to limb between the goldfinch and cardinals. The good Lord seemed so near, and I realized that he always is, but I too often fail to notice. I made a mental commitment to do better, and then I looked at the faces of my family and I felt blessed beyond measure. This day is so lovely that one could never imagine that only two days ago a cyclone passed over, leaving a trail of destruction.

Our farm structures were unharmed, but both Uncle Dick and Uncle Frank's barns lost at least part of the roofs. Uncle Dick had been gone on one of his missions for two weeks, and according to Katherine, Uncle Frank had gone to find him with some urgent information. Josiah and Benjamin helped Toby patch the barns until more lumber could be sawn and the uncles returned to give detailed instruction.

Life has been, well, I cannot think of the appropriate word, but *lighter* might do. Life is less heavy just knowing that the war is over. The conflict was so bad that the mystery of what the future holds is of no concern. I suppose we feel that if we could make it through the war's rampage, we can make it through anything.

Reverend Penn read about all of our needs being supplied, that we should seek first the kingdom of heaven, and all these things would be added to us. My thoughts were, for the most part, on those principles we survived the war, and our Maker's protection is the reason we are alive. And each time I think about still being here, I am reminded of our precious friends at Eden who are not.

Our Sunday service was interrupted by visitors riding fast up the lane.

Uncle Frank and the widow Huddleston obviously had something newsworthy to share. They seemed embarrassed to disrupt; clearly they were not aware that Reverend Penn was with us. Uncle Frank looked like death warmed over; I had never met the widow, so I had no opinion other than to question this unusual couple and their reason for being here. Uncle Frank asked our forgiveness for barging in, but that he had a grave report. The widow Huddleston never opened her mouth, but sat stone faced with a faraway look.

Four days ago the Seventh Cavalry of Kansas had been sent to break up and eliminate Uncle Dick's ruthless gang of bushwhackers and thieves. The soldiers found Dick Bozeman at the widow Huddleston's house at Yellow Bluff on the Eleven Point River. Like the coward I have always believed him to be, Dick ran as he saw the soldiers approaching, and as he climbed a fence, their guns were unloaded into his back. The seventh rode away, leaving Dick for dead. Uncle Frank knew about the widow's place and had gotten wind of the upcoming ambush, and he had traveled there to warn his brother. Alas, he got there too late because she told him what had happened.

A strange thing was that Uncle Dick's body was not on the fence. Evidently the bullets did not kill him because Uncle Frank followed a blood trail until the darkness of night fell. The hunt continued at the first light of morning to no avail; the blood trail was lost in a swift creek. The second day that cyclone came through, and searching was impossible. Uncle Frank's eyes clouded when he told of finding his brother on the third day. It appeared that Uncle Dick had sat down under a black locust tree, laid over, and blacked out. When the storm's wind blew, a huge limb from that thorny tree pierced him right through the chest. Uncle Frank said that it must have missed his heart because Uncle Dick was alive when he found him. He had lain there bleeding with a spearlike thorny limb pinning him against that rocky terrain for at least twenty-four hours. He had almost bled out, and wolves had tracked his blood in huge circles around the body. There were bites on his legs and arms, as they had attempted to eat him alive.

Uncle Dick's last words were, "It's hot! Move me away from that fire!" He never breathed after that, and his eyes popped wide open.

Uncle Frank and the widow buried Uncle Dick near the creek so that the family would not witness the horror of his maimed corpse.

I really wish that Uncle Frank had not been so graphic in front of the children. No wonder the widow was in shock. Josiah inquired as to what Frank intended to do with her, and his reply was that if we could not take care of her, he would get her to the hospital at Thomasville. Josiah told Uncle Frank that we were not qualified to attend to a person in her condition, and he would gladly accompany them to the hospital. They left right after dinner. Benjamin has just now asked if he could sleep downstairs near us. I understand just how he feels, and I am fairly certain that I shall not sleep either this night. As I sit here now and ponder the situation, Reverend Penn's voice reading that scripture keeps running over and over through my head: "Vengeance is mine; I will repay, saith the Lord."

JULY 4, 1865

Toby has been with us a few days. Although he has expressed no emotion whatsoever, it is obvious that his pa's death has touched his soul. This young man has come to the only place he knows of stability and safety. His uncle Josiah has taken extra measures to be exactly what this hurting, confused boy needs. Toby said that he was at a loss as to how to comfort his mother, and it was easier to stay away than to fail at an attempt. Josiah has worked hard to reverse that attitude, but is it not so very true that children learn what they live?

It was good for all of us to have company after dinner. Jeb and Tara stopped by on their way to Uncle Frank's. Toby was so pleased to see his cousin and she him. Tara may be the most compassionate person that I have ever known. She was so kind to Toby, and her actions were like a soothing tonic. Unfortunately the talk did turn backward, and the war was discussed at length. How odd to me the far different tone that the stories take on now that we are not in the midst of its rage.

Tara took me aside and asked if I could find Weti. Instantly, I became concerned for her and learned that she had lost another baby in the fall. She now suspects that she is expecting again, although only a few months along. Tara knew that I had no way to contact Weti, but she thought maybe her wishful inquiry would somehow conjure the old Indian here. Both Jeb and Tara desire to start a family, and I have no experience at what they are going through, so I feel completely powerless to help. All I know to do is seek the Master's face on their behalf. They left long before nightfall and promised to return on their way back home next week.

At supper, Toby announced that he would be leaving in the morning to help his ma. I suppose Tara's influence solidified Josiah's instruction. I will miss him but probably not as much as Lucy. That little girl simply adores big, bad Toby. I sense some jealousy from Benjamin by the way he dotes on her when Toby is near. The men are all asleep. Lucy and Carla are curled up beside me in deep slumber, and I am very, very thankful for our life these days, but I am sad for Tara. That issue I will attempt to leave at the Master's feet right now.

JULY 13, 1865

Weti was on the porch at sunup. She told Josiah that we should expect visitors within the hour. And as usual, she was right—Jeb and Tara's wagon rolled in just as we were finishing up breakfast.

The men went to field, and we girls gathered on the porch. Tara kept giving me that *you-know* look, so finally I took the hint and busied Lucy on a butterfly hunt. When we came back to the cabin an hour later, Weti was gone and Tara was wearing a mournful face. We convinced Lucy to rock Carla to sleep, and would you believe that they both took a nap? It was then that Tara shared the sad news.

"Weti says that I will lose this baby too. She says that I have bad blood, and that her medicine may help, but it most likely will not." She held up a leather bag of Weti's powder.

"Oh, Tara," I tearfully exclaimed. "I am so, so sorry! Whatever can we do?"

"I have no idea. Jeb is going to be devastated. Oh, Lenny, I have turned out to be a horrible wife! What if I can never have children? What do you think I have done to cause this curse? Lenny, I want a baby so badly! I want to be a ma and a granny! I want to make Jeb a proud pa and proud of me. Please help me! I just have to give him a child."

By now she was sobbing. I certainly had no answers for her, and I did not know what to do other than hold her and cry too.

We had gathered our wits and washed up before the men came back, but they were so engrossed in their own future plans that they did not notice our mood. Lucy sensed the atmosphere and climbed up onto Tara's lap. My little girl handed Tara her prized Carla and then began to stroke Tara's hair. It was all Tara could do to hold back more tears, but she hugged and rocked Lucy and Carla the rest of the afternoon.

SEPTEMBER 9, 1865

Toby came yesterday and stayed the night and brought us a few very unusual items. Come to find out, he had confiscated these from an abandoned Union camp some time back and hid them in an old holler log. The label on one can read, "Borden's Condensed Milk," and the other, "Van Camp's Pork and Beans." Toby remarked that he had tried both, and although not nearly as good as fresh, the contents would probably make a fabulous meal to a starving person; in fact, he had smuggled a large lot of it to those folks in the wilderness before they all disappeared.

Josiah added he had read that the Union had secured contracts with the manufacturer's to supply its troops these rations. Benjamin's nose went straight up in the air and vowed that he would only drink milk right from the cow, and who could possibly imagine beans and pork together in a can? So, these items went on the shelf, and I plan to experiment with them later.

Toby chatted endlessly about his experiences and of the lawlessness in Thomasville. He told that the hills and hollers there were filling up with smugglers, thieves, deserters, and freebooters, and those people were getting a stronghold, as the war had all but eradicated local government, and basically anarchy ruled. They were looting and plundering anything left and anybody crazy enough to return. Attempts by locals to establish civil authority were met with bloodshed. Even the new sheriff consorted with the hoodlums. I sure did not like the sound of all that, and I dreaded the thought of Josiah and Benjamin making their monthly jaunt there.

Toby confessed that he had already pledged his loyalty to Jim Jamison and was officially a member of the gang. Josiah thought that Toby's misplaced allegiance really lay with his pa, and Jamison was the next closest thing. He also believes that Toby may have been coerced to some degree and that his actions may be fear based. Whichever or whatever, I am heartbroken.

The thankfulness came when Benjamin shared his heart about the matter and assured us that he could not understand why Toby would even consider a life like that, and that he himself wanted no part of unlawfulness and could see a bad end to Toby's ways. Oh what a relief that was!

Before he turned in for the night, Josiah said, "And, oh, by the way, Toby left this for us." He flipped a coin my direction. It was new denomination—a two-cent piece, cheaper to produce than one cent, and was inscribed *In God We Trust*. Maybe that is why he left it.

OCTOBER 12, 1865

Have you ever formed an opinion of someone—maybe this someone had been in and out of your life for years at a distance—and then all of a sudden, circumstances change and you learn what that person is really all about, and it utterly changes your judgment? Well, that is exactly what happened today. Josiah's aunt Katherine rode up this lovely Monday morning, totally unannounced and completely unexpected. Uncle Dick has been dead four months, and this woman is already wholly transformed! She was seeking Josiah's assistance, of which he obliged.

Katherine's desire is to declare Rufus legally dead, since he has not returned from the war with his company, nor has he contacted any family member. His commander cannot confirm if he was killed or not. The benefit to this would be that she would receive a pension from the government as his beneficiary. Katherine's attitude was not of one seeking a handout, rather one of a desperate woman taking advantage of a gift. Since she has no income and Uncle Dick saw fit to leave her no legal recourse concerning their property or funds, she is indigent.

She expressed to us that she believed both Frank and Josiah would help support what remains of her family, but that she would rather have the opportunity to become an independent woman and never feel like a burden again. It was obvious that Katherine had thought this through and was adamantly determined. I was impressed! All this time I thought she was a mealy-mouthed, unintelligent, uncaring person, and now I realize that she had been dangerously enslaved to that beast of a husband.

Who would have ever imagined this turn of events?

Josiah gladly advised Katherine and offered to walk her through the process, for which she was very grateful.

When this woman described her profound pain at Edward's death, my heart broke all over again, and while she revealed the story of Temperance's conception, mental challenges, and all the dysfunctions that resulted, I formed a strong admiration for her endurance. Katherine divulged how she secretly pampered Edward and that she had great satisfaction in their relationship, which she trusts was well grounded. She described a side of Edward that none of us had seen, one of deep comprehension, and she added that he knew he would someday have to wait for her in the land beyond the sky. That boy's mother won my heart as she shared hers today; she confessed her treasures in heaven, and I learned to not judge a book by its cover!

NOVEMBER 10, 1865

Benjamin was rubbing the two coins in his pocket together as we rode the wagon home from Thomasville today. The town had changed so much; there was very little of the flourishing metropolis left, and the atmosphere was one of upheaval. Many buildings had been destroyed, and the citizens crept around as if it a necessary secrecy. I vowed to not return unless things changed drastically.

I asked Benjamin what he was so deep in thought about as he rolled those coins over and over in his hand. He looked at me startled and apologized for being so distracted. He told me that he had been processing the events of the past years through his mind and comparing Thomasville now to the one he knew as a little boy. He too was saddened.

"About the coins, Ma. It seems that all the time my head is thinking up ways to make money. And I do not know why that is such an important thing to me, but it is ever on my mind. While you and Pa were at the blacksmith's shop today, I visited with Mr. Woodside. He told me something that I cannot get off my mind. He said that life is like this coin." Benjamin held up one of those pennies. "You can spend it, but you can only spend it once. So I have been thinking, since he is successful, maybe I should take what he says very seriously, and I have been trying to figure out how to make money but not waste my life on what is not important. And in order to figure that out, I have got to determine what is important."

My goodness, that is deep thinking for a young man. I wonder if that mentality is a learned or an inherited trait. Josiah is a very deep thinker and so wise! Benjamin has been exposed to him, Weti, and a host of adult issues in his few years. I had made my own discovery today, but I have yet to share it as I too am mulling it over in my head. Last Sunday Reverend Penn came by and held a rather short study with us. He read from Malachi where it says, "And he shall sit as the refiner and purifier of silver." Reverend Penn expounded that this passage describes the nature of God. It seemed like Greek to me, and I do not know if I am getting old or what, but I just did not understand. So while we were in the blacksmith's shop today, I left Lucy with Josiah and slipped across the aisle to the silversmith and asked politely if I could watch him at work. That was acceptable to the old gray-headed silversmith, and so I did. He put the raw silver into a small cast pot and held it right in the center of a hot fire. He explained that the extreme heat would burn out all the impurities, so that the silver would eventually become completely pure and possess a much greater value. He apologized for not looking at me as he spoke, but he explained that he must keep his eyes on the silver at all times, else it might burn up and become worthless. I was fascinated at the process and asked my last question, "How do you know when it is pure?"

"That is the easiest part of the process," he replied. "The silver is pure when I can see my image in it."

FEBRUARY 18, 1866

Uncle Frank brought Katherine to consult with Josiah, and I was delighted to see Tressie. She clearly was happy to see us too. Benjamin ran and swept her up like a rag doll and twirled her round and round while she giggled her head off. Lucy watched with great concern, but when she heard the laughing, she joined in. Then, of course, she had to be twirled too. Uncle Frank was thrilled at our reunion, as he has been sincerely disappointed in the family riff and acts as though he is somehow responsible. Katherine had received a letter from the government requesting more information. Josiah helped her answer the questionnaire appropriately and was confident that for all practical purposes, her pension request would be answered and she should begin receiving payment within six months.

During the noontime meal, Katherine caught us up to date on Toby's well-being. He had stopped in for a few minutes while passing through yesterday. Toby had told her about running into a few of the men that had taken Temperance. They told him what really happened to her, although Katherine did not share those details. This group had invited Toby to join them, and he had considered it, especially after they told him that they had robbed their first bank in Liberty, Missouri. Toby had decided that his present position was all he could handle and kindly declined the offer. Katherine seemed rather proud of her young son for withstanding the gang's persuasion. Uncle Frank concurred, and the rest of us refrained from voicing our opinions.

Uncle Frank reported that Anna was basically well but had still not regained her memory or personality and that his hands were extremely full of the challenges associated with that bad mushroom day. He was considering taking Tressie to Tara. Uncle Frank thinks that Tressie needs more maternal attention than Anna can give her. I sometimes wonder about Uncle Frank.

Oddly enough, Tim Reeves rode up before we had finished eating. He joined in and told his own tale of being taken into custody, interrogated, and later released by the Union army last fall. He was very dramatic in his description of the firing squad lining up for his execution when a high-ranking Union officer discovered the ordination papers in his shirt pocket and ordered the execution stopped, as he could not be responsible for issuing the command to kill a man called by the Almighty. Reeves had been back to Eden and was attempting to rebuild all that had been destroyed during the war between the states. I thought that he was rather chatty with Katherine, even if he was only inquiring about the details of Uncle Dick's demise.

Benjamin said tonight that he thought Reeves had been spared by the mighty hand of God, and that proved that miracles do still happen. I did not have the heart to express my own feelings about this, but then who knows? Benjamin may be right. Tressie's presence made the day fabulous, and before they departed she was wearing that green velveteen hat and cuddling Carla. Uncle Frank had to threaten a spanking, as she did not want to give them back to Lucy. He promised Tressie a hat of her own, and I told her that I would ask Weti if she could make another dark-haired doll. Katherine reminded Tressie of the giant man that kept her safe that night in the woods, and she immediately apologized, hugged Lucy, and returned the treasures that they had shared for the day. I was so impressed with Katherine's wisdom and way of handling the situation. Lucy cried when they drove away, and I wanted to.

MARCH 17, 1866

This evening my entire family is at Eden, with one addition. Uncle Frank came to the farm yesterday with all of Tressie's things. He knew we were coming to Eden and asked us to move Tressie to Tara's care. Of course Tara did not mind, as she is delighted to have Tressie. Tara has always seemed more like her mother than her sister. Lucy was tickled to have a playmate on the trip, and Benjamin adores the little golden-headed darling! It was a delightful drive over.

Josiah and Benjamin have worked all day with Jeb to rebuild his barn that was partially burned by those Yanks in the rebellion. It was a great reason for a visit, but I never expected it to be so bittersweet. This is the first time that we have been back since Jeb's family and Miss Lessie were killed. Of course, nothing was the same. Mr. Van Winkle's home had been burned, and all that remained was a heap of ashes and rusted junk.

The most saddening thing to me is the change in Tara. She is no longer bright, bubbly, and full of life. She seemed sad, troubled, and lonely. Jeb had taken Tara to a doctor in Arkansas last week. They were expecting again, and this time was no different than the others. The doctor was certain that she would not carry this baby full term, and worse than that, his opinion was that she would never be able to deliver a child. Tara broke down while telling me, with good reason. She asked if I thought that middle wife's touching her head had anything to with this condition. My first instinct was absolutely not, but then what do I know? We agreed that it was uncanny that the old woman passed her skills of delivering babies to Tara, who could apparently never have a child of her own. That revelation really set her off, and when she finally stopped weeping, she explained that the old middle wife had no children either. "But, Tara, my dear, did you not tell me that she was a spinster?"

"Well, yes, but do you really think that she never ... well, you know," Tara replied.

"Evidently not. I am positive that she did not put a spell on you, Tara." I wanted to say something that would bring her comfort, but no words would come. I told her that the next time they came to our place we would take a visit to the rock and seek the one who has the answers. She agreed, and that cheered her up a smidgen.

From the look on Josiah's face this evening, Jeb has shared the bad news with Josiah, as his mood was serious. I could almost see the wheels turning while he was searching for the wisdom to share. Nothing came to him either. Benjamin told me later that he was genuinely concerned for Tara and feared for her life. His love for her is evident, and I attempted without explaining too much about a woman's body that having or not having a baby was natural and not dangerous. He reminded me that his real mother died delivering him. Oh my. I should pay more attention; that boy has every right in the world to be concerned. I asked him to forgive me for that inconsideration and that he was absolutely correct; we should seek help for Tara, to which he replied, "I will look for Weti as soon as we get home." I did not have the heart to tell him that Weti was already involved in Tara's situation, nor the sad prognosis.

APRIL 7, 1866

I think it was three days ago that Lucy and I were on the porch. She was playing dolls, and I was piecing Tara's lights and shadows quilt. Patches ran right up the rock step and laid a brilliant blue indigo bunting at my feet. The bird was visibly deceased! Patches just sat back on her haunches and stared at me. Lucy reached for the dead bird, but I waved her off, as I could see small mites crawling on it. That was odd!

Benjamin was building fence with his pa on the other side of the farm. I asked Lucy to play with Patches and scooped up the bird in a dishtowel and carted it off for the usual burial. The sandiest soil near was scraped up with my heel and the bird covered ever so gently.

When I went back to the porch, Weti was sitting there holding Lucy on her lap. Lucy was singing a song, and Weti looked older than I remembered. Weti kept staring at me too, and I wondered if my head had turned green or something. Patches eventually jumped off the porch and took off toward the barn. Lucy ran after her, and only then did Weti attempt to speak. Usually I could understand her broken words, but today her mumble was just not making sense. She finally gave up and sat very still, never taking her eyes off Lucy. Even the men's arrival for dinner did not change her mood. Josiah sensed a need in Weti, and after the meal he made a conscious effort to sit near her on the porch and engage in conversation. The words Weti delivered to him aroused a sense of urgency or seriousness; I could not determine which. Benjamin was more troubled than Josiah, so I joined them and learned that Weti was telling them that there was a disturbance in the force. "Whatever does that mean?" I quizzed.

"I am certain that I do not know, "Josiah replied. "But it has visibly upset this woman. And if it upsets her, then it surely upsets me, especially since I do not understand the source of her fear." His feeble attempts to assure this old soul that all was well prevailed not. Benjamin has this special bond with Weti, so we asked his opinion. He could not say for sure, but he too was greatly troubled. This is the only time that Weti has not disappeared. When I peeked out after midnight, she was still sitting guard on the porch.

I have never before seen Weti asleep, and when I looked out at sunup her eyes were closed. It scared me so bad, as I thought her dead. My squeal must have wakened her. She seemed a tad startled, but she just gave me a big nod. By the time the rest of the family got up, Weti was gone. Her behavior had all of us unnerved, but we did not know what to do about it, so at breakfast Josiah asked the good Lord above that he have his way and his will and to especially watch after our dear friend Weti.

Benjamin insisted that he search for her, but Josiah convinced him that if she wanted to be found, she would not have left. Ben was not happy with that, but he respected his pa's wishes and went about his usual chores, as did Josiah and I. Lucy donned her green bonnet, gathered her dolls, and set off for a day of flying or playing house or hatching eggs. She had a way of entertaining herself, which usually entertained the rest of us too. I had dinner ready, Josiah and Benjamin had come to the cabin to eat, but Lucy was nowhere in sight. We all called her to no avail. Alarm did not instantly set in, but after an hour of searching for her, panic consumed us! Josiah was beside himself and advised us to separate, spread out, and search. We searched the entire home place and found not a clue, so we widened the search. I headed for the rock, thinking that she may have wandered down that well-trodden path. I found Weti on the rock, but no Lucy. Weti's arms were outstretched to the sky, and her face was wet with tears. I was so consumed in alarm that I ignored her dilemma and screamed at her, "Weti, Lucy is missing! Have you seen her?"

Weti jumped off that rock and let out a fierce yell. My blood curdled. She grabbed my arm, and we took off down the holler toward Osage Spring and then followed the holler back to the farm in a full trot.

It is impossible for me to describe the scene at the cabin. Benjamin was just throwing himself on the ground wailing, and Josiah was rocking back and forth on the porch's edge, his face white as a ghost. Weti ran to him and began her own mournful howl. Perhaps *shock* would be the word, but it seemed like my feet would not move under their own power. I did not want to face what awaited me.

The green bonnet lay at Josiah's feet, and his arms were full of my baby girl. She had no breath. Her tiny body was covered with little black holes. Her white skin was now purple, her lips blue. I did not feel the rocks cut into my knees as they hit the ground, and I think I heard my own screams. That is all I remember.

It's a blur, but I think they were all here. Josiah insisted on building the small pine box and lined it with cedar boards. Uncle Frank and Toby helped Benjamin dig the grave near the patch of Cherokee roses that had only just begun to bloom. Tara never left my side, and Weti stayed on the porch in a trance, occasionally chanting a mournful cry in her native tongue. It was surreal.

I keep waiting to wake up from this nightmare. I keep trying to wake myself up because the pain in my chest is excruciating. I cannot wake up. I cry, jerk, fight, but I cannot wake up. The horror will not go away.

That was two days ago. I am still in the dream.

MAY 5, 1866

I think that I heard Josiah's voice this morning.

"Lenny, Lenny, Luvina! Speak to me!"

I think those were Benjamin's arms around me because that breath on my cheek smelled like him. I do not know why his face was wet.

It may have been Tara's voice that asked, "Josiah, what can I do? What do you need right now, this minute?"

A man's voice hollered, "I need to get that picture of her lying in that nest of copperheads out of my head!" Uneven footsteps swiftly left the cabin.

From the direction of the rock, I could hear the long, sorrowful wails. Those mournful cries filled the dark air, and I think they were coming from me. That is how it felt. It hurt. It would not stop hurting. I could not make it stop hurting. I ran to the herb garden, and I grabbed and pulled with all my might every last stem of sage. I slung it as far as I could! The dirt was flying, my eyes were full of it, but I kept pulling and throwing and pulling and throwing! They were all yelling at me. I clearly heard Weti shout, "Leave her alone!"

JUNE 3, 1866

"Doesn't she love Pa? Doesn't she know that I am still here? I need her! She is not the only one who lost Lucy! Why does she get to disappear inside herself and the rest of us have to keep on hurting? We have to watch the sun come up and then go down day after day for two months now, and it never stops hurting! Why does she get to stop the world and get off? I did not want to be angry at her, but I am mad, Reverend Penn! I am blooming mad! Seems to me that it is much harder to face this giant than to ignore it! I thought she was a rock! I thought that she loved me too! Why would God take two mas from me? I do not know what to do! I want to take off running and never stop! I want to go to sleep and wake up when this is all over!" Benjamin's voice was very loud, his anger evident.

My eyes were closed, yet I heard his words. My head was groggy; there was a mild pain in the temples, but those piercing words woke me up.

"Son, I am so, so sorry!" Reverend Penn finally spoke. "My heart's desire would be to answer your questions. Alas, I cannot."

"I know that you cannot, Reverend. I apologize for shouting at you. I really want to shout at God like I heard Pa doing a few days ago. He was in the woods, and I am sure that he did not know that Weti and I were within earshot. Weti grabbed my arm and stared into my eyes while shaking her head back and forth. Her eyes were full of tears, and I had none left. Pa was yelling at God and demanding that he send understanding. Weti told me that it was okay to ask our Maker. She said that the great Creator wants us to talk to him, even if we are angry. She said that he has all the answers and knows when we are ready to hear them. Is she right, Reverend Penn?" Benjamin's tone had settled some.

"I believe that she is right, Benjamin. Someday I hope to meet your Weti. It is obvious that she has the gift of discernment. Listen to her, Benjamin. She has a deep love for you and your family."

"Reverend Penn, she has been doctoring Ma since before we buried Lucy, and Ma is still in a trance," Benjamin rebutted. "I love Weti, and I have always trusted her, but—"

"She is a wise woman, Ben, but she is not God. Love Weti, but love God too, regardless," this preacher advised my son.

My son. Oh my word! *My* son! What have I done? What have I done to him? Some time elapsed before I could gather my body and make it move. I had to get to him; I had to hold him!

His eyes were wide and suspicious as I walked into their conversation. No one spoke. I walked straight to him and wrapped my arms around him. "I love you, Benjamin, more than you could possibly know," I whispered.

We both began to weep, and I could feel healing flowing through my body.

And then I felt another set of warm arms pull us tighter and together. Josiah was weeping too, and it was in this moment that my memory completely returned and I had a mental vision of Lucy lying with Carla in that cedar-lined box, the fluffy green dress pressed and shiny, and that matching bonnet's ribbon neatly cupping her beautiful face. She was asleep in Jesus, just like my mother. I remembered the burial, near the rock, and the huge crowd that gathered there. I even remember Anna hugging me with tears flowing down her face. The singing was angelic, and no one could see Weti, but I could hear her behind me, humming soulfully. I remember thinking that this was the first time that Josiah did not look ten feet tall to me, and Benjamin looked taller than his pa. What an odd thought. I remembered Josiah's soft whisper as he gently piled me on the bed that evening, "Lenny, we thought we had a baby, but we really had an angel."

Finally Benjamin spoke and broke the spell, "Ma, are you back?"

It did not seem appropriate to extend an apology. Benjamin did not require one, having me there was all he wanted or needed.

"Yes, son, I think I am."

I cannot be sure how long the silence lasted, but Josiah set a new precedence. "Now we can go on. But we can only survive with each other. You both *are* my life, you are important, and no words can fully describe my love for either of you."

It is like we had to start over, to start differently. Our bond is strong, our love stronger, the adhesive being our little Lucy. I do not know what will happen from this day on, but I believe that mighty prayers have been answered. And even in that, I know that I will forever miss Lucy, and never a day will go by that I do not sense her existence. I hope someday I have only gratitude that she was with us these short years, rather than grief and anger because she is not. Weti says that healing will come, and she of all people should know. I trust her. I do not trust myself.

The rock has just now crossed my mind, and I know that I cannot go there.

Oh, Lenny! How could you live through that? How could you possibly endure? I could not believe that Little Lucy is gone, and I never got to kiss her sweet face, or hold her tight. I felt cheated again! Perhaps it was a blessing that I was not near. You were stronger than me, Lenny! I wanted to crawl in the grave with my girl when she died. I knew your grief! I understood your pain! I was experiencing the killing pain again just reading your words. The pain never traveled very far away. No wonder you survived though. What I had never known is that love. The unconditional love of a soul mate. I did not understand those family ties that bind in total forgiveness and genuine love. Thank you, Josiah and Benjamin! Thank you for saving my sister.

SEPTEMBER 22, 1866

The days have passed rather slowly these past months, and our lives are as uneventful. Peace does subsist, but so does longing, longing for life as before. The mundane chores continue, and I constantly remind myself that my family's care is so much more than mundane, and it does come easier with each sunrise. The pain is strong, but I am realizing that there are more minutes between each time I think of Lucy. I do not believe that time heals, but I believe that we are learning to live with our lot as time does pass. I have attempted to write, but nothing comes, and this journal endeavor seems so unimportant now. I have not visited the rock either. Weti comes regularly; she is slower and quieter. Benjamin and Josiah are carrying on with vigor and have taken on the role of rescuers. Someday I hope to make them feel as though their mission is successful.

Feelings of being blessed are ever present, but those constantly battle moods of selfishness. My heart knows the winner, but time rules that war's conclusion. I just waft in the melee of it all.

Tara, Tressie, and Jeb visit often and bring great joy to this farm. Tressie is growing into a beautiful young girl and is so helpful to Tara.

Toby has not been back since the funeral. He is indeed an avoider, but I still care deeply for him and wish he would visit.

Yesterday Benjamin took some late garden vegetables to Katherine, and as he rode up to her cabin, Tim Reeves was sitting on the front porch, tying his boots. Ben thought nothing of this, and Josiah only rolled his eyes at the report. Of course I wondered what that character is up to now, but nothing was discussed further. Josiah did mention that Katherine was finally receiving the monthly pension from Rufus's military service.

A letter came from Miss Beth last week. She and Old Zeke were back in New Orleans. They had taken a steamboat down the mighty Mississippi. She does not know yet about Lucy, and I dread the day that we have to tell her. They loved her so!

I am weary this night and must close.

DECEMBER 8, 1866

It certainly does not bother me that those hoodlums stay away, but I miss those that I love. Benjamin has decided that we do not need a tree this year. He even removed the nail. I am not sure if that is because he is fifteen years old or because he does not want to be reminded how much Lucy loved Christmas. The holiday will be bitterly sad without her. Yesterday I was working on a quilt and remembered months ago when she played dolls as I sewed. The stitches turned fuzzy through the tears. Weti says that I must cry them out or else they will become like the poison and turn bitter in my soul.

Last night in the fire's glow we talked about what Christmas would mean to us from now on. We agreed that it is an occasion to be celebrated and that most importantly we should remember the birth that it commemorates. We decided that rather than give gifts to each other, we would make an extraordinary effort to help someone else in his honor. Lucy would like that!

This afternoon Josiah came back from Thomasville just before dark. There was only one letter that interested me in the stack of mail that he delivered. I did not know that Josiah had written to Miss Beth and Old Zeke while I was in that condition after Lucy died. Evidently it takes a long, long time for mail to circulate because she had written this card in September as soon as she received the news. I could read the heartache in her words, and her description of Old Zeke's reaction just tore me up! I do believe that they loved Lucy as much as we did. She wrote that Old Zeke had taken ill shortly after Josiah's letter arrived, and they could not get to us, but that they would come as soon as the weather would permit travel from the gulf. Her greeting was full of love and encouragement. She had obviously chosen her words carefully and apologized for not being here for us. I was glad that she did not use platitudes but rather expressed genuine compassion. If I learned anything through the tragedy, I learned not to say asinine things to people in pain. I do not remember everything that occurred, but I shake my head to think of the ridiculous statements voiced, and I wonder if those people actually believed that they were being helpful. If I hear one more time that everything happens for a reason, I may choke somebody. Only life itself lends wisdom, and I suppose some folks just have not lived long enough. I learned too that grace is indeed sufficient, and now we understand those instructions to sorrow not, even as others which have no hope, because that grace to live by includes that saddest part of life, *death,* and it was that grace that lifted us up and carried us through that fire! Only our faith continues to sustain us, else we would die of broken hearts.

Of course Josiah blames himself for not destroying that old trough when the wood busted and it would no longer hold water. He kept it behind the barn because he thought he might use it for something someday. Words do not change that for him either, so I have stopped speaking them.

It was Tara and Jeb that stopped by for a brief visit tonight. They had taken Tressie back to her mother. Tara was disappointed, but she had always known that Tressie would leave someday. It seems that something snapped inside Anna's head when Lucy died. I have no idea what, but several months after, they came to us and she apologized to me. She explained that Tara had told her what had occurred and how badly she had behaved. Anna claims amnesia, but her heart too was broken when Lucy passed.

For all practical purposes, Anna is acting like a different woman and attempting a rapport of friendship is much easier. Uncle Frank, on the other hand, has gone the other direction, and every time he comes around, there is a distinct scent of moonshine around his person. Uncle Frank has endured a horde of trauma since I have been a member of this family, and I suppose this is his choice of pain medication.

MARCH 14, 1867

Benjamin is sweet sixteen today. Oh, can I write that about a boy! He is sweet to me! Maybe I should write that he is a fine sixteen-year-old man! I prepared his favorite meal for supper and added a huge apple cake. I sincerely hope the half that he ate does not give him the green apple trots. Josiah ate the other quarter, and it just would not be right if I did not enjoy the rest of it, just in Benjamin's honor, you know. I asked Benjamin yesterday what he would like for his birthday, to which he replied, "Well, I will tell you if you promise to get it for me."

I told him that if at all possible, I promised! Then he told me that he would share his wish in the morning. So after breakfast today, he said, "Come with me, Ma. I want you to help me with my birthday present."

I was all for it until he took me to the herb garden. He had petitioned his aunts Katherine and Anna for a portion of their herb gardens. They were happy to oblige, and he had a basketful of sage seedlings for me to replant in my garden. I almost did not want to, but what could I say? Benjamin's one wish must be granted; I gave my word. This was a monumental task for me, and even though it hurt, I absolutely *had* to complete the chore. How did this boy become so wise? How did he know that I had to go back to that time and place, endure this pain, in order to heal? Josiah was in on it too because he came to help near the end of the undertaking. He surely had been watching from a distance. When completed, we all three stood, brushed the soil from our fingers, hugged in silence, and the bond grew stronger.

After he went to bed tonight, I wrote Ben a letter. I asked him to bear with me while I gave up the little boy and learned to love the man that he has become. That was hard too! Josiah has already gotten to that place, but it is a hard thing for a mother to do! Tonight is the first time that I have wanted to visit the rock. Benjamin's birthday has actually been a gift to me.

APRIL 10, 1867

I did go back to the rock after Ben's birthday, but I could not write about it until now. The day was perfect, a slight warm breeze, blue-bird skies, the foliage just beginning to burst forth in a pallet of greens, and the birds singing like there was no reason in the world to be unhappy. I was halfway there before I heard the footsteps, and a feeling of great comfort swept over and through me. I am not sure I could have continued the distance if Weti had not been there. She never showed herself, but I knew. I was not surprised to see a new patch of Cherokee roses, but I was astonished to see the beautiful stone marker. I did not know that Josiah had placed it there. I bypassed my rock and walked straight to her grave.

The stone was inscribed, "Our precious bequest." Tears did not fall there, and I was rather amazed. My arms ached, though, as I longed to hold that little girl and hear her giggle. I looked at the adjoining patch of flowers, and I thought of the years that Weti too stood near, longing for her daughter. She survived, and I knew that I would also. I did not touch the stone or the flowers, and I remembered the day long ago when Ben wanted to pick them, and I now understood why they seemed so sacred. Finally, I did climb on the rock. That is where the tears fell. The second that I addressed the Almighty, they flowed like Big Ozark spring. There was no powerful revelation received this day, nor any wise words of wisdom, but rather a deep, much-needed cleansing. I walked home lighter and sort of renewed. Do I miss Lucy any less? No. Has the pain disappeared? No. Can I continue on? Yes. Only because I know who holds tomorrow.

APRIL 12, 1867

The weather has been beautiful, and as promised, Miss Beth and Old Zeke rolled in this afternoon. I cannot express my delight! Most of what needed to be said had already been written, so we skipped that part and went straight to the tears.

Old Zeke had aged dramatically! Miss Beth expressed concern for him and admitted that she clearly understands that he will not live forever. They were indeed best friends if there ever were any! Josiah and Ben were thrilled at the visit also, and in Lucy's honor we enjoyed the last of the popped corn, and Old Zeke promised to help them plant a new crop in the morning. Miss Beth did not disappoint us, as she had a wagon full of newspapers from all over the country. Josiah will have reading material for months. Ben was given a stack of books too, and he is looking forward to getting back to reading. He has graduated from my school, as I know nothing else to teach him. It looks as though lately he is the one teaching me.

Miss Beth asked if it bothered me that she had worn the big hat, and I told her not at all, as that is who she is, and Lucy would be disappointed with anything less. I did notice that periodically Old Zeke would have to wipe a tear. That big dark-colored man has a mighty tender heart. He had whispered in my ear during our first hug earlier, "Death only hurts on this side." I shall always cherish his love and wisdom.

We had a few tales to share with them of our own. We knew little of Toby, but brought them up to date on Tara, Jeb, and the rest of the family. Miss Beth was pleased that the air had been cleared between me and Anna, and she was a bit astonished about Katherine's transformation. She said that only a man could do that for a woman, and I did not understand what she was talking about, but Josiah nodded his head.

We burned two candles completely down before Josiah insisted that we must get some sleep before the sun came back up in a few hours. Miss Beth teared up just now as she saw me pull the journal from the green velveteen hatbox. Why, I know just how she feels. I still hurt every night!

JUNE 16, 1867

Toby's appearance today was not as welcome as I would have hoped. He asked Josiah if he could lay low here for a while. Josiah told Toby that he would have no part in deceitfulness, but that he was welcomed to stay as a visiting family member anytime. Toby knows that Josiah is right, and I am a bit disappointed that he would jeopardize our safety. Then I remembered that he is the son of Devil Dick. Toby's actions were kind and generous, and he and Ben got along well. Ben was courteous to his cousin but was not as wide eyed as when he was a child. I could see Ben taking all of Toby's bull with a grain of salt. Although I refuse to accept it, I suppose Toby can be considered a formal member of the Jamison Gang because we were given complete reports of their activity.

Josiah asked Toby if he thought this behavior was acceptable, to which Toby had no answer. I really do not think that fellow knows. But he did understand our sentiments and did not stay long. I can only imagine the fear that must consume that community. I asked Josiah tonight if he thought we had shown Toby love or if we had pushed him away. Josiah said that setting boundaries was expressing love, and he believes that Toby knows beyond a shadow of a doubt that he is loved and wanted here, and his own choices drove him away. I hope that Josiah is right because I have a bad feeling about Mr. Toby.

OCTOBER 19, 1867

Josiah and Ben arrived home at dusk and were noticeably upset. While they were in the general store at Thomasville this morning, they witnessed Jamison pistol whip a man for commenting that civil law should be enforced and threatened to finish him off if he ever heard another word in favor of civil law enforcement. Before Josiah could get to this man's aid, Jamison had mounted and rode to the end of the street where the rest of his gang was waiting. Within a few minutes, they rode through the muddy streets and shot two men dead and swore to repeat this action if anybody rebelled against their rule. How horrid! But that was not the worst of it. One of the riders brushed by Josiah, pointed a pistol at his head, but at the last minute jerked it toward the sky as the trigger was pulled. Yes, it was Toby. At the last second he recognized his uncle Josiah.

Another shocking disclosure today was that Tim Reeves and Katherine had married.

NOVEMBER 16, 1867

Even though Tara and Jeb were visiting, Weti insisted that Ben go with her. Of course he did not mind, so they left around ten this morning.

Our company had already gone when Ben returned tonight. He was very reserved about his day and recanted carefully his experience with the old Indian. She led him directly to her cave, the place only he had been all those years ago on his birthday. They entered down the grapevine, and she once again showed him the natural shelf lined with those clay bottles of her powders. He had difficulty understanding what each was for, but he dedicated her broken words to memory. Ben said that the old woman got so weary that she had to sit a spell two or three times. Today she took him to another room in the cave where her greatest treasures were and instructed him as to who she wanted to have each after she was gone. Ben said that he did not listen that closely because he was upset to think of her leaving us. She taught him to make that dried bread—foodstuff that she routinely ate—and asked if he had any questions for her. She told Ben that she had seen far too many winters and was weary. She said something about the great light and hearing a call. Ben had no earthly idea to what she was referring and thought her a little mad. He is worried that Weti had dried and eaten some of the same poisonous mushrooms like Anna had gotten into. Josiah and I agreed that she had been very different since Lucy left us. I am not ready to say good-bye to Weti. Lord, please do not take her now!

DECEMBER 20, 1867

Josiah and Ben have spent hours in discussion, carefully and prayerfully seeking this year's special Christmas gift. Trapping this season was especially fruitful, and besides paying our taxes again for two years in advance, we have some extra money. A fur trader from Europe made unthinkable offers at the Thomasville buying station, so the pelts' values increased significantly. Ben purchased a new box of chalks for me, as well as another artist set of oils, brushes, canvases, an easel, and large pallet. That overindulgence produced a twinge of guilt in me, but Ben insisted that it was not a Christmas gift but rather an investment, and reminded me of the promise he made all those years ago on his first visit to the rock. That Ben may possess the traits of a con artist, or maybe he is a natural born sales-man. Whichever or whatever, he is precious to be so generous and thoughtful. His fascination with horses has grown over the years too, and the sorrel mare that caught his fancy also came home with him. This is the first major purchase that Ben has ever made, and he was rather proud of her. He spent all morning grooming this prized possession. He has plotted all day about where he might ride her (to show her off, I am thinking).

When Reverend Penn stopped by this afternoon on his way to Eden, it became apparent to my men that this year's Christmas giving opportunity had arrived right at our doorstep, and so when the good reverend left, he was riding that beautiful sorrel mare and had twenty dollars in his pocket for the old nag that had carried him through these hills and hollers for the last three years. I do believe that the reverend was riding taller in the saddle. The truth is that the mare is four hands taller than his old nag, and Reverend Penn is far too humble to ride in pride. I wish that I could say the same for myself, but alas, I cannot, as I am steeped in pride for my son.

A side note for this date; just before dusk, Ben brought in a per-fect-sized cedar. Josiah jestingly replaced the nail, and I dug out the box of chalk-colored shapes. The smell of popped corn still lingers in the cabin's air as I write. The fire's glow is bouncing off Josiah and Benjamin's faces as they read the latest newspapers and dime novels. Tonight there does seem to be peace on earth.

FEBRUARY 3, 1868

I woke up early and thought the sun was up, but it was only the moon shining on the new fallen snow, and it was beautiful! I laid back down and tried to sleep but never did. My spirit was troubled. I thought it might be that I ate too much leftover Christmas candy. Ben and Josiah rose early too, so we had griddlecakes and bacon. The coffee was especially strong this morning, and we were snug and warm.

Ben carried warm water to the chickens, but before he even had time to get there he was back at the door. "You had both better come!" he shouted.

Josiah pulled on his boot, strapped his leg, and then grabbed his jacket. I jumped into warm clothes and boots, and we followed Ben's tracks to the chicken house. Inside was a tidy stack of large woven baskets and smaller ones with lids. Ben was going through them when we approached. He was gasping as he informed us that the baskets contained all the things that Weti had shown him in her cave. He was beside himself and ran out of the building looking for signs of her. He found them too. Her footprints were clearly still in the snow. "I must find her!" he yelled and took off. Josiah grabbed my arm and held me back, as I had already begun following him.

"Please stay here, Lenny, I am not sure what Weti would have wanted, but I am certain that she would not want you tromping through the icy mess." Josiah was adamant. "Ben needs to be the one because she chose him to share her final wishes."

It was very, very difficult to just stand there and watch Ben disappear into that snowy forest alone. I did not weep then, nor did Josiah, but we held each other up and back inside. We did not touch the baskets.

Ben returned five hours later. His face was almost as white as the snow. He told that he had followed Weti's footprints down the path toward the rock, but instead of them going there, they went on across the ridge and right beside the elephant tree and stopped. Disappeared. "Where did she go?" he asked. "Did she just evaporate? Did she fly away?" Ben was confused and distraught. "I looked everywhere! I walked in every direction of that thong tree and never saw another footprint. I found her tracks leading from her cave to the chicken house; in fact, I could count six set of tracks, which proves to me that she made at least that many trips carrying the baskets. So she made those trips *after* the snow fell, so she had to leave after the snow came. Every step I made was left in the snow too. Pa, where is she?"

Josiah was shaking his head back and forth. "I am sure I do not know."

Our day was bizarre to say the least. I heard a racket on the porch and went to see what it was. There was a pair of indigo buntings happily dancing, squawking, and fluttering back and forth. I swear they looked at me, then each other, cocked their heads and as if being satisfied that they had been seen, flew off together.

Josiah said that he had never seen buntings this time of year.

MARCH 14, 1868

Saturday. Ben is seventeen today and very much a man. He wants to spread his wings and fly off on his own. He flew right into the huge dinner that his pa and I prepared. He flew right into the plowing of the garden spot too but mainly because he wanted to finish his chores and take off to Thomasville for the dance. I did not know that he knew how to dance! Josiah informed me that dancing had absolutely nothing to do with it, but there are girls at dances. Oh.

I am not ready for all of that, but I might as well get ready because that is the natural order of life. Josiah took to his seat for an afternoon of reading, and I journeyed to the rock. Today is my first visit since we found Weti's baskets. I paid very close attention all the way, but I never heard any footsteps. That only made my visit more sorrowful. I knelt at Lucy's stone and saw the Cherokee roses pushing up, as well as those over the little Indian girl's grave. I brushed away the dead leaves of winter and polished the stone with my skirt tail. Birds were singing, and a few squirrels were hopping from limb to limb. I heard the familiar chirp of the buntings, but I never spotted them. I climbed on the rock, and my mind wandered back to Lucy's happy antics, and the question came forth: why?

I fell asleep on the rock and woke up with these words running over and over through my head: *Sometimes the righteous are taken away from the evil to come.*

I pondered those words all the way home. They have yet to take root, and I heard no footsteps following me, but Josiah's big hug was just the medication that I needed.

I miss Ben tonight. I suppose I should get accustomed to it.

APRIL 9, 1868

We had not heard form Toby since the day he pointed his pistol at Josiah in Thomasville, until he rode up today. He was in a peaceful, repentant mood, and asked if he was allowed on our land. Josiah patted him on the back and told him not to be foolish. Ben shook his hand, and I received a strong, tight hug.

"I am leaving and may never come this way again. I know that I have disappointed all of you on many occasions, and I have committed my share of sinful acts for which I someday may be forgiven, but I could never forgive myself if I left without thanking you for all you have been and done for me and without saying good-bye," Toby spouted quickly.

I was not surprised that Toby felt that way, but I was shocked that he would go out of his way to say it. The citizens were demanding law be restored, Jamison had decided to go to Texas, and they would be leaving at dusk.

At the supper table we discussed Toby and his misadventures, from the broken arm in the barn to today's farewell. Anybody listening might have assumed that we were having a wake. In a way, it does seem like we have lost him too.

The conversation shifted, and Ben asked Josiah why men shake hands when greeting. Josiah explained that the practice began as a show that neither man was armed.

A handshake was the last thing that Ben shared with Toby, and Ben stated to his pa, "Well, if it still means that, then Toby's final act was a lie."

MAY 16, 1868

We had a picnic today. No, it was not a planned party but a giant surprise! That Ben pulled a good one on us. He drove his pa and me to Big Ozark spring on the pretense of sealing a deal with Mr. Greer concerning our crops this summer. No one was at the mill or spring, so we came right back home. I wondered why Ben parked the wagon near the front porch rather than take it to the barn. He climbed down with us and walked to the porch. No sooner had we stepped onto it than the shouting started. "Surprise! Surprise!" came from every direction, and people flooded out of each door and building.

Before I could get a handle on what was happening, a blue, checkered tablecloth was spread on the new grass and quickly covered with food. There were hugs from all—Uncle Frank, Anna, Katherine and Reverend Reeves, our precious Tressie, Tara and Jeb, Dr. Holcum, Mr. Woodside, Samuel Greer and family, and a few people that I was not acquainted with. The psaltery, fiddles, spoons, and juice harps were presented, and the music started. Ben and Tressie joined arms in a twirling jig.

Our spirits were lifted for the first time in years, and we actually enjoyed the day so much. Josiah dared me to attempt a jig with him, and I was not bashful and the dance was on. As we pumped water round and round the yard, the crowd cheered and clapped. Suddenly the noise became deadly silent. I noticed all eyes as wide as saucers, and when I realized that Josiah had danced his leg off, I fell to the ground right beside his leg in side-splitting laughter. Josiah may not have thought this was too funny, but everybody else did, and I have never heard such mirth in my life. Josiah was good natured about it, and as soon as he had strapped that leg back on, the music started and we danced around again.

Tara and Ben had cooked up this party to celebrate our anniversary, the war's end, the coming of summer, and for whatever other reason they could think up. Not only my family, but all of us needed the good medicine. The medicine only got better when Ben asked me to go into our bedroom and get his pa's harmonica. I wondered why he did not just get it himself, as I hated to leave one second of this fabulous time, but as soon as I opened the door I understood.

There on the bed sat Miss Beth, and Old Zeke was sitting in the rocker laughing and slapping his knee. "That, that, that Josiah! Plum danced his leg off!" and he burst into laughter that brought tears to his deep, dark eyes. Miss Beth and I lost our dignity laughing so hard, and we all joined the party.

Uncle Frank must have had some moonshine hidden because before the day was over his nose was bright red, his words slurred, and Anna had to drive the team home. Tressie stayed here with Tara and Jeb. I even enjoyed Reverend Reeves, as his hard edge seemed softened some. All the men bunked down in the barn, and we girls had a slumber party in the cabin. Oh, what a time! I could not believe it! I could not believe that we could actually laugh again and not feel guilty about it. This has been one of the best days of my life, and I am more grateful than ever—grateful that my family is so thoughtful and loving, that we have true friends, that God can and will still bless, and grateful to understand that I am still very much alive. I thought that I had died with Lucy and then again when Weti left. Honestly, it seemed like they were with us today, if only in spirit.

JUNE 30, 1868

We received a letter from Miss Beth today. She and Old Zeke are somewhere on the East Coast. She sent a preposted, addressed envelope and said that it was a matter of urgency that I answer the listed questions and return. Her letter read of meeting someone in New York that she suspected had a connection with my family. I obliged by sending her the formal names of my father and mother's families and approximately when and where they lived to the best of my knowledge. My heart hurt when I had to write that my mother, Pa, and sister were all deceased, and as far as I knew, I was the only survivor of my pa. The last question pertained to my own descendants. That was equally difficult to pen.

Well that was odd. Lenny would know, but I could not even remember our mother's maiden name or where they were originally from. Poor Lenny, you must have felt like an orphan. Oh how I wished she had known that I was alive! I am so sorry, Lenny, I never attempted to find you! I shall regret it to my grave and the pride that kept me from it!

JULY 6, 1868

A trip to the rock was in order this day. And thankful I am to have gone, as I believe that Weti's eminent and final departure was confirmed. A short distance from the two patches of Cherokee roses grew a third, and this patch had a similar but different tint and size. Oddly enough, they nodded in the soft breeze in my direction as I stared at them. Their slight bow was similar to the waves of pretty girls in parades, and perhaps it was my imagination, but I felt a surge in my spirit, and a feeling of warmth blew across my face. The little hairs on my arms stood straight up, and a shiver went up my backbone. It was not a fearful fixation, but more of an enlightening experience. It is extremely difficult to explain with words. I dusted off Lucy's stone and ran my fingers over those engraved words. After an hour on the rock, I picked one flower from each of the three patches, kissed them, and tucked them in my shirtwaist.

OCTOBER 25, 1868

Anna drove her team up the drive in a huff this afternoon. She had clearly been weeping , and Tressie was unusually distant. Ben saddled up two horses and took Tressie on a ride to the river. Anna was in a tizzy! It was only after she asked us to take care of Tressie in the event of her demise did she explain her troubles. There is a strong possibility that Anna has not fully recovered from the poisonous mushrooms because she laid out her plans to take her life. Josiah eventually got to the heart of the real issue. His uncle Frank's drinking evidently affected his common sense because when the widow Huddleston was released from the asylum, he assumed the responsibility of her welfare. That only manifested infidelity, and Anna blamed herself. She thought that her illness had made her less of a woman, and perchance, an appalling wife. Josiah assured her that was absolutely not the case, and that strong drink was like an adder that ultimately released its poison. He told her that infidelity was *never* about the act itself or the spouse but was a direct result of an unmet need deep inside the perpetrator.

Anna had not a clue of what Josiah was attempting to explain to her, so he changed his tone and instructed her to consider other options than rather self-destruction. He could see that he was getting nowhere, so we just let her vent her troubles in hope that it was just all talk. He asked Anna where Uncle Frank was, to which she replied, "Yellow Bluff."

I feel bad and angry both at Uncle Frank. I suppose a war of some kind must rage in this old world at all times.

DECEMBER 1, 1868

Dr. Holcum's colorful wagon arrived today, and he jumped out asking if we were having another party anytime soon. He laughed loud and slapped Josiah's wooden leg. "You sure can cut a rug!" He guffawed.

Josiah remained solemn, and I only grinned. Josiah inquired as to his visit, and he told us that he did not expect us to purchase his goods, but he did have a special delivery and then produced a parchment-type envelope.

As soon as that noisy wagon was out of sight, we gathered round the fire and opened the large New York postmarked package from Miss Beth. It contained a great number of certified papers, certificates, and legal documents. Josiah's eyes widened when I pulled out a large stack of stock certificates. I had not a clue what they were, but he gave Ben and me a short lesson about the New York Stock Exchange being established over seventy-five years ago and the process of buying and selling stocks. It was all confusing to me, but Ben soaked it in like a sponge. These certificates had been purchased years and years ago by an English immigrant named Johnson, who took ill, perished, and had only one known living heir, Paul Johnson. Miss Beth's letter explained that she had befriended an attorney in New York and over supper one evening he told her of a mysterious portfolio that had baffled him. The documentation declared that this Englishman had worked the docks, but in order to live out his dream of success, each week he invested a small portion of his wages in the growing stock market. These investments had matured, split, and doubled again many times through the years, and at present there was a huge quantity of bonds worth thousands of dollars sitting idle. She wrote that this sounded so much like the stories I had shared of my grandfather (not the investment part, but the immigrant dock working part and the name), and that is why she had me answer all those personal questions in the letter some time back. The information that I mailed back matched the information in the portfolio, and after an exhaustive search, records indicated that I was the only surviving descendant, and that I could legally claim this property.

"What does this mean?" I asked.

Josiah said that if it was all true, it meant that I was far wealthier than I ever knew. That put sincere fear in my heart! "I know nothing about being wealthy. I do not want to be anything other than what I am right now. I do not know what to do."

"I do not suppose that you have to do anything," Josiah concluded.

Ben was still digesting this new information and had no comment.

I am troubled! My pa and sister should have that wealth, not me, and they are gone.

MAY 4, 1869

The past six months have been rather mundane. The only change was Ben's new venture. Markets have already been established for furs, beeswax, roots, wooden implements, and a multitude of other products. Ben's experience and observation of the goings on in Thomasville gained him the acquaintance of many suppliers, craftsmen, and businessmen. The chicken business taught him to identify a need, and he has recognized that there is a lack of transportation for these goods to reach the waiting markets. Ben has mapped two possible routes. One would require wagon trains that could travel the trade route from Piedmont to St. Louis. The other would require boats to float the goods down the Eleven Point River to Black Rock, Arkansas, where ships waited to haul the stuffs to New Orleans. He had haggled with a boat builder in Winona and knew the costs of the boats, and he had received quotes from a wagon miller near St. James for a fleet of four wagons. Given the upfront expense, the time investment in each direction, and the potential perils, Ben had decided that the wagon route would be most productive. His plans laid out before us, the excitement in his eyes turned to sadness. "Pa, Ma, only one obstacle holds me back from jumping on this opportunity with all four," he declared.

"And that would be?" Josiah asked just as Ben had hoped he would.

"Funding," came the answer. "I have priced all that I own and applied for loans, but I could not scrape enough dollars together.

So I have offered silent partnerships to a few men in Thomasville. They have agreed, but I do not have confidence in their honesty, and I have not found an attorney that will attest to the guarantee of my venture. I am at the point where I can proceed, and the big risk is not that I cannot make this business profitable, but that I will be duped by ruthless scoundrels. At this point, I am willing to take that chance because I believe so strongly and am reasonably secure in my business plan." That was quite a delivery!

Josiah hung his head in mental deliberation. I left the two alone and from the closet pulled down the green velveteen box. Ben's eyes questioned me as I handed him that parchment envelope. "Cash these in," I told him.

"Oh, Ma, I could not possibly take your inheritance! Not your stock certificates!" he spouted.

"Of course you can. You are my only heir. You can have it now or later, and it looks to me like you could use it right now," I replied.

He looked at his pa. Josiah smiled and shrugged his shoulders. "You are the man, Ben. Decisions will come at you from every direction; might as well start right now making them."

"Are you sure, Ma?" Ben asked me. "Are you sure that you are sure?"

"I can think of nothing else that would make my pa happier than to see his grandson aspire and realize his own father's dream. You take this with all of their blessings and make them proud."

So, Eleven Point Transport Line was born right there in the front room.

APRIL 10, 1869

Jeb and Tara arrived five days ago at dusk. After a good night's rest, we loaded up in two wagons, and the four of us headed for Kansas. Tara has been ecstatic ever since she had seen the "Homes Wanted for Orphans" notice in the St. Louis newspaper and convinced

Jeb that perhaps this could be their mission, and the very reason that they could not have children of their own. Tara was obstinate about making a home complete with children. These trains have been running since '67 from New York. Josiah thinks that the published information is most likely not the entire truth. Supposedly the streets of New York City are teeming with an estimated thirty thousand abandoned children. Some are truly orphaned, other simply tossed aside like garbage. Some were believed to be runaways from abuse or drunkenness while others were from families that just had too many children to care for. The pitiful little ones are hungry, dirty, and extremely needy, living in doorways and under streets. The Children's Aid Society and the New York Foundling Hospital joined forces to establish placement for these waifs, and the Orphan Train was born. Great strides were taken to make sure that these children were placed in good homes all across the Midwest. Tara convinced Josiah and me to go along. There is no way that I would consider taking a child to replace Lucy. I was, however, open to the idea of offering a home to a destitute child. Mainly we went along to support and vouch as to Jeb and Tara's character and to the well-being and safety of their home. Upon arrival I noticed as many as fifty wagons already parked in front of the Methodist church. The local committee had been chosen and instructed by the train's organizers to line up and approve prospective families. Our information was documented, and we joined the other folks to wait for the train. A whistle sounded far away. Tara jumped up and nervously wrung her hands. Her eyes misted over, and Jeb put his arm around her shoulders. Josiah moved closer and took hold of my hand.

All the while I was imagining what must be going through those children's minds and how fearful they must be. I wondered why their Creator would have them abandoned and left helpless. It occurred to me that this train was the help that they needed and must have been inspired from above. Immediately I was grateful for the thoughtful people who put this together and asked for blessings on them. By now the train had pulled to a stop at the platform. Smoke was still boiling from the tall black stack, and the sound of gushing steam overpowered all other noise. A young woman in a stiff, starched dress stepped off first and then stood with arms motioning the children. We watched as they were escorted back to the church and lined up on the podium.

My heart melted for those children that were put on display like livestock. Many women smiled and waved at them. Yet fear emitted from the little ones' eyes. The prequalified families were called in the order they had registered and walked back and forth before the youngsters eyeing them and even touching occasionally. One to three children at a time were chosen and removed from the lineup. Papers were signed, and the children were formally adopted and rode off to their new lives. Josiah watched with disdain, I believe. Jeb and Tara's names were called, and they tenderly approached the few remaining orphans. The two that had initially caught Tara's eye had not yet been chosen. The tiny girl protectively cuddled a younger boy, obviously her baby brother. He was crying, and she was attempting to hush and comfort him. I saw Jeb nod his head at Tara, and she knelt before the young duo. She offered her hand, to which she received no response. So she gently touched the little boy's face, and he stopped crying. She reached in her pocket and produced one of those beautiful rag dolls. The young girl took it and held it to her chest. The paperwork was being executed before they ever left the stage.

To my surprise, I heard a deep voice call, "Josiah Bozeman family." Josiah and I strolled to the process desk and were told that we had not been approved as a family. The reasons being that Josiah was a cripple and that our age was a deterrent. Instantly I was angered, but Josiah's tug calmed my pride. We had agreed that if the good Lord had wanted us to care for one of these, it would have worked out; his plans for us must be otherwise. Perhaps he was right, but I still take it a bit personal.

We were introduced to Sarah and her brother, Seth. Their names alone made me think that their parents must have been knowledgeable and had vast hope in the Word. Perhaps someday we will hear their story. We welcomed them to our family and made every effort to convey love and comfort. No way would we know what was going on in their pretty little heads. Sarah was seven, and Seth was four years old. They were skinny but clean and dressed in new outfits.

Tara is already a wonderful mother. She had packed special snacks for her new children, and they gulped down the cool water from her crock. The sugar cookies disappeared long before the jerky, and she was well on the way to their hearts. The day was young, so we departed Kansas for the rugged hills of Missouri. The Huddlestons' wagon was ahead, and I watched little Seth crawl over the backboard and into Tara's lap. Shortly thereafter, Sarah climbed over too and took her seat between her new parents and then laid her head on Jeb's side and went to sleep.

The two-day trip home was uneventful, other than Sarah finally speaking. Her voice was soft, but she had a harsh accent. We learned that she could not read and was ignorant of proper manners, but her spirit was sweet and her personality bashful. She possessed feminine mannerisms and was super protective of Seth. He never uttered a sound and seldom released his clutch on Sarah. They had a long way to go, but so far, it did not appear that there were any serious obstacles.

The new Huddleston family stayed the night and met their cousin Ben. He was wonderful with the children and was thrilled see his prayers being answered.

SEPTEMBER 20, 1869

Last year's surprise picnic has turned into an annual affair; however, this year was postponed until today. The usual crowd gathered in our front yard with a feast, lots of music, and frivolity.

Last June we spent two weeks at Jeb and Tara's adding new rooms for Sarah and Seth. Those children have blossomed and are thriving at Eden. Seth is beginning to speak, and Sarah will not stop talking. They cling to Jeb and Tara like little chimps. Tara's glow is back, and she is elated with her new charges. She whispered today that she wished that Weti could see her babies. So do I. Missing Weti is an understatement; our lives are richer for having known her and emptier with her gone. If it is possible, I think, that she left part of her spirit here because I can sense her sometimes. Maybe it is my imagination, but it feels good and brings comfort.

Tressie being ten years old now, and the oldest child, has assumed the role of boss where the other young ones are concerned. She had them playing school and camp meeting, and at the end of the day all three were worn tee totally out!

Reverend Reeves and Katherine came all the way from Doniphan and were unusually quiet. Anna told me later that they had some trouble with the church. Because Katherine is still receiving a pension from Rufus's military service, she and Reeves did not get a formal marriage license, else she would lose the income. The church asked for the legal marriage certificate, and since they could not produce one, the Baptist church kicked them out. So their membership was moved to the Methodist church where he now preaches. "That's the trouble with churches," Uncle Frank mouthed. "They are forgetting from whence they came, forgetting who is supposed to be in charge, judging when they are not the jury, wearing that holier than thou attitude, casting stones, and turning the rest of us away."

I had to wonder if this is Uncle Frank's justification for his current addictions and the excuse he must convince himself with that it is all right to live his double life. Uncle Frank's nose was red again, and he could not have danced if he had wanted to at noon because he was stumbling already. I am thankful that he does not get mean when he indulges; he simply gets silly. Ben did not join us the entire day, as he was almost ready for the trial run of his new company. He had hired three drivers, and the wagons arrived two days ago. He took the idea from Dr. Holcum and painted them special with his designed logo, so that eventually anyone who spotted them, even at a great distance, would recognize them as the Eleven Point Transport Line. He is so clever! Josiah helped him remodel a feed room in the barn for a temporary office until he can locate the most practical town for the enterprise's home base. His hired hands are also bunking in the barn, and they really enjoyed our party today and the meal, especially since they will be traveling in three days. Ben estimates that he will be at this home base every two to three weeks. His excitement is contagious. Josiah beams with pride. I have mixed emotions. I am not sure if I can tolerate the empty nest.

The big surprise of the day was when Sarah began singing. Someone played a melody that she had words for, and she stood and sang as if she had done so all her life. That voice was angelic, and we were all stunned and charmed. At the song's end, the clapping and cheering only inspired her to continue, and she entertained us the balance of the day. Tressie harmonized in the background. It was beautiful!

Josiah takes great strides to avoid being the center of attention; so much in fact he avoided dancing at all this year. That may have been my only disappointment of the day.

OCTOBER 1, 1869

The wagons are partially loaded and ready to roll. Ben and I painted in three shades of green "Eleven Point Transport Line" over an iridescent blue background, and a bunting in flight through the O in the word *transport,* completed his logo. They look great, if I may say so myself. Ben seemed pleased as well, and Josiah gave us a huge smile and a nod. Uncle Frank stopped by just after supper and delivered our mail that he had been carrying since last week. The letter from Miss Beth caught my eye, and it may have been rude, but I opened it before he left. She and Old Zeke were making their way south and had taken a break on the outer banks of North Carolina. She was thrilled to hear about Ben's latest venture and wished him well. Since the Central Pacific and Union Pacific Railroads met in Utah, and the final spike, a gold one, was driven last May, it was her opinion that Ben's business could now span the entire country. She and Old Zeke offered their services, should he ever need them. I was thankful that her letter came before he left, so he could set off knowing that help was available, just in case. Ben appreciated all the support and said that he felt in his bones that this was finally the calling that he had been made for.

Looking backward, it is easy to see how things fall into place. I write that because Miss Beth asked if I had made any decisions concerning the stock certificates. She said that she hoped that I had cashed them in because on September 9, the stock market's attempt to corner the gold market caused the market to crash and was dubbed "Black Friday." I know so little about such things, I was not as impressed nearly as much as Josiah, but after he explained, it is crystal clear that our well-being was blessed yet again, because we had indeed cashed those certificates before the crash. Miss Beth believed the timing of the sell was divinely inspired. No doubt!

Those four wagons lined up the lane, Ben was in the lead hack, and I do not know what he was waiting for unless he was giving the fear time to evaporate and the excitement to come under his control. I saw him gazing upward, and the flutter of those indigo blue wings caught my eyes too, and their sweet chatter was welcomed approval. Finally, he turned, looked at us, raised his left hand high in the air, waved, smiled, turned his head forward, and slung that arm forward while yelling, "Roll on!" Those drivers yanked the reins, the horses' heads jerked, and their feet began moving, the wheels turned, and it was a beautiful sight to see our son's dreams become reality! Josiah's arm tightened around my waist, and I did not dare look into his beautiful, dark eyes. We stood there until those wagons were long out of sight and we could no longer hear rocks popping under the rolling wheels. He pulled me into a full-fledged hug. The moment we walked into the cabin, I understood how those mama birds feel when their little ones learn to fly. Our nest was empty. It does hurt.

Neither of us knows exactly what to do tonight. I am certain that we will adjust to this new phase of life, but we realize that our mission has changed. Josiah is hammering on his leg, and I have just now put the sewing away. I cannot concentrate. One thing is for sure: this night will bring many sincere prayers.

I may sleep in the loft. And tomorrow I may go to Uncle Frank's and ask if Tressie will come stay with us for a while.

DECEMBER 9, 1869

As promised, Ben did come by today. How could anybody change so much in two months? He was indeed a sight for sore eyes! How handsome! Josiah said that he had always been that handsome. I suppose he is right. Truly I had never paid attention to just how much he looked like his pa, and oh my, how dashing that man is! Josiah said that I had been looking at him through the eyes of a mother. It matters not; we were overjoyed to see him—handsome or otherwise! He had made arrangements with his drivers to take a few days to visit their families and then meet up in Thomasville Saturday to pick up a load of locally made goods. Ben was impressed that he had been able to procure shipments back this way, and very few miles did they travel empty. He had stopped by Winona, ordered four more wagons, and hired more drivers. There was a wooden box packed with receipts and invoices for me to sift and sort. I sure hope that I can make heads or tails out of this pile and keep up even half as good as he has done already.

Ben's big surprise was the beautiful young lady riding in the seat beside him. Her name was Felina, and her waist-length, shiny hair was pitch black. Long, thick lashes framed those equally dark eyes, and her skin looked like a fresh baked loaf of bread drenched in butter. Her beauty was breathtaking, and it was plain to see how any young man could have been infatuated with her. Felina was quiet but sweet. We would have liked to have learned more about her, but they only stayed a few hours. Ben said that he met Felina on the docks where she was looking for a ride to Oklahoma to catch up with her family. They were separated when the steamboat that her mother and siblings were traveling on up the Mississippi sank during a thunderstorm, and there was only room for the younger children and the mother on the next passing ship. Her pa had already started the homestead and had sent for the rest of his family. She was the eldest, and her ma was rather sickly. What man would not rescue such a beauty? I suppose all those Saturday night dances polished Ben's rough edges and taught him social skills with the ladies. Josiah says that I have no idea. I guess not and furthermore do not want to know. Anyway, while they were here, Ben was a perfect gentleman, and Felina was likewise proper.

After they left this afternoon, it dawned on me that someday Ben will start his own family and that will be yet another change in our lives, a welcomed change, I might add. Seeing what has transpired in Jeb and Tara's family, I am looking forward to ours increasing as well. The place feels empty again but not as bad as it did last October. At least we know that when he can, Ben will stop by to see us. Well, he has entrusted his accounting to me, so we are assured that he will be by regularly. *Entrusted,* now that is a word of enormous proportions, and it means everything to me that Ben trusts me. That is perhaps the greatest honor ever bestowed upon me.

MARCH 12, 1870

The Eleven Point Transport Line's owner stopped by today with a huge leather bag of paperwork and a great big smile. Ben was as excited as ever! His boat maker had finished the river vessels, and the aquatic division of his business would launch in three days.

Josiah had a long visit with Ben after supper while Felina and I cleaned up. We had our own little chat about family, friends, and, of course, Ben, or Benjamin, as she calls him. Now that's funny! He requested that we stop using that infantile name when he turned sixteen. She talks of her big dreams and tells of all the exotic gifts that Ben showers her with. Felina's family has settled on their homestead, but she did not want to join them and told us that she was nothing more than a glorified babysitter. Granted, the two life-styles differ, and I remember myself having such a great desire to leave that desolate old farm. I also picture how I broke my poor pa's heart. I suppose getting older adds multiple points of view.

Felina's dreams include grandeur and prominence, and her tastes are expensive, so should the two make a commitment; it's a good thing that Ben knows how to make money. On the other hand, she is down to earth, and has made herself at home in ours, and that pleases us because any friend of Ben's is special here.

Ben and I spent some time going over his books, and he is very satisfied. Those wheels in his head just turn harder. He asked if Jeb and Tara were doing okay, to which I said that I thought so, and he made sure that he had my undivided attention and continued, "I mean financially."

Well, I did not know because that is a subject not discussed, but for all appearances, they seemed fine. Ben made me promise that if they ever needed anything I was to let him know. And if Tressie had a need of any kind, I had to promise to tell him. He actually left ten dollars for her just in case. Ben told me that he fully intended to repay all the money from the stock certificates, plus interest. I told him that the money was his and not a loan. This was as near to an argument as we had ever had, so I dropped it and encouraged him to keep up his fabulous work.

I heard who I thought was Ben and Felina moving around out-side sometime during the night, and that was confirmed at breakfast when Felina flashed a fancy diamond under Josiah's and my eyes. Ben was proud to tell how he proposed to his sweetheart under the stars and placed that fancy ring on her finger. She was ecstatic, and Ben was beaming. Right after breakfast they packed up and drove away. It gets easier every time, but this time our joy was multiplied, for this time we have gained a daughter. It is so good to know that Ben will not be alone.

MAY 30, 1870

Ben has worked a monthly stop here into his schedule. His business has boomed! Not only did he put four more wagons into service, but the five river boats are taking products and goods down the Eleven Point River to Black Rock, Arkansas, where they are packaged for shipment to New Orleans. Every other trip Ben has had Felina beside him, and we have gotten to know her a little better. Ben adores her. That man has the most amazing stories to share. Earlier this month he delivered the first stove in Oregon County, which was purchased with peanuts. A family had grown and harvested enough peanuts to pay for a cook stove. Ben told of a strange machine that he had delivered to St. Louis that would write with ink on paper when the letter key was punched. He said they called it a typewriter.

He often brings strange new products, and we are amazed at the brilliance and improvising of inventors these days. They make gadgets that are supposed to make work easier or quicker. We cannot decide if they really do, but we are having difficulty finding room to store them. Josiah says that we should actually use these new-fangled objects, and then he says, "It is hard to teach an old dog new tricks."

We are grateful for Ben's generosity and still so proud of his accomplishments.

The daily chores are taking less time, but our new assignments with the Eleven Point Transport Line take up the balance of our day, so unless something unusual or earth shattering occurs, this journal may not get much attention.

SEPTEMBER 8, 1870

Old Zeke's teeth were shining as he turned the horses right in front of the porch. Miss Beth hopped out and ran around to offer him her hand. Now that is a switch!

That was not a cap on Old Zeke's head, but a thick cover of white hair. His eyebrows were white too; his shoulders drooped, his steps were shorter, and his breathing more labored, but he moseyed on to the barn to find Josiah. I was so, so happy to see Miss Beth! We spent the entire afternoon catching up, and by the time the men came to the cabin, we had supper on the table. The rest of the evening, Josiah and I listened intently to their tales of travel up and down the East Coast.

Miss Beth was thrilled to hear about Tara, Jeb, and their children and was very, very excited about Ben's venture. We were glad to fill her in and crow about our son's accomplishment.

Miss Beth asked a hundred questions about Felina. One would think that she was his court-appointed advocate. She told me to keep my eyes open, and I asked what could I do, as Ben was a grown man making his own choices. "Pray harder then," she snapped. I thought she was a bit overbearing, but I do not love her any less, as our own best interests have always been in her heart.

Miss Beth asked Josiah if he was familiar with a place called Falling Springs, and he asked if she would like to visit. The sky was so blue, that autumn nip was in the air, and the leaves were beginning to turn, so we decided that it was indeed a perfect day for a trip. I packed a picnic and off we went. Old Zeke rode this trip as Josiah manned the reins, and we girls took in the magnificent beauty of these hills and hollers. The spring actually exited the earth high up that bluff; the pool below had an unusually blue tint, and it was ice cold! The cave was a short distance to the north of the spring and cabin, and it too was high up the bluff. Josiah told stories about when he first came to this country and explored the cave with his uncles. They built ladders of tree trunks and shimmied up, only to discover that the cave was laden with artifacts, but they did not stay long because they also found ancient skeletons draped in deerskin. We laughed so hard when he told about the three of them running over each other and jumping out of the cave rather than taking the ladder, and then they ran for two miles before any of them would stop. The picnic tasted so much better on the bank of that millpond. If a day could be perfect, this was one. The ride home was just as enjoyable, even if Old Zeke fell asleep the first mile. Miss Beth carefully placed a lightweight blanket over her friend and a pillow under his head.

Josiah insisted that Old Zeke sleep at the cabin this visit, as the stairs to the barn loft are steep and too dangerous to risk a fall. Old Zeke seemed embarrassed to cause concern, but deep down he was thankful to avoid that trek this time. Miss Beth hugged Josiah later and thanked him for his compassion toward her longtime driver and best friend. We did not stay up and talk into the wee hours tonight; I think we talked it all out today. Tonight I am ever grateful for friends, "What I found at the rainbow's end."

DECEMBER 15, 1870

Tressie is here, and oh my, how wonderful it is to have a little girl in the house again! She is growing more beautiful and lovely every day. Tressie and I had some very deep discussions about life and death and heaven and Hades. She lost Edward and then Lucy, and she fears that she too will die. I never thought about her thinking that. What a huge, real dread for a beautiful little girl! This day the sun was shining, and the temperature was lukewarm, so I thought a visit to the rock was in order. Tressie and I enjoyed the walk, and I found myself listening for the footsteps, but alas, there were none. We climbed on the rock, and I pointed to the spot where the Cherokee roses grow. Tressie already knew that and began to weep to think of Lucy buried there. *Perhaps this was a bad idea,* I thought until she hugged me real tight and told me how much she loved and missed Lucy. Then she told me something that shook my very soul. She said that about a month before Lucy passed, the two of them were playing in the barn, and Tressie had one of her fuzzy feelings and she shared the story of the winter that she was lost in the sleet and about the giant, dark man who had kept her safe and warm all night. She shared with Lucy how that man told her not to be afraid and not to worry about her family because they would come to her when the sun came up. Tressie told me that she was very surprised when Lucy asked what that man smelled like. Tressie began crying at this point in her story, and when she finally gained her composure, she continued by saying that Lucy asked if that tall man smelled like rain. I was mystified and simply sat spellbound. Tressie said that yes, in fact, that is exactly what he smelled like, and she asked Lucy how she knew. Lucy told her that she had met him a few days before at Osage Springs when she and Ben had a picnic there, and Ben had gone to sleep. Lucy had climbed to the top of the bluff and could not get back down. Rather than cry and wake her brother, she decided to pray to the God that her pa always talked to and ask for help. She could not see the man, but she could smell him as he was telling her the direction of each step to take on her climb down to safety, but the strangest thing was that he told her that she would soon come live in the rainbow. Lucy told Tressie that Weti was waiting at the bottom of the bluff. She jumped in her arms, and the man was gone. Tressie said that Lucy told that story very nonchalantly and changed the subject when a she spotted a black snake eating a rat behind the haystack. I asked Tressie why she had never shared that story, and she just shrugged her shoulders.

"I don't know. I thought if I said it out loud, it would disappear and not be true. I want it to be true so bad, Aunt Lenny!"

Of course, I was speechless. I was so baffled that I did not know what to say to her or how to comfort her. I pulled her close. She asked me to pray, and I did.

We walked home in silence because the mood was like a powerful spirit, too vital to break. Tressie went to bed early, and as she slept, I repeated her story to Josiah. He too was awed and said that he needed to go for a walk. He never said another word, but strapped his leg back on. He has not come back yet, but he will. And he will come home different, just as I did this afternoon.

DECEMBER 25, 1870

The Christmas tree never fell over one time today! (Perhaps because it is tethered to the nail back in the wall.) We enjoyed a marvelous day! Jeb, Tara, Sarah, and Seth have been with us the last three days. Tressie helped me decorate the tree with Lucy's chalk-colored paper ornaments. I determined that we should stay busy, which was very easy to do.

Uncle Frank, Anna, Reverend Reeves, and Katherine arrived just before noon with a wagon loaded with scrumptious food. Ben and Felina rode up right behind them, and lo and behold the next wagon was the one with the fringe on the top. Miss Beth and Old Zeke had planned for years to spend Christmas with us and finally made it. Oh, we ate and ate and ate! We laughed and shared stories until I thought the cabin could not possibly contain the joy. Sarah directed a skit where Seth was a shepherd boy, and Tressie was Mary. Baby Jesus was one of Weti's beautiful dolls, and Sarah was the angel that delivered the good news. I must admit they did a marvelous job! The spirit really moved because tears ran down Old Zeke's face while the parents' faces beamed with pride, and my own heart was about to burst open. Ben enjoyed that never-ending story yet was glad that they did not ask him to play a part, and Felina listened intently but acted like she did not totally understand. Miss Beth was impressed, and that was something in itself, as she is an avid theater patron. The great treat of the night came when Sarah slipped Jeb's psaltery from its case and began to play and sing the most beautiful song of the baby in the manger. That child is clearly blessed with enormous talent. And how did she know how to play that instrument? I was awestruck! That was remarkable enough, but then Seth climbed up into Josiah's lap, stood straight up and began reciting the Christmas story from the book of Luke. This was the first year of my life in Missouri that Josiah has not read that story directly from the Book. Obviously Sarah was not the only gifted child here today. Josiah made his way to the untracked snow under the pines and dished my wooden dough bowl full of the beautiful, fluffy, white matter. He opened a can of the Borden's condensed milk that Toby left years ago, stirred in a cup of sugar, and then spooned each person a bowl of this delicious snow ice cream. There is no way that I can pen all the wonderful things that transpired this day, sufficed to say that it was very blessed!

The temperature was not freezing tonight, but a light snow began to fall just as the wagons were leaving. I am saddened that Tressie had to go home, and I do so hope that Miss Beth can stay a few days. Ben and Old Zeke have their bedrolls spread out before the fire, and Felina and Miss Beth are in the loft. I can hear them softly talking. Josiah's leg is leaning against the door, and after he went to sleep I put a red sock on it, and a candy cane, a note of sweet nothings, and a poem.

DECEMBER 26, 1870

Today was less busy but emptier somehow. The entire family was thrilled that Ben and Felina had set their wedding date. They have decided that they would like to get married at the Big Ozark spring next March 24. I do wish that Tara and Jeb could have stayed over, but Miss Beth and Old Zeke are still here, and she helped Felina design the wedding invitations. I have no experience with such fine things, but thank goodness for Miss Beth and her knowledge of etiquette. All was going great until Miss Beth insisted that Felina get Ben's approval of the invitations before we cut and addressed them. Felina refused and almost became angry with Miss Beth. I did not like how the cabin filled immediately with tension. The atmosphere changed when the men came in for dinner, and Miss Beth made certain that Ben saw and approved the invitations before she would help one minute more. Felina was obviously aggravated, but she did not voice her disgust, for which I was thankful.

Katherine was a dear yesterday and shared the last address that she had for Toby, and told us what little she knew of his recent adventures. Ben said that he would really like to invite his cousin to the wedding, so I added Toby to the list, which keeps growing, as do Felina's plans. We started off planning a small, simple ceremony, but it has become a colossal gala. Clearly Ben is excited as well and has been pouring out his plans for his bride's fabulous home to Josiah and Old Zeke. They have been all ears because Ben has not given them an opportunity to speak, but Josiah's grin says it all, and Old Zeke just nods with pride. I think that Ben and his Aunt Katherine struck a deal on the farm left by Uncle Dick to build on. How wonderful that he and Felina will be nearby!

Ben and Felina packed up and left after dinner, and Miss Beth let me have it. She unloaded her opinion of Felina and her mislaid plans and the horrible way that she was treating Ben. She was very upset with my soon-to-be daughter-in-law. I was surprised and did not know how to respond, other than to tell her that I had great confidence in Ben's choices, and my love for Ben would transfer right on to Felina, as the two become one, and that I will accept her as my own child and treat her as such. As hard as it will be to do, Josiah and I must cut the cord and respect that our son will soon leave us for good and should cleave only unto his wife. I believe that being friends with Ben will be quite rewarding because the experience of being his parent has been a great blessing. He is the kind of man that will make a wonderful friend, and I will think no differently of Felina. We both agreed that she is young and has a lot to learn. Nothing I said changed Miss Beth's opinion, but she promised to help with the wedding in any way that she can and that she will attend the ceremony in honor of Ben, whom she loves dearly!

Miss Beth and Old Zeke left for Thomasville for the night, on their way out west. She carried a huge package of beautiful wedding invitations to post there.

Josiah and I sat by the fire in silence this evening. Isn't it odd how quickly an unfortunate turn of events can steal a happy, happy day?

FEBRUARY 28, 1871

Winter has been rather harsh thus far, but today it had warmed up quite nicely, so I decided that since the big day is near, I must seek some solace and wisdom. The rock awaited me, and off I went. Very little green was showing anywhere, not even a hint of the trees leafing, and I could see a long distance through the forest because the pines' boughs were well above eye level.

The rock humbly overlooked its earthly post, but before I climbed into that well-worn seat, I knelt at Lucy's grave and gave her another tear. Will I ever not miss her? I glanced at Weti's daughter's resting place and a thousand questions came up. Without consideration or thought, I rose and headed toward the elephant tree. I had not been there since Ben described Weti's footsteps that disappeared in the snow. The walk was a bit eerie, as the forest was unusually quiet. The eyes of the elephant tree stared as I approached, and no matter which route that I walked, they watched me; it was a bit unnerving. The woods were completely undisturbed as far as I could see; not even a turkey scratch disrupted the scene. I stood in the spot where Ben explained Weti's dead-end tracks, and I looked very slowly in every direction and could see nothing out of the ordinary. I do not know what I expected to find: a sign, a clue, or maybe even Weti. Naturally, disappointment flooded in. I reached out and touched the elephant tree with my right hand. Nothing. I walked around it and stopped directly in front of it. I thought it odd that a hollow stump was only a few yards down the hillside. I have not a clue what urged me to go to this stump, but I did and knelt beside it. The deepest area of the stump held that black water that old witchy women say takes off warts, but in the shards of unrotted wood lay a leather bag. I am positive that it was the pouch Weti always wore on her belt. It was damp from the seasons, and I was not sure what I wanted to do. Would it be sacrilege to remove it from the resting place, or would leaving it be abandonment? Looking away, I thought perhaps I was dreaming and that when I looked again the leather pouch would have been a figment of my imagination. But no; it was still there. A very long time passed before I decided that if Weti had wanted me to have that bag, she would have left it with all her others things. I could not, however, resist the temptation to look inside, and against my better judgment, I did. There was a lock of midnight black hair, several baby teeth, a tiny wooden cross, and a grayish-green leafy substance that smelled very familiar. Yes, I was as baffled as I expected to be.

After replacing the contents and bag as near as to how I found it, I walked away, almost hating to turn my back on the stump or elephant tree. The forest was even quieter as I made my way back to the rock, and I began wishing that I had not come. I ran to the rock and climbed on, seeking a refuge, I suppose. I began to visit with my Maker. As it so often happens, my mind wandered to another place and time. I was remembering the beautiful spring day that was so windy that our laundry was blowing at a ninety-degree angle from the line. Josiah thought it a perfect day to teach Ben to build and fly a kite. He said that children in the Orient made a great sport of this, and they did indeed put a kite together from the old newspapers that Miss Beth left and tiny saplings. Josiah used a ball of twine on a stick and ran like the wind, holding that kite over his head and unrolling the twine at the same time. (This was before he lost his leg and before Lucy came.) The fast breeze grabbed the kite and took it up, up, up, and Benjamin was fascinated. The going up was not so bad, but each time the kite came down, new saplings and paper had to be put on. Benjamin finally got the hang of it, and as the breeze died down some, the kite stayed way up in that blue sky. Josiah took the twine from Benjamin and tied it to the picnic basket's handle while we enjoyed dinner on the ground. The kite just gently swayed one way and then the other at the end of that twine.

The nervousness that had consumed me when I reached the rock had now dissipated, and I pondered why this particular day played itself out in my thoughts.

Then those inaudible words answered: "Benjamin is planning to marry next month. You have concerns of his well-being. I just wanted you to know that he is like that kite. He will gently sway this way and that through life, and sometimes he will crash and need repair, but be assured that I will always be holding the end of the twine. When he needs reeling in, I will do so, and when he crashes, I will heal him. His pa gave him back to me long ago, and he will be safe. To worry is to doubt me. Pure love casts out fear, and I love him."

My walk home was without fear and no following footsteps.

MARCH 24, 1871

The big wedding has taken up most of our time these past few weeks. Ben turned twenty on the fourteenth. He was not here, but Josiah and I celebrated anyway with an apple cake. It was quite a surprise when Toby came by Monday. We could not believe what a handsome man he has become and so polite. He did not share any details of his whereabouts or shenanigans for the last three years, but he seemed more interested in what and how all the family was doing. He had received the wedding invitation and was happy that he was still welcome here. Our place looks like the camp meeting grounds. There are folks everywhere! Felina's family is huge, and we were glad to at last make their acquaintance. Of course, Jeb, Tara, and the children were busy helping with the many preparations. Miss Beth excused herself from the hustle and bustle with a head-ache and was lying down until it was time to go. All the other aunts and uncles had been assigned jobs, and Tressie was Felina's personal assistant, jumping at her every whim.

Felina had her dress tailor made in St. Louis, as well as her attendants' gowns. A fancy food service from Kansas City had hired a subcontractor in Alton to cater the food, drinks, and cake. That did help a lot, but my, at the expense! Ben told Felina to have whatever kind of wedding she wanted, only tell him where to be when. Even the weather was on Ben's side, as the day was spectacular. Two days ago, we began hauling decorations to the spring, and Josiah was told exactly how to build an arch just beside the cave spring. I must admit the whole setup was unbelievably beautiful! The biggest scare of the day came when the wagon carrying the harp and violinists from St. Joseph got a tad too close to the edge of that steep embankment, and they all squealed in fear of plunging down the bluff. They were fine, but Josiah had a big laugh. He is not that fond of uppity city people who put on airs. Here again, I have to admit, their music is magnificent! *Hectic* is not the word to describe the last two days, nor the scene; it was much worse than that.

Early this morning things began to come together and hearts became merrier, which is a good thing. People were donning their finest, and there were some gorgeous clothes, but nobody outshined Miss Beth. Perhaps in Lucy's honor, she dolled up in emerald green. Her hat was wide and round, and the feathers and toile dripped from it. Her gown was elegant, and she appeared to be floating as she walked with that lace parasol. Old Zeke was not to be outdone and had a long-tailed jacket and vest. I am not sure which shined more: his shoes or his teeth.

Wagon after wagonload of guests arrived.

A photographer was one of the first on the scene and sat up a tripod contraption. He would duck his head underneath a black cloth attached to a wooden box and hold up a flashing light of some kind and then come out from under that cloth and lift a plate from the box, replace it, and repeat the process.

The crowd had taken their places, and when the harp began to play a certain song, Josiah and I walked this pathway and took our seats. Felina's mother followed and sat across from us. Felina's pa was to walk her up and give her to Ben, so they were out of sight at this time. Ben, the preacher, and his groomsmen filed in from the bluff over the cave. They looked so handsome! The bride's court came down the path one at a time, swaying with the sweet music, and lastly the little flower girl pranced down the aisle dropping the imported rose petals while stopping to wave at everyone that she recognized. It was then that the music changed tempo and became louder, the preacher asked us all to stand, Ben's eyes were peeled to the opening, anticipating his beautiful bride, so we all turned to watch her parade down the path. The music played and played and kept playing. The song was repeated twice, and only when Felina's pa slowly came into view alone did it stop. He just stood there with this dumbfounded look on his face, shrugged his shoulders, and shook his head.

Felina never did show up. Nor did Toby.

MAY 13, 1871

I sat on the rock most of the day, with the last two months running over and over in my head. Ben has not made his monthly visits and is sending his paperwork via a courier. His humiliation is heart wrenching! I can completely understand why he has no desire to show his face, but Josiah says that it does not have as much to do with pride as it has to do with the fact that he is pushing himself onward, away from the pain. Ben has stepped up his business ventures by adding yet another three wagons and four more boats. He has saturated his life with work. Before the wedding he had given Josiah a huge amount of money to invest in the bonds that Colonel Woodside was selling for construction of a new courthouse in Alton to replace the one burned during the war. Now that he had the exorbitant bills from Felina's freewill wedding, he had to hold back on the initial investment, which embarrassed him even more. Josiah says the shame comes not from the money situation, but from the fact that he was so blind to her true nature. Josiah gladly purchased the bonds in Ben's name and used the rest of the money from the stocks that we cashed in to purchase the balance of Ben's original request. I couldn't care less about all that money stuff; I am sick over Ben's broken heart. I am so full of anger toward Felina. Mess with me, but do not mess with my child! Some days I think I could choke her with my bare hands. Then there is the matter of Toby. No person has ever disappointed me so! Not a soul that I know of has heard a word form either of them. And that is a good thing, I suppose, as they have ripped their britches with all people in these hills. Forgiveness is due, but I cannot muster it yet. Weti would be unhappy with me about that, but I can be certain that she would be far more upset with those two wedding crashers! I realize that like Ben, I must move on and come to terms with this sad turn of events.

I tried so hard to concentrate on the here and now, but my nose was running, so I reached into my pocket for a hanky and wondered why that piece of twine was there. Then I remembered cutting a piece too short to tie up the journal and stuffing it into the pocket last week. And then there it was, the kite analogy.

Let it go, Lenny. Let it go.

I began to laugh and cry at the same time. I am so ludicrous! How could I forget that so soon? Thank you, Lord, for reminding me that you have Ben in your grasp. He has crashed, but you are mending him. He is swaying to and fro, but you have a hold on him.

I walked home with more spring in my step and power in my spirit.

SEPTEMBER 9, 1871

Our lives have gotten back into a routine of sorts. The garden has finished producing for the most part, so there is very little to do other than the usual chores. Miss Beth and Old Zeke stopped by a few hours last June on their way to San Francisco and left Josiah a huge stack of books and me a crate of fabric. Ben was here two days, and his stories never ended. Josiah enjoyed seeing the world through his son's eyes. All those tales and experiences were fabulous, but not once did he dwell on the debunked wedding or Felina. I am proud of Ben for pressing forward. His visit was like healing salve for all of us, and I believe that his stops here will become more frequent now.

Josiah gave Ben the bonds from the courthouse construction project, and Ben immediately returned all the funds that Josiah had pitched in, plus interest. From the books that I am keeping, it is evident that his business is still growing by leaps and bounds, and he has not missed a cent from the frivolous overspending on the wedding that never happened. He told Josiah that was nothing more than a bad investment and that he had learned a very difficult lesson and would be much more aware before he ever invested his heart again.

Ben drove away in much the same fashion that he did the very first day. I could feel a depression setting in until I spotted the indigo bunting singing from the top branch of that huge cedar and reached in my pocket to feel that piece of twine. Ben is doing great!

DECEMBER 31, 1871

I hear sleet falling on the roof. Usually Patches would be whining on the porch, as she so often did when ice came, but Josiah found her on the barn loft last month curled up in the straw. She apparently died in her sleep. We had been expecting that for some time, after all she was seventy-seven years old in dog years. Josiah buried her in the corner of the barn's dirt floor and painted her name on the old wooden wall just above. Her passing reminds me of Ben's childhood passing too, because I will never think of her that I do not see that little boy in my mind. They were good for each other, and I will always be grateful to Reverend Reeves for bringing her that day.

Maybe that is a thought to end the year on: change. Everything changes, doesn't it? And no matter how good things are, they always get worse. And no matter how bad things are, they will always get better.

APRIL 3, 1872

We have just returned home from an exciting camp meeting near Eden. What a wonderful time to spend with Tara and the children, well, Jeb too, but he and Josiah spent most of the time together. This meeting was much like the first one we attended so long ago, except that there was no war between the states. The only conflict came from the daily battle of good and evil. The crowd was massive, and yet I longed for my friends of old. It was not entirely sad, as their memories live on, and I can recall those anytime. We made many new friends. The terrific surprise came just before the evening worship when a familiar wagon with fringe on the top rolled into camp. Sarah and Seth ran at great speed to jump up and hug Old Zeke before he even climbed down. Miss Beth's big red hat was certainly out of place, but that did not faze her; she plowed right in the big middle of the service. What did faze her was the reverend's sermon, and on the last day, she was hatless, right out in the middle of that beautiful river's flow with a hundred other sinners, including Sarah and Seth. Old Zeke cried and cried and told us about the time his grandpa "dunked him in dat ole Missoury river and held me under 'til dat ole muddy river washed my sins away." Old Zeke said that he was "waitin' on dem golden slippers and to fly away." He said that he "had been tellin' Mizz Beth for years dat she outta b'lieve; she outta b'lieve, 'cause de Maker iz comin' foe uz."

He may have been the happiest man at the meeting. He dropped that cane and was running around hugging everybody.

The last night of the meeting, Sarah jumped up and ran down the aisle, grabbed her new little redheaded friend, and dragged her to the podium. Somewhere on the way, she had picked up Josiah's psaltery and she began to play. Those two little girls' voices blended like smooth cream, and surely no angels could sound so heavenly because the Spirit filled every heart there that was open to receive it. The reverend was nearing his last call when Seth went forward, walked up to the reverend, and told him of his call and surrender to preach the gospel. That was the loudest the shouting ever got.

MARCH 14, 1873

The mantle clock has just struck three, and the apple cake is almost done; its aroma fills the cabin. Ben is twenty-two this day and has come to spend it with us.

Ben picked at his pa earlier about the graying hair around his temples. Josiah told his son that gray hair is the crown of old men. Ben thought that was funny until Josiah showed him that in the Scripture; then he took it a bit more serious. Work suits him well, and his monthly bookwork increases. I expect he would really like to take these logs to a professional, but he uses the accounting as an excuse for regular visits. That is fine with us because we need to see him occasionally.

Ben was wearing a new watch today. It must have cost a fortune! The cake is done. Ben ordered a birthday supper menu exactly like the one in '62. His request was granted, and he told me the supper was worth far more than his gold watch, and until I was better paid, he thanked me. That boy! Oh, I meant to write *that man!*

DECEMBER 31, 1873

Hardly a newsworthy moment comes to mind this evening as I pen the year's final entry. Our family is healthy, our needs are all met, and I dare say that we are happy enough. Tressie is fourteen and moved in with Tara's family. Uncle Frank has his hands full with Anna, whose health has deteriorated considerably. She never did quite recover from those poisonous mushrooms. Tressie adores Sarah and Seth, and we understand that those two girls have been traveling around to country churches singing. Tressie has become an avid seamstress like her big sister and wants me to help her with a quilt for her hope chest. Josiah constantly picks at her and asks her exactly what she is hoping for. Tressie's cheeks will blush, and she will say, "Oh, Uncle Jo, you know." Jeb is teaching Seth to handle the johnboat up and down the river, and they are building onto their cabin again. Tara seems so content and is glowing in her motherhood.

Ben came for Christmas. Josiah agreed that he acted preoccupied during the holidays, and we hope that whatever is on his mind is a good thing. Miss Beth and Old Zeke did not make it here this year, although we did receive several letters from them. In fact, we received a postal card, and I understand that it was one of the first ever printed. It came from San Francisco, where they rode some contraption called a cable car. We laughed at the thought of Old Zeke's wide eyes and big grin, holding on for dear life riding on a horseless vehicle going up and down hills.

Probably the worst thing that happened all year was on a cold day in October. Josiah was hunting near the forest, and when he stumbled, the gun fired and shot him in the wooden leg. He spent an entire afternoon filing the splinters off. He has discovered that an extra rolled-up handkerchief fits perfectly in the hole.

I have spent many hours on the rock this year. The Cherokee roses were more lush and lovely as ever, perhaps because of the tear showers. I returned to the elephant tree only once, and Weti's pouch was still in the stump just as I had left it. And as far as I know, it remains undisturbed. I am learning not to look back as often and to not spend as much time thinking of the future but enjoy this season of my life with the most wonderful husband in the world.

FEBRUARY 6, 1874

Saturday. Ben's wagon was a sight for sore eyes. Snow has covered these hills for over three weeks, and travel has been impossible. He probably had no business out in this mess either, but *impossible* is not a word in Ben's vocabulary. Hell or high water, he is pushing on. That trait could perhaps be both his greatest and worst attribute. He was much more attentive this visit and unknowingly revealed the source of his distraction, at least we think.

Ben asked if we remembered the group of men that Temperance met her demise with. Of course we had never actually met them, but we certainly recalled that horrible event. Josiah said that he had seen the elder brother, Frank, at Wilson's Creek, but only from a distance. The newspapers are full of the accounts of the Jesse James Gang and their misdeeds. Josiah has never appreciated the way reporters romanticize those crimes and write heroes out of wrongdoers. Ben agreed with his pa and told that only last Saturday, Frank, Jesse, and their gang robbed their first train at Gad's Hill. Ben thought that they were having an unspoken contest of sorts with the Younger Gang to see which could be the biggest and baddest. Chills went through me as he told of the robbery, and I should have known that was not the rest of the story. That Ben set me up for what he really wanted to tell us. It seems that he had taken a short vacation last month and was entertaining a lady friend by taking her on a trip to the resort area at Hot Springs, Arkansas. Well, that was a shock in itself! The stage coach was filled to capacity with other tourists, and they were having the best time watching the beautiful countryside pass by, sharing stories of their lives, and bragging on their accomplishments, when suddenly there was yelling, gunfire, and the drivers jerked those horses abruptly to a stop. The stage was surrounded by men on horses, their faces half covered with bandanas and guns drawn. The dark-headed man was shouting for all the passengers to disembark, of which they gladly obeyed. Two of the men took all the money from their pocketbooks and the women's purses while the other gang members stayed mounted on the horses and kept their guns pointed at the travelers' heads. The second insult came when the robbers made another pass through the tourists and collected all their jewelry. At this point in the story, Ben pulled out the empty pocket of his trousers, revealing the missing watch. *Doggone! They took Ben's prized watch!* Satisfied that all the worthy goods were stolen and this group of people completely terrorized, the gang rode off at breakneck speed. Once the dust settled, an account was taken between the passengers and drivers, who agreed that those crooks had made off with about three thousand dollars' worth of goods and money. One of the gentle-men took off his black derby hat and pulled out a crumpled wanted poster picturing the James brothers, and they all agreed that it was indeed the James Gang that had just made their acquaintance.

I was appalled and upset about the whole ordeal, but Ben was laughing and said that nobody got hurt and that he felt just a lit-tle special because he had had a personal encounter with the most famous gang of all times. I still fail to see any humor in this dreadful act. Ben said that the watch was just a thing; a material good that could easily be replaced.

The sun came out late this afternoon, and nearly half of the snow has melted. After supper Josiah popped the last of the pop-ping corn, and the three of us sat around the hearth, reminiscing the years gone by. Both tears and laughter were conjured during the Lucy stories. I was not sure that we should be talking about all that, but Josiah thinks that it brings healing. I suppose he is right, as usual. Ben has more fun telling his pa of things that Josiah has no knowledge. I imagine that Ben is always on the watch for new and interesting facts that he can shower on us. We play right along, as it is a win-win for all of us. The one thing that Ben did not tell was about his lady friend, and no, we did not pry.

As I close this entry, I am thinking of Ben's missing gold watch, and I remember the story of the rich young ruler that was told to sell all he had and follow Christ. The young man walked away sadly. Our Ben could be so different, and my heart feels pleased to remember the time at the Eden camp meeting when he walked that aisle. I do believe that is the difference. Having not of silver and gold is not such a bad place to be. I would much rather sit on the rock than on a throne.

SEPTEMBER 5, 1874

Thunder and lightning woke me up before the clock tolled five this morning. *This will be a miserable day for a funeral.* I lay still until I heard footsteps in the loft and knew that Ben too was awake. I put the coffee pot on the fire and began stirring up the biscuits. He wrapped his arm around my shoulders and asked how I was holding up. I assured my son that all was well and asked how he was, to which he gave a weak nod. Josiah joined us shortly and we had a quiet breakfast. The men hitched the wagon, and we dressed for Anna's funeral. On the trip to Uncle Frank's, we shared our memories of her and our heartfelt sadness for Tara and Tressie. Reverend Reeves and Katherine's wagon was just ahead of us as we turned the last bend to the Bozeman home place. I noticed a bouquet of oxeye and one of Tara's stunning quilts awaiting their ride to the burial.

Not surprisingly, we found Uncle Frank tipping the jug. His nose was red and puffy. Jeb, Tara, and the children had been with him the last three days, and he was obviously ready to get this over with. He wanted to bury Anna near Edward. Most of our consoling was spent on Anna's children. They are all so ashamed of Frank's drunkenness and lack of concern for their mother, and the shock of all shocks came when the widow Huddleston rode up. Josiah flashed his eyes in my direction and lifted those eyebrows as to remind me of my place in the matter. So my mouth sealed over. Uncle Frank kept glancing her way, and I thought that he might as well have pulled her right beside him. Tressie and Sarah sweetly sang "In the Sweet By and By," and we all joined in on the last chorus. Seth asked his pa if he could say a few words. Permission was granted, and that elegant presentation of the gospel was the only tear-provoking event of the day. Josiah called Seth a prodigy; I called him precious! There was no point in wishing that the little fellow's effort would have an impact on his adopted grandfather because the hard drink was in control by this time. When discussing this matter on the way home, Ben remarked that he had noticed in his travels that on every bottle or jug of commercial alcohol, the word *spirit* could be found. He believed that there are two kinds of spirits in this world, good and evil, of course, and proven by his own experiences, the spirits in those containers were definitely *not* the good kind. I am positive that Anna's children would concur.

All the women, save the widow Huddleston, left the graveside and returned to Anna's home. The men stayed to close the grave. Tara asked if there was anything of her mother's that I would like to have, and I told her no. I may have offended her, to which I was very sorry, and I explained that having the opportunity to love Anna's children was the greatest honor and I required nothing more. Tressie packed every last item of her belongings and told us that she never intended to come back here, and that if it was acceptable to Jeb and Tara, they were now her parents. As soon as the men returned, Josiah, Ben, and I said our farewells and headed home.

By nightfall, there was little left unsaid about the day's episode, so our conversation turned directions. Ben told us that he would be leaving at sunup to get back to his commerce. From a bag he retrieved a strange-looking heap of metal. He explained to his pa that this was a new invention and that he had been shipping wagons of it to load on westward bound trains. He called it barbed wire and said that ranchers were stringing this on wooden fence posts around and across their properties, not so much to keep their cattle in, but to keep grass hogs like buffalo out. What will they think of next?

Where did the idea get into my head that getting older meant life getting easier? Because it certainly is not! Tonight I feel very empty.

JULY 4, 1875

Yesterday the wagon with the fringe on the top rolled up the lane at midday yesterday. Miss Beth was driving, her frown evident from a good distance. I did not see Old Zeke, and my heart raced. She stopped the horses and motioned for me to come. The old, dark man was lying in the back, ill and almost unconscious. He barely had the energy to help us get him to the bed. His head was as hot as fire. We put cold compresses on it, and I dug out Weti's old bags of powders. The pink one had worked on me, so I mixed with water and gave it to the old soul. Josiah took over when he came in from chores. He was deeply concerned and wished that he had someone to send for the doctor. I told him that I would gladly go, and he agreed, but I should wait until morning.

Not a one of us slept all night, but took turns sitting by our dear, dear friend's bedside. Old Zeke was so delirious that he was talking out of his head. He would squeal like a little child and clap his hands, and then he would cry like a baby. We could not understand his babble, except for the word *light*. Shortly after the mantle clock tolled three, the old man got still and quiet. Josiah encouraged Miss Beth and me to lie down a while. We did go to the front room, but neither of us could doze off. Less than thirty minutes later, Josiah came from the bedroom and told us that the old soul had passed. He just went to sleep and stopped breathing. Miss Beth was devastated and cried and cried. There was no consoling her and nothing to do but join in. Her first words spoken when she could speak were, "How did you stand the pain?" There was no answer from either of us, and we wept some more.

At sunrise, I was going for the undertaker. Josiah was going to go, but Miss Beth was fearful for two women to stay with a dead body. That really surprised me. I thought that she was a rock. Miss Beth insisted on an undertaker; a simple pine box would just not do for Old Zeke. Josiah sent me to Alton, where he had met the Clary brothers a few months back. They were opening up a funeral parlor and livery stable. Finding the funeral parlor was easy, and within ten minutes the brothers were escorting me back home. They came right in and took care of Old Zeke without asking for any assistance. Miss Beth was well pleased with their treatment of her dear friend and told them that she had decided to bury Old Zeke in that beautiful cemetery that we had visited together at Falling Springs.

All the activity and the lack of sleep had my head a bit woozy, and Josiah reminded me that today was July Fourth. Oh my! Jeb, Tara, and the children would be waiting for us at the river where we had planned to meet and celebrate the day. Ben had even left fireworks from the Orient for Josiah to light after dark. We had a bonfire planned, and Jeb's watermelon patch had yielded an abundant crop that we intended to devour. I had forgotten all about our plans, and Josiah made sure that Miss Beth would be all right here with me before he left to tell the family what had transpired. The Clary brothers arranged for a graveside funeral service tomorrow in the afternoon, so Miss Beth entrusted Old Zeke to their hands until then. Josiah and the rest of the family arrived at dusk. The children were visibly upset, as they adored the old man. Tara was good medicine for Miss Beth; she was well acquainted with the depths and pangs of death.

Miss Beth is as lost as a goose. I have never seen her out of command, not even once. Life has played its hand to the in-charge woman. As bad as this may be to write, I am happy that Old Zeke died here. What in the world would she have done had she lost him on the road in some strange place? God really does work things out. I can smile now as I remember Old Zeke giving his testimony about being baptized in the Missouri River by his grandpa. Wherever heaven is, I am sure that Old Zeke is there wearing dem golden slippers that he always sung about.

JULY 10, 1875

A smooth, squared stone is embedded in the rocky soil just under the hill at the Falling Springs cemetery. Josiah and I went yesterday to water the sod that covers the fresh-shoveled dirt. Miss Beth asked us to mark the grave, and she would have a special monument set later. This fall, I will transplant an almond bush and maybe a few spider lilies that Old Zeke loved so much. With the grave in order, Josiah and I walked to the spring's outlet and ate our packed lunch of biscuits and ham. Josiah hummed softly the tune that took me back to the funeral.

The Clary brothers did a marvelous job. I suppose that I was impressed because this was the first commercial funeral that I had ever attended. Josiah insisted on helping dig the grave. He said that it was the last thing he could do for Old Zeke. I do so wish Ben could have been here. Tressie and Sarah played and sang several precious songs. That music drifted up the bluffs and down the hollers and was so sweet that the birds hushed their singing. The sounds were so heavenly that if Old Zeke could have heard, he would have tears streaming down his cheeks. One of the Clary brothers said a few words, and then Seth boldly walked before the small crowd gathered but addressed Miss Beth directly, or so it seemed, and delivered a sermon that could make us hear the angels' wings . If people left this place feeling down or sad, they did not listen, because that boy had a way of bringing glory right down on top of us all. He told us we need not weep for Old Zeke because the man was finally home. Evidently his words were the appropriate and right ones because Miss Beth snapped out of her deep grief and began planning her next move on the way home. Now, I mean this in a good way; it is not as if she is forgetting Old Zeke and jumping right back into life, but she seemed to harness the power to make calculated decisions.

Miss Beth had Josiah take her to Thomasville the day after Old Zeke died, and she must have sent fifty telegrams. There was not time for people to travel the country over and get to our remote hills, but every day since, at least two telegrams have been delivered back with condolences and words of sympathy. One of those telegrams was from Ben. His words of compassion were of great comfort to Miss Beth, and his offer to help in any way was also welcomed. In fact, yesterday Miss Beth took the reins and drove that fringe-lined wagon down the lane all alone. She insisted. Her first stop will be at Ben's home near St. Louis, where she will place an ad for a driver if Ben does not have a recommended employee that would be acceptable to her. Sadness consumed our hearts as we stood on the porch as she disappeared into the trees. We offered to take her, but she would have no part of that. Her determination will either save her or become the source of her demise. Helpless may better describe our emotions this night.

I am getting rather weary. I mean weary in my soul and spirit. The same must be true for Josiah, as he is very quiet and withdrawn. I am too tired to even walk to the rock and have not the desire to go.

DECEMBER 1, 1876

Josiah is ill this evening. He has carried a fever for five days now, and his energy is spent. Proof of his illness comes in the form of him hopping around the house without his leg. When that man does not feel like strapping on the leg, he is seriously ill! His diet has consisted of chicken soup and sourdough bread lately. He will not let me go for the doctor. I fear for his life and have vowed to myself that if he is not better by next Thursday, I am going for help. In the meantime, I keep praying for it!

The year is swiftly coming to an end, and little different has transpired in our modest section of Missouri, although we understand from our sources that the world at large is changing drastically. Miss Beth really likes her new driver, a young man with looks that would stop a train but sports a speech impediment. Miss Beth says that his handicap is irrelevant to the job, but Davy is convinced that it sets him apart as a freak among people and has no desire to seek a normal life. So far the setup is working fabulously for the both of them. Miss Beth keeps the young ladies at bay with a shotgun.

Eleven Point Transport Line has grown beyond belief, and Ben has diversified his business into several other fields. He laughs really hard when he makes the statement that he does not want to put all his eggs in one basket. Our son has indeed come a long, long way from Bozeman's Eggs and Other Oddities. Had I known back then where he is and goes these days, I would have never sat on the porch all night worrying about the coyotes getting him. Constantly I am reminded these days of how little in charge I am of anything. Nor is anyone else for that matter.

Reverend Reeves and Katherine can be counted on for two visits a year. Their updates consist of their church doings. Each visit they stop by Edward's grave and seem genuinely interested in the rest of the family's well-being. After all these years, I should think that my distrust of the fine Reverend Reeves would change, but it has not.

Tressie is seventeen years old and is sparking with a young man from Alton. Sarah's jealousy over this relationship is the only adverse behavior that she has ever exhibited. Tara has her hands full with two teenage girls, which reminds me so often of me and my sister so long ago. Jeb and Seth have a bond as great as any father and son, and not only is Seth an incredible preacher, he has also become very proficient at boat building. Those two have built and sold a number of river boats to folks up and down the Eleven Point River. Tara is still quilting, tatting, and although her hair is fading to gray, she is as beautiful as ever!

We seldom hear from Uncle Frank, and when we do it is usually about a tavern brawl or fistfight over some insignificant matter. We love him dearly, and it breaks our hearts to see his goodness drowned in alcohol. Josiah says that we do what we want to do, but I wonder if his drinking is not so much a habit, but maybe an addiction, or even a curse. We never want to be judgmental, but rather helpful. Alas, unless it is wanted, 'help' can not be rendered. Whatever it is, at this stage of his life, it is unlikely that he will make any changes. The widow Huddleston died in early spring, and rumor has it that Uncle Frank already has another companion. That we are aware of, he never contacts his children. Evidently, Ben's mystery woman did not pass his test or live up to his expectations, as she has not been the object of conversation at all this year. Being single has no adverse effect on him, and we do not broach the subject. I expect that Tressie will be the first to bless the family with a baby.

We have met her beau and like him very much. They have that look toward each other, so we are certain that it will not be long before wedding bells toll again.

I hear Josiah coughing, so I must close.

Oh, Josiah! Lenny needed you! Benjamin needed you! I know you did not die, but did you ever get well? You did not forget me, Lenny, did you? Tara's girls and other things reminded you of me often, just as often as I thought of you. You missed me as much as I missed you. Only I had been bitter because I thought you did not care, and you had been lonely because you thought I was dead. I felt great sadness!

AUGUST 23, 1879

Several years have passed since my last entry. I feel the need to apologize, but know not to whom other than myself. After reading the previous page, it is necessary that I report here what came of Josiah's ills. I suspect that he had yellow fever, as there has been an epidemic sweeping the country, especially in the South. Three times during the past two years I nearly lost him. I have never prayed so hard or so long! The Lord saw fit to let him live, and my gratitude is unmatched! Ben had come by during the final episode and as a last resort went to the chicken house and rummaged through Weti's old baskets. He confessed that he too was on his knees petitioning the Maker to spare his pa when he felt compelled to unpack a specific basket and found a clay jar of brownish fluid. He thought back to the day that Weti took him to her cave and explained what her medicines were for. At that time Ben did not understand, but this day on his knees in the chicken house he recalled from memory her babble. She was describing delusion set on by hot fever, and she pointed to this red clay jar, and it was the only container of that shade, hence his recollection. Ben rushed back to the cabin with this find, and we administered the liquid to Josiah. By the next morning, the man was coherent, breathing normally, and the fever had completely vanished. Weeks passed before Josiah's energy and muscle tone returned, but he did get back to his old self. Not until months later did Ben tell me about the golden light that he imagined seeing when he lifted his head from that fervent prayer in the henhouse that day

Ben's latest venture is a new wholesale business where he sells directly to retailers. His largest customer is the Woolworth Brothers, who have opened stores on the East Coast and all the items sell for either five or ten cents.

Ben's hiring of a professional accountant was of mutual consent, as we all knew that the Eleven Point Transport Line had long outgrown our capabilities. Ben vowed that his visits would remain as frequent as possible, and he has held true to that promise. He also brought a lady friend home once or twice, but as far as we know still has no serious relationship.

Tressie, on the other hand, married her beau.

Sarah has graduated from school and is training to be a teacher herself. She has pursued a music career, and thanks to Miss Beth's connections, has been in touch with a blind gospel music composer named Fanny Crosby. Mrs. Crosby has taught Sarah to write her own songs and how to compile a melody.

Seth has almost completed every lesson in all the books at school even though he is not nearly old enough to finish. He is still preaching at every opportunity and only gets better and better.

Miss Beth and Davy have not been here in almost two years, but they do send postcards and letters. The rest of the family remains unchanged, and that is both good and bad, depending on which ones. Josiah is slowing down, and I am afraid that soon we will attempt to find Dr. Hanger and have another leg built. That poor limb is worn to a frazzle. He spends each night picking splinters out of his overalls and oiling the metal parts. The foot has ceased to swivel at the ankle, and a huge chunk has fallen out just above what should be a knee.

I too have felt better. My heart is happy, but there is something wrong in my right side. I have not said anything to Josiah or anyone else. I just keep hoping that it will go away. I have noticed that the whites of my eyes are yellowing a bit. They do not hurt, but my vision is blurring. I am attributing all these symptoms to aging.

DECEMBER 1, 1880

The only thing of any significance this year came in the form of a package from Toby, and a very well-written and informative letter. His colorful adventures out west paled to the gravity of the lengthy apology and plea for forgiveness. His only mention of Felina was that she dumped him in El Paso for a fancy cowboy.

The package contained an incredible artwork that would rival any at the Louvre and was painted by a Buffalo Soldier who saved Toby's hide in a shootout. He asked that we enjoy this treasure until the day he came back to Missouri, and then he would only claim it if it affixed our pardon.

Josiah carefully hung the stunning canyon painting over the mantle. It will suffice as a reminder of betrayal and forgiveness. It will serve as Toby's place in the family and force us to face our own heart's condition.

To me, it is as if one of my own has come home. That Toby is a prodigal! I dare say if he showed up tomorrow, Josiah would kill the fatted calf. It is hard to say what Ben might feel, and that is important to me also!

JANUARY 2, 1881

A few nights ago, Josiah and I enjoyed a houseful of company. Miss Beth and Davy were passing through on their way to Florida, and Ben, after spending the holidays with his lady friend, had come for a belated Christmas.

I knew eventually that it would, but far too early into the evening Miss Beth asked about the painting. While I hesitated for the right words, Josiah jumped right in and explained its origin. Ben became extremely quiet and slipped to the porch. I went out and sat beside him.

"Ma, I was humiliated and devastated when she stood me up at the altar. I pushed harder and harder just to forget it, to prove my worth, or for whatever reasons, but now I realize that the only emotion I have left at all is pity. That pity was directed toward Toby because Felina was bad news, and without knowing, Toby actually saved my life. In my heart I know and believe all that, but hearing his name tonight brought back the pain. I just need to work that out. I want to see Toby again, and I am glad to know that he is alive."

The smell of popping corn drifted from the cabin, and we wasted no time getting back in and enjoying this priceless pleasure that can only be truly appreciated by those who know from where it comes.

DECEMBER 30, 1881

Tara finally got to use the blessings that the middle-wife rubbed on her head all those years ago when Tressie had twins on Christmas day. Because a baby was expected, none of that family attempted to make the journey here, but no one was prepared for two babies—a boy and a girl. Tressie was staying with Tara for that very purpose, and now we are sewing as fast as we can to make another of everything. Jeb rode over with the news a few days ago and was as

excited as if they were his own. Tressie named the babies John and
Mary. Jeb said that Sarah is a natural big sister, and Seth has been
fascinated with the entire experience and is thrilled to have a better
understanding of creation. Christmas this year will be remembered
for a long, long time! Is not a new baby the reason for the season in
the first place?

When Ben stopped by in October I had had all I could stand
and tried my level best to ask Ben this question with care, concern,
and genuine interest. I just *had* to know about this mystery woman
who had been taking up so much of his time. Thank the good Lord
that Ben was not offended at me, and he actually apologized for
keeping us strung along. Ms. Samantha is a widow living in Memphis. Ben said that she was extremely timid, sweet, and dead set
against moving anywhere else. Ben thought that the umbilical cord
had never been severed with her mother, with whom she boards,
and he found safety in the relationship because they both knew that
it could be nothing more than a good friendship. He assured us that
if he ever became involved again in a serious relationship that we
would be informed. Was not that a kind way for him to tell me to
mind my own business?

Since there is a large possibility that we will never be grandparents, the new twins have already gained special entrance into our
hearts, and we have not even seen them yet. John and Mary. Oh my
arms are longing to hold them!

It is so good to close another year on a positive note. Josiah is
hammering on his leg again, so I will sign off for now and go get
the sanding paper.

APRIL 30, 1882

I went on an unexpected trip last week to St. Joseph with Miss
Beth and Davy. We attended an estate sale. Not just any sale. The
items were none others than those of Jesse James's widow. That

notorious outlaw had been gunned down for reward money by his own cousin, and now his widow had to sell everything they had to feed her children. Miss Beth had those auctioneers eating out of her hands. Never do I remember having so much fun in one weekend. My sides hurt from laughing so much. Would you believe that the one item that Miss Beth purchased, and left here was a beautiful gold watch with the initials BWB engraved on the back. I would have never believed it in a million years! Yes, it was Benjamin's watch, the very one that Jesse James took from him at the stagecoach hold up. That Miss Beth is as good as gold; a gold watch that is. Which speaks to me, Ben was not materialistic, as he never bought another, and that good things do return, just like the bread cast upon the waters.

Lenny, you actually learned to laugh! And I was not at all surprised at the depth of your faith. You grew into an even more incredible person. I desired that kind of faith, Lenny. Oh, how I wish you had written more of these last few years. I wish I could have known more, learn more. Surely during these missing months you were not ill. Perhaps you were only tired of writing, or maybe age slowed you some, or life just became unexciting.

I supposed I would never know for sure.

DECEMBER 26, 1886

Another four years have rolled by, and I have had little to write about in the last several, so I shall attempt to catch up.

Sarah has been away at college for three years to the University of Missouri, compliments of Miss Beth and Ben, her studies in music, of course. Seth has taken a church pastorate in Texas, and Jeb and Tara are aging gracefully. Tressie's family has moved to her old home place, and besides the twins has two more children, Matthew and Luke, and they are the best neighbors in the world. Josiah has built a private lane for the children to use, and they visit us frequently. We are not their grandparents, but they make us feel that special. Miss Beth and Davy came through in early October on their way to South Texas, where Miss Beth has officially designated her final place of residence, a place near the gulf. Josiah called her a snowbird. She laughed and told him that there was a lot of truth in that. Davy seemed content to follow her around and settle down too. Josiah thinks that we might not see them again, as Miss Beth really aged fast after Old Zeke passed, and her traveling days are becoming limited. Uncle Frank has never returned, and we seldom hear his name mentioned. Ben comes by maybe twice a year but keeps in touch through cards, letters, and an occasional telegram.

The landscape has changed drastically since the timber company has cut most of the pine. We both regret having our timber harvested and would rather have the trees back than ten times the money. Hindsight is indeed twenty-twenty. We no longer go to Thomasville, as it has merely turned into a residential community; the commerce takes place in the county seat, Alton. It is difficult to see any signs of the struggles that took place twenty years ago during the war, and to young people, the stories are simply tall tales. If it were not for the *thump, thump* of Josiah's leg, I might think that I dreamed the whole thing. These days I spend a great deal of time going through what we have left of Weti's things and just trying to recapture that feeling of what she was and did. In the warmer weather, I spent many hours on the rock, and Josiah spent as many fishing in the river. Often I accompany him, but we seldom go to the rock together. The Cherokee roses bloom thicker and fuller every year, as they never lack for tears, for we still water them.

Josiah put up the Christmas tree again this year. In fact, we have never missed a year of tying one to the wall in all this time. Rather than Tressie, now her children help decorate it, but we still use Lucy and Ben's chalk-colored shapes and string the popping corn. Josiah cannot bear to break tradition, and I wholeheartedly agree with him.

In some weird way, Christmas just would not seem like Christmas without that tree. Two days ago Ben came home for the holidays, and he brought the angel for our tree. She was out-of-this-world beautiful. Her name is Rachael, and she climbed right into our hearts.

APRIL 5, 1887

Twenty-eight years ago today, Josiah and I rode those horses across the Eleven Point River and onto this place. And twenty-eight years ago I saw that little boy run out from behind the cabin yelling, "Pa! Pa!"

Today we received a telegram from that same little boy. It was an announcement of his marriage to that beautiful young woman. They have eloped and are getting ready to move into their temporary home in Kentucky.

Tressie made a mad dash across the path as soon as she received the same telegram. We had a good cry. I am not sure what kind of tears they were—joy, I suppose. Ben would have been proud of the celebration that we had in his absence. Josiah was thrilled as well. Ben commented that someday soon they plan to rebuild on that farm where Edward is buried, if Tressie would not mind having them for neighbors. "He is ridiculous!" she shouted. "I would not have it any other way!"

It is certain that we all share her delight. The children had no idea of what all the to-do was about, but they danced and laughed anyway.

Writing for the both of us, I dare say that we are completely satisfied in our hearts for Ben and his new bride. He looked long and diligently, and this companion is a mighty special individual. We know nothing about her family, but it is assured that she will be deeply loved and honored by this family. Ben promised that they would visit as soon as possible, but to not be disappointed if it was not tomorrow. That Ben!

Just anticipating their visit was enough to get me on my feet and sprucing up the entire cabin. I washed curtains, scrubbed floors, and planned meals, and on and on. Josiah warned that I was pushing. He was right, and before nightfall I was back in bed.

Josiah made me go to the doctor in West Plains last month. I did not want to go and begged him to not make me. I believe that this pain will eventually go away, and I only mention it when he asks. It has not kept me from the chores that must be accomplished, so I think he is making a big to-do about nothing. Nevertheless, he took me, and the doctor said there was nothing he could do, but that I needed to eat good food and move around as much as I could. See! I told him!

I did notice this morning when I peered into the looking glass that the whites of my eyes had turned yellowish, and I remember my pa's toenails yellowed. I think all old people get tired easily; maybe yellowing goes along with that.

I am rather sleepy. And I must close for now.

NOVEMBER 15, 1890

Ben and his bride have been here only once this year in early spring, but they plan to spend the Christmas holiday with us. He has drawn out plans for a three-story home on his aunt Katherine's old farm, so I am sure they will spend a great deal of time there also. We cannot wait to see them again. Josiah goes on and on about what a wonderful match they are and how handsome and how happy; well, I can honestly say that I am in agreement 100 percent. We both agree that this marriage was worth waiting for!

The sky was as blue today as I have ever seen it, and the colorful leaves are just beginning to fall. Where the fires burned the tops and limbs of the sold pine timber, hardwood trees emerged, and the color is magnificent! I felt relatively good today, so took the box of chalks and strolled to the rock. It does take longer for me to get there these days. The buntings were out; it is rather late in the year, but maybe they were enjoying the unseasonable weather just like I was. If I might say so myself, today's drawing would rival any other amateur. The picture seemed to run from my fingers that were moving under a power other than my own. On the canvas before my eyes appeared the landscape as I had viewed from this spot for over thirty years. Even I was surprised that it came from my own hand.

Sleep must have overtaken me at some point because I woke and shook off an odd dream. Josiah was on my mind heavily, and I began to pray about him. I wish that there were better words than *thank you* because those really do not have the supremacy or muscle that I needed to convey. I trust that the good Lord understood my heart in thanking him for filling my life with Mr. Josiah Bozeman. I begged my Maker to not take him away from me, as I could not possibly continue on without him. I thanked him for all the other wonderful people in my life, and before I left that heart-shaped clearing I watered Lucy's grave again. I miss her as much this day as the day we laid her there, but really, she has never left my heart.

The way home this evening seemed longer than ever; in fact, I had to stop and rest twice. Maybe I just wanted to listen. But the only thing that I heard was the bold words that blared through my mind: "Get your house in order." The demand was so strong that no question could overpower it, and as ludicrous as this may sound, all I could think to do was gather my treasures.

So when Josiah fell asleep tonight, I carefully cleaned the velveteen hatbox, the object that represents to me my baby girl and all that she was. I pressed Ma's apron, held it to my face, and felt the kiss of Mother. I breathed in its love and then neatly folded and placed it in the round green box. I ventured to the old smokehouse and broke off the dried sage, and with Weti's *mano* and *metate*, ground that herb into the finest powder possible and then poured into the clay jar. I thought of how this represented wisdom and happiness to me and conjured Weti near as I gently placed it too in the hatbox. When this journal is completed, it will be tied with the short piece of twine in my pocket and will join my other treasures.

Thinking of closing the lid causes a chuckle inside because I treat these worldly, irrelevant objects like my own personal little ark of the covenant. Thankfully, I cannot worship material goods, for I know in whom I have believed, and I am persuaded that he is able to keep that which I have committed unto him against that day.

FEBRUARY 28, 1891

Josiah did not want me to, and told me so in no uncertain terms, but he let me overrule him and have my way. I was determined to get to that rock, even if he had to carry me. Although the pain was great and each breath was difficult to take, I did go under my own power. From my concave seat in that marbled rock, I could see that the flowers were not blooming yet, and no birds were singing, but the ground wore its pine needle carpet elegantly, and the few hardwood leaves were blowing in a rolling fashion across the clearing. Lucy's grave kept beckoning my gaze, and I did look, but I saw nothing unusual. I began thinking of the events that brought me to this very place so many times, and suddenly my entire life scrolled through my mind. I became so absorbed in this that I did not notice the clouds rolling away and the sunbeams shining on the rock around me. A familiar sound startled me, and the source of the noise flew into view. It was a pair of indigo buntings in the middle of the mating dance ritual. They too were as absorbed and never noticed my intrusion.

Only tonight do I realize that this is not the time of year for birds to nest, so I suppose some weird weather phenomenon will introduce spring and the planting season will be different too.

On the rock today I had no questions for the Creator, only thanks. Even in that, no words would come, but my heart was grateful. I did not receive any mighty revelations, and I did not ask why I am sick or how long I will live, but I was just glad to be there and near Lucy. Josiah was nervously waiting for me on the porch, his new leg bumping on the wooden planks, and he jumped up as soon as he saw me. He ran and held my waist the rest of the way. I thanked him for letting me have that special time, but I did not tell him about the footsteps that followed me home.

MARCH 18, 1891

Lenny died four days ago, and we buried her next to Lucy. I have been perched on her rock for two days. I have now read through this journal twice. As a mere, common man, I do not deserve the esteem that she held for me, but I am blessed above all men to have shared a life with this vivacious, tender woman. It is only fitting that I pen the final entry, so as to document the rest of the story. I deem it a great privilege. *Josiah.*

No need to recant her life or describe who she was, as any reader has already formed an opinion. But I promised Lenny that I would record her final minutes. In the wee hours of March 14, she went into a peaceful sleep and never woke again. Approximately seven hours before that final slumber she called to me, "Josiah." Her breathing was labored, but she insisted on speaking. "Josiah, I will not be with you much longer. I know that I am going because I have just now seen it. I saw it, Josiah!"

"What, Lenny, what did you see?"

"I went to the light. The light is alive, Josiah! And they are all there! My mother, and Pa, Edward, and Lucy were holding hands, jumping up and down, squealing and waving to me. Weti and her daughter had flowers, Old Zeke's white teeth were shining through his big smile. And I knew everyone of them, and they all knew me! The sweet music was like a gentle breeze, but it flowed through me; yet it was me, like my pulse. The air was like being inside a rainbow, all those brilliant colors were sparkling, yet I was breathing them, and it was strength. And, Josiah, I did not see Jesus, but I could feel him, and his aroma was of rain. It was as if the glowing light *was* him, and everything I saw was enveloped in his glow. I felt him love me. Not for anything that I did or did not do, other than chose him; he just simply loves me! This whole life, the good and bad, is so surpassed by the brilliance and glory that the things of this life simply faded away, except for the treasure that I stored there. And I understood, there is specific purpose in our earthly existence. It *is* a gift. And I am going there only because I accepted him. You have to tell them, Josiah. You have to tell everyone. You have to!

It's real! Josiah, it's real! And it's bigger than anything you can possibly imagine; it's completely indescribable! And, Josiah, Mother was right! About heaven, about s*age*. There is Perfect Happiness!

Benjamin got here the day before Lenny passed. I do believe that is what she was holding on for. She went without knowing that Benjamin's wife, Rachael, is in fact her own niece, and that they are expecting my grandchild. Regretfully, I have only just now discovered this myself. Also, the revelation that the Johnny Simmons, who befriended me near Wilson's Creek is indeed my brother-in-law has stunned me to the core. Had Lenny known these things, it is certain that the full circle of her life would have made more sense, and many of her unanswered questions understood. I look forward to the day that I can make Johnny's acquaintance again, hold my grandchild, and deliver Lenny's missing hugs and love to her sister, who is very much alive and well.

It was not the little hands tugging at my skirt, but rather the soft, sweet whisper, "Granny, Granny," that brought me back, and a few seconds passed before I could open my eyes. Bryson's hands reached for me as I laid the journal aside, and I swept that precious child into my lap and hugged him with a love that no man can describe. It was all sinking in, slowly. My mind was over absorbed as I stroked his fine, soft, dark, wavy, hair, and I felt his small fingers sliding down my wet cheek, and I heard that gentle voice ask, "Granny hurt?"

"Granny is not hurt, sweetie," I spoke, and that is when I saw them. They had been there all along, and I never noticed until that very moment. But there they were, looking up at me, full of love and trust; yes, those are *his* eyes. Josiah Bozeman's eyes. And thinking back, I realize that Ben has those same eyes and stature and charisma. No wonder we all fell in love with him, especially Rachael, and Johnny and I had instantly felt such a kindred spirit. I could not believe it! And I could not stop crying. How did she do it? How did Lenny pull this off? She had Josiah for thirty-three years, and now I have *his* son and grandson to love forever. *Oh, Lenny, I have wasted all these years thinking that you let me down. Lenny, I never stopped loving you. I was only bitter—bitter because I did not know the truth. I did not have all the facts. I assumed wrong. I am not bitter anymore. I have cast that poison to the wind, just as* Weti *instructed."*

Bryson insisted that we have a bite to eat, and so we did. Then I insisted that we light a lantern and go to the garden. I took the garden scissors and a basket. The lantern was set high out of the baby's reach, and with muddy feet we tromped into the middle of the herbs and cut to our heart's content, the basket full of sage.

Bryson is fast asleep now, and it was all I could do to stop staring at him. Johnny will be home day after tomorrow, and I cannot wait to share this amazing discovery; the man who saved his life at Wilson's Creek is Bryson's grandfather, Josiah Bozeman. I have never felt so content; it is as if a great burden has been lifted and life finally feels good and whatever seemed missing is no longer. The stars are as vivid as I can ever recall, and I realize that the strong storm from earlier has dissipated. I lay my head on Mother's apron, and her voice fills my memory. I can hear her saying, "Sometimes he calms the storm. But sometimes he lets the storm rage and he calms the child." I realize that is exactly what he has done for me this night, this life. Only the Creator himself could devise such an unraveling and deliver such joy and peace in a world where good and evil sleep together. I have made a decision to live the balance of my life as if it is the last minute and allow the Lord to take charge. I did not know how desperately tired I was of kicking against the pricks. I am ashamed of living my whole life as a crybaby; as in comparison to Lenny, my live has been charmed and pain free! I vow to live forward with a more thankful heart, to recognize that bad people are not all bad, and good people are not all good, and I intend to pay closer attention to the birds, in fact, all of creation. My heart is sad that Lenny is really gone forever from earth. But I *shall* see her again, and I shall forever share this blessed bond with Josiah, and someday thank him I shall!

Somebody's coming, I thought, and looked to the direction of the footsteps.

Oh my! It's a tall, handsome, dark-eyed man. Bryson's pa.

THE SERIES IN THE RUGGED HILLS CONTINUES ...

Read about your favorite characters in future volumes. Like the pieces of Lenny's quilt, they stitch together all the missing squares and triangles of these years long ago and become a thing of great comfort.

Watch for coming publications and learn more at www. intheruggedhills.com.

e|LIVE

---

listen|imagine|view|experience

AUDIO BOOK DOWNLOAD INCLUDED WITH THIS BOOK!

In your hands you hold a complete digital entertainment package. In addition to the paper version, you receive a free download of the audio version of this book. Simply use the code listed below when visiting our website. Once downloaded to your computer, you can listen to the book through your computer's speakers, burn it to an audio CD or save the file to your portable music device (such as Apple's popular iPod) and listen on the go!

How to get your free audio book digital download:

1. Visit www.tatepublishing.com and click on the e|LIVE logo on the home page.
2. Enter the following coupon code:
   f55e-a466-1ce1-ec1b-989a-9ff0-1122-2596
3. Download the audio book from your e|LIVE digital locker and begin enjoying your new digital entertainment package today!